SHADOW OF THE ALPHA

THE ALPHA KING'S BREEDER
BOOK EIGHT

BELLA MOONDRAGON

For Meagan

CONTENTS

1

―――――

CAME UP SHORT

Kenna

IT'S QUIET HERE. The golden walls and spiraling columns soak up the sun as I walk steadily toward my dad's office. Beyond giant ceiling-height windows, the sparkling city of Moonrise, the capital of Eastonia, spreads out in a sea of cream and gold until it touches the banks of a lake the color of polished turquoise.

On the opposite shore, at the base of a towering network of mountains, sits Old Moonrise–the original witch coven native to the Roguelands. Once, twenty or so years ago, there used to be a palace built of crystal sitting on a ridge overlooking the old village and the lake.

Until, well, my mother destroyed it.

I smile softly at the thought of my mom and pick up my pace, my sandals clacking against the white marble tiles.

I turn a sharp corner, nodding hello to a trio of maids who pass me, and slip into my dad's office like a shadow.

He looks up from the massive mahogany desk in the center of the room, his dark brow lifting as I gently close the door behind me.

1

Behind him, bookshelves stretch toward the domed, muraled ceiling.

A map lies on his desk beneath untidy papers and a scattering of old paperweights. He sighs heavily, checks his watch—a rather expensive and gaudy gift from my uncle Isaac, the Alpha King of Crescent Falls—and leans back in his leather office chair.

"You're supposed to be packing," he says, crossing an ankle over a knee as I edge toward his desk and lean my hip against the side of it.

"I'm packed."

"That didn't take long."

I roll my eyes to the ceiling, to the sweeping depictions of some battle that took place during the Great War when the Moon Goddess rebelled against the gods who wanted to tether her, to leave her powerless, and her people in shackles. I click my tongue and look down at my manicured nails. "Aunt Maddy is my size. She said I could borrow whatever gowns I need while I'm there. I didn't see a point in bringing any of my own. They take up so much room!"

"The fashions in Crescent Falls are different from here, Ken. Are you sure?"

I run my hands down the vibrant violet pants I'm wearing—made of silk with swirling embroidery—that cuff around my ankles. My top, with its long, loose sleeves that gather at the wrists and shows off my midriff, is made of the same fine fabric. I shrug.

"I want to fit in."

Dad stares at me for a long, long time saying nothing.

I run my tongue along my lower teeth and give him another little shrug. "I packed two gowns of my own."

"Good," he finally says softly, and looks back down at the paper he's reading.

I can tell by his gruff demeanor that he's as wound up about this upcoming trip to visit my cousins in Crescent Falls as I am but for completely different reasons.

To him, this is an opportunity to stress about my safety for two months. I imagine he'll pace back and forth in front of his desk, or the magic mirror he uses to call my uncle, until the floor turns black from scuff marks. Mom, too, will worry. They always do.

It's because I'm not like them.

I watch my dad, Alpha King Ryatt of Eastonia, mark a few lines on the paper before signing the bottom of it. He's all sharp lines and rigid muscles. He has a spine of steel, and a heart just as strong.

He met his match in my mom, Ella. The Queen of Eastonia. The Luna of Moonrise. The Firestone Witch.

While my parents would cut someone down just for looking at them the wrong way, I've always been more of a pacifist. I lean toward kindness, and I'm far too trusting, too soft, too willing to please.

My soft heart isn't interested in conquering kingdoms or squashing my foes. No, there's only one thing I want, and I have two months to find it in Crescent Falls before it's too late.

I roll my lower lip between my teeth and smile as my dad meets my eyes again, his gaze softer than before. "Say what you want to say, Dad."

"I don't like this at all."

Sighing heavily, I hop onto his desk. "Why not?"

"You're practically putting yourself out to auction–"

"It's a Moon Festival, Dad. There's going to be balls every night to help people like me find their mates."

"There will be more balls held here, in Eastonia."

"I went to every mating ball and festival held this spring, Dad. I even went to Tarsian, remember? I didn't find anyone."

Dad narrows his eyes and blows out his breath at the mention of Tarsian, the desert kingdom across the river boundary that used to be the marker between the Roguelands and Rifthold. Now, Alpha King Jaxon rules over Tarsian and maintains a strained relationship with my parents, although deep down, I think he and my dad might actually be good friends, but would *never* admit to it.

"You only turned twenty-one this spring. You're so young–"

"But I'm old enough to take over Veiled Valley this fall when Grandpa Westfall steps down."

A hush falls over the room.

When Dad doesn't say anything, I continue, "I did everything you wanted me to do, Dad. I graduated from college. I trained with you and Grandpa. I trained with Mom...." I taper off. "I need one summer of freedom before I take over as Luna of Veiled Valley, one summer to try to find my mate, and then..." And then my real training begins. Training that includes preparing myself to be queen of this entire kingdom one day.

My stomach curls in my belly at the thought.

I couldn't be farther from my mother in temperament and poise. During my childhood, I was wild, practically uncontrollable, but that changed as I matured. I excelled in school. I learned to keep my enormous and varied powers under lock and key until I needed to harness them, and I can harness those powers *well*.

I attended the exclusive Moonrise Academy of Mystical Arts–a school for witches and shifters with special gifts–and graduated this spring as valedictorian of my class with a specialty in healing and midwifery.

I'm a skilled healer. I have knowledge of, and can harness the use of, dark magic, including curses. I can create and control magic fires that burn cold and silver and turn my body into a mere shadow of mist.

But I'm nothing like them. I haven't ever used my powers in battle. I've never needed to.

I've never wanted to.

"I don't want to rule alone," I say, and my voice breaks around the words.

Dad looks at me with so much love in his eyes that it makes me consider not stifling the tears now brimming on my lashes.

"I don't want you to go and come home disappointed, Kenna."

His words ring through his office.

I chew my lip, unable to meet his eyes. As a family, we've skirted around this subject for a long, long time. While I am, most definitely, a witch, my wolf abilities are minimal in comparison. Shifting is fine and dandy, but I'm clumsy, tiny, and comparatively weak in my wolf form, and there's question about my ability to feel any kind of mate bond whatsoever because of it. My witch side is just too strong and overwhelms my wolf gifts.

That hasn't stopped me from obsessing over finding my mate, though.

"And you won't be ruling alone," Dad says, rising and organizing the papers. "Evander will be your Beta, like Granger is mine."

It's like a knife to the chest.

I stifle my emotions, turning my expression to a mask of steel, but he catches the single flicker of uncertainty behind my eyes.

"He'll come around, Kenna."

"I haven't spoken to him in five years."

"He's been busy."

"Mhm…" I nod. Busy, sure. If that's what they want to call it. Busy roaming whatever kingdom he's called to serve as a *Ghost*, the greatest and most lethal kind of spy the Allied Kingdoms have.

Right now, I think he's in Celestoria. I honestly don't know. I haven't seen him since the day after my sixteenth birthday. I haven't talked to him, either. I doubt he wants to give up a life of danger and adventure to stand beside me in Veiled Valley, just like I doubt he ever thinks about me at all.

I slide off Dad's desk and cross my arms under my chest, my mind reeling over the past twenty-one years of my life all at once, picking through every memory of Evander despite my internal desperate pleas not to.

He was my best friend. We grew up together. We played in the woods and at the lake shore. We had sleepovers and trained together until we started school and went our separate ways for the first time.

It was my fault we grew apart. One day, I didn't want to play in the woods anymore. My interests shifted from climbing trees to playing with dolls, then shifted further to my piano and the romance novels that cover every surface of my room. Evander fell to the wayside, and it was natural. He is a boy, and I'm a girl. I'm a witch, and he's a shifter. I'm a princess, and he's… *a lethal machine trained to inflict quiet, swift death.*

I find it hard to swallow as I turn from Dad and pretend to be invested in his bookshelves. My mind races to our last encounter. Evander, having been gone for years while training in Tarsian, returned to Moonrise shortly after my sixteenth birthday.

I'd been sitting outside reading a book on the terrace overlooking the private garden in the back of the castle. I didn't realize he was there until he said my name, and I turned.

It's hard to describe it. I didn't recognize him at first. The goofy little boy with freckles, copper blond hair, and startling emerald eyes had turned into… something *beautiful*, but also dark and empty.

The rest of the encounter is buried deep, deep down in my memory. I refuse to think about it, or how much it hurt when he tore through the friendship we'd built and left ashes in his wake, with no remorse for my sensitive feelings. For my *heart*.

"Kenna?"

"Did you say something?" I ask Dad. He's staring at me right now, his brow furrowed.

"Are you all right?"

"Where's Mom?" I clear my throat, giving him my best smile.

He arches a brow and sighs. "She had a meeting in Old Moonrise with the mystics. She'll be home in time for dinner, she said."

I nod, trying again to swallow past the lump in my throat.

"Are you sure you're okay? You look pale. Are you sick? Maybe we should postpone your trip–"

"I'm fine," I say hurriedly, shaking my head.

Dad walks over to me and lays a hand on my shoulder, squeezing. I have to look up at him to gaze him directly in the eyes. I'm several inches shorter than my mother, which means I'm over a head and a half shorter than my dad. I don't know how I lost the genetic lottery in terms of height and emotional composition, *but here I am*, short and trying not to burst into tears.

"Don't rush into anything. You'll find your mate one day. It shouldn't be your priority right now."

He's right. I hate that he's right but… I've looked all over Eastonia for any flicker of a mate bond. I've attended countless balls, visited almost every village here, and nothing.

In two months, I'll move to Veiled Valley and rule as their Luna, alone. My opportunities to find my mate will be significantly diminished.

I know I sound pathetic. I know that I have everything I could ever want. I've never needed for anything, never gone hungry, never been brutalized or scared.

But I want what my parents have.

I want love, more than anything. Even if I can't feel the mate bond, I at least want something close to it.

Dad kisses my forehead. "Don't let Ryan get you into trouble, either."

"I can't make any promises about that," I laugh.

2

GHOST

Evander

THE NONDESCRIPT WAREHOUSE in the Crescent City commercial center smells like cleaning solution and sweat.

I rack my weights, panting, catching my reflection in the dirty mirrors overlooking the makeshift gym in one corner of the massive building. Above me, light pours from several half-broken windows at the juncture of the galvanized roof. A single pigeon flies from one rafter to the other.

I take off my headphones, the thrumming music giving way to the sounds of my colleagues, my brothers in the *Ghost* forces, continuing their workouts.

Flynn walks into view, his reflection in the mirror coming to rest beside mine. His dark hair is brushed away from his face, his dark eyes locking on mine as he nods and asks, "You still using those fifties?"

"No." I shake my head, motioning for him to take the dumbbells I just racked.

He pulls them off the shelf and sits on a weight bench, rolling his shoulders. "Fuck, man. How are you doing curls with these?"

"Ev's gonna need to buy some new shirts while we're here. He can barely walk around without the seams busting loose." An agent named Connor chuckles somewhere behind us. I glance at him and shake my head as he drops into a squat with a bar over his shoulders.

"I already have," I reply coolly, giving him a flash of teeth as I pull my sweaty shirt away from my skin. It's hotter than hell in here. It's dead of summer, and we've been housed in an old warehouse with no ventilation whatsoever. One would think the Allied Kingdoms would put a little extra care into housing their most lethal defense.

Flynn rolls his eyes back to mine in the mirror as I take my shirt off and toss it on the cracked cement floor. "We've got a meeting with General Howard today."

I run my tongue along my lower teeth. "Why?"

"Maybe we're finally getting an answer about why we're in this city."

I catch my own reflection in the mirror as I run my fingers through my dark blond hair. Before this, we'd been in Maatua for three months doing some reconnaissance for Alpha King Anthony. The old king won't stop picking fights with the rulers of KiloKilo, and when a few of his best generals went missing, the Allied Kings, Alpha King Isaac and Alpha King Ryatt, called on the Ghosts to go find them.

So, I spent three months in the sun, lounging on sparkling white sand beaches, which turned my skin a deep bronze and my hair a rich shade of gold. My green eyes are brighter now, contrasting with the tan.

Now I'm here, sweating my fucking balls off without a reason as to why.

I rub my jaw, noticing the week-old stubble. "Fuck, I need to shave before he gets here." General Howard is a stickler when it comes to the rules. When he gets here, we have to be clean shaven, clean, and dressed in our order issued uniforms.

The idea of standing around in this gods-forsaken warehouse in leathers and long sleeve, scaled armor makes me want to vomit.

Just as I turn to get my water bottle with every intention of going to take a shower, the massive metal door leading into our makeshift gym bursts open.

General Howard, tall, lanky, and all business, strides in. He comes to a stop, crossing his arms over his chest.

I glance at Flynn, who smirks at me. General Howard is our manager. He's good at the paperwork aspect of our missions, but when it comes to being in the field… I doubt the man has ever raised a claw to an enemy before.

Instead, he sends us out to do the secret dirty work for the Allied Kingdoms.

"Is this what you've been doing for a week? Fucking around?" His gaze sweeps around the room before landing on me. "Go take a shower and meet me in my office in ten minutes, Agent Evander."

"Your office?" I ask, my voice laced with mischief. "Is it behind the crates, or the old shipping container by the bay doors out front–"

"Now," he growls.

I run my tongue along my lower teeth and shrug, clutching my discarded shirt. I look back at the group of men still standing around the gym, all of them watching me and the general closely while I brush past him.

As I walk over the metal threshold into the main area of the warehouse, I hear the general say, "The rest of you miserable lot are to dress and prepare for a mission tonight in the inner city. There's an underground auction ring that needs to be disbanded–"

The door closes behind me. The bay door overlooking the street is open, a large black SUV parked just within sight. I heave a breath and turn toward another set of rusted doors, which lead to a network of dimly lit, dusty hallways. There's a few bunk rooms back there where we sleep and house what belongings we have.

I take a cold shower because the hot water is nonexistent. I dress, putting on a worn out gray cotton shirt and black athletic pants instead of my leathers, and walk out to the SUV.

It's unlocked, and Howard is sitting in the back behind a driver wearing sunglasses and a suit. Likely one of King Isaac's men, by the look of it.

The people of Eastonia still prefer to keep their paws on the ground.

I grind my teeth and slide in beside Howard, closing the door behind me with a snap.

"What is this about?" I ask.

He hands me a folder. "You're going out in the field for an undercover mission."

I open the folder and feel my breath catch in my throat. I slowly scan the page and then the picture of the woman staring back up at me. Her glossy brown hair falls in thick waves over her shoulders as she beams at the camera, that button nose of hers scrunched and silver eyes creased with pleasure. Beautiful. She's always been beautiful.

I shut the folder and hand it back to him. "No."

Howard raises a brow. "You're saying no to the Allied Kings–"

"Fire me, then. My contract is up in two months, anyway."

"Agent–"

"This isn't a mission. This is babysitting–"

"From this moment forward, you are the Princess of Eastonia's personal bodyguard."

"Find a warrior from Alpha King Isaac's ranks for this. I'm overqualified."

"Alpha King *Ryatt* has asked for you personally."

"I highly doubt that," I growl, reaching for the door handle.

But the driver locks me in. I frown.

"This is undercover, like I said. You're not to be seen. Not by her, or anyone else, for that matter. She's to remain unaware that she's being watched."

"So, I'm stalking her."

"Not–not stalking. Keeping tabs."

"And reporting back to you with her movements? What would you like to know, General? Where she shops? Who she talks to? How many times she licks her thumb when turning pages in her little books?"

The general narrows his eyes at me. "This isn't up for debate."

"What is the reason for this?"

I know for a fact Alpha King Ryatt wouldn't put his spies on his daughter. He trusts her. Kenna is powerful. She's smart, sharp, and able to defend herself. At least, she was trained to be like that.

But knowing her like I do, she's oblivious to the evil of others. Too trusting, too fucking sweet for her own good.

And then there's me.

"You have to find someone else."

Howard thumbs through the folder. "You know her the best, according to the king."

"Then tell me why—"

He sighs heavily. "The Moon Festival is going to be the biggest event the United Packlands has seen in two decades. There's going to be thousands of people in Crescent City and the nearby territories. She'll be there for the festival. She needs protection. Quietly, however. Her parents don't want security getting in the way of her... agenda."

I keep my face trained on an expression of boredom, but instead I'm starting to reel. "Agenda?"

"She's looking for her mate, and King Ryatt wants to make sure she's still allowed her freedom while keeping her safe from anyone who might try to take advantage of her."

"Her cousins are Alpha Sydney of Shadowcrest and Alpha Ryan of Lighthide. She doesn't need *me*."

"They're unaware of this plan. Only the Alpha Kings know you're here. This isn't up to us. It's been decided. Plus, from what I hear, you will be her Beta shortly. This is a good way to get to know the woman you'll be ruling beside as her second. She won't even know you're there."

I eye my general. I've spent the last five years of my life avoiding Kenna. I spent the last five years trying not to think about what this fall will look like as I ascend the title of Beta beside her and whoever she ends up falling in love with and marrying.

I've been a Ghost for years now, moving from one territory to the next. I've killed dozens. I've moved unnoticed, like a shadow, leaving no traces behind. I've never felt guilt or remorse for my actions, for the blood on my hands.

I am trained to kill. To fight. To protect Eastonia and aid the other kingdoms who come calling for my skills.

I am not trained for *this*.

I grind my teeth and snatch the folder back from Howard, giving the pages inside another once over. I ignore Kenna's picture. Her image is already burned into my mind, as is the look on her face when I told her we could never be friends again, that I never... that I *hated* her…. It haunts my dreams.

"Is she in danger?" I ask. It's the only plausible reason Ryatt would send a Ghost to protect his daughter. Kenna's parents love and trust her, and she has family here in Crescent Falls. Her cousins are Alphas. Her aunt and uncle are the Luna and Alpha King, for Goddess' sake.

"The rest of the men are going to find out that aspect of this tonight. She might be, or it might be another of the princesses currently in town for the festival. All we know is there's been rumors of a rebel group planning a kidnapping of a royal, and the Allied Kings want their princesses secured."

I think of Misty, the fifteen, almost sixteen-year-old princess belonging to the royal house of Crescent Falls. I've only met her once when her entire family came to Moonrise. She's good friends with my younger sister, Piper. She'd just been a kid when her family visited, and she's still a kid in my opinion. Luna Madeline and Alpha King Isaac are her parents.

Which makes her Kenna's cousin.

"You'll be housed in an apartment near the Silverhide territory, just outside of town in the neutral zone. She's staying with her cousin, Alpha Ryan, during her trip."

I nod, because there's nothing else I can do. I can't get out of this.

The driver unlocks the door, and I leave the car without another word.

Within minutes, I've packed the few belongings I have, which is nothing more than a few changes of clothing and a picture of my family–my parents, Granger and Amanda, and my five siblings.

I told myself leaving Moonrise and following this path, even though my parents protested, would be the best course of action. I didn't want to be Kenna's Beta, but it's my birthright. It's a role I am destined to play.

But Kenna and I were destined for other things, too. Things that would ruin the sweet, kind, compassionate girl I loved when I was just a kid and everything was easy.

So, I ruined what could have been. I told her I hated her, that I felt nothing for her, that the childhood crush I had on her for years, the crush she admitted she shared, meant nothing to me now.

Five years ago, I broke Kenna's heart.

This is what I deserve, I think, as I walk into the apartment near the gates to the sprawling, wooded pack territory within view of my window. I deserve watching her try to find the happiness I can't give her.

Because she's my mate.

And she'll never know, because she can't feel the bond, and maybe that's a blessing.

3

MEATHEAD

Kenna

A SHARP SCRAPING SOUND PULLS my attention from the book in my lap. I blink then whirl in the chair I've been lounging in for the better part of three hours to find my cousin Ryan dragging a massive grill across his back patio.

"What the hell are you doing?" I ask.

"Dinner." He grins then picks up the grill like it weighs nothing and walks to the far side of the patio where the concrete gives way to a stretch of emerald green grass before it meets the woods.

I huff out a breath as Ryan continues his show of strength. "You're such a show off, Ryan."

It's true, and he knows it. He simply winks at me and walks back into his house—a large log home with several bedrooms, sparse furnishing, and an assortment of manly decorations like the mounted buffalo head over the fireplace... with a glittery blue thong hanging from one of the horns.

This place is a party house, plain and simple, and I'm not surprised in the slightest. Ryan has always been the wild one of the twins, and the pack he rules over, Silverhide, emulates that energy perfectly. Everyone in the wooded village nearby is young and mostly single. The village square is sleepy during the day but a wild party at night, with live music and dancing and street food.

Compared to the cityscape a few miles away, this place feels like… I'm not really sure how to describe it. It's not like Eastonia, but Ryan and his pack remind me a lot of the smaller packs dotted throughout the Roguelands. Tight knit, secluded, and more in tune with their wolfish ways.

Ryan returns from the house with several packages of meat wrapped in wax paper and dumps them unceremoniously on the table in front of me.

"Are we feeding a small army?" I laugh, pushing my sunglasses down the bridge of my nose. "I thought we were going out to dinner tonight!"

He motions to his body, arching a dark brow. "This is a pre-dinner snack, Ken."

I roll my eyes and curl into the lounge chair, trying to find where I left off in my book, but Ryan is purposefully being noisy and annoying.

He's probably right about the six steaks and dozen or so sausages being nothing but a snack before dinner. Ryan is *huge*. Huge in a big, stupid way that doesn't seem necessary. He's the tallest man in our family, with Sydney only an inch behind him. But he's also broad and so heavily muscled that all of his shirts are always too tight.

The girls drool over Ryan. No wonder he has a thong hanging from his mantle.

"Are you going to sit around being boring all day, or are you going to help me with this?" he asks, cracking open a beer.

"Help you with what?" Sydney's voice sounds from the house behind us, and I turn, smiling up at my cousin as he walks through the back door dressed in a white button down shirt and gray slacks. "Hey, Kenna." He squeezes my shoulder. "It's good to see you."

"Thank the Goddess," I groan, rolling my eyes to Ryan. "Now that you're here, I can actually have an intellectual conversation with someone."

Ryan glowers at me from over the rim of his can of beer.

Sydney sits down beside me and eyes the table. "I thought we were going out to eat before the festival?"

"I'm hungry now, and Kenna hasn't even started getting ready."

I close my book with a snap. "You never gave me a time to be ready, Ryan!"

"Make yourself useful and go start the grill."

"I don't know how to start the grill," I argue.

Ryan wiggles his fingers. "Use those powers of yours."

I turn to Sydney, giving him a pleading look. "Can I stay with you instead?"

Now Ryan's laughing and digging in the pocket of his jeans for what I assume is a lighter.

Sydney just smiles apologetically. His pack is closer to his parents' home, the castle of Crescent Falls, and his pack is... all business, to say the least.

"You're going to be bored out of your mind staying with Syd, trust me. I fall asleep the second I pass through the gates into Shadowcrest."

"It's true." Sydney nods then smirks. "Plus, my house is going through a renovation right now. You'd be stuck in one of the pack houses in the village, and I doubt your parents would be happy about it. You could stay with our parents if you want."

"Dad can read you the complete history of the pack lands every night before bed."

I frown, but wave them both off. Ryan turns to walk over to the grill, but I light the coals with a flick of my finger from all the way across the patio, and he turns, giving me a dramatic bow in thanks.

Despite the constant bickering and teasing, it feels great to be here with my cousins. I'm an only child, and Ryan and Sydney have always felt like brothers to me. They also couldn't be more different.

Ryan is a playboy. He loves the ladies and can charm anyone out of their clothes with a single heated look in their direction, whereas Syd is more reserved and serious. Ryan's sense of humor is sarcastic and loud, while Syd is on the dry side and prefers to just sit in contemplative silence.

Ryan and his pack members own a garage that works on luxury vehicles. He's a mechanic and is usually covered in oil or other grime after a day's work while Syd is an engineer with his own firm that helps their father, the king, when it comes to city planning and updating infrastructure.

I assume their differences are genetic, but also... Sydney is going to be the Alpha King of Crescent Falls one day. He's always had that burden on his shoulders. He's always had to be the serious one.

"How's your mom?" Sydney asks, leaning back in his chair and sliding a pair of sunglasses onto his face.

"She's great," I reply.

"Mom and Dad want a family dinner soon," he says, resting his elbows on the armrests.

"I'd love to see them. Misty, too."

Sydney nods as he stares absently at the woods beyond the backyard.

I chew my lip and look him up and down. Though naturally a quiet person, right now he seems slightly out of sorts. "What's wrong?"

"Just a long day," he sighs.

"You're still going to the festival with us, right?" I turn in my chair. "You can't leave me with him. Ryan will have me dancing on a table by the end of the night, and you know I can't handle alcohol very well."

Sydney chuckles. "I'm going, don't worry. And don't worry about Ryan. He's just not ready to settle down yet."

"Are you?"

Sydney looks at me, a ghost of a smile touching the corners of his mouth. "I might be. I'm considering it."

"So you're going to look for your mate during the festival?" I grab his arm as excitement blooms through my veins.

"Sydney is going to end up with some princess from a far off land," Ryan grins as he walks to grab the meat for the grill.

"I have to find someone to fill Mom's shoes," Sydney corrects, "regardless of her societal standing. She has to be–"

"Don't start," Ryan says in warning. "I don't want to hear any of that 'she has to be dutiful, responsible, blah blah blah' shit tonight, Syd. You're getting drunk. I swear on the Goddess, I will drink you under a table tonight."

"That's not going to happen," Sydney laughs.

Ryan shrugs, a playful gleam in his eyes. "You gotta get out, man. You need to have a little fun before Dad retires and makes you sit on his throne. Right, Kenna? See, that's why she's here, to have fun before taking over as Luna of Veiled Valley."

"So that's still the plan?" Sydney asks, ignoring Ryan completely.

I nod, trying my best to smile. "Yeah. Grandpa Westfall was always going to retire when I finished college and turned twenty-one–"

"Speaking of which," Ryan cuts in from across the patio, where he's now laying fat steaks on the grill. The smell of roasting meat fills the air and suddenly, I'm just as hungry as he is. "You and I are going to shift one of these nights. I want to see what you can do."

"You'll be terribly disappointed, Ryan. I'm not much of a wolf."

Sydney eyes me curiously. I haven't seen them since I finally came into my wolf powers. I've only been able to shift for a few weeks now, and it hasn't been going well.

I sigh and turn to fully face Sydney. "I'm a really small wolf, and I'm clumsy."

"Okay… that doesn't really mean anything, Kenna. You have to get used to being in your wolf form. It takes training, sometimes, for some people."

"Shifting… hurts."

"Oh," he says. "It shouldn't hurt."

"I know, that's what my mom said." I swallow and glance at Ryan, who is looking at us over his shoulder, likely listening to every word we're saying.

Sydney considers my dilemma for a moment. "What do you think is wrong?"

"My powers are overwhelming my wolf abilities for sure. So, there's no way around it. I'm a witch. A Firestone, at that. This is just who I am, I guess."

"What about the mate bond aspect?" Sydney lowers his voice and leans in. "Have you felt… anything?"

"No, and I went all over Eastonia this spring during our mating season. I went to, like, every ball and festival held in the villages. I felt nothing. That's why I'm here. Maybe my mate is on this side of the border." Or maybe I can't feel the mate bond at all. All I know is that if this fails, I can return to Eastonia and take over Veiled Valley without feeling like I didn't leave a single stone unturned. I can rule alone, not having to worry that my mate is still out there, looking for me as much as I'm looking for him.

And maybe I'll meet someone. Someone special, someone I can fall in love with despite not having a mate bond between us. I mean, before the veil between Crescent Falls and Eastonia fell, a lot of people in Eastonia did something called imprinting, which is the act of marking and pledging to be with each other forever.

I think of Evander's parents. Granger imprinted on Amanda, because as a fox, and the only fox at that, she was mateless. But from what I heard from my parents, Granger felt the mate bond with her regardless of if she could feel it.

Maybe my mate is out there, and I'm just incapable of feeling it.

Ryan sets a plate in front of me. "Eat. We have a long night ahead of us."

"Do you ever eat fruit and vegetables?" I tease, staring down at the steak taking up the entire surface of the plate.

"This body," he grunts, flexing his arms, "isn't built on broccoli, Kenna."

Sydney slides his tongue along his lower teeth and laughs. "No wonder you got stuck in our mom when you were born. Your head is just as big as your ego."

Ryan chokes out a laugh, "Damn, dude. Don't let her hear you say that. You're the current favorite and that might knock you down a few pegs."

Sydney and I sink back into silence while I eat a few bites, but then he clears his throat, momentarily checking his watch. "Have you talked to Evander lately?"

I set my fork down. Great. I really don't want to have this conversation. Sydney and Evander were friends as kids when our families used to meet in Maatua every year.

"No, not in a very long time."

"I haven't either. Last I heard, he was some kind of specialized warrior who can shift into a fox and a wolf interchangeably. Is that true?"

"It is." I slouch in my chair, not wanting to even think about what Evander has to do for work.

Sydney licks his lips. "But he's going to be your Beta, right?"

"So many questions," I tease, giving him a big, sparkling smile that I hope hides the hurt behind my eyes. "I need to go dressed for this party, huh?"

"Sure," Sydney says, but there's an edge to his voice I've never heard before. In fact, as I walk back into the house, I glance over my shoulder at the twins, who are now talking quietly as if they don't want to be overheard.

I have a sudden feeling that something is amiss.

But, I'm not here for drama and politics.

I walk into my guest room and throw open the closet, looking past the boxes and cramped workout gear on the floor, and pull out one of the dresses I packed.

Tonight, I'm going to find my mate.

Or, at least, I'm going to try.

4

IS HE MY MATE?

Kenna

THE MAIN TEMPLE of the Moon Goddess sits beside a lake which is currently illuminated by lanterns that make the water glow. Large tents cover the wide, grassy plain between the lake and the temple, and music rises to the star filled sky.

I've never seen so many people in one place at one time. Eastonia is big, sure, but my people are more secluded than the packs that hug that territory surrounding the Alpha King of Crescent Fall's lands.

Over two dozen packs bleed into Crescent City, their territories separated by walls, or woods, or even just a single street.

On the far side of the lake, I can just see the castle where my aunt and uncle live.

I smile, my cheeks straining. I'm glad I came here, even if I don't find my mate. The city is intoxicating.

Ryan and I lost Sydney some time ago as we moved from tent to tent, checking out the different music and entertainment. The main mating ball is taking place in the temple tonight, but we haven't made our way there yet. I'm too busy soaking it all in.

"So," Ryan says, nudging my shoulder as we walk side by side toward the temple, "what do you think?"

"Is it always like this?" I ask, motioning to the crowd.

"This busy? No. No way. There're people from other kingdoms here right now. We have smaller festivals throughout the year where all the packs come together, mostly around specific holidays, but Celestoria and Crescent Falls just signed a new treaty, opening up some more territory for my dad to expand into, and with the borders opening up between here and Eastonia, my parents decided this summer is the perfect time to put on this show of unity." He looks down at me with his cocky smile.

"Is that what you think this is? Just a show?"

"Nah, I think this is a good thing. It's always a good time when the packs around here open their gates and mingle with each other. It keeps spirits high and communication open." He's quiet for a moment, as if lost in thought, then asks, "Is it true you're here to try to find your mate?"

"Yeah. It's true."

"So I have to watch you flirt all night? Gross."

I give him a playful punch to the arm, and my knuckles sing with pain.

"Don't hurt yourself." He chuckles, roping a burly arm over my shoulders. "Let's go find this mate of yours, then. I'll be your wingman."

"You're the last person I want as a wingman," I reply tartly, trying to shrug his arm from my shoulders. "Secondly, I have this under control."

"Do you even know what a mate bond is supposed to feel like?"

Like a pull you can't ignore. Like an electric pulse is moving through your very soul at their touch. Like you can get lost in the way they smell, and taste, and...

"Do you know?" I ask, and Ryan smirks.

"Yeah, of course."

"You don't sound all that convinced."

"I'm a few months older than you, Ken. Who says I haven't felt a spark yet, huh?"

"Judging by the sheer amount of random bras I've found lying around your house, I highly doubt you've found your mate."

"Unlike you, I'm not ready to settle down. I'm waiting."

"Waiting for what? Why would you ignore the mate bond if you've felt the pull?"

"There's loads of reasons. Jeez, Ken. You act like we all still live in caves. The bond isn't just about breeding anymore, you know. It's... shackles–in more ways than one."

"You just don't want to give up your life of bouncing from one woman's bed to another."

Another cocky grin. "So what?"

"So, what if you meet your mate out here tonight, then what?"

"I won't."

"What makes you so sure?"

"Because I've already met her."

I whirl on him, and he drops his arm to look down at me with that patronizing look that runs on my mom's side of the family. He looks like my Grandpa Maddox right now. "Shut up. You've met your mate?"

He nods then shrugs like it's nothing at all.

"What? When? Why–"

"Kenna, drop it. It's not that big of a deal."

"It's a huge deal! Who is she–"

"She's–she doesn't feel the bond yet. And I'm not saying another fucking thing about it. You're going to drop it."

Of course I'm not.

"What do you mean she can't feel the bond yet?"

"We're done, Kenna."

Ryan starts jogging up the stairs leading into the temple three at a time, and I hurry after him, much slower in my heels. "Ryan!"

But he reaches the top of the stairs and gives me a teasing look before disappearing into the swelling crowd of party goers standing on the veranda overlooking the festival.

"No!" I huff out, standing on my toes to try to see where he went. He seriously thought he could drop a bomb like that and run away? This isn't over. Not even close.

I wade through the sea of finely dressed people attending the mating ball. I blend in with my fuchsia silk gown, my thick, dark brown hair curled and piled on top of my head. I'm wearing a little makeup today, which I rarely do. I feel pretty.

A few people glance in my direction as I pick my way deeper into the temple. Some stares linger longer than others, but I'm not approached. I doubt many people know who I am. Even though the veil came down shortly after I was born, Eastonia is still shrouded in myth. The borders between our lands are tightly monitored, almost impossible to cross. Why would these people need to know about the Princess of Eastonia?

I smile to myself, happy to be a faceless, nameless stranger in the crowd for once.

Finally, I reach Ryan, who is standing next to Sydney near the back of the temple's main room where a statue of the Goddess rises several stories over our heads.

I'm panting and flushed, my ears ringing from the music, when I lurch to a stop and grip Sydney's arm for support. "Ryan, you–you better tell me–" I fight for air as Sydney and Ryan turn around to face me, Ryan looking smug, and Sydney looking concerned.

"Have you been running?" Sydney asks.

"Ryan just told me about his–"

A third man comes into view when Ryan whirls to fully face me, giving me a warning look. But my eyes are on the handsome man between them, the man who's leaning against a marble column with the first three buttons of his shirt undone and his tie loosened. His brown hair is swept back away from his face, and his dark eyes lock on mine while he gives me a soft smile, a kind smile.

He dips his head. "Hello."

"Hi," I manage to say, my chest locking up. I nudge Sydney, hoping for an introduction.

Sydney's jaw flexes as he slowly turns from me and back to the mystery man he'd just been talking to when I so rudely interrupted, apparently. "This is Ella Westfall, Princess of Eastonia."

"Wow, it's an honor," the man says, and promptly bows to me.

I blush.

Sydney exhales deeply, his eyes flashing with annoyance. I'm not sure if it is directed at me or his companion. He says, "Ella, this is Markus Aberfeldy, Alpha of Emerald Shore."

"It's very nice to meet you," I say, holding out my hand for him to shake, as is customary in Crescent Falls, I think.

But he takes my finger and bends them, pressing a kiss to my knuckles. "Very nice indeed."

Sydney and Ryan exchange glances as Markus straightens, his touch lingering on my fingers for a moment longer than necessary. "What brings you into town? You're far from home."

"This festival," I tell him, wondering why my heart is beating so fast. Is this the mate bond? Is this breathless feeling what that first moment of clarity is supposed to feel like, or am I terribly out of shape and just spent the last five minutes chasing Ryan?

"Have you been dancing?" he asks, smiling around the words.

"No, I just arrived."

"Well, you shouldn't waste any more time standing around with these guys," he says, and at first I think he's telling me something along the lines of 'get lost, the Alphas are talking,' but he takes my hand and whirls me into the crowd.

I look over my shoulder at my cousins and notice their frowns. Ryan leans in to say something to Sydney who nods, looking grim.

I'm not here to get involved in the complicated pack politics of Crescent Falls. The rest of my life will be nothing but politics. I'm here for *this*.

Markus sweeps me into a dance–some kind of old-school waltz that has me tripping over my feet immediately.

"Do you not know the steps?" he asks in a teasing tone.

I look up at him, taking him in. Handsome, sure. I haven't ever considered what my type would be, but he is *nice* to look at.

"I wasn't ever trained in formal dance," I tell him, and he smirks wider.

"What were you trained in, then?"

My stomach twists. While my parents always told me my powers were gifts, and something to be proud of, there was an unspoken rule about not showing them off while visiting family across the border. Eastonians are used to us and our magic, but here?

What am I even supposed to say?

"My grandfather is an Alpha, and I'm going to be filling his shoes at the end of the summer," I say, and it seems to be enough for Markus.

"That's odd. Do you not have brothers?"

"No, I'm an only child."

His eyes brighten. "I only know of one female Alpha, Alpha Emery of Obsidian Temple."

"Well, now you know two." I grin.

He smiles too, but there's something unreadable flashing behind his eyes as he says, "Then you'll take over as Queen of Eastonia someday?"

"Not for a long time, but yes, eventually I will be queen."

"Ruling second to your husband—"

"No," I laugh as he leads us into another turn. "No, Eastonia is a matriarchal society now. My dad is actually my mom's second."

"I find that hard to believe."

Something in his tone makes my skin crawl, and I briefly try to pull away, but he has a hand locked on my back, keeping me fixed in place. "What's so hard to believe about that?"

"It goes against our nature, doesn't it? Men lead; women follow."

I scoff. "Maybe in Crescent Falls, but not in Eastonia. Plus, my parents have always treated each other as equals. It was my dad who actually battled to ensure my mom would rise as queen of his lands—"

"Then it wasn't law, and your dad could have ruled as king. It might be subject to change, then."

I narrow my eyes at him. He has a far off look in his eyes as he absently scans the crowd over the top of my head.

The exquisite string quartet music fades, and the dance draws to a close, but Markus keeps his hands on my body regardless of the Alphas coming to fetch their daughters off the dance floor.

Then I realize why.

Another song starts up, something recorded and new age. Music booming through speakers situated throughout the large ballroom. The crowd cheers as a ripple of relief washes over everyone around us.

I look around, trying to untangle myself from Markus. More women are being led off the dance floor, some arguing with what I assume are their parents. These must be the high bred ladies of the packs whose parents aren't okay with them staying for what I imagine is about to be a huge party.

Again, I try to pull away from Markus, but... something inside of me shifts. At first, it's a scent. Something... something faint, but delicious. Something that causes my body to tremble, and my breasts suddenly ache with the need to be touched. I find myself blushing and inhaling deeply, leaning closer to Markus to see if that scent is coming from him.

"What is that?" I whisper to myself, and then it hits me. It's like a flicker of electricity zooming over my skin. My heart races. My blood hammers in my ears, blurring with the music.

I look up at Markus, confused, wondering if he feels it too.

Is he my mate? Is this... is this what it's supposed to feel like?

I open my mouth to say something, anything, but then the feeling fades so abruptly it steals my breath with it, leaving behind a kind of emptiness I've never felt before.

Sydney suddenly grabs my arm. "Time to go, Kenna."

5

INTERVENTION

Evander

THE COLUMN at my back is smooth and cool to the touch, which is a welcome relief. In front of me, the crowded ballroom in the temple writhes with color and noise as the ball takes on a new vibe. There's a darker edge to the music now compared to the soft, classical music that was playing before. The dancing has changed as well, and couples are glued to each other as they sway and grind to the music.

I exhale deeply, crossing my arms over my chest, my feet firmly planted in place.

A tall, dark haired man dressed similarly to me—all black, wearing a finely made dress shirt and matching trousers—makes his way through the crowd clutching a bottle of what might be beer, his face shadowed and distorted by the strobing light now suffocating the dance floor.

But then I realize who's walking in my direction.

Flynn huffs out a breath as his back meets the wall behind us. "Fuck, man. This place is getting rowdy. I had to wait twenty minutes to get this warm beer." He inspects the bottle, frowns, and proceeds to drain the contents in full.

I glance in his direction before locking my gaze on the crowded dance floor again. "It must be nice having the night off."

"Yeah, well, all the other guys hung back. We were awake all night in the fucking catacombs under the city. Did you know about those? Creepy, man. Anyway, I figured I'd see what the hell you were up to tonight, given you're on some top secret mission."

"You wasted a perfectly good opportunity to rest." I take a step deeper into the shadow currently keeping my body veiled from view. "This is all I'm doing." Standing here, trying to stay hidden. Trying not to tear into the crowd and pull the man who has his hands on Kenna out of the temple and take him apart piece by piece.

Flynn rolls his eyes and frowns at his empty beer bottle. "Who are you spying on?"

"Confidential."

"So is everything we do. Don't leave me hanging. Which Alpha fucked up?"

I sigh, wishing I had a drink to nurse, but I'm on duty. "Not an Alpha."

"Beta, then?"

"No."

"Ev, tell me. Everyone back at the warehouse is wondering. It was a shit show not having you around last night while we were taking out that auction."

I roll my shoulders and wonder if maybe I should tell him, but once he finds out who I'm here for, he'll have nothing but questions.

Fuck it. "I'm guarding the Princess of Eastonia."

Flynn grunts in surprise. "*Kenna?*"

Here we go.

"Dude, Princess Kenna? She's here?"

"She is, and it's not that big of a deal."

"Uh… does she know *you're* here?"

"No, and it needs to stay that way." I swallow hard, keeping my eyes locked on the crowd. I can't see her right now. She's short, which makes this vantage point a terrible one, but there's no upper level overlooking the ball room, so I'm stuck looking at the fucking man touching her right now, looking down at her like she's a snack.

"Why?"

I finally tear my attention back to Flynn. He knows more about the Kenna situation than anyone because we went to school and then trained in Tarsian together. "I was told it's because she's looking for her mate."

Flynn raises a brow. He doesn't know *that* aspect of our relationship, thank the gods.

"How does that make you feel?"

"Are you a therapist now?"

"No, but I remember you coming back to school after visiting home that one time, when you were fifteen or sixteen. You were a fucking wreck, man. You used to talk about her all the time. You used to write her letters, and then it was like she didn't exist."

"We were childhood friends. Nothing more. It was hard to avoid that since we were practically raised together."

"But something happened between you guys?"

I bite my lower lip. Flynn catches the motion before I can stop myself and gasps, then laughs. "No way."

"No way, what?"

"Oh, don't do that whole, *'I'm a big tough super spy with no emotions'* act with me, Ev. You love her."

"I don't *love* her. I don't feel anything for her. I am here because General Howard demanded it of me. This is just a mission, and right now, you're distracting me."

Flynn smirks. "You got it bad, don't you?"

"Shut. Up."

Just then, the crowd parts enough that I finally catch a glimpse of Kenna and...,

I'm moving forward, cutting through the crowd, careful to keep my head down. Thankfully, the lights are dimmed, and it's easy to blend in. Kenna's back is to me. She can't see me. She *won't* see me.

It takes all of the self-control I'm capable of to not launch myself at this man, this man who's gripping the back of her dress hard enough his knuckles are turning white as she places a hand on his chest and firmly tries to push him away.

My blood boils.

I'm not supposed to intervene. I'm not supposed to make myself known at all, but I can't sit back and watch this happen.

Kenna is too polite to tell someone to fuck off. She's always been that way. I'd been the one, when we were kids, who slammed bullies into the dirt and told them if they ever touched, spoke, or even looked at Kenna again, I would end them, slowly, mercilessly.

Kenna never knew about it, either. I made sure of that.

I'm almost at her side when I notice another man barreling in her direction.

I immediately stop moving, letting the crowd swell around me, but he sees me.

Sydney, now an Alpha, meets my eyes with the same feral, protective expression I'm sure is on my own face as he slows but doesn't quite stop. A look of relief mingled with confusion, then understanding, passes behind his eyes. He nods at me before putting himself between the man and Kenna, whispering something in her ear while taking her hand and giving the man who was so roughly clutching her a look that conveys the man overstepped.

But I'm close enough to feel her. To feel that pull... gods. Her scent. Like the lilacs that bloom in the gardens around the castle where we were raised. She smells like home, and it hits me like a punch in the gut.

She looks wildly around as Sydney leads her away, but her cousin doesn't let her turn around to look at where I'm still standing, unable to snap out of the sudden haze gripping my senses.

When the crowd starts to swallow them again, and Kenna is lost from view, Sydney turns to look at me over his shoulder.

We can't mind-link, but the look he's giving me right now is clear enough.

He will find me later, and we will talk.

I pull myself back out of the crowd, and it takes all of my strength not to turn around and go to her, to make sure she's fine, but another sense is taking over.

"Change of plans," I tell Flynn as I reach his side.

Flynn raises his brows as I roll up my cuffs.

"See that guy, right there," I jab my thumb toward the man moving out of the crowd to join a group of men who look roughly our age.

"Yeah. Why?"

"I want to know who he is and what pack he belongs to. You can be seen, I can't. Go talk to him."

"Bossy," Flynn grumbles. "You owe me a drink for this." He pushes off the wall and makes his way toward the group. Flynn can charm anyone. He can schmooze his way into any crowd, and within twenty minutes, he returns to my side and leans against the wall clutching a glass of whiskey.

I don't ask where he got it, but he's smirking at me as he dips into the shadow I've been lurking under.

"Markus Aberfeldy. Twenty-five. Just took over as Alpha of Emerald Shore after his older brother's... unfortunate *accident* involving a stairwell."

"Huh," I muse, crossing my arms over my chest. "What else?"

"He's looking for a Luna. I asked about the girl he was just dancing with, and he was smug as hell. He told his buddies he might be selling himself short talking to the daughters of Betas. He made a comment about how an advantageous match might be in his cards."

I wonder what Kenna said to him. If he's an Alpha, she was likely introduced to him by her cousins. He would have known she was a princess, but what else?

"Are we kicking this guy's ass?" Flynn asks, smiling.

I lick my lips. "Sure. Why not?"

Flynn grins like mad and hands me his drink. I drain it, catching movement out of the corner of my eye. Sydney is leading Kenna out of the temple, his hand wrapped around her upper arm. Ryan follows close behind. It's hard to miss the twins, even in a crowded place like this. Tall, imposing, and handsome, all eyes are constantly on their movements. The disappointed looks of the women watching them depart briefly makes the corners of my mouth twitch into a ghost of a smile.

I used to be friends with them. My family sometimes joined Kenna and her parents when they did their yearly trip to Maatua for Winter Solstice. I'd been particularly close with Sydney, but it's been at least ten years since we last saw each other.

Still, he'd recognized me in the crowd. That brief moment of clarity in his eyes makes me wonder if he knows exactly why I'm here despite General Howard telling me the princes were as in the dark as Kenna.

Kenna is pointing an accusatory finger at Ryan, and he's laughing, as they cross the threshold onto the veranda and out of sight.

She's fine. She's safe with them.

For the first time since I arrived at the ball, I feel like I can breathe.

So, I turn my attention back to Flynn.

"Have you been briefed about the kidnapping threat?" I ask Flynn.

"Not really, but I assumed something was going on the second you said you were here to guard Kenna."

"It's a rebel group," I tell him. "With ties to both here and Eastonia." I did a little digging today before the ball. It's not hard to find information about the underground in the neutral zone, where my apartment is strategically located.

Flynn nods. "Yeah, we picked up a few guys from the auction who were from Eastonia. They won't tell us who they work for, but they have ties to both kingdoms for sure. Something's brewing."

We know enough to understand the dissent in some spaces is about the borders opening up between Crescent Falls and Eastonia. Once, a veil of magic prevented the two kingdoms from contacting each other. Now, twenty-one years later, border crossings aren't nearly as tight. The kings are allies and bonded by shared family.

Not everyone agrees with the way either kingdom is moving, ushering in a new era of unification and peace.

"I'm going to introduce myself to Markus," I tell Flynn. "Maybe he knows something about this underground network of rebels."

Flynn snorts. "That guy? Doubt it. He's as dense as a brick."

"Everyone is until they're in a situation where they're about to be flayed open," I say and scan the crowd for the Alpha in question. He's leaving.

But he's not going to get far.

"Let's go."

6

———————

AUNT MADDY

Kenna

MIDDAY SUNLIGHT DRIFTS through the open windows in my Aunt Maddy's personal sitting room. The pale pink wallpaper glistens with delicate floral patterns that glow a soft gold in the sunlight, and all of the furnishings are pale wood and soft, creamy colored fabrics. The scent of Grandma Isla's rose garden just outside the windows is thick and rich, and I find myself closing my eyes for a moment to breathe it all in.

Ryan and I drove from his pack territory to the castle, where his parents live, after a quick breakfast. Ryan got a call from his dad, my uncle Isaac, that he needed to speak to him immediately, and I decided to tag along in hopes of seeing some of my family members.

Unlike our yearly family gatherings in Maatua, this visit has been a little boring and lonely. My aunt, uncle, and cousins work, and I just… sit around, smelling the roses, apparently. But I also need to borrow one of Maddy's gowns for tonight.

Just as my eyelids flutter closed, a sharp female voice cuts through the air as she whines, "You're not my dad, Ryan!"

A smacking sound follows, and I feel the corners of my mouth ticking up at the corners as Misty, Ryan and Sydney's sixteen-year-old sister, whirls into the room.

"You're a teenager!" Ryan shouts as he rubs his cheek, following her into my haven of quiet solitude and wrecking my peace. "Also, Mom and Dad already said you're not allowed to attend *any* of the balls this summer. Why are you mad at *me* for it?"

"Because I can be," Misty huffs, throwing herself on the couch next to me in a very dramatic fashion. "I can just sneak out and go to the festival pretty easily."

"Oh, yeah? What are you going to do? Climb over the front gate and run past the warriors dad has on guard twenty-four hours a day? Or are you trying to get me to let you spend the night so you can sneak out of *my house–*"

Misty bares her teeth in an aggressive snarl that cuts Ryan off. He bites his tongue, narrowing his blue eyes at his sister.

"You're a witch," he tells her flatly.

Misty rolls her eyes to the ceiling and crosses her arms under her breasts.

"Hey," I laugh, pointing an accusatory finger at Ryan. "I'm an actual witch, remember?"

"Sorry," Ryan grumbles, but he runs his fingers through his hair and slouches into an armchair across from us.

Misty flips her thick, golden blonde hair over her slims shoulders and glowers at her brother. She has the same bright blue eyes, but other than that, she looks nothing like Ryan or Sydney, for that matter. The twins take after their mother in coloring, even though their hair is a dark shade of reddish brown.

Misty, however?

She is the spitting image of our Grandma Isla in every way. It's honestly impossible to tell them apart when looking at old pictures of Isla in her youth.

"What exactly is going on?" I ask, looking from cousin to cousin.

"She cornered me the second we got here and demanded I let her spend the night tonight so she can attend the masquerade ball taking place on the festival grounds," Ryan says testily, stretching out his legs. "And I said no, obviously."

Misty sticks her tongue out at her brother. "I don't see why it's such a big deal. I'm sixteen! I'm going to Wellington next fall. It's not like I won't be around parties, boys, and alcohol there!"

"Are you trying to get me in more trouble than I already am?" Ryan hisses through gritted teeth.

I lean forward. "What are you in trouble for?"

Ryan's gaze slides from Misty to me, and he huffs out a breath. "No reason-"

She barks a laugh. "No reason? Ha! Dad has been in a horrible mood the last two days because you and Syd beat up an Alpha-"

"What?" I ask, shocked. "Ryan-"

"Syd and I had nothing to do with what happened to the Alpha of Emerald Shore, first of all. Secondly, Dad agrees that the asshole had it coming."

"Markus? The guy I danced with two nights ago?" I blink, trying to remember his pack name. I'm sure it was Emerald Shore, but there are so many packs...."

"Yeah, him." Ryan runs his hand down his face and scratches his jaw. "Apparently, he got jumped while leaving the temple. He's causing a scene now, trying to get Dad to do something about it. He thinks me and Sydney were involved."

I glance at Misty. She looks smug as she inspects her bubblegum pink painted nails.

"Were you involved?" I ask. I haven't given this Alpha much thought, honestly. I didn't like the way he talked about my parents and what my role should actually be when it comes to ruling ahead of my eventual husband.

But for the past two days, I've been wondering about the... *reaction* I experienced while in his arms.

Was that the mate bond?

I feel like I need to see him again to be sure.

But judging by the look on Ryan's face right now, I doubt that's going to happen easily, if at all.

"He's a cocky, arrogant bastard who might have killed his own brother to take over their pack," Ryan deadpans, crossing an ankle over a knee. "He's been trying to get on Syd's good side for a while now, to form some kind of alliance. But we didn't like the fact he took you to the dance floor without even asking us."

"Do I need your permission to dance with someone?" I cut in, my tone sharpening to a fine edge.

"No, but I'm an Alpha, and you are my family member. Practically a sister. It's my responsibility to have your back."

"I don't need your protection." I scooch to the edge of the couch in preparation to stand, but soft footsteps drift into the room, and both Misty and Ryan relax.

Ryan gives me a look that says we're going to continue this conversation at another time just as Aunt Maddy comes into view.

She's beautiful as always with her dark red hair pulled back away from her face. Dressed in a pale blue, finely tailored suit, she glides to a stop in the center of the room with her hands planted on her hips. "Misty, you're supposed to be at training right now." She checks her watch. "You're actually twenty minutes late, missy. Cassian is going to be livid."

Misty sighs heavily and stands. She glares at Ryan, who makes a face back at her as she practically stomps out of the room.

"What's her problem?" Maddy asks, looking between me and Ryan.

"She wanted to spend the night at my house so she could sneak out and go to the ball tonight," Ryan says with effort. He suddenly looks exhausted and groans as he rises. "Is Dad out of his meeting?"

"Yeah, he should be. Where's Syd?"

"I thought he was here with Dad," Ryan replies. "Is he not here?"

Maddy shakes her head and shrugs. Ryan simply walks away and out of sight.

"Well," Maddy sighs, rolling her shoulders. "Come here, Kenna, and give me a hug!"

I do just that.

"Goddess, it's been too long. How was your birthday? How has it been staying with Ryan? Tell me everything!"

"My birthday was fine," I laugh, "and staying with Ryan has been great. It's nice to spend some time with him, just us."

"I knew it was a good idea. I suggested it, actually. We thought Ryan could use the company."

"I think he has plenty of company," I chuckle, then promptly shut my mouth and turn pink.

Maddy smirks. "Oh, trust me, I hear all about Ryan's reputation as the kingdoms most notorious flirt."

He does *a lot* more than flirting, but I just smile and nod as Maddy motions for me to follow her upstairs.

She takes me into a room on the second floor, closing the door behind us before flipping the light switch. I blink to adjust my eyes to the brightness and take a deep breath as I scan the room coming into view.

Of course, the Luna of Crescent Falls would have an entire room in the castle as a dedicated closet.

It's nearly as large as my bedroom back in Moonrise. Shelves are full of shoes, gowns hang from racks, and ceiling height shelving units are stacked with sweaters and pants.

"So," she says, rifling through a rack of gowns. "I talked to your mom this morning."

"Oh, yeah?" I ask, momentarily blinded by the torrent of color making the room spin.

"She says you haven't checked in with them since you left Maatua last week."

"Yeah… I haven't. I've been busy." It's true, in my defense. Dad spirited me to Maatua, which is also called 'jumping,' the act of basically walking through space and time and landing somewhere completely new. It's incredibly difficult and taxing on our powers to do long jumps all the way here, so once in Maatua, I spent a few days with my grandparents before catching the ferry to the mainland.

But… that was a week ago, and I did tell my mom and dad I'd be checking in weekly.

"Don't worry, I talked to her and let her know you were fine and having a good time. You are, right?"

"Having a good time? Yeah, I am."

Maddy eyes me for a moment before pulling a few gowns from the rack and hanging them on a hook next to a huge full length mirror. "Ella told me you're here to find your mate."

I purse my lips and tuck my hands in the pockets of the cream colored silk pants I have on. "Did she?" Great. My mom and aunt are best friends, and nothing has ever been a secret between them. I should have known Mom was going to share every detail of my plans.

"She wanted me to talk to you about something. About the mate bond, actually. Here, do you like this one? Red is always such a good color on you and your mom." She holds up a crimson dress, but I shake my head. She frowns, putting it back on the rack.

"What about the mate bond?"

Maddy chews the inside of her cheek for a moment before pulling out another gown, this one a muted sage that shimmers in the sunlight. "Look, I know you're wondering if you can even feel the bond. Your mom told me about how training in your wolf form is going. I lost my wolf when I was your age."

"You did?" Well, apparently this is one secret Mom left out. "How?"

"I'm sure you've heard a few tidbits of the story of how Isaac and I met, and my life in Celestoria. I was abused, starved, and worked nearly to death. I was weak, and that reflected in my wolf powers, and then I lost the ability to shift altogether. I couldn't feel the bond with Isaac, not at first. It wasn't that crazy pull and feeling that knocks you off your feet." She smiles to herself, carrying the sage dress toward her shoe rack. "Honestly, not everyone feels that way around their mates when they first find each other. Your parents are the exception. Those two, well, their bond was stronger than any I've ever heard of. They were woven together from birth, whereas I needed a little... nudge, to feel anything with Isaac."

She turns to me with the dress in one hand and a pair of beautiful strappy heels in the other.

"What kind of nudge?"

"I thought I'd never feel the mate bond, and I was okay with it. I was fine being with Isaac knowing he wasn't my mate, but then he... he marked me, and our bond snapped into place."

She hands me the gown and smiles, squeezing my hand.

"You'll find your mate, honey," she says softly. "You don't need to rush."

"I'm going to be a Luna soon, Aunt Maddy." I don't want to be alone. I don't want to rule–alone. I don't want to be stuck in Veiled Valley waiting for my mate to find *me*.

She must pick up on the unsaid words dancing behind my eyes because she tucks a rogue lock of hair behind my ear and says, "Evander will be there with you, right? You won't be alone. You'll have your best friend with you."

My heart feels incredibly heavy as she leaves my side to start going through her jewelry.

I stand in silence, my mind reeling back to that strange, all-consuming sensation I felt at the ball.

Maybe that wasn't the mate bond.

Maybe that was... something else.

"Where is Syd, by the way? He's supposed to join us for lunch today."

I sigh, smoothing my fingers over the dress. "I have no idea."

7

—————

SUSPICIONS

Evander

I NORMALLY DON'T GO on runs on bright, sunny days like this, but the swatch of forest beyond the city center is a shaded, welcome relief from the glaring heat as I sprint back into the neutral zone in my fox form.

It's been ages since I was able to shift into my fox. I can't do this often in Eastonia. Only me and my mom are foxes. There's none of us left, from what I understand. My three brothers and two sisters don't carry the ability, which would have shown up in their early childhood.

Foxes can shift from birth. At least, that's what Mom assumes. I could shift from the age of two. My wolf abilities came later, in my late teens, like most wolf shifters. I guess having the ability to shift into either form is even rarer than being a fox.

I dart through the trees and across the first paved road I've come across for miles. The city rises just down the road, the first gates leading into neighboring pack territories coming into view.

While it's common to see wolves running here and there all over

49

the city, a fox is another story. I'm sure there are other foxes around–
wild ones, not shifters. But one this close to the city?

I'm better off shifting into my wolf form now but decide against it,
needing to stretch these powers I normally keep buried deep, deep
down.

I edge along a fence that runs along the boundary of the Silverhide
until I reach the outskirts of the neutral zone, which is a small neigh-
borhood that borders four packs. A few shops teem with people as I
cut through an alleyway. The coffee shop across from my apartment
is particularly popular, which is working against me as I debate my
next move.

I can't run out into the open as a fox and dart into the apartment
building unseen.

I look up at the fire escape, and the window into the apartment I
left open for this purpose, and wait for a group of people to pass on
the sidewalk before leaping up, my claws catching on the first rung of
the ladder hanging several feet above the ground.

Within a few seconds, I'm four stories off the ground and
squeezing through the window.

When I hit the floor, I'm back in my human form, panting,
covered in sweat and feeling better than I have in days. Maybe weeks,
if I'm being honest.

I shake out my aching, tired muscles and walk into the bathroom
to shower, my mind blissfully clear and empty. I needed this today. I
needed this emptiness to prepare for tonight.

Another night spent watching Kenna from afar.

The thought of her springs through my head before I can shake it
away. I imagine her turning to face me, a book in her lap, her hair
falling in soft curls over her shoulders. She smiles at me, and it guts
me. I missed her sixteenth birthday, and she had no idea I was coming
back to Moonrise to see her, to give her a present I found in Tarsian.
A present I carried with me all the way back home.

I can still feel the cool touch of the necklace made from beads of
polished turquoise and lapis lupus in my pocket. I can still feel the gut
punch the moment I stepped into the shade of the awning she was

sitting beneath while reading, and her scent hit me—no, stop. I won't think about it.

Not today, not ever.

I'm just pulling on a pair of pants when a sharp knock sounds on my door. I freeze.

No one knows I'm here other than General Howard and maybe the Alpha King. Neither would be visiting me. I'm just a grunt, a tool to be used. I'd be summoned if they needed me.

I slowly straighten up, grabbing a shirt off my bed and walking carefully toward the door.

Another knock as I lean toward the door, careful to not make a single sound.

"I know you're in there, Ev."

I chew my lower lip and close my eyes, cursing silently as I open the door a crack.

Sydney, the Alpha of Shadowcrest and the Prince of Crescent Falls, smiles smugly at me, clutching two iced coffees.

"Are you going to invite me in?"

"How did you know where to find me?"

"I didn't. I just happened to be visiting the coffee shop that just opened across the street and saw a fox dangling from a fire escape." He winks at me, stepping inside uninvited. "Nice digs. Let me guess, this is included in whatever operation you're performing in my kingdom?"

"Your *dad's* kingdom," I correct, closing the door behind him with a hint of annoyance flowing through each word. "What are you doing here?"

"I'm here to ask you the same thing. I figured you weren't here to pay old family friends a visit."

I pull on my shirt, smoothing it over my chest. My skin is already sticky and hot from the unforgiving heat beating down on Crescent Falls today. "What if I am?"

Sydney hands me an iced coffee, his stormy blue eyes locking on my own. "As prince, and heir to my father's title, I'm privy to more information than you realize. It didn't take a lot of effort to find out the Ghosts are in town and that there's a rebel threat. But you weren't listed as active on the mission that took place three nights ago, the mission that took out that illegal breeder auction, which makes me wonder why, exactly, you're *here*, and not staying in the warehouse across town where your comrades are hiding in plain sight."

"I prefer AC," I grin.

Sydney narrows his eyes.

I slowly bring the coffee to my lips, sipping dramatically from the straw.

"Why are you–"

"Princess Kenna," I cut in, smiling at the way he bristles. "I'm here to guard Kenna, privately."

"You could have just said that," he grumbles, turning to get a better look at the single bedroom apartment. He sits on the couch and stretches out his legs, crossing his ankles on the coffee table. "Does she know?"

"Of course not." I sit in a chair across from him, thankful for the cold coffee now chilling my veins. "She won't know about this either."

"So you're spying on her." He jabs a thumb toward the window. "You have a view of Silverhide, I see."

"This wasn't up to me at all."

He leans back, looking remarkably casual despite his smart, freshly ironed white dress shirt and black slacks.

Sydney has always been all business. He's my favorite of the twins. But he's also sharp, cunning, and slightly manipulative.

Just like me–which is why we've been friends for so long.

It's also why, now that we're older and hardened, that we know better than to fully trust each other.

"I haven't seen your face in years. I thought I was seeing a ghost in the temple," he murmurs. "I guess I was, actually."

"I don't get holidays off, Syd."

"No, I imagine you don't." He looks around again, taking in the sparse furnishings. "How long are you in town?"

"However long Kenna remains in Crescent Falls, I assume."

"So that's it? You're just going where she goes?"

"If she's out in public, yes. I don't have jurisdiction in Silverhide or the castle where your parents live, obviously. She has more than enough protection when she's with the family."

Sydney nods. "Whose idea was this?"

"Alpha King Ryatt, and your dad, I imagine."

"This has to do with the kidnapping threat." Sydney looks down at his coffee for a moment, lost in thought.

"That is a rumor, not a confirmed threat."

"How much do you know about the rebel situation?"

"Very little, honestly."

He grinds his teeth before exhaling deeply. "So, that's it? You're just here to follow Kenna around while she looks for her mate?" There's an edge to his voice I hadn't expected.

I lean forward, my mouth quirking into a smile. "You're not happy about it, either."

"It's a fucking stupid idea. Coming here to party and spend a summer with her family, fine. Sure. Coming here to find her mate when she can't–" he cuts himself off, shaking his head. "She's vulnerable out there in the festival, which you know, based on what you saw at the ball two nights ago. The first Alpha she came across happens to be a rival, and he's already started running his mouth about the fact the Royal Princess of Eastonia is here looking for a husband, and now I have every Alpha and Beta from here to Celestoria blowing up my phone asking for an introduction."

My blood boils, but I ignore it, asking, "And you're mad about that? This is what she wanted. Now she has options."

"She might have options, but these men aren't interested in meeting her because of *her* but because of the fact she will one day be queen of an entire kingdom. They only care about her status and future influence. Not Kenna. You know her, Evander. She's not like *us*."

There's so much fire in his voice. Syd is the kind of guy who was born an Alpha. That kind of dominance radiates off him as he straightens up a bit and continues, "She leads with her heart, not her head. She's too Goddess-damned nice and has always been taken advantage of for it. I've never seen her use her powers besides lighting the occasional candle from across the room. She is prey out there at the festival, and she refuses to acknowledge the position she's putting herself in."

"That's why I'm here."

Sydney eyes me skeptically. "Did you have anything to do with the Alpha of Emerald Shore's assault?"

"Of course I did."

He smiles softly, shaking his head. "Markus has been telling everyone who will listen that Ryan and I had him jumped. I'm sure my dad is ripping into Ryan right now about it. I'm supposed to be there."

"But you're here instead."

"I needed to get my facts straight before confronting my father about the fact the Ghosts are in Crescent Falls, and especially why one was keeping tabs on my cousin."

I shake my head. "No one can know. *You're* not supposed to know."

"I knew something was up the second I saw you barreling in Kenna's direction at the ball."

"That Alpha had his hands on her," I growl. "That was just business. I was doing my job–"

"He might've been the first, but he won't be the last to try to put himself in her way. And the look in your eyes... no, that wasn't *just business*."

I stare at Sydney. Sydney the Alpha, the heir, my old childhood friend. He knew me back when Kenna and I were close. He knew, judging by the look on his face right now, that my feelings for Kenna went beyond friendship from an early age.

He also knows there's nothing I can do about it.

I am a Beta's son.

She is the future queen.

"I've known you my entire life. You've always been so protective over my cousin. You kicked Ryan's ass once for pushing her in the waves when we were all in Maatua together–"

"What are you trying to say?" I stand, towering over him.

Sydney remains seated, smirking. "Kenna won't tell us what happened, but I know something changed between the two of you. Anytime I mention your name, she clams up. Practically curls into herself like she'd rather think about anything else but you. Why?"

"That's between me and Kenna."

"Fine." I grit my teeth as he rises, tucking a hand in his back pocket.

"You might have blown my cover by coming here. Thanks for that."

"It's a shitty apartment. I can get you closer to Kenna. Ryan can put you up in a house in Silverhide."

"This is close enough."

His eyes flick to mine, narrowing into cat-like slits.

He knows. It's obvious in the way his nostrils flare, trying to pick up my scent. Some people have that uncanny ability to scent a mate bond on others.

"Kenna can't feel the bond. She thinks it's because her magic overpowers her wolf. Do you think that's true?"

"Possibly. It isn't stopping her from trying to find her mate, though."

"Do you think she'll find him?" he asks, and I know it's a trap. He's trying to bait me into telling him what I assume he already knows, or at least suspects.

So, I give him the only answer I can. "No, she won't. But perhaps she'll find something close enough, and I can get on with my life."

Sydney nods, but his eyes don't leave mine as he raises his coffee and sips. "I'll see you tonight, then?"

"You won't see me, but I'll be at the ball."

"It's a masquerade. Wear a mask if you want to blend in."

With that, Alpha Sydney leaves my apartment.

8

PANIC ON THE DANCE FLOOR

Kenna

THE BALLROOM at the temple has been totally transformed since the last time I came here just a few days ago. Dim, blue-hued lighting highlights the silver streamers falling from the ceiling, shimmering like starlight. Fresh flowers cover every surface, and string music whispers through the air over the rising voices all around us as I stand with my cousins toward the back of the room.

The dress I borrowed from my aunt Maddy hugs every curve like a glove. It's a little long for me, but a pair of heels keep the hem from dragging on the floor. The sage green silk makes my sun-tanned skin glow.

Again, I feel very pretty tonight. I pinned my hair away from my face and let it fall loose in thick, bouncing curls down my back. A mask of sage and gold covers the top half of my face as I look around the ballroom.

A few formal dances take place. Young men and women twirl in tight circles, smiling and laughing. Others congregate near punch bowls or over flutes of champagne.

But no one stands near us, or even so much as takes a step in our direction.

Ryan shrugs beside me, trying to get comfortable in his impressive suit jacket that hugs his muscles.

"Stop fidgeting," I tell him, looking up into the navy blue mask covering his upper face. "You're scaring away people who might want to come talk to me."

"It's not me scaring anyone away," he grumbles, jabbing a thumb in Sydney's direction.

I sigh heavily, knitting my gloved fingers together. The gloves match the dress, and I feel incredibly fancy wearing them. "What's his problem?"

"You," Ryan says honestly, nabbing a glass of champagne from a passing waiter.

"Me?"

"Haven't you been wondering why we've been here for two hours and no one has approached us?"

I frown and look around, catching a few people staring at us, at me. They glance at Sydney before turning away.

"What exactly did Sydney do?" I ask, whirling toward Ryan to face him fully.

"Well, there was the whole *Markus* thing."

Ah, that. I heard the Alpha of Emerald Shore got assaulted after the last ball, but Sydney and Ryan swore they had nothing to do with it. At least, that's what they told my uncle. I'm not sure I believe him.

"Rumors spread fast," Ryan sighs, "and Sydney didn't even attempt to tell the other Alphas and Betas that he had nothing to do with the attack. He simply... let them believe that anyone who so much as looks in your direction has to answer to him first."

"Are people that afraid of Sydney?" I glance at Sydney, who's talking to a group of stale looking men a few feet away.

"He's the heir of this kingdom." Ryan shrugs again, mumbling a curse before handing me the flute of champagne and taking off his jacket to reveal a white dress shirt. "Look, I'll take care of him, okay? I'll distract him so you can have a good time."

"I came here to find someone," I tell him, desperation creeping into my voice. "It's not his responsibility to–to protect me, or whatever it is he thinks he's doing!"

"I know," Ryan hisses over the music, which is growing louder as the formal part of the ball draws to a close. Soon, a band will start up, and the night will shift into something new. Something more intimate and fun. "I'll work on it, okay?"

I sip from Ryan's champagne glass and look down at my dress. What a waste of an outfit.

Sydney steps up to us again with a severe expression drawn across his mouth. His eyes are visible behind his mask, and honestly, it's obvious who the twins are despite the camouflaged theme of the night. If they'd been a little shorter, or carried themselves a different way, maybe I'd have a chance tonight, but because of them, I stick out like a sore thumb.

Everyone in the kingdom knows who I am and who I'm connected to now.

I drain the rest of the champagne and narrow my eyes at Sydney, preparing to give him a piece of my mind, but Ryan ropes an arm over his brother's shoulder. "You said you'd try to enjoy yourself at *one* of the balls. You haven't done that yet."

"I had business to attend to–"

"Dude, come on!" Ryan groans, gripping Sydney's shoulders. "Lighten the fuck up. Let's get some drinks."

A group of women walk by. One of them slows and looks at Sydney, her long platinum blonde hair bouncing down to her waist as she gives him a smile that could light up the ballroom. She coyly looks away as she follows her friends through a break in the crowd but looks over her shoulder again before disappearing from view.

I look at Sydney and notice him watching her, wide eyed.

"Ah, *there we go*. See, Ken? I told you I'd keep him distracted. All right, Syd, let's go hunting."

"No–"

Too late for Sydney. Ryan yanks him away, and Sydney knows better than to make a scene. I watch my cousins move through the swelling crowd as the final song played by a string quartet comes to a close.

I exhale deeply. Finally, I'm alone.

I proceed to watch the crowd as I slowly sip a second glass of champagne. A band starts up, and the ball turns into more of a party than before. Ten minutes pass, then twenty, then thirty.

And, I'm still alone.

I don't know what I was thinking. I know I can't feel the mate bond. I knew, even before planning this trip, that I wasn't going to find my mate across the borders of Eastonia.

At least in Eastonia, when I visited the various mating balls during the spring season, I had fun. I had friends to be with and people to talk to. Eastonians couldn't care less about their status when it comes to approaching people like me—people with titles. It's an easier, more open kind of communication.

Crescent Falls is entirely different… and no one will speak to me because I'm a princess, and Sydney is my cousin.

Apparently, they need his permission to approach me now, and he's unwilling to give it, or they're too scared to skirt his boundaries.

I close my eyes, wondering if I should try to find a third glass of champagne before giving up and planning an early trip back home, when someone bumps into my shoulder. I stumble forward, my ankles no more than limp noodles in the impossibly high heels, and nearly fall over when I'm caught around the waist and steadied.

I gasp out a breath as a man in a pale blue mask quickly hauls me upright and steps away, giving me an apologetic bow. "I am *so sorry*," he says, only his mouth visible beyond the mask.

In the dim light, I can just make out a gleam of soft, light brown hair, but that's it.

"It's all right. It's these—these damn shoes. I can barely walk in them, let alone stand," I reply, giving him a wobbly smile. How embarrassing! I need to get myself together, but the two glasses of champagne I've ingested aren't helping. "Thank you for saving my life."

He chuckles. "I wouldn't consider that a lifesaving act, Your Highness. It was my fault. I bumped into you."

"I was likely standing in the way."

He looks over the top of my head at the wall behind me. I wasn't in the way. I've been glued to the wall for the better part of an hour at this point wondering if it's time to throw in the towel and be alone for the rest of my life.

"You have a nice view of the party from here," he remarks.

I eye him, watching the way his mouth moves. "You have a Tarsian accent."

"Is it that easy to pick up?"

"You're from Eastonia, then?"

"Guilty as charged." He brings a glass of scotch to his lips.

"Are you here to find your mate?" It's such a forward question, but I haven't run into anyone from Eastonia yet.

"Oh, no," he laughs. "I'm here with my sister."

"Oh," I reply, trying not to sound disappointed. Am I really this desperate for attention? Goddess above.

"Well, again, my apologies, Princess." He bows low and is gone as quickly as he came.

"You're a desperate idiot," I say to myself, toying with my gloves. I could be home right now, enjoying my last few months of freedom with my friends in Eastonia. I could be with my parents, helping Mom and the mystics with the upcoming Rite, that religious festival that takes place every decade or so during a full lunar ellipse. There hasn't been one in twenty-one years, and one will take place at the very end of summer this year, but I'm here doing... *this*.

Tears prickle along my lower lash line. I quickly and discreetly brush them away, trying to maintain the makeup I plastered on my face.

Why is this so hard? And why is it so hard to explain to everyone why I feel the need to find my partner, even if it's not my mate?

I'm not cut out to be an *Alpha*. A Luna, ruling beside my husband, sure. I need someone to fill in the gaps, to be the hard, dominating force beside me because I cannot be *that*.

I want other things. I want children. I want a warm, sunny home. I want to cook meals and sit by a fire with the love of my life after we tuck our children into bed.

I want to be a midwife. It's the only thing I've ever truly wanted.

But I want to make my parents proud. I need to be the queen I was born to be. One day, my mom and dad will be gone, and it will be me on the Firestone Throne, ruling over an entire kingdom full of magic and danger and….

A tear works its way down my cheek before I can wipe it away.

I close my eyes tight, stifling a sob.

I feel a touch on my arm; it brushes up to my elbow. I open one eye and find a tall man dressed in all black standing before me, his face almost entirely hidden by a jet-black mask.

In the dim lighting, I can't make out any of his facial features beside a sharp, clean jaw. His shirt is halfway unbuttoned, the promise of the hard, sculpted muscles beneath just visible to the naked eye.

"What?" I ask rudely, sniffling.

"Would you like to dance?" he asks. His voice is low and rasping, and it does something to my insides that I can't explain. There's a familiarity to the way he speaks–somewhat slow, as if he ponders every word that leaves his lips before he says them.

"No."

"Are you sure?" He reaches up and swipes the tear from my cheek. He's wearing gloves–black leather. I wonder why, but his touch on my skin brings me back to the moment, to the ballroom, to the reason I'm here.

"I don't know," I reply, but he takes my hand and starts to lead me away from the wall, and I let him.

He guides us to the very center of the ballroom where a crowd is swaying to the music coming from the stage. It's a deep, rumbling, ethereal kind of noise that works its way into every muscle, down to the very marrow of my bones. I've always loved music, and this song does something to my brain that eases the tangled web of emotions threatening to drag me under.

I sway, closing my eyes, as the stranger wraps an arm around my waist to keep me flush against his chest. My head fits perfectly in the crook of his shoulder. He smells divine—like leather and sweat and something deeper... sandalwood and the vanilla candles I hoard in my room back in Eastonia.

It's comforting. I feel instantly, wholly at peace in this man's arms and I...

A shout rings through the crowd. He stiffens, but the music continues to play. Another shriek, and then more shouting, and suddenly the man snaps into action and picks me up like I weigh nothing at all.

"Wait!" I cry out, but he places a hand on my back and rushes through the panicking crowd. The muted lights overhead flicker before going out completely, and the entire room is consumed by near pitch-black darkness.

Howls pierce the air, and people are bumping into us, some crying and screaming in their haste to find an exit.

And this man is still running with me in his arms.

"Wait! My cousins!" I cry out again, trying to push him away, but the sounds of the ballroom grow distant as he darts into what I think is a corridor of some kind and then steps into an alcove.

"Do not make a sound," he pants, lowering me to the ground and caging me against the wall. My hand is on his chest. I can feel his heart thundering.

Another howl, somewhere distant, makes my entire body lock up.

9

SHIELDING THE PRINCESS

Evander

I'M GOING to regret this. I shouldn't be dancing with Kenna, her body glued to mine. She's a perfect fit as she lays her head against my shoulder and wraps her arms around my waist.

She's zoned out right now, completely overcome by the music. She's always been like this. As a kid, we'd get stuck in the square in Moonrise for hours because someone would be playing a fiddle or singing a song that would have Kenna locked in place, unable to look away.

She has no idea who I am. It's been long enough now that she wouldn't recognize my voice. It's much deeper than the last time I saw her. I'm taller, stronger, leaner....

Right now, I'm just a stranger to her, and it will never be more than this.

But her arms around me make me want to take her somewhere else, somewhere private, so I can keep touching her. So I can strip her of the gown she's wearing and feel her skin, so I can smell past the floral perfume she's wearing and find that scent that makes me feral.

That can never happen.

But this... this is fine. This is comfortable. This is all I can ever take from her.

I simply couldn't take seeing her cry anymore. I'd moved through the crowd the second I saw that tear slide down her cheek.

I can handle a lot, but not that.

My hand is flat on her back. She's warm and soft, curvier than I remember.

I shouldn't say anything to her, so I stay quiet. Once this song is over, I have to pull us apart and return to the shadows.

I'm dipping into a haze of feeling brought on by her touch and the music when I sense something... else.

There's been a shift in the air. I can taste... magic.

My muscles lock up, and I clutch Kenna hard. She's not paying attention. She has all of this power and won't use it.

A ripple rushes through the air. Everyone around us keeps dancing, unaware of what I'm sure is a threat.

A threat to the woman in my arms.

Someone shouts. I wait.

The sound of clothing shredding cuts through the music, and I move.

Kenna gasps as I lift her up and shove my way through the crowd just as the panic begins. The lights cut out. Darkness swallows the crowded ballroom whole. People are crying out for friends, confused and terrified as howling kicks up behind us.

Kenna is telling me to stop, to wait, that her cousins are in the ballroom, but I'm running toward the archways lining one side of the room, archways that lead into the network of corridors I scoped out during the first ball.

I let some of my wolf powers flow through me, just on the cusp of shifting, to allow me to see more clearly in the dark. Not many people can control their abilities like I can. I had to train for years to hold off that urge of transformation to use my gifts to their full advantage.

I spot an alcove just big enough for the two of us leading off one of the corridors and cut into it, lowering Kenna to her feet.

"Do not make a sound," I rasp, clasping a hand over her mouth.

She's breathing hard, her fear glazed eyes looking up at mine.

She can't see me clearly at all. The lack of power to the temple is the only thing working in my favor right now. She doesn't recognize my voice, but she'd recognize my eyes right now. I'm sure of it.

But with my wolf powers coursing through my veins, I'm… on the verge of losing control. My mate is *right here*. I'm touching her. The smell of her fear makes me want to shift and kill everyone in that ballroom.

Her hand curls on my chest, bunching up my shirt.

A few people gasp and stifle sobs as they run past the alcove we're hiding in, looking for an exit.

Her mouth is slightly open against the palm of my hand.

I find it hard to swallow as my whole body hones in on the feeling of her lips against the thin fabric of my gloves, gloves that turn into armor to cover my wolf in the event of an emergency, like this very situation.

I pull my hand away, lowering my head as I keep us glued to the wall, my body shielding hers from view.

She takes a breath as quietly as she can.

"It's okay," I whisper.

"What's happening?" she whispers back.

"We're being attacked."

"By who?"

"Rebels." It's the obvious answer.

"What–"

I shush her as another group runs by. I can hear the chaos taking place in the ballroom. I imagine Flynn and the rest of the Ghosts knew this was going to happen tonight. In fact, I had a feeling something like this would take place eventually, which is why I allowed myself to get closer to Kenna than before. Royal guards and warriors had been crawling through the temple in plain dress all night.

Everyone else is safe with this much security involved, but not Kenna.

Because the Rebels are here for *her*. I'd bet my life on it.

Kenna continues to suck in breaths. She leans closer to me like I'm an anchor in the storm we're weathering. She pulls me closer while I battle the conflicting emotions rolling through my body right now. Anger at the situation. Frustration over the fact that Kenna is more powerful than anyone in this kingdom yet she doesn't use those gifts to protect herself. Desperation because she's terrified right now, and I am the only thing guarding her.

I close my eyes, trying to focus less on her scent and her touch burning into my skin and more on the noises of the battle taking place in the ballroom, but Kenna's hands brush up my chest.

"Why," she whispers, drawing in a breath. "Why do you smell like this?"

Fuck. I close my eyes as her hands travel back down my chest. Her breath hitches in her throat, and I can smell the change in her. It mixes with that warm, sweet scent she gives off. It's something… headier and richer. Something that gnaws on the shred of self-control I have left as her hand cups my jaw.

She knows. She has to feel it too. Even if it's just a flicker of the bond we share, she's aware of it now. I open my eyes to find her looking up at me, at my mouth. Her lips part, and if she wasn't wearing a mask, I'm sure I'd see her brow knitted in confusion.

"Who are you?" she whispers.

My restraint slips at the desperation in her tone. I lower my face to hers, my nose brushing against her nose, my lips coasting over her jaw. She smells so good. Her skin is so fucking soft, and my wolf is screaming in agony, pleading with me to claim what's mine.

When she lets out a soft, whimpering moan, I lose it.

"Fuck it," I rasp, clasping her neck to keep her still while I press my lips to hers.

She melts into my arms as I press her into the wall. Her breasts brush against my abdomen, full and heavy. I'm out of breath, but I deepen the kiss, my tongue sliding over hers. She gasps and gathers me closer until there isn't any space left between us.

Nothing else matters. The world around us fades entirely. I am locked in place, unable to stop, and I can't get enough of her.

My free hand slides down the slope of her hip, down the generous curve of her thigh. She hikes her leg, and I press into her, gripping her leg and losing myself to the soft weight of her in my arms.

'All clear'

'We got one.'

'Bring him outside, we need him alive.'

'Where is Agent Evander? Has anyone seen him?'

I pull away so suddenly Kenna slumps forward, and I have to steady her. My heart is racing as I look down at her, at her flushed cheeks and swollen lips.

Oh, fuck. What did I just do?

The mind-link is going haywire as my fellow agents check in. I hear my name called through the link, over and over, but my attention is split between my duties and the woman before me, the woman looking up at me, breathless, her hands still clutching my shirt.

She lets go and reaches for my mask, and I immediately snap out of the haze.

It's still dark, but quiet.

I step away from her, panting for breath, letting my wolf powers simmer and ease away.

"Who–"

I grab her arm and lead her wordlessly out of the alcove. I ignore the way she tries to dig in her heels as we reach the empty, trashed ballroom. She tells me to stop, but I can't even look at her. I shake my head as a group comes into view, a dozen or so people standing on the veranda overlooking the festival beyond the temple.

Ryan of Silverhide is with them, thank the fucking Goddess.

Ryan turns to us, his attention wholly on Kenna.

"Ryan?" she squeaks.

Ryan looks so relieved. His body slackens as he steps forward and catches her in a hug.

I slink back, unnoticed, at least I hope.

But Ryan looks at me over the top of Kenna's head, his eyes narrowed.

I nod at him, wondering how much his twin brother had shared with him, and turn from the crowd of confused partygoers lingering on the steps before disappearing back inside to find my fellow agents.

I feel Kenna's sudden panic and desperation through the bond. She's looking for me right now, trying to spot me in the crowd.

I can't believe I let myself do this to her.

I need to get out of this situation, right now.

It doesn't take long to find Flynn and the rest of the Ghosts. I walk into a chamber toward the back of the massive temple, following their scents, and rip off my mask, letting it fall to the ground.

Flynn turns around, rolling his eyes as I stride up to the group standing in a semicircle around the man kneeling on the ground. "Nice of you to finally show up," Flynn grumbles.

"I had to secure the princess."

The space is illuminated by a single shred of moonlight beaming down from an angular window in the ceiling. Flynn looks me over as I stalk toward the captive. His brows raise as I wipe my mouth on the back of my hand, noticing the smudge of pink lipstick.

I give Flynn a sharp look, and he purses his lips looking more than amused as I crouch in front of the kneeling man and rip off the pale blue mask concealing his face.

Stormy, dark hazel eyes meet mine. His brutally split lips curl into a devious smile.

I know who he is, and what he's doing here, immediately.

"I can smell her on you," he rasps, his voice choppy from what I assume was a punch to the throat. "They can't protect her for long."

Gabriel, from the Draven Coven east of Tarsian, a coven led by followers of the long dead King Kane, smiles up at me.

Gabriel's father, Atticus, is enemy number one in Eastonia and the biggest threat to the royal family there.

Kenna's biggest threat.

A sharp explosion of darkness swallows the room for several seconds.

I rear back, grabbing Flynn's shoulder. He bends at the waist, coughing, choking for breath.

When the smoky magic clears, Gabriel is gone.

10

MORNING AFTER

Kenna

I'VE BEEN LYING on my side looking out the window for hours. I haven't slept a wink.

I curl my knees into my belly, nuzzling deeper into the flannel print sheets in one of Ryan's guest rooms. It's 6:00 in the morning. We didn't get back to his house until well after 1:00.

And I haven't moved from this position.

I run my fingers over my mouth, closing my eyes at the memory of the kiss—my first kiss. My first kiss *ever*.

That's probably why the whole thing felt so magical. Being pressed against a wall and ravaged by a masked stranger was the most delicious thing that's ever happened to me.

So, that's probably all it was. Shocking, delicious, and desperately wanted.

Not the mate bond.

Right?

I roll onto my back and look at the ceiling. Milky streams of morning light start poking through the blinds, dancing across the textured ceiling hanging over my head. I can feel the rain in the air before it starts, and the ticking sound against the windows feels like the kind of gentle wakeup call I need to get up and ready for whatever today brings.

I'm sure I've overthinking what happened between me and that man last night. I didn't see his face. I didn't catch his name. But his smell and his taste is imprinted on my mind, and I can't shake the memory of how his body pressed into mine or how it made me feel.

Also, I shouldn't be thinking about this at all, given the circumstances of how the kiss happened. From what Ryan told me, an all-out brawl started in the entrance of the temple and bled into the ballroom, where panicked chaos ensued. I can't help but feel like there was more to it than a simple fight. He couldn't explain why the power went out, and Ryan doesn't have powers beyond that of a wolf, from what any of us in the family know, so he couldn't taste that strange, metal flavor in the air before everything started happening.

But I had. I can still taste it now as I walk out of my room in a pair of pajama shorts and a tank top, my unbrushed hair pulled up in a huge bun on the top of my head.

A door at the very end of the hallway opens just as I close my own door. A woman steps out carefully, quietly, wearing nothing but the pale gray dress shirt I swore Sydney had on last night. But that makes no sense. Was it Ryan's?

The woman I saw—the woman with long, platinum blonde hair who'd smiled at Sydney at the ball—this is *her*.

She looks toward the kitchen, then back down the hallway, going rigid when she sees me standing there.

"Good morning," she whispers, smiling kindly, but her cheeks turn a bright, ruddy pink.

"Good morning," I whisper back and find myself smiling too. She grimaces as she slowly shuts the door behind her. It squeaks, and she mumbles a curse under her breath.

"I was going to make some coffee," I tell her, "if you want some."

"I'll be late for work if I stay," she whispers, but grins. "Thanks, though."

"Yeah–"

She hurries down the hallway toward the kitchen and living room, disappearing around the corner. I stand in place for a few seconds until I hear the front door open and close.

I huff out a breath. Did she come back here with *Ryan*? After making eyes at *Sydney*?

I didn't see Sydney after leaving the ball. Ryan said Sydney left his side, and he never saw him again and figured he might have just gone home to Shadowcrest.

I run my tongue along my lower teeth and stalk into the kitchen.

Sitting with a hot cup of coffee in my hands at the kitchen counter, twenty minutes later, I watch Ryan walk in. But, his bedroom is a floor above us, not down the hallway where my room is located.

So, he slept with her, and then kicked her out into one of the guest rooms, huh?

"You're a dog, Ryan," I hiss.

Ryan, barely awake, blinks and turns to me. "What?" He runs his hand over his face, scrubbing sleep from his eyes.

I open my mouth to tear into him about his devious behavior when a door down the hallway creaks open.

Sydney stumbles out into the open concept kitchen and dining room looking dazed. His formal slacks are undone, and he's barefoot, and *shirtless*.

"What are you doing here?" Ryan and I ask in unison.

Sydney groans, holding his head in his hands. "Stop talking so loud."

"This is my usual voice." I look from Sydney to Ryan.

Ryan smirks, shaking his head. "I should have known you'd come back here instead of to your own pack territory." He points at his brother, but his eyes meet mine. "If anyone is a dog, it's him."

I stand, clutching my coffee as a laugh works its way up my throat.

Sydney blinks like the faint, stormy daylight is painfully bright. "Did you guys take my shirt?"

"Oh, my Goddess," I laugh. "Ryan actually got you drunk last night!"

"Obviously," Sydney growls, making his way to the coffee pot. "I couldn't go back to my pack like this. Plus this place is uh... a closer walk from the temple."

I lick my lips and glance at Ryan, who's grinning at his brother. "So, what was her name?"

Sydney smiles to himself, but then his brow furrows. "I don't remember. Shit, I don't remember.... She told me, I'm sure. I'll remember it after a few cups of coffee."

"Well, you just missed her. She has your shirt, too."

Sydney looks over at me with so much annoyance behind his bloodshot eyes that I momentarily bristle.

"Don't look at me like that," I tease, sipping from my mug. "I'm happy for you."

"At least one of us got lucky," Ryan remarks, chuckling.

Sydney closes his eyes and whispers a prayer to the Goddess to give him the strength not to lose his mind before he turns with a steaming cup of black coffee in his hands.

"I don't believe you didn't get any action. Who did you bring home this time? Is she still hiding upstairs?" he asks Ryan.

Ryan shakes his head. "I'm taking a break from the ladies."

Sydney arches a brow. "Sure you are."

"It's true. You are, in fact, the only one who got any attention last night–"

"I got kissed."

The twins look at me, practically snapping their necks in surprise.

I lean against the counter, which bits into my ribs.

"No you didn't," Ryan says, snorting a laugh.

"It's true."

"When?" Sydney asks, looking more than shocked.

"When everything was going on." I wave a hand in dismissal, but Sydney looks confused and Ryan looks... suspicious.

"What happened?" Sydney looks between us.

"Well, you left early with your lady friend so you missed the whole thing," his brother says to him, but his eyes are still on mine. "Kenna, who did you kiss?"

"What happened, Ryan?" Sydney orders, but Ryan shakes his head, holding a hand up to silence his brother.

"I don't know. He asked me to dance and then the power shut off, and he hid me in an alcove for a while until it was safe."

Ryan looks so severe right now. Sydney, too, straightens.

"He was wearing a black mask, and all black, and he had black leather gloves on," I rattle off. "I don't know why he was wearing gloves–"

"The man who brought you out to me on the veranda last night?" Ryan says in shock. "That's who you kissed?"

"Yeah. Do you know him?" Hope blooms in my heart but is quickly squashed by the look the twins share. They're using the mind-link, I can tell. Bastards.

Sydney looks at me for several seconds before storming out of the kitchen and back into the guest room.

"What's his problem?" I ask.

"Kenna," Ryan says slowly, easing toward me. "Did you... feel anything, during the kiss?"

"Like, what, the mate bond?" I laugh, because I'm not about to give myself hope that that bright, shiny feeling in my heart right now has anything to do with the mate bond instead of everything to do with the excitement of last night in general. "I don't know, Ryan. It was my first kiss, so I don't know how to feel."

He lets out his breath but continues to look at me skeptically. Sydney returns with his phone pressed to his ear, his eyes clearer than a few moments ago.

He lowers his phone for a moment, glaring between me and Ryan. "A brawl?"

Ryan shrugs, but I can tell from the look on Sydney's face that he doesn't believe it for a second. In fact, that suspicious feeling that whatever happened last night was a lot more than a brawl creeps in again as he slowly brings the phone back to his ear. His eyes meet mine. "Kenna, go get dressed right now."

"What? Why?"

"You, too." he says to Ryan, shaking his head.

He crosses his arms over his chest. "What the fuck is going on, Syd?"

"We're on our way," Sydney says to whoever is on the line and hangs up. "Kenna," he repeats sternly, "go get dressed. *Now.*"

A prickle of unease shoots up my spine. I obey because Sydney has never talked to me in that kind of tone before. He sounds… angry, yeah, but there's more to it. An underlying current of nervous panic settles in the house as I pull on a pair of pants and matching shirt I brought with me from Eastonia, something that probably seems very formal for day-to-day wear here in Crescent Falls, but I have a feeling we won't be out and about at the festival today. The pink satin fabric makes the sunny, peachy coloring of my skin stand out so I like it. I meet my cousins in the kitchen again, both of them dressed for the day.

Sydney, completely sober now, turns to me. "We're going to the castle."

"Did something happen?" I ask hurriedly.

Ryan looks like Sydney just told him what really went on the night before. His cocky smile is nothing but a tight, flat line as he nods.

"Family meeting," Sydney says gruffly and turns around to walk out of the house.

Family meetings aren't a good thing in my family.

A family meeting means something went terribly wrong.

I lock up my spine and follow Ryan out of the house, letting the memory of my time with the stranger slip away and be replaced by a cold, nagging sensation that threatens to let my powers come to life. I keep them so clipped, so under control, but right now, I can feel the shadows I inherited from my dad sliding over my skin. I cross my arms over my lap as I settle in the back of Ryan's car–a massive SUV with a third row. I've been deposited in the way-back so the twins can speak privately in the front.

As Ryan steers us toward their parents' home, my stomach curls.

Their conversation is muffled by the AC, but I catch Ryan murmuring, "If he's here, then it's serious."

"I know," Sydney replies, and I look up to see Ryan looking at me through the rearview mirror.

I sink into the seat, my powers dancing to life.

"Does she know?" Ryan asks. "About... *them.*"

"No," Sydney says. "It's not our place..."

I look out the window as I lose Sydney's voice to the radio Ryan just turned on. We cross through a gate and start driving down a long, winding, paved road. A security checkpoint looms in the distance, and beyond that, the Alpha King of Crescent Falls's castle rises above the trees.

What the hell is happening?

I look down at my hands, letting my shadows curl around my fingers in a glimmer of dark, twisting mist.

11

SHE'S COMING HOME

Ella

EASTONIANS DON'T HAVE cell phones.

It's not like I didn't try…. Hell, I spent the first ten years of my tenure as Queen of Eastonia trying to convince my people that at least *some* of the technology in Crescent Falls is a good thing.

But Eastonia is home to skeptical, superstitious people. They like their privacy and unobstructed views, apparently. They weren't about to let me mar that by building cell towers on the mountains that separate my kingdom from my brother's.

But, a cell phone would be fantastic at a time like this.

I whirl toward Ryatt, my mate, my husband, and the love of my life, and ball my hands into fists.

"Ryatt," I say as steadily as possible, "why are the Ghosts in Crescent Falls?"

Ryatt swallows hard, his jaw tensing as he looks into the whirling depths of the magic mirror at my back. Isaac is already gone from view, and so is Alpha King Jaxon of Tarsian.

The two kings were just filling Ryatt in on the little inconvenience that turned into a massive problem, and I happened to walk into the room at the mention of Evander being tasked with seeing Kenna safely back *home*.

I look from Ryatt to Granger, who is leaning against the wall on the far side of the bright, airy room I use as my personal office. The sweeping views of the Moonrise Valley cast sprays of golden sunlight across the muted crimson carpets, but the dizzying view does nothing to quell the sudden fury raging to life within my chest.

"Why is your son in Crescent Falls?" I ask Granger hotly, my cheeks flaring nearly the same color as the carpet beneath my feet.

"Kenna is unaware," Ryatt assures me, but I shake my head.

What happened between Evander and Kenna isn't our fault. It's not the fault of Granger and Amanda, either, but as their parents, we're involved.

Both Evander and Kenna are secretive in their own ways. My daughter, the ray of sunshine, brushes things off like specks of dust on her shoulder. Nothing can affect her–at least, from the outside.

But I know her. She sits up in her room, playing her piano, letting those feelings play out on the keys like I do with a brush and canvas while painting.

Evander is like his father. He buries things so deep, and for so long, that they turn to ash and dust and simply drift away.

I hold Granger's gaze, unflinching. "Does she know he's there, Granger?"

"No," he says, and I allow myself a single breath.

Evander shredded Kenna's heart five years ago. I know vague details because Kenna tells me almost everything. I know that Evander returned from training in Tarsian and came to see her before anyone knew he was back in Moonrise. I know they fought, and Kenna made it sound like she said something to him about missing her birthday, and he… absolutely lit into her.

Then, he ended their friendship and stormed back to Tarsian, leaving destruction in his wake.

Kenna felt awful about it for a long time. I tried to reason with her, telling her that this happens between friends sometimes. I told her about the time I abandoned her Aunt Maddy in the plains outside of Crescent Falls–pregnant and unable to defend herself. Maddy should have hated me forever after that, but somehow she's still my friend.

But Kenna made it sound like they could never, ever, be friends again.

Evander steered clear of all of us, including his family, since then. He's a Ghost now, a highly specialized warrior working in the shadows of both kingdoms to ensure peace.

I know it guts his parents–especially Amanda.

Evander is in danger all the time.

Which means if Evander is around Kenna, she's likely in danger, too.

"Why is he guarding our daughter?" I say with more force since both men are reluctant to tell me anything.

I'm well aware of the rebel threat. It's all Ryatt and Isaac meet about lately. It's been brewing for years now, dissent festering from a small, obscure group of King Kane sympathizers who have been holed up on the far edge of Eastonia for two decades.

But their numbers were minimal then and have remained as such.

At least, that's what I thought.

My memories flood with images of my time spent underground with Petra and her cronies. That was the start of all of this. Her coven, the Draven coven, survived, even though I killed her.

I didn't kill her brother, though.

"Atticus is making moves," Ryatt says with remarkable calm. "Isaac confirmed what we thought might happen. He has his followers in Crescent Falls now."

"What happened?"

It's Granger who speaks up next. "Commander Artyom has his Ghosts in Crescent Falls looking for the rebels. They busted an illegal auction, and that led them to believe an attack was being planned during the festival at one of the balls."

My blood turns to ice as I slowly swivel to my husband, whose eyes are pure steel and locked on the mirror.

"Where is Kenna?" I ask as steadily as I can.

"She's safe. She's with the family," Ryatt says, his tone strained. Fury shines behind his eyes as his gaze locks on mine. It's been so long since I've seen that furious, unholy fire come to life there.

Ryatt is, by all accounts, the most powerful man in the known world.

But the most powerful thing about him is his love for our child.

"Who is behind this?" I ask him.

I already know the answer, but I need to hear him say it. I need to confirm that Ryatt is about to bring hellfire down on the rebels without restraint or remorse.

"The Draven coven," he rasps.

"Atticus's son Gabriel was briefly detained by Evander and the Ghosts at the temple before he spirited elsewhere. They're trying to track him." Granger shifts his weight against the wall.

"Gabriel can jump?" My hands curl into fists. "Ryatt, we need to get Kenna out of there. Now!"

"It's already being arranged. She's on her way to the castle in Crescent Falls as we speak."

"And Alpha Jaxon is gathering his own forces to try to track down the coven near Tarsian. He believes they're underground," Granger adds

Of course, they are. Petra dragged all of those witches into the depths and committed unspeakable acts, while her brother, their new leader, stood by and watched.

I met the man once—when he led me out to be tortured by his sister. He's been in hiding ever since and only recently allowed his followers to start causing problems in the surrounding territories. Jaxon has been on it, to his credit. No one gets away with anything in Tarsian without Jaxon putting a firm end to it, but the Draven coven has proved to be slippery.

If they're in Crescent Falls, there's no telling what they're capable of.

"Kenna is safe," Ryatt says. He steps forward, gently wrapping his fingers around my forearm. His touch is immediately calming.

Grounding, even. But my mind still reels, and my chest feels like it's caving in as a truth hits me right in the gut.

"He's going after the princesses. Misty–" Oh, Goddess. My sixteen-year-old niece. This is the coven's attempt to get at me somehow, to force me into a conflict I've been avoiding for years. Kidnap the princesses. Kidnap my daughter, and my brother's daughter, to get the Allied Kingdoms to act, to bring on the war they so desperately want.

"She's being moved as well."

"To where?" I look at Ryatt then Granger.

My husband replies, running his hand down the back of his neck, "Maatua. Isla and Maddox are being filled in as we speak. They're safest there. I will jump to Maatua tomorrow to fetch Kenna and bring her home."

"Evander is going to be escorting her to Maatua personally," Granger adds from across the room.

I know I'm supposed to feel better because of this. Evander is like family to us. I was in the room when he was born. I was one of the first people to hold him.

That baby–that scrappy, wild little boy–is gone now.

I look at Ryatt, seeing the same thoughts flashing behind his eyes.

"Granger," he says softly. "I need to speak privately with our queen."

His Beta's footsteps recede. I don't look back at him. I know he's going to go talk to Amanda about the same thing we're going to talk about now.

"Kenna won't want him to do this, Ryatt."

"I know," he says, pinching the bridge of his nose. "I know–"

"She hasn't spoken his name since her sixteenth birthday."

He intertwines his fingers with mine, drawing absent circles on the palm of my hand with his thumb. "What do you think happened between them?"

"He tore her to pieces. I don't know." It had to be something major for Kenna to completely shut down like she did.

Kenna's soft heart is what I love the most about her, but it's sometimes her greatest weakness. She sees the best in everyone and loves them despite their flaws. She will be an amazing queen one day–the kind that leads with kindness and bravery... with her heart, unlike me. I lead with my head and with my powers. My people respect me, honor me, and follow me, yes, but I am not wholly loved.

Kenna will be.

But she doesn't have the grit we do. That's been clear from a young age. She's nervous, afraid to be disliked, to make enemies if necessary.

But she made an enemy out of Evander somehow, and it shredded her.

"Ella, are they mates?"

"Wh-what?" I almost laugh. "Where did you get that idea?"

"It would make sense. Most young men start coming into their powers as teenagers these days, especially now that the veil is gone. Evander came home and saw her, maybe felt the bond for the first time–"

"Ryatt," I sigh, letting go of his hand. "If they were mates, I doubt something like this would have happened. They haven't spoken in years. They haven't seen each other–"

"Do you remember how much you hated me in the beginning?" he smirks.

I roll my eyes. "I did hate you."

"The mate bond isn't always wanted. It can be scary for young men especially. I went through it. I felt the bond with you before you could feel it, and it made me question a lot of things."

"You were scared," I correct, giving him a teasing look, "of being shackled to me your entire life."

"I was scared of not being the man you deserved, Princess."

My heart squeezes as I feel a tug down our bond, a gentle caress against the little threads binding us together as he uses the nickname he gave me so long ago.

I don't believe him, though.

"She can't feel a mate bond, Ryatt. That's the truth of this. She's more witch than wolf."

"Time will tell. She's still young. She's only been able to shift for a few weeks."

I relax a touch. "What else did Isaac say? Also, why wasn't I notified about your meeting?"

"It was an emergency. You were with the mystics when he called. I didn't have time to alert you." He glances around my office, his gaze absently grazing the ceiling-height shelves full of books and knick-knacks. "Evander will bring Kenna home. She'll be safe in Moonrise. But I need to put up wards around Eastonia."

Wards. Ryatt's magical shields to keep things hidden and protected. It's been so long since we've needed them.

He continues, "Once she's safe and home with us, I will close the borders and ward them so no one can cross, and no one can get out of Eastonia until the Draven coven is dealt with."

"I want Atticus and his son alive, Ryatt." I whisper, and he catches my gaze, seeing the silver fire behind my eyes. "I have unfinished business with Atticus, two decades in the making."

1 2

CONSUMED BY THE SHADOWS

Kenna

THE DINING ROOM table in the castle can seat twenty-four people. It's insane, really. I've been to both formal and informal dinners here during my brief and scattered trips to Crescent Falls. Normally, the family only gathers in Maatua, and there we like to spread out on the grass, or the patio, or the beach for dinner....

But there's no food laid out. No breakfast spread, no snacks. Nothing to drink or fiddle with.

I lace my fingers together in my lap while I sit on one of the chairs near the head of the table. Ryan sits across from me, his legs crossed as he drums his fingers on his knee.

Sydney and Aunt Maddy are upstairs with Uncle Isaac.

Misty walks into the room, her eyes red, bloodshot, and full of tears. A smear of mascara peppers her left cheekbone as she looks from me to Ryan.

I shoot to my feet. "Misty, what's the matter?"

She pouts, her lower lip jutting out. "They're sending me away for the whole summer!"

Ryan and I exchange glances as she sinks into a seat beside me. I gently rub her back in little circles as she absolutely comes apart at the seams. Her bright pink T-shirt rumples under my touch as she leans into my shoulder and starts to sob.

"It's all right." I coo, but down the mind-link I ask Ryan, *What is going on?*

'I don't know.'

'Why aren't you upstairs with them–'

'I'm not a future king, Ella.' His voice is stern and hoarse in my head as he meets my gaze, narrowing his eyes. *'Whatever's happening, I'll find out with you.'*

I inhale sharply through my nose and continue comforting Misty, who is absolutely beside herself.

"M-my friends–they get to go to the festival and the concerts this summer but I–I have to go to Maatua and hangout with Gramma and Papa instead!" She's practically wailing.

"We love Gramma and Papa," I remind her, patting her head like I would a little kitten. Her silken strands of golden hair feel like satin between my fingers. "You'll have the best tan out of your friend group when you return for your first year at Wellington. And... your hair might be blonder, too."

She sniffles. "I don't care. I don't want to go!"

I give Ryan a pleading look, but it's lost on him as Isaac and Sydney walk in, followed by a forlorn and nervous looking Maddy.

Steel seeps into my spine as I sense the unease pouring off all three of them.

Uncle Isaac looks down at Misty, his bright blue eyes darkening with sympathy and guilt, before he clears his throat and meets my gaze. "I just spoke with your father."

"Okay..." I manage to reply. My chest feels heavy, and it's not because Misty is wrapping her arms around me and trembling with sobs. I continue patting her head and toying with her hair just so my fingers have something to do.

Maddy steps up, placing a hand on Isaac's forearm. "Kenna, darling, you and Misty are being moved to Maatua for your own safety. Your father is going to meet you there and escort you back to Eastonia."

"Why?" I ask.

Maddy inhales deeply but shakes her head, her lips parting as she tries to find the words.

I realize that everyone in the room is uncomfortable saying anything with Misty, who just turned sixteen, in attendance.

Something serious must have happened for my family to want to move us to Maatua for our safety, which is the only reason why they would. I'm here for the festival.

There isn't a festival on Maatua, that's for sure.

I suck in a breath. I'm an adult. I can handle whatever it is they're about to tell me with grace and bravery. My mind reels over the possibilities. I know something happened last night–something that was a lot more than a brawl.

"Misty?" I say, giving her a little nudge. "Can you do me a favor and go up to your room and find me a different color for my nails? I want something more colorful than this if we're going to the beach."

Misty lifts her head to inspect the glossy, cream colored manicure on my fingertips.

She meets my eyes–eyes the same shade and shape as Grandma Isla's eyes–and nods. She's smart enough to know this is just a distraction to get her out of the room. She doesn't want to be here anyway.

She's gone in a flash of golden hair and purple pajamas.

I roll my shoulders, putting on the face I've practiced in the mirror for years. The face of a Luna, of a queen, of someone much braver and more capable of making hard decisions than I am.

Sydney catches the change and seems impressed, but only a flash of that shows behind his eyes.

Isaac looks at us–the adult children. "The rebel threat has arrived in Crescent Falls, and they've made themselves known. Your father and I, Kenna, believe they're here for you."

I nod–because it's all I can do.

He continues. "Maatua is the safest option. You can't be in Crescent Falls until this threat is taken care of."

"I understand," I choke out, biting back the strangled sob built by sheer disappointment and heartbreak.

I think of the man from last night. It's like a dagger in my heart. When I woke up this morning, he was the first thing on my mind. I can still taste him against my lips even though I brushed my teeth this morning.

I won't get a chance to find him again.

I know, without a shadow of a doubt, that I won't be leaving this castle until I'm escorted by armed guards to the port.

I feel myself sinking into the seat, trying to make myself as small as I can as Isaac continues telling us what's happening. I barely hear him over the thundering echo of my heartbeat in my ears. He's saying something about… about a plan. How me and Misty are going to put in separate vehicles taking separate routes to the port tomorrow morning before sunrise.

I hear my mother's name and blink, looking at my uncle. "Is she all right?"

"Your parents are fine but worried about this situation. They want you home."

"I'll be okay," I say, more to myself than to anyone currently staring at me. "I'll go home."

I feel Ryan nudge my foot under the table in solidarity as I drop my gaze back to my lap and try to not to look like I'm about to burst into tears.

It's not that I'm scared. I'm just… I hate putting people in the position of feeling like they need to protect me because I'm not capable of protecting myself. I know how powerful I am. I know how to use those powers. I've trained for something like this–a threat to my freedom and my life–since I was a child.

Because I am the sole heir to an entire kingdom.

It's a crushing burden.

I wish I was more like my mom. If she were in my position, she wouldn't be slouching in her chair like I am. She would be standing, shoulders squared, as she made the calls instead of listening to the plans being made for her.

I just wanted to find love. I wanted to find my person. Maybe even my mate.

And as the memory of the kiss last night drifts back to the forefront of my mind, I feel another crushing blow to my chest as the man's scent gets stronger, almost like he's here.

"General Howard," Isaac says, his voice full of gravel from talking for the last half hour while I zoned out completely. "Thank you for coming."

I look up and freeze. My blood stops rushing through my veins. I'm sure the floor is falling beneath my feet as two men walk into the dining room.

Evander is dressed in all black–the familiar uniform worn by the warriors of Eastonia. The scaled onyx armor fits him like a glove, and he's so… big. So strong. So different from the last time I saw him five years ago.

He towers over the unfamiliar general by five inches at least. His golden hair shines with copper undertones in the hazy light pouring through the windows behind him.

But his eyes–the color of polished emeralds–don't shift in my direction at all.

I can feel Sydney's gaze on me, burning into me. Ryan, too, shifts his weight in his seat, but his foot remains against mine as if he's trying to keep me grounded.

This day couldn't get worse.

But then Evander says, "Princess Kenna has been followed for the last week by a band of three wolves, all of which are confirmed rebels from the Draven coven. I've seen them at every ball she's attended and spotted them following her and Alpha Ryan around the festival during the day. Last night, we killed them during a raid on a safe house in the woods toward the far edge of the Silverhide territory. It's confirmed she was their target."

My stomach hollows out. "You've been following me around?" I speak without meaning to, and the heartbreak and confusion in my voice is clear. I'm looking right at Evander, but he will not look at me.

No one else speaks. My voice echoes through the room.

"How long have the Ghosts been following me around?" I ask, tearing my gaze from Evander to my uncle and aunt.

"Since you arrived," Isaac says, and Maddy looks stricken.

"Isaac, why didn't you tell me?" I hear her whisper.

What the hell is going on?

My gaze falls on Sydney, and my heart cracks. "You knew, didn't you?" He knows what I mean. He knew Evander was here following me around while I tried to find my mate. Sydney knew, and he made it impossible for anyone to approach me, to talk to me. He knew I was in danger.

I look at Ryan who looks so angry that it gives me a shock.

Ryan didn't know anything.

"What exactly is going on here?" Ryan asks in a low, dark tone that sends ripples up my spine. "Was Kenna brought here as *bait*?"

"No." Evander's voice is edged to a fine point. He finally looks at me, a brief glance. "She was not. We weren't aware that the Draven rebels infiltrated Crescent Falls' underground until the night of the first ball."

I stand abruptly and walk out of the room. I can't hold in my tears any longer. Several emotions flare at once. Guilt for putting my family in this situation. Disappointment for spending a single week in Crescent Falls and being so close to finding someone and failing. Heartbreak…. Heartbreak because… that kiss….

I duck into an alcove just as my powers ignite. My hands turn into shadows that creep up my arms, then over my chest, and down to my toes until I am nothing but a shadow.

It's a gift of mine, a special one, something passed down from the Shadowsynger line. Even my dad can't do this–turn into a shadow so dark I'm unseen by the naked eye.

I wipe my nose, sniffling.

Footsteps echo down the corridor I'm hiding in.

Evander comes to a stop roughly ten feet away, tucking his hands in the pockets of his leather pants. He looks around. I don't know how he can do it, but he knows exactly where I am.

"I'll be escorting you to Maatua personally," he says.

I say nothing. I just watch him, watch the empty, emotionless look behind his dead eyes. These are the first words he's said to me since our fight five years ago.

His lips part like he's about to say something else, but then he grits his teeth.

He turns and walks away, leaving me in the shadows of my own making.

13

CHASED THROUGH THE WOODS

Evander

THE MOON IS STILL high in the sky when the first blacked out SUV pulls out of the driveway moving toward the security gate. Princess Misty is inside the vehicle with her suitcases. I didn't watch the heated exchange she had with her parents. I could hear it, though. The Princess of Crescent Falls is not happy she's being sent away for the summer.

I cross my arms over my chest and lean against the hood of a similar SUV, checking my watch. It's 4:00 in the morning. Kenna and I will set out for the port in twenty minutes, taking a different route than Misty and the Ghosts assigned to escort her to Maatua.

Royal warriors in their wolf forms move through the surrounding woods like shadows, searching for threats.

I check my watch again. Fifteen minutes. Fifteen minutes until I'm stuck in a car with Kenna, alone–for two hours, if I respect the speed limit.

I roll my lower lip between my teeth and let it go with a pop, then straighten and whirl toward the footsteps sounding behind me in the dark.

"Jumpy this morning," Flynn drawls, cracking his knuckles. "I was trying to walk as heavily as I could to let you know I was coming up on ya'." He kicks a pebble across the cement before coming to a stop at my side.

"What are you doing here?"

"I got reassigned," he sighs, giving me a shrug.

"To what, exactly?"

"Reassigned to you. I'm your backup on this little road trip."

I eye him skeptically. "On whose orders?"

"Commander fucking Artyom," he grunts. "Howard practically dragged me out of bed an hour ago–panicked. This is a pretty big operation now. We've got Ghosts coming in from Eastonia to relieve us of our current mission in Crescent Falls while our unit returns to Eastonia to do the gods know what."

This is odd. Normally, only a few Ghosts have feet on the ground in one place while the others remain scattered across the Roguelands with other warrior units in the various packs. Never in the history of the Ghosts has the entire fleet been dispatched at once.

Flynn nods to himself, meeting my eyes. "If you're thinking this is madness, you're right. I don't know what's going on yet, but everyone's been called to action. From what I heard while spying on Howard through his mind-link with Commander Artyom, Alpha King Ryatt has called on his commanders in Eastonia to start preparing for war. The King and Queen of Eastonia are closing the borders, putting up wards." Flynn's special little gift of penetrating through the veiled walls of the mind-link certainly comes in handy in moments like this.

"War?" I turn to Flynn. "With the rebels…. How many are there to constitute this many–"

Footsteps break over the cement–light and hurried. I turn to find Kenna hustling toward me, her eyes downcast on her pair of pearly white sneakers.

I hate her outfit. She looks like any other woman in Crescent Falls dressed in jeans and a white T-shirt, her hair tied in a bun on the very top of her head.

When she's dressed in the vibrant, silken fashions of Eastonia, she's… magnificent.

Flynn nudges me hard, smirking down the mind-link, 'You're blushing, dude.'

'Shut the fuck up and get in the car.'

I move toward Kenna, snatching the suitcase out of her hand. It's lighter than expected as I toss it in the back and open the door for her. She climbs into the back seat without a word.

I start the car, my hands curling around the steering wheel. Flynn gets in the passenger seat and immediately turns on the radio. I shut it off again without a word.

I wait for Agent Connor, who is stationed in his wolf form a few miles ahead of us, to give me the green light through the mind-link.

Flynn turns in his seat to look at Kenna, smiling. "How's it going, Princess?"

"Uhm, it's going about as good as you'd expect. How are you?" Her voice is kind and gentle, and I know she means every word. Kenna is the type of person who actually cares when asking how someone is doing.

Flynn arches a brow. "I'd rather be sleeping than be stuck in the car with his asshole all morning, but what can you do?" He winks at Kenna, and she grins, her cheeks going a little pink.

I grind my teeth and hit the pedal, lurching us forward.

Flynn, who hasn't buckled his seatbelt, hits the dash with a crunch and mumbles a colorful curse under his breath.

"Sorry," I say dryly. "I don't get to drive these often."

He glares as he buckles his seatbelt, but through the rearview mirror I see Kenna smiling down at her lap, biting her lip….

I look back at the road just as Connor's voice rumbles through my head, 'You're green.'

We pull away from the castle, taking a back road that weaves through the royal family's private land for several miles. I clock each wolf we pass, taking stock of how many warriors the king has patrolling the grounds. It's a quiet, thirty minute drive through a dense forest along a dirt road before we finally reach pavement again.

The city stretches before us in the distance, a soft electric glow against the millions of stars overhead. The first ferry of the day is set to leave at 6:00 A.M., an hour and a half from now.

"Repeat the plan to me," I say to Flynn, the first time any of us have spoken since we left the castle. I glance in the rearview mirror, watching Kenna stare absently out the window looking withdrawn and... sad.

I bite back what I want to say to her. That I'm sorry this is happening. That I'm sorry she didn't get what she came here for.

"The first scheduled ferry of the day leaves the Port of Crescent Falls at 6:00 A.M. Princess Misty of Crescent Falls will board at exactly 5:45, and we have a fifteen minute window to get Princess Kenna aboard before the ferry leaves the port. The ferry will leave on schedule, no exceptions. The only other passengers are warriors in plain clothes. Once aboard, the princesses will be secured in the cockpit for the duration of the trip to the Island of Weatherby, a roughly six hour journey. From there, they will board a royal vessel under the flag of Maatua and be escorted by ship for another twenty-seven hours, approximately."

I nod. Weatherby is a small island territory of roughly two-hundred people. The princesses won't be stepping foot on the island, however. They will be going from one boat to the other.

"Once in Maatua," Flynn continues with a jaw cracking yawn, "Agent Evander and Princess Kenna will meet up with Alpha King Ryatt and be escorted to Veiled Valley, via jump. Princess Misty will remain in Maatua under the guard of the Ghosts until further notice."

Another glance into the backseat. I notice Kenna listening intently to every word Flynn says. Her eyes shimmer in the darkness as we turn off the pavement onto another dirt road, purposefully taking a longer, more rural route to the port. Trees hug either side of the road, leading us deep into a forest. Her view of the city vanishes, and that shred of hope in her eyes does as well.

"What will you do when you reach Veiled Valley?" Flynn asks a moment later.

I ease my death grip on the steering wheel. "Stay there."

Flynn furrows his brow. "What?"

"My contract with the Ghosts runs out in a month and a half. I got the order from Commander Artyom this morning that they're waving those last weeks of service. Once I set foot in Veiled Valley, I am the Beta." My words ring over the engine like a death knell.

Kenna heaves a breath but stays silent.

She knows that once we arrive, all of this is over. She will become Luna, and I will rule by her side as her unwilling second.

And we'll both be miserable–together.

Flynn twists in his seat to look at Kenna. I want to smack him, but the mind-link steals my attention as Connor's voice echoes through my head. 'Rat in the nest–' he cuts off, and I grip the steering wheel again.

"Kenna, are you buckled?" I ask.

Surprised, she meets my eyes in the mirror and nods.

An uneasy feeling settles around us. Suddenly, the lone, unlit dirt road feels too silent, too wide open despite the trees choking the easements on either side. Flynn senses something too as he twists to look out his window and slowly pulls a pair of black gloves out of the front pocket of his jeans.

'Connor–'

'I heard him. We're being followed.'

Behind us, shadows drift in the dark–three large, swiftly moving shadows.

"How close are we to the port?" Flynn asks as he carefully puts on his gloves. He curls his fingers, testing the fabric.

"Thirty-five minutes," I say, keeping my eyes split between the road and the shadows catching up to us in the rearview mirror. "Kenna, unbuckle your seatbelt and lie down flat in the backseat."

"Why?"

"Do it."

She swallows with effort and obeys my command, lying as flat as she can.

I sit up a little straighter as the shadows edge closer. Three large trucks come into view, their lights shut off as they move through the darkness. I press down on the gas, slowly accelerating.

"Get in contact with the caravan transporting Princess Misty," I tell Flynn. I'm not making any sudden moves, not yet. Not with Kenna in the car.

A wolf runs out in the middle of the road ahead of us, caught in the glare of the headlights. Stark gray against the amber glow, its head snaps in my direction.

"Princess Misty just boarded the ferry."

"Tell them to pull up the anchor."

"We won't make it in time—"

"Tell them to pull up the anchor and get away from the port!" I shout, knowing full well that Kenna can hear every word I'm saying. Her fear radiates down the bond and rips into my chest.

The wolf in the headlights turns to face us fully as we gain ground. The trucks continue to close in, and now we're surrounded on all sides as wolves sprint out of the shadowed woods.

"Now," I growl, and Flynn opens his door, disappearing into shreds of plain clothes as his wolf leaps into the night, his gloves turning to obsidian, scaled armor that covers almost every inch of his lean, powerful body. He blends into the darkness immediately, disappearing from view. The car door slams shut on its own accord.

Somewhere behind me, Kenna lets out a choked breath.

More wolves are coming out of the woods and running alongside the car.

I reach back with one hand and grab Kenna's shirt. In one swift motion, I haul her between the gap in the front seats and deposit her where Flynn was just sitting.

She yelps, surprised, when I reach across her and grab her seatbelt, locking it in place. The last thing I need is for her to fly through the windshield when I hit the wolf still standing in the center of the road.

I'm really lying on the gas now. The pedal reaches the floor, and the engine whirs, filling the car with so much noise it drowns out Kenna's desperate protests to watch out, to stop.

With one hand on the wheel, I cover her eyes.

The wolf is a second too late. He should have known I wasn't going to stop.

A ball of gray fur flies over the top of the SUV, but I keep going, the trucks behind us gaining ground.

In the distance, I spot a trail into the woods. It's going to be tight, but the SUV will fit– I hope. I honestly don't know, but I don't have time to ponder the logistics of it as I yank on the steering wheel and send us bounding into the woods.

"Evander!" Kenna shrieks, gripping my arm for dear life as I keep it clasped over her chest, pinning her to the seat. We fly over bumps and uneven ground, and behind us the trucks are still following, turning on their headlights to guide them down the trail.

"Hold on," I grunt, yanking on the wheel again. We make a sharp turn between two trees. Metal grinds and splinters as the side mirrors shatter and disappear behind the vehicle.

I cut the lights, driving blind through the woods, dodging trees and rocks. The trucks are still following me but losing speed as they try to navigate the path I'm carving. I edge against an embankment that stretches into complete, rocky darkness.

A flash of light in the rear view mirror catches my attention as one of the trucks hits the truck beside it, sending it barreling into the rocky abyss.

I take another sharp turn and speed back out onto the main road. We have a flat tire and something is dragging on the road beneath us, but I still have speed and power.

"Evander, please!" Kenna pants, her nails digging into my arm. "At least drive with both hands on the wheel."

"What's the fun in that," I smirk, and we look at each other.

We look into each other's eyes for the first time in five years.

I open my mouth like I have something to say, but then headlights through her window tear the unspoken words from my lips.

A truck smashes into Kenna's side of the car.

14

FREE FALL

Kenna

I BLINK. I blink again, confused about the sudden rush of night air against my right cheek. Evander's voice is nearby, distorted and hazy. Sparkles cover everything... or maybe that's just my vision coming back.

"Kenna? Goddess, Kenna? Are you okay?" Evander sounds frantic.

I reach over and try to pat his hand, but I suddenly lurch forward. The sound of metal on metal erupts in my ears, causing them to ring. I scream, and then I'm thrust back into reality.

We're moving at what feels like the speed of light. I'm in a car. The window at my side is shattered, and the door is crushed inward. By some miracle, I'm okay. I'm covered in glass. The windshield in front of me is splintered but intact, and on the horizon, the lights of the port come into view.

We're barreling toward a private dock. The ferry sits at the very edge of it, but it's raising its ramp.

We're rear-ended again. Evander grabs my arm. "Are you okay?"

"I'm okay," I rush out, reaching up to wipe tears from my eyes. "What happened to Flynn? He's out there all alone!"

"He can handle himself. Don't worry," Evander says through gritted teeth.

I feel like I'm in a daze. I'm just sitting here, watching us sped closer and closer to the dock. The ferry is pulling away. We're not going to make it, but Evander isn't stopping.

He can't, I realize.

Wolves are running along each side of the car, and behind us, two trucks are swerving back and forth, trying to ram the car.

I look at Evander, realizing the situation we're in. "They're here for me," I say. "There must have been a spy in the castle. They knew we'd be taking this route."

He nods.

"You have to stop the car."

"I'm not going to do that." He revs the engine. We're closing in on the dock with each passing second.

"Evander, please! We're going to go into the water if you don't stop!"

"We have to jump, Kenna."

Fear chokes my senses. I've never spirited before. My dad tried to train me, but I haven't been able to tap into those powers if I even have them at all.

"I can't," I cry out, terror ripping through me. "I can—If you stop, I can use my powers on the wolves—"

"Have you ever killed anyone, Kenna? Because that's what we're going to have to do if I stop this car."

"You're going to kill us both if you don't stop!" I shout. We bound onto the wide planks leading up to the dock. The ferry blares its horn. People are running along the deck of the ferry, waving their arms in warning.

"Kenna!" Evander shouts. "Do it! You have to do it now!"

"I CAN'T!" I scream, tears streaming down my cheeks.

Evander grunts with effort as he lays on the gas, giving it all he can. I clutch his arm, screaming at the top of my lungs as the edge of the dock disappears.

Time slows to a crawl as the dock gives way to nothing but the horizon ahead of us. The first hints of sunrise cast light over the waves lapping the shore. For a few seconds, it's peaceful.

"DO IT NOW, KENNA!" Evander shouts, and then the horizon disappears from view and is replaced by nothing but water.

Nose down, the car hurtles toward the waves.

"Evander!" I cry out, my nails sinking into his forearm.

My scream is the catalyst for something untapped in my soul. My mind explodes with light, and then I'm being ripped apart, hurtling through blank space and an endless, beginningless kind of time that makes me wonder if we went into the water, and now I'm drowning. Everything is slow and fast at once. I feel like I'm spinning, falling, and then–

The air is forced from my lungs as my back hits something solid and hard.

I smash through it, unable to scream as the sound of splintering wood echoes all around me.

I fall onto something soft this time, and the smell of hay penetrates my senses.

Something–several somethings–hit me in the face. *Pop, pop, pop.*

I can't breathe. I try to open my eyes, but it's so unforgivingly bright.

Flailing, I throw my arm out and connect with someone's chest.

"Ev–Evander?" I rasp, my throat on fire. My entire body is in agony as I clutch his shirt.

Evander groans and coughs just as my vision clears, revealing a hole in a shabby roof.

Shingles fall from the roof. One hits me on the cheek, and I yelp in pain and surprise. Dust and… and feathers? Yes, feathers. Feathers are drifting through the air all around us.

"Where are we?" I pant, unable to move. I'm afraid I'm broken. Something has to be broken. My legs? My back? Goddess forbid, my neck.

Something pinches my leg.

I squirm, giving whatever is repeatedly pinching my knee cap a gentle kick.

A squawk yanks me back into my body, the situation, and the fact I'm lying prone.

"Evander!" I screech, rolling over to face him. Four chickens burst into the air, making a terrible racket as I crawl to Evander's side and take his face between my hands.

He looks dazed as he peers up at me. His pupils are dilated, and his eyes are unfocused.

Where are we? Oh, gods, what have I done?

I shake him. Nothing. Nothing but a groan. I give his cheek a gentle pat. Nothing.

Should I slap him? Would that wake him up? It's only a matter of time before our enemies catch up to us, and we're found.

"Evander, please," I whisper directly into his ear. "Wake up!"

I give him another shake, and this time he blinks, sucking in a breath. His eyes meet mine, his pupils expanding to the point they take up nearly all of his emerald green irises.

I suck in a breath as his hand clasps the back of my neck–hard–keeping me fixed in place with my face hovering only an inch above his.

"It's me," I whisper. "It's Kenna. We're in a chicken coop."

"What?"

His grip doesn't slacken. My heart is racing, and I can honestly say it's not because we just fell through the sky and through a barn roof. No....

He's so close. My lips are nearly brushing his.

"I did it," I say, giving him a wobbly grin. "I jumped."

"To where?" he whispers.

The squawking of the chickens hits a peak, but they're the last thing on my mind. I'm just... looking at Evander. My friend. The person I loved the most in the entire world before... before everything happened.

"Evander?"

His breathing is rapid, and I can feel his heartbeat racing since my hand is flat against his chest.

He suddenly lets go of my neck and gives me a little shove. I fall back on my ass, and for a moment, feel a shred of something heavy lacing its way through my heart. It feels like… rejection.

But, I don't get a single second to process it.

Evander rushes to his feet but sways violently as four men scurry to the entrance of the chicken coop. I jump up, throwing my arms around Evander's waist to steady him.

He raises a hand, motioning for the men to stop.

I don't think they were going to even attempt to approach us, though. They look shocked, maybe even dumbfounded, as they look from us to the hole in the roof.

"What the hell?" one of them asks.

I raise my brows, unable to stop myself from smiling. Delirium is setting in, for sure, because I start laughing like a lunatic.

Now, Evander is looking down at me. In fact, everyone is looking at me.

"Say something else," I beg the men. "Please."

They look at each other. One of them has a hand on his knife belt. "Uh, which one of you fell through my fucking roof?"

The eldest of the men, likely the father of the other three, steps forward with a blade drawn.

I almost fall to my knees in relief.

His accent is thick and rumbling, and *oh so familiar*.

"We're in Eastonia," I choke out, squeezing Evander. "I jumped all the way to Eastonia." I look at one of the younger men. "I've never done it before, you know."

No one knows what to say. Even Evander is standing motionless.

A muffled female voice drifts into range, accompanied by the swishing of homespun fabric.

A pretty, but exceedingly surprised, woman comes into view. She's shorter than the men by several inches, and her pale brown hair is piled on top of her head. She's clutching the skirt of her apron—something sewn by hand and embroidered with delicate blue flowers.

"Oh my gods! Who are you?" she asks, her eyes sliding from Evander to me.

"My name is K–"

Evander claps a hand over my mouth. "I need to speak to your Alpha. Immediately."

The man—possibly the woman's husband, narrows his eyes. "Where did you come from?"

Evander ignores him completely. "I'm a warrior in Alpha King Ryatt's army. My name is Evander, and this woman is my charge. We're lost. Where are we right now?"

The family glances at each other. It's the woman who speaks up first, "You're in the Highlands. The village of Tiscoln is five miles south of our property."

Evander looks confused as he lowers his hand from my mouth. Obviously, he doesn't want me to say my name, but these people don't seem like the murdering type to me. "I'm not familiar with a village called Tiscoln. Or the… what did you call it?"

"The Highlands," the husband says skeptically. "Where do you think you are right now, boy? You're a long way from the Roguelands."

Evander takes my hand and yanks me behind him before moving toward the entrance of the coop. The family separates to allow us to pass through the threshold into the sunlight, into the fresh, mountain air.

I gasp. I've never seen anything like this in my life, and I live in the mountains. But this is… wholly different.

Towering, snow-capped peaks spread out as far as the eye can see. Huge mountains. Mountains bigger than anything I've ever witnessed.

I know where we are.

And the husband was right about being a long, long way from the Roguelands.

"This is the mountain range between Eastonia and Crescent Falls," I say to Evander in a mere whisper. "I had no idea people lived here."

"Me neither," he says in a low, gravelly voice.

"This used to be within the veil." I stand on tiptoes. The view is just… breathtaking. Everywhere I look are more mountains and valleys. There aren't any trees this far up, but it's still summer, and green grass stretches for miles over rolling hills. A stone house and barn sit nearby, chimneys puffing smoke. Cows and sheep graze lazily in a fenced in pasture, and a huge garden chokes several outbuildings.

I turn to the family, smiling. "This is incredible. Is this where you live?"

The woman nods, returning my smile with a warm smile of her own.

"Is that your garden?" I ask enthusiastically.

Now, she's really smiling. "Oh, yes. I pride myself on my squash. It's the best for miles. Are you hungry, sweetheart?" She looks me up and down from where her feet are firmly planted in the entrance of their nearly destroyed chicken coop. "Maybe a bit cold? What are those things on your legs called?"

"Uh, blue jeans." I feel a blush creeping in.

She nods, but I notice Evander and the men are staring each other down. I nudge him in the ribs.

"Chill out, please. We're safe."

"I can't mind-link with anyone, Kenna. We need to leave as soon as possible."

One of the younger men steps forward, his brow furrowed. "Did you just say *Kenna?*"

Evander curses under his breath and reaches into his jacket, probably for whatever blades he keeps hidden in the inner pockets. I grab his wrist, digging in my nails.

"Yes. He did. That's my name. I'm Kenna Westfall, Princess of Eastonia."

15

PRINCESS IN A SHED

Kenna

Cleo, the wife, mother, and matriarch of the property where Evander and I fell through the sky into their chicken coop, sets a huge clay platter on the kitchen table–an old, gnarled table graying with age and wear–and smiles brightly as she lifts the lid. Fragrant steam wafts into the air as roast chicken and an assortment of vegetables come into view.

I'm starving and still riding a high from jumping for the first time. I honestly can't believe I did it.

But now we're in Eastonia, and we're so far away from the Rogue-lands that neither of us can mind-link with our families back home.

So, we're stuck. For the meantime, at least. I don't mind in the slightest.

We've been here for several hours. Cleo immediately took me inside their cozy home and found me a change of clothes–her youngest son's shirt and pants that are so long I had to cuff the sleeves and roll up the pants by several inches–but I'm warm, and my body isn't as broken as I thought.

My back is sore from breaking through the roof. My mind is a little hazy from the events of the last few hours. I haven't quite come to terms with the fact that we almost died by launching a car into the water and that I had to be escorted into hiding in the first place.

Also, I'm with Evander. I'm with Evander, essentially alone, for the first time in years.

I wordlessly watch Cleo fix me a plate. She smiles as she sets it in front of me.

I thank her and look out the window overlooking one of her many sprawling gardens and can just see the chicken coop. Her sons are on the roof, inspecting the damage.

And Evander and her husband, Neiman, are off doing... something. Something, I assume, has to do with finding a way down to the Roguelands from here.

"Do you like tea?" Cleo asks as she sets a kettle on the stovetop.

"I do."

"Dark, light, floral?" she asks, reaching for the cabinet above the stove where an assortment of glass jars house a TON of herbs.

"Uhm, floral," I whisper, but my attention is on the sheer amount of jars–on the tiny ones, especially, no bigger than my thumb. Before I can stop myself, I'm standing on my tiptoes beside her, pulling down a jar of dried, dark green berries.

"I've never seen these in real life," I tell her, meeting her sharp hazel eyes.

She inspects my expression for a moment. "I grew them."

"That's impressive," I reply, pulling the cork from the jar and sniffing deeply.

"Do you know what they're used for?" She turns from the stove and fetches a stool, walking it back to where I'm standing.

I drop a single berry in my palm and turn it over, marveling at it, shocked that I'm actually holding one. It has a waxy sheen to it and leaves an oily residue in the palm of my hand.

She takes a few other jars down, all of the contents more interesting than the last.

"Hunter berries are used for... healing."

"In some cases," she whispers, glancing at me before going back to arrange the herbs on the counter. "What else?"

I watch her closely. The average household in Eastonia would have teas, spices, and an assortment of healing herbs, sure, but this?

"They're also used in the cure for the occulence curse that turns people into rogues by force." I swallow. I can almost taste the berry, as if its powers are sinking into my skin.

"How is the cure made?"

"Bloodbane, taro root skin, and moonstone dust are crushed with two hunter berries and steeped in a tea, with a pinch of the blood of the afflicted," I rattle off, digging deep to remember my yearlong study in the Dark Arts, curses specifically. "To be drunk hourly, for three days. The afflicted blood curse will resolve a week after that with continued care…." I close my eyes, trying to remember. "It takes ten days for an occulence curse to resolve with treatment, and after that, a single hunter berry per month on the full moon will prevent the afflicted from turning back into a rogue when they shift."

"Very good." Cleo smiles, her eyes meeting mine as she opens a jar of something sticky and rather stinky.

Stems coated in a silver, pungent oil drop into my palm.

"Silvervain."

"Good."

Another jar opens.

"Severfell."

"Good. And this?"

I sniff deeply, the smell coating and briefly numbing my nose. "Wolfsbane, of course."

She grins. "Gotta be careful with that one."

I smile, too.

But then I take another look around. I see her mortars, her jars of steeping tea, and tonics. "You're a healer," I say, and she nods.

"I'm not a witch, if that's what you're wondering."

"You have witch herbs, though."

"I just have a green thumb and enough time on my hands to try to grow as much as I can," she replies as she closes all of the jars. "And

Tiscoln isn't known for their healing, that's for sure. We don't have a coven nearby. No witches for hundreds of miles."

In the distance, I hear the echo of a hammer. I wince.

"Evander and I can fix the roof. It was our fault."

"You weren't climbing on the roof like he said, were you?"

I feel like Cleo has uncanny abilities of sight despite being full shifter.

"No... I'm... well, what do you know of my family?" It can't be much, given that these people live in villages not even marked on the maps I've studied in my dad's office.

She motions for me to sit, and I do. I take a few bites of my food while she watches with a smile, then turns to pour the tea she started while I was staring in the cabinet. "Our people left during the beginning of King Kane's reign. That must have been... two hundred years ago, now. He wasn't the first King of Eastonia. There were a few before him, all worse than the last, and some folks scattered into this mountain range rather than fall prey to the kings. What I know of your family, Princess Kenna, is simply... rumors. Your mother is a Firestone Queen, which our people have been waiting for, but they are weary and superstitious. So, if your mother is a Firestone, I'm assuming you have her same gifts."

I nod. "My dad is a Shadowsynger, too."

"Oh," she smiles. "I didn't realize there were any left. Old magic, you know. From a time before the veil."

I take another bite of food as she sets a cup of tea in front of me. I mumble a thanks around a mouthful, but she doesn't seem to mind my terrible manners right now. I'm famished, and this is the best roast chicken I've ever had in my life.

"My dad can do this thing where he disappears and appears somewhere else. My mom can, too. But I've never been able to do it until this morning."

I go on to explain to this nearly complete stranger how I used my powers to spirit us back to Eastonia. We're lucky to be alive, honestly. The first time my mom did this, she nearly destroyed the castle in Veiled Valley.

And the fact I was able to jump this far is… astronomical. Impossible, really.

I'm still buzzing with pride.

I just have no idea how to do it again to get us home.

The door leading into the kitchen garden opens, and Neiman darkens the doorway, followed by Evander, who looks severe. He's still in the plain clothes–athletic joggers and a black shirt–that he wore on the not-so-secret failed mission to get me to the port.

Evander's eyes sweep over me, looking for any traces of harm.

My heart aches at the concern behind his eyes, but then I remember I'm nothing more than a mission to him. I'm his charge, just like he said.

I look down at my food as the men come inside. Neiman whispers something to his wife and walks through an archway into the depths of the house I haven't been given a tour of.

I don't think we're welcome guests despite Cleo's kindness.

Through the windows, the sun is beginning to set. It's probably only midday in Crescent Falls, however.

"Kenna, come," Evander says, but his eyes are narrowed on Cleo.

I look down at my unfinished food.

"She's safe here," Cleo says hotly. "Let her at least finish her meal before you boss her around like she's nothing but chattel."

Evander's nostrils flare.

I take another bite, watching the exchange through my lashes.

"I have guest rooms set up upstairs–"

"We're not staying. We have a two-week-long journey to the nearest village in the Roguelands–"

"Stay for a night, at least. Please. There's a storm rolling in, and you'll have to seek shelter overnight anyway, and the people of Tiscoln won't be nearly as friendly as we are." Cleo's words are laced with ice that works its way down my spine.

I look at Evander. I can practically see the gears turning behind his eyes as he decides what to say next. He's always been like that. Every word he says is well thought out before he says anything at all.

"We'll sleep outside."

"Outside?" Cleo and I exclaim in unison.

Evander looks at me, holding my gaze. I feel the intensity of it in the marrow of my bones. He doesn't want me saying anything right now.

He'd probably be livid to know I just told Cleo I could jump, and made it very, very clear I have a profound knowledge of herbs, potion recipes, and curses.

I chew my lower lip as the tension in the room falls over us like a wet blanket.

I should say something. I know I should. But being around Evander makes me nervous in a way I didn't expect. He's... different now. Handsome and imposing. And the way he's looking at me makes me feel like I'm very small and insignificant.

It's a horrible feeling.

I swallow my last bite of food and stand. Cleo looks at me with sympathy in her eyes as I thank her for the food once more.

But Evander doesn't move toward the door when I do.

"We'll sleep in the coop, which is about as much hospitality as we deserve," he begins. "I'll spend the rest of the evening fixing the roof before we leave... in the morning."

Cleo heaves a breath and waves a hand, motioning for us to wait. She disappears into a side room and returns with bedrolls and an oil lantern. "Sleep in the shed attached to the coop if you're serious about making the Princess of Eastonia sleep outside tonight," she huffs, thrusting the bedrolls into Evander's waiting arms.

He doesn't even thank her for them.

I follow him out to the shed in question. Dust lifts in the air as he opens the door and steps inside.

"You could have thanked her, you know. Instead of being a total asshole."

Evander looks at me over his shoulder in surprise. "I've never heard you cuss before."

The shed door slams behind me, and I flinch. "I'm not a sixteen-year-old girl anymore. I grew up, Evander. I cuss... sometimes. I'm tougher than I used to be. You don't need to treat me like a child."

"Tougher? You were crying at the ball last night."

I meet his eyes. Holes in the shed roof let in a little bit of light, though not enough to see him fully. But it's enough to see the hard look behind his eyes.

Fury I hadn't known I was capable of comes bubbling to the surface, and I can't shove it down, no matter how hard I try. Unlike Evander, I rarely think before I speak, so I say, "I know you hate me, but we're stuck together right now. You need to be nice to these people. They're kind. They offered us a place to stay–"

"We don't know them at all, Kenna. You've always been far too trusting–"

"You don't know me anymore."

We stare at each other for several seconds.

I push, "You left and never came home. You don't get to tell me who I am and what I'm capable of. You especially don't get to make fun of me for–for crying at the ball, of all things. We could've died t-today.." Tears sting my eyes. "I don't want to be here with you anymore than you want to be here with me."

"Kenna–"

I storm out of the shed.

He, unfortunately, follows.

16

———

WHY I MUST HATE HER

Evander

I'LL GIVE credit where credit is due and admit that Kenna is fast. She darts across the grassy expanse of wide open farmland at a speed I hadn't expected, and I find myself jogging to try to catch up to her.

She cuts between two barns and disappears into a shadow of silver mist.

"Kenna," I pant, looking around for the tell-tale signs she's near.

A twig crunches in the distance. I whirl around to see footsteps shifting through the grass. They disappear as Kenna–invisible to the naked eye–climbs over a fence and down an embankment.

She came into this ability as a child. I vividly remember the day it happened and how jarring it had been. One second, we were playing in the woods surrounding Old Moonrise while her grandmother, Cressendra, forged wild herbs, and the next, Kenna was simply gone.

But not really. I could hear her screaming for help but couldn't find her. I felt her grabbing my arms, but it was a phantom touch.

Her scream alerted nearby warriors, who then alerted Alpha King Ryatt that his daughter was missing despite me telling them she was

119

right there, but invisible. That I was holding onto her for dear life while she begged for help.

She didn't know how to change back, and it took several hours for Alpha Westfall of Veiled Valley, her grandfather, and her dad to calm her down enough to try to walk her through it.

We were seven when it happened, and after that day, Kenna spent most of her time training her newly budding powers.

It was also the first day I realized my role in her life.

From that day forward, I promised to protect her at all costs.

I remember Ryatt thinking it was stoic and honorable of me to pledge such a thing at the ripe age of seven. I knelt before him in his throne room, wearing a ragged pair of overalls I'd grown out of the year prior. I wanted it to be formal, official.

Because I meant it.

Little did he know that keeping that promise meant breaking her heart almost a decade later.

I walk down the embankment, meeting a rocky, shallow valley with a creek bubbling through it. Through the glare of the setting sun, I can just make out her shadow perched on a distant rock, those shreds of silver light glittering against rich, vibrant gold streaks of sunlight.

"Go away," she says.

I sit down on a rock several feet behind her and wrap my arms around my knees.

She begins to come back into view.

"I don't need you to follow me around wherever I go. It's creepy."

"It's my job."

"It's not."

"It is, Kenna."

She whips her head to look at me. Her eyes are the purest silver I've ever seen, but I know if I were closer, I'd be able to see flakes of blue around her pupils—the same color blue as Sydney's eyes.

I hold her gaze as the sun dips below the horizon, casting the mountainous landscape in deep shades of violet.

"Evander," she says, turning in her lounge chair with a smile bright

enough to blind. "I missed you yesterday. I thought you'd be here for my party–"

Her scent hits me like a punch to the gut. Sparks fly up my arms, settling deep in my chest as something–something unbreakable weaves around my heart and squeezes tight.

"No," I say aloud, confused, finding it hard to focus as the... the mate bond snaps into place.

I blink, the memory of the moment I knew, without a shadow of a doubt, that Kenna was my mate drifts back into the recesses of my mind where it refuses to fade away entirely.

She's looking at me like she did that day–broken, confused, and scared.

"Why are the Rebels after me?" she asks quietly.

I stand and hop to another boulder, putting less distance between us as I sit back down. "What do you know about the Rebels?"

She draws her knees against her chest, resting her chin on her left kneecap as she faces the inky dark horizon.

"Not much. I know there have been whispers of conflict brewing, but the past few months, my priorities have been preparing for the Rite and–" She cuts herself off.

"And finding your mate," I finish for her, the words like acid on my tongue.

What I'm doing to her is unforgivable.

In my defense, and it's the only defense I have, I did reject her. At least, I thought telling her I hated her, that I never wanted to see her again, would count for something.

But the bond didn't break.

She tilts her chin toward the stars as heavy clouds start to rush in, a stiff breeze rippling over the rocks.. "I can't feel the mate bond. I don't know why I wanted it so badly when I knew, deep down, it was impossible. I can barely shift, did you know that? Did whatever file you had on me for this mission tell you that I can't shift?"

"You can shift, Kenna."

"It hurts, Evander." She mimics my tone, but doesn't look at me.

"Shifting hurts so bad, and I can't–if I try to shift, I get scared of the pain and back out."

I watch her pick at a crop of moss covering the rock she's sitting on.

She continues, "And then when I am in my wolf form, I'm just... I'm tiny. I'm clumsy and can't seem to get my feet under me. My wolf senses are... minimal, at best."

"But you're a powerful witch. Don't forget that."

She sighs. I'm still watching her slender finger absently toy with the moss. I refuse to think about last night, in that alcove, when those fingers had been clutching my shirt as she drew me in for a deeper kiss.

I look down at my own hands and flex them.

"Have you been looking?" she asks just as the first drops of rain fall from the sky. The clouds swallow the stars whole, blocking out whatever light from the sunset is left.

"For what?"

"For your mate?" She turns to look at me.

I hold her gaze, debating my options, studying every combination of words I could say to her.

"No."

She swallows, nodding as she turns back to the stormy horizon. Lightning flashes, thunder rumbling through the valleys below us.

"I guess we just be... miserable and lonely together," she huffs, tilting her face to the rain.

"I don't think you're capable of being miserable, Kenna. You've always been... happy. Kind and sociable–"

"Why aren't we friends anymore?"

I suck in a breath, gritting my teeth. I do owe her an explanation, I just can't... I can't tell her the full truth. "You know what line of work I'm in–"

"I would have still been your friend no matter what. No matter what you were training for, or what you did with your gifts and I... I'm sorry, Evander."

"You have nothing to be sorry for, Kenna. What–"

Her eyes meet mine in the dark. "I didn't know how strongly you felt about missing my party and when I told you I *liked* you, it was…." She bites her lip, and I'm about to lose control of the restraint I've let build for all these years.

"Kenna, listen–"

Lightning cracks over our heads, so close I can smell the charred remains of whatever rock just exploded in a deafening sound several yards away.

I rush to her as she screams, covering her ears.

"We need to go," I tell her and guide her upright, helping her maneuver over the rocks.

"Cleo was right about the storm."

"Yeah, she was." The grass is saturated with rain as we edge toward the shed.

"Why didn't you let us just sleep in the house?"

"We don't know these people."

"Is everyone a threat to you?"

"If you're involved, yes. Everyone is a threat." What I don't say as I lead her into the shed and roll out her bedroll is that I'd flatten armies in her name. I'd use my bare hands, my claws, and my teeth to turn the sea at the edge of Tarsian red if anyone so much as raised a hand to her.

One day, she will be Queen of Eastonia, and I will be her Beta.

But I can't be her mate, not when there's so much at stake.

Being around her makes me weak, dizzy, and unfocused. She is the only thing that takes up any space in my head when she's around, and how am I supposed to protect her when her proximity makes me so wholly unfocused on the dangers all around us?

This lie is for her own good. She'll find someone, one day. Someone who deserves her pure heart. She'll have his children, and together, they will rule.

He won't have to worry about her safety because I'll be there watching, taking out anyone who threatens to lay a finger on my queen.

While she lives out a dream I once dreamt for myself…

And I'll be doing… this.

I sit up. It's been several hours since we came back to the shed, and Kenna is fast asleep beside me. I haven't slept at all. I can't when I'm around her. I've been listening to the sounds of the farm for hours, trying to determine what's normal and abnormal at this time of night.

The rain is stopping, but the tin roof overhead still thumps with heavy drops that blur the night sounds beyond the shed.

But I hear wolves–several of them. Their scents mingle as they approach the property.

I'm out of the shed in a matter of seconds, pulling on my armored gloves and preparing to shift as four wolves come into view.

They can't see or scent me, I've made sure of that. Training to be a Ghost for over a decade has had its advantages.

A low howl breaks through the air, petering off in a whimper. Something's wrong…. These wolves aren't aggressive, and I can sense an underlying ripple of desperation as the group approaches Neiman and Cleo's front door.

I pick up pounding footsteps on stairs before the door opens and the couple steps out into the night, just as I walk into view.

Cleo glances at me but turns back to the wolves.

They're using the mind-link. I think they are , at least. Because no one speaks aloud.

But Cleo nods before turning to her husband and saying, "Run upstairs and grab my cloak and bag."

I eye the group of wolves. One of them takes off at an insane rate of speed, disappearing into the night, but the others remain.

They don't pay me any mind as I edge toward the house. The group parts to allow me to walk up the front steps and across the threshold.

Cleo is in the kitchen pulling jars of herbs from a tall shelf, a smattering of supplies covering her work table.

"Is something wrong?" I ask.

"I have to go into Tiscoln," she says hurriedly. "There's a young woman there struggling in labor. They let her suffer for two days before trying to find help. This is her first baby, and they're not sure the child is alive anymore."

She curses under her breath as a jar falls and shatters on the ground.

I'm at her side in an instant, waving her away as she stoops to pick it up.

Tears cloud her eyes as I straighten, dumping the glass shards in a waste basket.

"Tiscoln's midwife is away for a birth higher in the mountains."

"Have you delivered a baby before?"

"My own," she admits, smoothing a hand over her face. "But this woman is very sick, from what I was just told. I don't know how helpful I'll be."

I take a deep breath and study her face. As much as I want to keep Kenna as hidden as possible... She is the only person who can help right now.

"I'm going to go get Kenna. She's a midwife."

Cleo nods but winces. "Tiscoln won't take kindly to a witch in their village–"

"Do you want this woman and her baby to live, or not?"

17

SOMETHING ABOUT BIRTHING BABIES

Kenna

"Kenna."

I reach up to rub my eyes, my back stiff from sleeping on the ground.

"Kenna, wake up."

Someone shakes me gently.

"Hey!"

"What?" I groan, blinking into amber light shining directly in my face. I squint, and Evander's features come into view, his expression washed with concern. "Ev? What's going on?"

"You need to get up and come with me."

As I come back to reality, unkindly thrust out of a dream I think had to do with the upcoming Rite, I hear voices outside.

Evander wastes no time. Suddenly, I'm standing, and he's laying a cloak over my shoulders, clasping it over my sternum. He works deftly in silence.

Fabric brushes against my collarbone, and I feel a sudden spark of familiarity at the touch. I step back, feeling like I just experienced a shock to my system.

Evander is wearing gloves–black gloves. The same kind of gloves the man I kissed wore.

My lips part as I begin to ask what those gloves are for, but he takes me by the elbow and rushes me out of the shed into the crisp, night air.

The question flutters away into the dark abyss of my sleep-raddled mind as I spot Cleo standing with Neiman, the two of them flanked by three unfamiliar wolves.

"Is she old enough to shift?" Neiman asks with a nod in direction.

"No, she'll ride on my back," Evander replies, masking the cold hard truth about my predicament with a lie.

I look around, noticing the huge bag Neiman has slung over his shoulder. I can smell the herbs from here.

"Is someone hurt?" I ask, my powers prickling to life.

"There's a woman in labor in Tiscoln, and she's struggling," Cleo says. "Her family came to me for help, but I'm just an alchemist. We need your help."

I look from Cleo to the wolves. "Of course. I'm happy to help."

Excitement flares in my chest, but also… nerves. For the past year, I worked in a midwifery clinic in Moonrise. I've delivered dozens of babies–mostly witch babies, though. Shifter births are always more complicated, more likely to have something go wrong.

I swallow hard to tamp down that nervous energy rushing through my body and nod. "Let's go, then."

I turn away from Cleo as she begins to undress, one of the wolves from Tiscoln taking her supply bag in its jaws.

But turning around puts me in view of Evander, who is taking off his shirt.

I lower my gaze a second too late. My eyes sweep over his broad chest–over the roping, tight muscles that coast down his chest and abdomen before disappearing in a sharp V below his waistband.

Goddess, when did he start looking like *this*?

I blush so brightly I'm sure my cheeks can be seen from the heavens as I turn to look at the shed while he takes his pants off.

"What are the gloves for?"

"Armor, if I need it while in wolf form," he says behind me.

"Do you need it right now?"

I'm met with silence, and when I glance over my shoulder, Evander is replaced by a huge golden wolf with piercing green eyes.

He's not wearing armor. I look down at his paws, which are as big as my face, for sure, and wonder where those gloves have gone.

His pants and shirt are neatly folded beside him.

I feel a little tickle in my... chest, not my brain, as Evander says through what I think is the mind-link, 'Can you hear me?'

'Yeah, but this doesn't feel like the mind-link–'

'Get on.'

I square my shoulders. The idea of riding on his back makes me squirm, but I obey. I wrap my arms around his huge neck and get a mouthful of fur as I pull in a surprised breath when he tears off into the night without warning.

He smells very good, honestly. As a witch, I grew up hearing all of the jokes the others would tell about the shifters. How the shifters smelled like wet dogs, or dirt, or a damp forest, but Evander smells like... vanilla candles.

Weird, right?

Where have I smelled that scent before?

I keep my eyes firmly shut as we barrel through the barren, rocky landscape into a deep valley. Soon the smell of smoke rises in the air, and it's clear we've reached a village.

It's nearly sunrise now as I lift my head and blink into the clear, pinkish hue of early morning.

Evander skids to a stop in front of a cottage toward the edge of the village. Spruce trees tower overhead as I get off his back, but then I feel it.

Death hangs nearby, like a ribbon of smoke hugging the air above my head.

"MORE HONEY. It's going to taste awful and she needs as much sugar as we can get into her," I tell Cleo in a soft whisper as we grind herbs in the corner of the room. Behind us, nineteen-year-old Elsie whimpers as her mother lays a cold wet rag over her forehead.

No wonder she's struggling so badly. She's not even old enough to shift. Her baby is full term and ready to be born, but the child is bigger than her small frame can handle.

"Is the baby alive?" Elsie's twin sister, Jessa, asks quietly as she comes up to my side to fetch the cup of tea Cleo just made for the struggling young mother.

"Yes," I assure her, resting a hand on the woman's shoulder. "But I need to turn the baby. She's not in the right position."

"It's a girl?" Jessa asks with a watery smile, her eyes filling with tears.

I nod, hoping I didn't just give away a surprise.

The cottage is full of women—young and old. I've been met with skepticism since arriving here an hour ago, and I'm generally given a wide berth as I tend to the laboring mother, but no one has outwardly tried to stop me yet.

I understand some packs are still weary of witches.

I just hope I can convince them that not all of us are evil.

I kneel at Elsie's bedside while her mother and sister help her drink the tea—a concoction Cleo and I made to help ease the labor pains. The honey is just to help give her energy, but after two days of hard, painful labor, I can tell Elsie is ready to throw in the towel.

The idea of putting her under and cutting this baby from her stomach makes sweat prickle across my hairline. I do not want this to come to that.

I wait for Elsie to finish the tea, which she does with a grimace. "I know it tastes horrific," I say with a tight smile. "But it will help you feel better."

"I don't want to die," she whispers, her skin a pale cream in the sunlight pouring from the window behind her.

"You won't, I promise."

A few of the women in the room glance at each other. I wonder how many women in their pack they've lost to childbirth. It's so common for shifters to struggle, especially the young ones. My own grandmother, aunt, and mother suffered greatly delivering the members of my family.

I flex then curl my fingers, making sure they're warmed up.

Cleo waits for my command nearby. She's been incredibly helpful when it comes to convincing these strangers that I am capable of delivering this baby.

I just hope I'm able to save the mother when this is all said and done.

Elsie screams as I turn the baby into position. Her agony tears at my resolve, but I don't let it show. I've done this many times.

Finally, the herbs we used to calm her kick in, and the energy in the room changes from quiet panic to something happier, sunnier, and more at ease.

"All right," I tell her, roughly an hour later as I feel between her legs. My fingertips graze the top of the baby's head. "Wow, a full head of hair."

A soft laugh ripples around the room, and a very sweaty, beet red Elsie grins deliriously at me from over the swell of her belly.

"She's ready to be born. Are you ready to guide her into this world?" I ask Elsie.

"I am," she says softly, nodding.

I notice the blood between her legs. It's more than I'd like to see, but there's no stopping this baby now.

I need to get her out, and once she's safe, I'll save Elsie's life.

"Push," I say, and her family gathers around her shoulders to help guide a new soul into their pack.

I feel hands on my shoulders and back. A few of the women—possibly aunts or the grandmothers of Elsie—are behind me, giving me the same kind of encouragement Elsie is receiving from her mother, sister, and friends.

It's a magical, sacred moment. Prayers to the Goddess are raised in both murmurs and loud, booming songs that shake the windows in time with Elsie's cries of pain, desperation, and eventually relief.

The baby girl is born in a ray of sun in the afternoon on a cloudless, perfect summer day.

But I don't place her in her mother's arms.

"Take her, dry her off," I say hurriedly to Jessa, who jumps to my side. Elsie groans and trembles, saying something unintelligible. Blood rushes between her legs.

I'm panting, covered in sweat, as I shout, "Everyone out!"

Cleo jumps into action, herding the concerned family out of the bedroom where Elsie has been laboring for several days now.

They gather in the living room beyond the door. I can hear muffled sobs as their prayers and praises to the Goddess turn to desperate pleas to save Elsie.

My heart is in my throat as I turn to Cleo. "I need valerian root and silvertongue. Steep it only for two minutes, I'll be done by then."

"Done with what?" Cleo asks but immediately moves to the table where she keeps her herbs and boiling water.

I have no time to answer. Elsie starts to shake violently. I'm almost out of time.

"Why do shifters lose so much blood during childbirth?!" I say through gritted teeth as I pin her arms to her heaving chest. My powers fly out of my hands in ribbons of blue, shooting over her pale skin.

I hear Cleo startle behind me, but I don't stop. My eyes flare a bright shade of silver as I will all of my healing powers to converge at once, forcing life back into the dying mother.

"Come on!" I urge, imagining the broken parts of her knitting themselves back together again. I imagine blood rushing to her heart, to her brain. I imagine air filling her lungs. "Cleo! The herbs! Now!"

Cleo is beside me in a second, holding a teacup.

I blink, then blink again, digging deep to bring forth an old trick of mine from my youth.

Tears spring along my lower eyelashes—tears that glow a pale gold in the sunlight. Tears I inherited from my grandmother, Isla.

I swipe them away into the palm of my hand and squeeze my fingers so that they fall into the teacup, then raise it to Elsie's mouth. I watch the tears swirl over her lips, then disappear.

She stills.

I take several steps away from her, panting, sweat pouring down my temples.

Elsie takes a sharp breath, a hand flying over her heart.

A strangled sob erupts in the living room, and then Jessa is rushing in with the baby.

"Elsie," she sobs, kissing her sister's cheeks. "Oh, Elsie."

The rest of the family comes in as Elsie returns to life. The baby is placed in her trembling arms as her cheeks flush with healthy color again.

I walk on unsteady feet toward the corner of the room, finding it hard to breathe. My powers are going haywire.

"Here," Cleo whispers, handing me a cup of tea. "It's just chamomile."

I drink it down, trying to ease my thundering heartbeat.

"You just performed a miracle," Cleo says.

"I'm just doing my job," I pant, meeting her eyes.

But Cleo shakes her head slowly from side to side, tears lacing her lashes. "No, child. That was a miracle if I've ever seen one."

As she says it, the family begins to approach me, closing me into the corner and peppering me with tearful gratitude.

But I'm overwhelmed, and other powers are edging toward the surface.

"I need some air," I say, keeping a smile plastered on my face as I hurry out of the crowded room and into the daylight.

There're people everywhere, everyone looking at me, everyone talking to me all at once.

"It's a girl," I croak, and rush around the outside of the cottage toward the woods.

I'm barely in the cool, humid shadow of the spruce tears when my powers erupt, and I'm sucked into a sightless shadow.

I rest my back against a tree and slide to my ass, stretching out my legs.

I turn to a crunching sound nearby, and Evander steps out of the cover of a tree in his human form, dressed in his all black Ghost armor.

So, that's where the gloves went.

How he can see me still, when I'm lost in my powers, I'll never know.

"I think I kissed–I kissed a Ghost at the ball," I say, panting between the words. "I think–did I kiss Flynn?"

Evander cracks an uncharacteristic smile.

18

A MOMENT OF QUIET

Kenna

EVANDER STEPS CLOSER, but I'm still draped in my shadow. I love this power of mine, honestly. It's my favorite of the arsenal of magic that dwells in my veins. I can just... disappear, or harness the power and turn myself into a writhing mass of the darkest kind of shadow and cause all kinds of chaos, but I've never done that.

Blending into the shadows? Yes. All the time.

But Evander can see me. He crouches in front of me, knitting his fingers together while resting his elbows on his knees.

"Your uniform looks stupid," I grumble.

"I've been told women love men in uniform."

"You look like an underfed dragon." It's true, in my defense. Black, thick fabric envelopes him from his neck to the tips of his toes–every inch of him covered in strange scales of a depthless onyx. Leather armor covers his chest, forearms, and thighs. It hugs them like a glove, which makes sense, given that all of this is possible because of a pair of black gloves.

Ghost armor is incredibly complex, and only the highest ranking warriors in the Ghost army have it. The armor makes it impossible for enemies to pick up their scent, is impenetrable, and can turn to a full coat of armor if they shift from human form to wolf form, and back again.

I only know this because I was there the day my Uncle Isaac unveiled the first prototype in my father's office. Sydney and Ryan had come to Eastonia with him, and all three of us watched our fathers marvel over what Isaac had been able to create with the raw materials Dad supplied from some mystical mine in the Roguelands.

Uncle Isaac has unique powers of manipulation. He can unlock anything. He can forge anything.

"A dragon?" Evander huffs, his eyes meeting mine despite my shadow. "Thank you."

"It wasn't a compliment."

"Is there a reason you're out here pouting in the woods and not letting the villagers pepper you with compliments and gifts for saving one of their own? I know you like gifts. And especially, compliments."

"If you came out here to tease me, you can leave."

"It's my job–"

"I don't care if it's your job to follow me around. I want to be alone right now so I can cry and try to catch my breath in peace, just for a minute."

"I wanted to make sure you were all right," he says. "That's all."

"I'm fine. I just need a moment to get back in control of my powers."

"Okay," he says.

"Okay," I echo, sniffling.

He rises and backs away but sits several yards from me with his back turned in my direction.

I'm not sure how long we sit here like this, with me staring at the back of his golden head and him quietly picking pieces of grass and weaving them together. But eventually, my heart stops racing, my mind clears, and soon that flight or fight feeling that sends my powers into a tailspin eases enough for me to let my shadow power dissolve around me like wisps of smoke.

"It's impressive, you know," Evander says from several yards away. "The way you can just disappear into nothing."

"You can see me still, so I wouldn't say I'm completely invisible."

"Well, the shadow does nothing to hide your voice or your whimpering, so…"

I huff a breath. He's right. I should work on that. But… "I don't care what you think of me, Evander. I want to get home as much as you want to be rid of me, so let's not sit here and pretend like we're eight again and you're teasing me relentlessly for no reason."

He's silent for several moments. I wait on pins and needles for his response. He used to be so witty–so sharp and cunning with his words. I remember several instances where he left our fathers speechless after he pleaded our cases when we got in trouble for being absolute menaces to society as kids, and we got away with it more often than not.

But he only says, "You didn't kiss Flynn at the ball."

I blink, having forgotten I'd even said anything about my kiss. "Oh–"

"The village would like to thank you, you know. They're setting up a party in the town square. There's going to be food, and dancing. Everything you like. It's a celebration for you and the mother."

"How do you know all of this?"

"I… might be spying through mind-link."

I frown. "You can do that?"

"Not as well as Flynn," he admits. "It's part of our training, though. The average wolf isn't nearly as guarded as the people in power I'm normally working with–or against…. It's easy to tap in. Someone is saying something about chocolate cake with… raspberry icing–"

I'm on my feet in a second flat, and Evander chuckles, rising and dusting off his fancy, ridiculously expensive armor.

But I hesitate leaving the private, sheltered sanctuary of the woods.

Evander keeps his distance, but I can feel his gaze boring into the side of my face as he says, "You've been given a room at the local inn. It's a nice place, I scoped it out already. Some of the local village women have laid out clothes for you to change into, since those are... bloody."

I look down, realizing I'm still in my jeans and what was once a white shirt. The events of leaving Crescent Falls are a blur. It feels like a lifetime ago that Evander and I were involved in a high speed chase. In less than twenty four hours, I nearly died, spirited to Eastonia, delivered a baby, and saved a woman's life.

"What else do you know about the cake?" I ask, finally looking at him.

***

NIGHT FALLS over the village of Tiscoln. I've been making the rounds–splitting my time between checking on Elsie and her baby girl and conversing with the ever curious and mystified villagers. I've learned that Tiscoln itself is small, and most of the people who call this place home are spread throughout the nearby mountains, coming to this village to trade goods and commune with each other.

It's very... how do I explain it? I've never met people like this before–people so in tune to their wolfish sensibilities. In fact, most everyone is in their wolf form as the celebration continues on into the night. It's like these people have been trapped in a place lost to time, locked within the veil, and they had to resort to an older way of life to survive.

It's a full moon too, so no wonder everyone is shifting.

My social battery runs low rather quickly. I take a cup of mead down to a creek that runs along the far side of the village while music and livery continues in the background. Lantern light reflects off the water's surface as I sit on the banks, dipping my bare toes in the cool water.

I sip honeysuckle mead and listen to the music, finally letting my mind adjust to our peculiar situation. Evander has been mostly gone all evening, talking to various men and wolves about what I assume has to do with where we are and how we can get to the Roguelands.

He hasn't asked me to jump again. I doubt he will, given that fact I brought us all the way here. I have no idea how to tell those powers of mine where to land.

The mead is a calming presence in my system, but my powers are stronger right now than they usually are because of the moon. I need a moment to clear my head.

But I also knew Evander will find me if I walk out of sight, so I'm not surprised when his footsteps sound out behind me, and he stops a few feet away.

I turn my head to look at him over my shoulder. He's dressed in a pair of dark pants that hug his legs more than they should. He probably borrowed them from someone, and given that fact he towers over most of the men here, it was probably the best they could do. His shirt, however, fits him like a glove as he sighs and edges closer, sitting down beside me.

"What was that sigh for?" I ask lightly before taking another sip of mead.

"Am I not allowed to breathe in your presence, Kenna?"

I glare at him, but his sly smile does something to soften my heart toward my old friend.

I roll my eyes back to the creek. "So, what's the plan, then?"

"There's a road system that leads out of the mountains, but it's treacherous this time of year. There're a few river crossings we need to worry about, but I've been assured the people of these mountains are generally friendly."

"So we're going on foot?"

"I'll shift, and you'll ride on my back, unless you want to give shifting a try."

I swallow back the sharp, "NO!" that springs to mind.

"You don't have to shift. Carrying you isn't an issue."

"I'm not too heavy?"

"You're rather heavy, but I've been through worse."

I glare at him again, but it's obvious he's just teasing and… for the first time in many, many years, a glimpse of the funny, witty personality he must have buried deep down is coming to the surface.

"Your mouth is the reason you haven't found your mate yet," I quip, offering him my cup of mead. "You've always had a sharp tongue. Maybe if you were nicer, women would be more interested in getting to know you."

"I already told you I'm not looking for my mate or anything like that."

"Why not?"

His brows pinch together. "Why do you care?"

"Because your wife, or mate, will be the High Lady of Veiled Valley, like your mom is until we take over. You need to have one, eventually."

"My lifestyle isn't conducive to maintaining close personal rela- tionships–"

"But it will be. Really soon, actually. You and I are supposed to take over in… just a few weeks, you know."

He looks down at me, his eyes the color of raw emeralds in the dim lantern light. "What would you do if you didn't have to be Luna of Veiled Valley?"

I sigh heavily and rope my arms around my knees. "I'd be a midwife."

He chuckles softly. I look at him at just the right moment, catching the brief smile that touches his lips. Gods, he's so handsome when he smiles. That flicker of something like a crush comes to life in my chest again.

"You are already a midwife."

"Yeah, but… I can't be a midwife and run a pack the size of Veiled Valley."

"If you had–" he cuts himself off abruptly.

But I know what he was about to say.

"If I had my mate, or at least someone equivalent to rule beside me, I'd have time. I know."

Evander says nothing for a long time. I let the silence fall between us, enjoying the momentary quiet. We haven't spoken like this in years. I never thought we would again. He used to know all of my hopes and dreams, and now?

"I'd like you to be settled at the inn soon," he says after several minutes. "Cleo and her mate have warned me about how rowdy things are going to get once the moon is high, and I don't like the idea of you being out here–"

"I'm ready to go now," I tell him. He's right. That slight, ever present pull I feel toward my wolf is sharper right now, and I'm not sure if the strange, electric sensation in my body has to do with my wolf or if it's because Evander is here, and we're talking like the old friends we used to be. But I'm tired, and tomorrow sounds like the beginning of a long journey.

I follow Evander through the town and what remains of the party. I check on Elsie one last time. She's fine and surrounded by family and friends.

Finally, I let Evander lead me upstairs at the inn, which is rather loud and lively as those who haven't shifted gather inside for drinks and music, but the hallways and rooms upstairs are more subdued.

My room is nothing more than a bed, a dresser, and a wash basin. I came here to change into the flowy, cream colored dress that brushes my ankles and shows off a rather large amount of cleavage, the look rounded out by slightly puffy long sleeves that taper at the wrists and a cinched waist.

In the darkness, however, the room feels plain and empty–and surprisingly cold.

"Goodnight," Evander says, moving toward the door.

"Wait," I say, fighting the urge to reach out and grab his arm. "Where are you sleeping tonight?"

"Outside your door."

"What?"

"I'll be right in the hallway in my wolf form. It's the safest option–"

"You're going to sleep on the floor?"

"Of course, where else would I sleep?"

"In here. With me. There's plenty of room in the bed."

The look he gives me rattles me to my core. I feel my breath catch in my throat as he says, "I can't sleep in the same bed as you, Kenna."

"Why not?"

Again, the intensity in his look does something to my body–

setting every nerve on fire. I sense something… off. Something shifts between us, and a scent tickles my nose faintly, but enough for me to catch a hint of leather and vanilla.

"You didn't kiss Flynn at the ball," he rasps.

"Then who did I kiss?"

19

FEEL THE HEAT

Kenna

EVANDER SHUTS THE DOOR. The lock clicks, and for a moment, the only sound I can hear is my heartbeat racing in my own ears.

He looks... conflicted. Unsure—and unsteady.

"You—you smell like vanilla candles," I whisper, unsure if I say the words out loud or only in my head.

But he looks at me, holding my gaze. "I do?" he asks quietly, his voice taking on a tone I'm not accustomed to. It's softer than before, less on edge.

I nod, finding it impossible to swallow past the lump forming in my throat.

"Why?" I ask, because it's the only word frantically bouncing around my skull.

"Why do I smell like the vanilla candles you like so much?" He takes a step toward me, then another, but there's still an incredible amount of distance between us.

"Yeah, why?"

Evander's jaw clenches, and his eyes dart to his boots. Guilt clouds the fine features of his face.

But I don't care that he feels guilty. I've been feeling guilty for years, thinking I was the reason our friendship ended.

"Why did you storm off when you came to visit me five years ago? What did I do to you, Evander, to make you hate me so much?"

"I've never hated you," he rasps, meeting my eyes again. "Not for a second–"

"You said you did!" Tears begin to burn along my lower lashes.

"I couldn't be what you wanted me to be–"

"I just wanted you. I didn't care–"

"You knew what I was training for!" He shouts, and I feel the urge to cower. Fury, then guilt, flashes behind his eyes as he runs his fingers through his glossy hair and shakes his head. "You knew I was training to be a Ghost. You knew we weren't going to see each other again for a long, long time. You knew I couldn't match whatever you felt–"

"But did you feel the same?"

Five years ago, I stood from my chair on the veranda overlooking the city where we'd grown up together. I vividly remember the dress of pale pink dotted with gold and cream colored beads I'd been wearing, and how the silken fabric fell over my legs as I stood, facing Evander.

He'd just shouted at me, saying *no*. I'd laughed and asked what was wrong, and he backed away, backed away like I'd hit him.

"You told me you couldn't talk to me anymore. That I needed to stop sending you letters."

"Kenna, I don't want to talk about this–" Evander looks like he's considering moving back toward the door. "I can't talk about this."

"Then I asked why I couldn't send you letters anymore, and you said–"

"I said," he growls, "I couldn't take it–"

"What couldn't you take?" I plead, my tears threatening to spill down my cheeks. "I told you I loved you, that I missed you so much, and you told me you hated me. That we could never be friends, and that you never wanted to see me again. Why?"

Evander exhales deeply, nostrils flaring. His hands are clenched into fists. "I can't be your friend, Kenna."

"Still?" I swallow hard, the second blow of his rejection sweeping through me and tying my heart into a knot. "Why?"

"I can't answer that–"

"I don't care. You have to. You owe me–"

"I don't owe you anything," he snaps. "I couldn't bear it, Kenna, seeing you again. Seeing you grown up, a woman, just–just fucking beautiful and you–" He stumbles over his words, which is not the Evander I know at all.

"You're mad at me for growing up?"

"No. Gods, that's not it."

"Then what happened, Evander?" I shout. "We were best friends. I loved you. Every day you were gone, I missed you. Do you understand? Whatever I did to you, I'm sorry. I am so, so sorry. Okay? I thought–I thought we'd always have each other. I wanted you at my wedding one day–"

"Your *wedding*?" he seethes, and a chill snakes down my spine as he takes a step toward me.

"Y-yeah," I stammer, tucking my arms behind my back and lacing my fingers together to stop them from trembling. "I thought we'd–I thought we'd be friends forever. That one day our kids would play together like we used to do, and our mates would be friends and we–we could all live together and be happy–"

"That is my worst fucking nightmare."

I blink at the coldness in his tone. "Evander?"

He takes another step, his chest heaving with each breath. "You and I can never be friends. We can't have that life you've cooked up where it's all rainbows and butterflies and family fucking dinners–"

"Why are you being like this?" I cry out, my voice shaking. "Is it because of the letter–"

He goes still, the fury in his eyes fading away almost entirely.

"Because I said…" I trail off. "Because I said I had a crush on you?"

He runs his tongue along his lower lip and takes another step in my direction, nearly closing the distance between.

"I didn't realize admitting that meant I wouldn't have you as a friend anymore," I grind out, but my heart is threatening to leap out of my throat.

"I came home because of that letter," he says in a near whisper. "I needed to see you. It had nothing to do with your birthday. I just needed…"

I close my eyes as his proximity invades every sense, every nerve ending, every blank space in my mind.

"Then why did you leave?"

"Because I couldn't be what you needed. The consequences were too great."

"What consequences? We were sixteen!"

He shakes his head, but we're chest to chest, and I keep my eyes closed as he lowers his head, his lips brushing over my temple.

"My duty to you is clear. I can't be your friend when I am the one who vowed to protect you. You… Kenna, you are distracting in every way. I can't focus on anything when I'm near you. I can barely breathe in your presence, and I…." He inhales, letting go in a shuddering breath.

"I don't need your protection."

"You do."

I go to shove him away, my hands planted on his chest, but my fingers curl into the light fabric of his shirt, feeling the taut muscles beneath.

A spark of truth wraps its way around my heart and tugs.

"You kissed me at the ball."

He steps away. I drop my arms to my sides.

"You kissed me," I repeat, tears beginning to slide down my cheeks. "It was *you*."

"Kenna, I'm sorry–"

"You don't deny it, then?"

"Do you think I'd lie to you about that?"

"Of course, I do. I don't know you anymore. The Evander I knew and loved wouldn't yell at me, or tell me my dreams were his *fucking* nightmare!"

"The thought of having to stand by and watch while you fall in love with someone else," he says, each word brutal and heavy with emotion, "is like someone is twisting a knife in my gut. I can't do it, Kenna. I pledged my life to the Ghosts to try to prevent becoming your Beta. I stayed away, stayed silent, because I couldn't–I couldn't–"

My mind is empty–a blissfully, peaceful darkness that swells with the meaning behind his words. Maybe I'm reading him wrong. Maybe he means something else, something entirely different than what my body is telling me is true.

"Kiss me again," I say so quietly I'm sure he doesn't hear it, but his eyes meet mine.

"No," he whispers, shaking his head, he reaches out and wipes my tears away with his thumb. His touch lingers on my skin and I feel it *everywhere.*

"Please," I whisper, and his thumb traces a line over my lower lip. I close my eyes, relishing his warm, steady touch.

I don't why I want him to kiss me so badly. Maybe it's just to confirm that what I felt that night wasn't anything more than excitement and longing for attention. There's something here, though. Something between us that's different and uncommon.

I think I would know right away if I were feeling the mate bond. It would be a snap, an electric pulse, something tangible that I could sense, smell, and taste.

I'm still clutching his shirt when he leans in, his mouth hovering over mine. I'm on pins and needles as he softly brushes his lips against mine, and then I'm pressing myself against him, and my lips plunge into his.

He tastes like salt and a hint of scotch. He smells like leather, vanilla, and the air after a heavy storm. His arms wrap around me, caging me in, holding me steady as my knees give out, and I lose myself to him.

He pulls away enough to suck in a breath, and I do the same, but I don't want to stop.

"Evander," I murmur, opening my eyes enough to look up at him, and I find him looking down at me, his gaze heavy and hooded as he leans back in and kisses me again.

There's nothing soft about it this time. He presses me closer, gripping the back of my neck to guide me as his tongue slides across my lower lip. I let out a trembling moan.

His other hand slides down my back, his touch sending ripples of feeling coasting over my skin.

I feel… heat. Heavy, luscious heat that settles in my belly before exploding through my upper thighs.

"Kenna," he whispers before dragging his kisses down along my jaw and neck. His hand slides around from my back to my sides, then up to my breasts.

Oh, Goddess…. I let out another moan, his name on the tip of my tongue.

Should I be feeling like this for *Evander*? My childhood friend? My teenage crush?

He tugs at the bodice of my dress, and I gasp as cool air touches my skin. He frees my breasts from the gown, and suddenly his mouth is grazing over tender, sensitive places no one else has ever touched.

I know about sex. My mom told me about it. She was never weird or uncomfortable in preparing me for womanhood, but this… this feeling is not what I expected in the slightest.

I choke out another gasp as his tongue flicks over my right nipple. I tangle my fingers in his hair, finding it hard to stay upright. I know the bed is behind me. Another step backward, and the back of my thighs will hit the mattress.

I want this. I want him. I want him to take me to bed and lay claim to me, and it's a desperate, overwhelming feeling that doesn't entirely make sense.

I almost voice it, but nothing but a strangled moan escapes as his teeth scrape back up my chest, then my neck, and then his lips are on mine, and I burn for him.

But when I start pulling on my sleeves, desperately hot and

needing to get out of my clothes, he stops, his lips hovering centimeters away from mine.

We're both panting, out of breath.

No, no. I'm not ready for this moment to be broken. I try to clutch his shirt to pull him back to me, but he steps away, just out of reach.

"I'm sorry–"

"No," I tell him, shaking my head. "I want–"

"We can't," he interrupts, but the look in his eyes tells me he desperately wants to continue. Maybe more than I do.

"L-lock the door behind me," he rushes out, turning to leave.

"Where are you going?"

"I need to shift."

20

NOMADS

Evander

I have two options.

Option one: Run like hell. Find the nearest village where I'm able to finally mind-link with someone, anyone, from King Ryatt's forces and find a way to get Kenna home so I can run deeper into the mountains and disappear forever.

Or option two: Turn around and claim her as mate, like the Goddess intended, forever shackling her to a murderous, violent man who is grossly unable to give her everything she deserves.

I keep running–sprinting–my paws overturning raw earth as I tear through the forest and back up into the mountains until I'm past the tree line and far enough from Tiscoln that I can't feel the overwhelming pull toward her anymore.

In the distance, I can just see the faint lights of Tiscoln shimmering in a shallow valley, nothing more than a muted glow in a thick crop of trees.

I skid to a stop on the peak of a lower mountain, my paws sliding over late summer snow and ice.

I don't question why I just did such a thing to Kenna. I don't need to. I already know why–I can't control myself around her, not anymore. Not now that I've tasted her, and the more I'm with her, the worse this is going to be.

I have to get her back to her parents. I have to come clean to King Ryatt. I'll tell him the truth, that I'm her mate, and that I can't be her Beta.

She needs someone kind and gentle. She needs someone who wants a herd of children. She needs someone she can talk to, who can empathize with her, who wants to be with her and is capable of loving her as much as she loves him.

She needs someone who doesn't have to worry about protecting her every hour of every day for the rest of her Goddess-damned life.

I sink to my belly and lower my head to the ground. Wind whips through my thick, golden fur. The urge to shift into a fox is strong, but I ignore it. If I'm going to spend the night in the mountains, I need to be in wolf form for warmth, at least.

I just need to cool off. I'm confident Kenna is safe at the inn. I interviewed several of the higher ranking men in the village and even spoke to their Alpha during the celebration tonight, and while they're a wild, rural pack, they aren't the violent type, at least not toward women.

They also want nothing to do with the Roguelands or the witches who inhabit it and are more than happy to give Kenna space.

It's the only reason I feel I have the ability to leave her alone in Tiscoln at all, but tomorrow, something has to change. We need to move. We need to pick our way down the mountains to the Roguelands.

'Can anyone hear me?' I send through the mind-link to any and all Ghosts who might be in range. I find it hard to hope anyone is even remotely nearby.

Nothing.

I get up and shake snow from my coat two hours later before maneuvering down the mountain and into the forest. I'm sure Kenna is asleep by now. Hopefully. She'd better be, given that she has to be up at the break of dawn.

I edge into Tiscoln just as the first glimpses of sunlight break over the mountains and cast the valley in ribbons of gold, but I'm not alone.

The Alpha of Tiscoln, a man of thirty, trots out of the woods and stops abruptly when he sees me cut between two buildings in the town square. He lowers his head, ears twitching. I lower my head in a show of submission. This is his territory, after all.

Pleased, he ticks his ears to the left in a motion for me to follow, and I let him lead me down the sleepy cobblestone street until we reach a large, unimposing three-story stone cottage that stretches toward the forest canopy.

Breakfast smells hit me right in the stomach as I follow him inside.

He goes up the stairs off the foyer, but I remain near the front door.

A young woman steps out of an archway to my left and pauses, her smile fading to one of marked concern as we look at each other.

I shift, my armor coating my human body in scales and leather, and her fearful expression fades.

"Would you like something to eat?" she asks.

I roll my neck and crack my knuckles, easing the tension from my muscles. "I'm waiting on your husband. If he allows me to eat, I will."

"He might be the Alpha of Tiscoln," she smiles, her light brown eyes creasing, "but I am the Alpha of this house, so whether you eat breakfast is up to me. Come." She motions for me to follow.

I glance up the stairs. I know better than to cross an Alpha's boundaries, especially when it comes to a wife or mate, but I doubt this woman is going to let me decline her offer again.

I wordlessly follow her down the hallway and through the archway, which leads into a wide, spacious kitchen. A table is set, and two small boys sit on one side, their curly red hair gleaming in the morning sunlight starting to stream through the window.

A third child, a little girl and the oldest of the bunch, narrows her eyes at me as I sit at the table next to her little brothers.

"Who are *you?*" she hisses.

"Mirabella, mind your manners," her mother says behind us.

The girl tilts her chin toward the ceiling. Her bright red curls are braided away from her face as she looks down her tiny nose at me. "Who are you, *please?*"

"Saying please doesn't count," comes a booming male voice from the archway.

I turn to the Alpha of Tiscoln as he enters the room. I begin to rise from my chair, but he waves me away, giving me a friendly smile. "No need for formalities at my family breakfast table."

I ease back into my chair, nodding once.

But Mirabella is still eyeing me coolly.

"This is Mirabella, obviously," the Alpha says, motioning toward his daughter. "That's Andrew; he's six. And James is four."

I give the boys a nod, and they go a little pink in the cheeks.

"My mate–"

"Katherine," she smiles, setting plates piled with eggs and sausage in front of us. "Please excuse my children's terrible manners. They get them from their father." She gives her mate a look, but he's gazing up at her lovingly.

It makes something twist in my gut. Something like jealousy, which I hadn't expected.

"Why are you wearing scales like a fish?" Andrew asks before popping a piece of egg into his mouth.

All three children look at me expectantly.

"It's for protection."

"You're a warrior, then," Katherine says as she sits down with her own plate.

"Yes, I am."

"He's been tasked with escorting the princess of Eastonia back to her homeland," the Alpha says.

I realize I've never caught his name. I doubt it matters. I glance at him, wondering how a man his age is able to have all of this–this family who eats breakfast together in the morning–while running a very large pack.

He's only thirty at the most. His wife might be younger, but it's hard to tell. They're both young, fit, healthy, and seem remarkably... happy.

I eat a few bites to be polite, but I have no idea why the Alpha would bring me back here. I'm a stranger in their lands. I have a witch with me. We're not planning on staying.

Within minutes, the children are bouncing in their chairs, ready to be dismissed from the table, and Katherine gathers their plates and shoos them into the depths of the house.

It's just me and the Alpha now.

The air takes on a new feeling as tension roils between us, thick enough to cut with a knife.

He leans back in his chair and interlocks his fingers, his eyes meeting mine. "My pack talks. I'm sure it's the same all over. Gossip spreads like wildfire in these Highlands."

"What gossip are you alluding to?" I ask, keeping my voice low and level, damn near uninterested.

"The Highlands do not have an Alpha King. We never have because this area wasn't populated until two hundred years ago or so. We used to be nomadic, more wolf than man. But times are changing, and with the packs in the Roguelands spreading out along the base of the mountains, we're closer to civilization than ever before."

I need him to get to the point because I'm burning daylight, and Kenna and I need to hit the road as soon as possible.

I almost say as such, but he bluntly continues, "I know about the rebel threat. The packs in these lands are close knit, forged by familial bonds and marriages. Several of the packs in the lower Highlands, toward the edge of the Roguelands, have encountered your rebel outlaws. Just last night, I met with the Beta of the Redwood pack, which is twenty miles south of here, and they've learned that Alpha King Ryatt is calling on his army to prepare for war."

Flynn was right. This is bigger than we thought, and the royals are making moves.

"Which is why I need to leave here as soon as possible to bring the princess back to her family. She's in danger here. She's in danger anywhere that's not the capital of Eastonia."

"Moonrise, isn't it?"

I nod.

The Alpha purses his lips in thought. "You cannot take the direct route into the Roguelands. We have a small road system now that leads into the river basin, where the Opal Hill pack resides. That's your closest pack affiliated with the Roguelands. But you have to stay off the roads."

"Why? Are you telling me you have Draven Rebels in the Highlands?"

"Possibly, or a small faction of their coven. We've killed at least thirty in the past month. The Alpha of Redwood took out an entire group of them in a cave near the edge of his territory two weeks ago. He left no survivors, but his pack suffered casualties."

"You realize by telling me this that I have to report it to my commander, who will then relay this information to the king–"

"I'm telling you this because the packs of the Highlands are prepared to fight for the crown."

I'm stunned into silence for several seconds. "How many packs?"

"Six. We have roughly five thousand warriors willing to fight. We already have bands patrolling the borders of our pack territories."

I nod but then meet the young Alpha's eyes. He's serious. His eyes are set and cold as his gaze bores into mine.

"You'd be fighting for the Witch Queen, you know."

For a split second, a new emotion flashes behind his eyes.

It's humility–a rarity amidst the Alpha's I've met in my life.

"She is Firestone. She was meant for the throne my people are willing to fight for." He stands, and I follow. "Do you need escorts into the Roguelands?"

"Will the people of this territory attempt to stop our progress to the Roguelands?"

"No, they will not. I've already spread the word about your princess. You will both be welcome in any pack you come across."

He walks me to the door. Bright, morning daylight filters through the windows, casting his rustic home in peels of gold and amber.

But I pause before crossing the threshold. "You're giving up your freedom from the reign of another Alpha King. King Ryatt and Queen Ella will view the Highlands as part of their kingdom once I tell them this. Are you sure?"

"My people have survived here for two centuries—but barely. We've had several terrible winters and ever worse harvests. Now that the veil is gone, hunting has been less successful, and unless the Alphas of this land act, we will have to resort back to our old ways."

He'd mentioned they were once nomadic, likely following whatever game they could hunt from breeding ground to breeding ground.

"I want better for my people. For my children," he sighs with a nod. "This is the way forward for my people. They will never forget the heroic actions of your princess, warrior. One day she will be Queen of Eastonia, and that is who we truly follow into battle."

I leave the Alphas house with a heavy chest. I reach the inn and find Kenna sitting at the bar picking at a plate of fruit.

She glances at me before sliding off her chair. She hikes a leather bag over her shoulder—likely a gift from the village for her services—and finally looks me in the eyes.

"I'm ready to go home," she says and brushes past me into the open.

2 1

CHOSEN FOR THE RITE

Ella

AMANDA SHIFTS her weight beside me as we stare up into the ceiling of the remains of the observatory.

After I destroyed Ravenna's crystal castle in Old Moonrise to save my friends' lives, I offered to have this palace rebuilt.

The mystics refused–flat out.

They said it was a gift and a message from the Goddess that the orrery survived the devastation. It sits in the remains of the palace, warded by Ryatt's powers against the elements, and has a view of the night sky as I wait for the mystics to arrive. Metal arms twirl in a circle, holding up the planets of our solar system–the moon and the stars around it.

This room has been the meeting place of the mystic's for millennia, since long before the veil ever came down around Eastonia.

And one thing I've learned about the mystics during my time in Eastonia is that they cannot handle *change*.

A woman in a pale silver robe appears, her face obstructed by a glittering mask of pure moonstone.

Amanda jumps, startled, but I've grown accustomed to their strange ways. I have a theory about them, and that's that they simply regenerate. I've never met a baby mystic. I've never met a family who had a daughter go into the trade. They just... appear, wearing the same robes and the same masks.

I never know their true names, either. Sister this, sister that. That's all they are.

Another trio of mystics appear, and I briefly wonder if Amanda is going to have a heart attack, but she steadies herself with a tight grip on my forearm. Amanda steers clear of the mystics if she can. Her work as the wife of the Beta generally has to do with the public, especially when it comes to entertaining and appeasing the high ranking families of the packs under our rule.

I need her at my side for this meeting, however.

If anyone had told me that the two of us would one day be running an entire kingdom together, I would have laughed in their face. We're doing a good job, I think. We can be serious when we need to.

Right now, I'm deadly serious.

Because we have a date for the Rite.

"When?" I ask, and my voice sounds unfamiliar in the echo of the towering columns of pure crystal all around us.

The orrery keeps spinning, and the *click clack* of the gears puts me on edge as I wait for the mystics response.

In unison, they say, "The third Saturday of the month. Two weeks from now. A Blood Moon Eclipse."

I find it hard to swallow. Has it really been twenty-one years since the last eclipse?

Beside me, Amanda looks from mystic to mystic.

One of them steps forward, her robes brushing against the mosaic tiles. "Everything is in place. We will hold the ceremony and celebration in tandem."

"That sounds like a plan." I sigh, unable to hold back my nerves any longer. "Have you seen... anything else?"

Amanda tenses. I know we're both waiting for them to tell us our children are dead, or captured by the enemy, or something equally as bad.

The past two days have been torture, to say the least. Evander and Kenna never made it on the ferry. They never arrived in Maatua.

The only clue we have is that Ryatt felt *something* in the protective wards he put in place the same morning Kenna was supposed to board the ferry with Misty. Someone broke through the veil in the furthest reaches of the Roguelands—from Crescent Falls.

I know Kenna is alive.

And I know Evander is risking his life to bring her home.

He will. He will bring her home.

"No, Your Grace."

Great. Just great.

I glance at Amanda, who says into my mind, 'Can they really not tell us where they are?'

I sigh again and give her a little shrug. I'm barely holding myself together as it is. Ryatt is off in the Roguelands tearing the place apart looking for them with only a hunch to go on, and I'm here, being the queen, pretending like my heart hasn't been ripped clean out of my chest.

"Do we know who will be performing the ritual?" I ask.

The mystics confer in their strange, silent way before one speaks up and says, "A young witch by the name of Vivienne has been chosen. She's been notified of her fate and has accepted."

Amanda and I glance at each other. "And the man?"

"Evander of Moonrise."

Amanda's grip on my arm tightens. I choke down an alarmed, "What?" before the word can escape.

"Very well," I manage to say and give the mystics a slight bob of my head.

Without another word, Amanda and I hustle out of the orrery and into the village of Old Moonrise. I could spirit us across the lake, back into the city, but I know by our silence that we both need to walk and process what we just found out.

Amanda lets go of my arm and walks steadily through the village toward the lake shore, her shoulder squared, and her body absolutely rigid.

I follow her, passing the trail leading to Ryatt's old house nestled in the trees, until we reach the docks lining the lake.

It's practically empty here. A single fisherman sits in a canoe just off the shore, eating a sandwich while waiting for a fish to take his bait.

Amanda plops down on the edge of the dock.

I sit next to her, and we stare out over the lake for a long time, watching the sun go down over the mountains in the distance, and the lights of the new city I forced from this lake twinkle alight.

"He'll do it," Amanda says in a small, sad voice. "Evander will perform the Rite."

"He has a choice," I tell her, but she shakes her head.

"He's so–so stubborn. He gets that from me." She huffs a breath. "But he's so… he's so much like Granger. He loves order and performing his duties. He's every commander's dream."

"He doesn't have to do this," I repeat.

"It's not up to me," she whispers, shaking her head. "He's an adult. He'll see this like everyone else does–a blessing on his family, something to be proud of. It's why I did it. I knew my parents would be proud that I was the chosen one… not that it mattered."

Amanda's entire family perished when King Kane's forces attacked her pack and village shortly after she and Granger performed the Rite.

It took them both several years to tell Ryatt and I some of the details of what took place during that night when they were chosen by the mystics to bring back the moon after the eclipse.

Amanda's fate was read to her. She was told she'd have many children–all healthy, all strong and capable. She was told she'd find her fated mate, and together they'd usher in a new era of peace and prosperity for Eastonia.

But like the women before her, she had no idea who would be entering that cave with her, and then Granger was at her side.

"I was told he'd be special," Amanda says as she watches the last streams of sunlight dust over the lake. "That Evander would have many gifts and a divine purpose. He's a child of the Rite. He now has the ability to shift into both a wolf and fox and flew through his Ghost training. I just–he's shy, Ella. He's always had a hard time making friends, and I doubt he's even ever had a girlfriend."

I chuckle, giving her a look. "You really think he hasn't gotten into his fair share of trouble across the river in Tarsian during training? If he's as much like Granger as you say, I'm sure he's been with plenty of women." Ryatt and Granger had quite a reputation during their days as young warriors. I've heard plenty of stories from that time, whether I like it or not.

"He's more tender-hearted than he'd ever admit, and I worry he'd accept this and–and it would eat at him."

"What do you mean?" I ask, generally confused.

Amanda runs her fingers through her long, copper-blonde hair. "He just always does what other people tell him to do. He always does what he thinks is right for the greater good. I don't think Evander has ever done anything for himself, and it breaks my heart."

"And you think he'd do this because it's expected of him?"

"Yes, I do. He won't refuse."

"And what if he finds his mate within the next two weeks, and it's not this Vivienne girl?" I ask, giving her shoulder a little nudge. "Do you think he'd still do the Rite?"

"I don't know, Ella. Maybe I'm thinking about this too deeply." She fidgets with the seam of her blue silk skirt. But then she cracks a smile and chuckles to herself.

"What's so funny?"

"I was just thinking about how we used to wonder if Evander and Kenna were mates. They were so close as kids."

I smile, but it's wistful. "I remember that. I remember how they used to play mates and set up little houses in the woods together with her dolls and all of his play weapons so he could hunt for her."

"Times have really changed them," she sighs. "I'm worried about them right now."

"So am I," I readily admit. "I'm sure they're fine. I know they're together, at least."

"Evander would never let anyone hurt Kenna," she says. "She's the one person he's ever really cared about."

Her words do something to my heart as the stars come into view above us. I take Amanda's hand in mine.

"What do you think they're doing right now, besides fighting?"

She smirks. "Hopefully making up for lost time."

Our room in the castle is massive but feels cold and empty without Ryatt. I sit on the edge of the bed, freshly showered and wearing sweatpants and a tank top. It's late at night. Probably past midnight, at this point. I've already used the mirror to contact my brother, and there's been no news about any sightings of rebels, or of my daughter, in Crescent Falls.

At least my niece is safely tucked away in Maatua.

I lie back on the bed and knit my fingers over my stomach, gazing up at the domed ceiling and the mural painted across it thousands of years ago.

When the city first appeared, Ryatt and I brought in as many skilled artisans as we could find to bring the castle and surrounding city back to life.

It took years–five years, exactly–to return the castle to its former glory.

It's been home since then, but I miss the castle in Veiled Valley. I miss it especially on lonely nights like this, when there's no one but me and the staff.

At least in Veiled Valley I had the magic that lived in the house to keep me company.

But a tickle in my chest breaks me from my musings.

'I have news about their whereabouts,' Ryatt says through the mind-link, also sending a little tug down the silver thread of our bond.

164

I sit up, sighing with relief. 'Where are they?'

'Commander Artyom is sending a Ghost into the mountains. There's been rebel activity there, and a scout from some rural packs said a witch helped deliver a baby high in the mountains yesterday.'

'We don't have any witches stationed as healers that high in the mountains. That's outside of Rogueland territory–'

'I know. It's her, isn't it?'

'It has to be her. Who else could it be?'

I think of my beautiful, talented daughter and her midwifery skills.

'I'll find her and bring her home.'

'I know you will.' I debate telling him what Amanda and I just learned about Evander but decide it isn't my news to share.

Granger is with him. Amanda likely already told him what was happening.

'Goodnight, Princess,' Ryatt says, and my chest warms with newfound hope, love, and relief.

22

THREE WOLVES AND A WITCH

Kenna

NIGHT FALLS, and Evander and I haven't said a word to each other. In fact, he's been pretty much unseen for most of the dozen or so miles we hiked today, all of which were done with me blanketed in my shadow and him running somewhere in his fox form.

Or wolf form. I honestly have no idea. All I know is that whatever happened between us last night has made us both unwilling or unable to even look at each other.

I know better, which is the worst part. I know better than to kiss a friend and think everything will go back to the way it was before. That's like, a cardinal rule in friendship between opposite sexes, right?

Maybe it did go back to the way it was before, actually, because now we're not speaking, and I have no idea where he is or what he's up to.

I let my shadow fade and huff out a breath as I come to a full stop in a moon-soaked clearing, my legs aching and feet blistered and sore.

"I'm done, Evander. I'm not going any further." My voice carries in the cool night air.

'You're out in the open, Kenna. Keep moving. I found a cave.'

"Great," I grumble, swinging my new leather satchel. It's laden with herbs and supplies for our journey. Little treats like cake and sandwiches, a few packages of dried meat and oats. All of which I plan on eating myself and not sharing a crumb of.

I edge through the clearing back into the dense forest we dropped into a few hours ago. The forest was, at least at first, a welcome relief from trying to navigate the rocky cliffs and winding trails down the mountains, but now I'm wading through chest deep heather following Evander's distracting scent.

Clouds roll in, sending a stiff, cool breeze through the trees. I'm a little cold when I finally break through the trees again and find myself walking along a large rock face where a soft glow is visible around a corner.

I round the corner and find Evander–dressed in his leathers–crouching next to a fire.

"It looks like you've been here for a while," I grumble, shrugging off my satchel before sliding onto my ass. I let out my breath and briefly close my eyes.

"You weren't in much of a hurry," he says, annoyance lacing each word. "I had to do something to pass the time after I found this place."

"For someone who was tasked with stalking me back in Crescent Falls, you seem to not care enough anymore to stick close by."

"I was close by. You have powers, Kenna. Have you forgotten how to protect yourself?"

I glare at him and reach for my bag, pulling out one of the sandwiches. He doesn't even bother to look in my direction as he says, "Rest for three hours. We're leaving again before dawn."

"What's the rush?"

Now he's looking at me. I take a bite of my sandwich, holding his gaze. I want to say something, anything, about the kiss we shared back in Tiscoln, but after today, that feels like it happened a lifetime ago, and I can't come up with the words I need to ask him what exactly happened between us.

Because I'm sure kissing someone isn't supposed to feel like *that*.

A blush prickles across my cheeks at the memory of his lips on mine, and then his lips lower down, and heat immediately pools between my thighs. His eyes scan my face, then his nostrils flare, and I wonder if he can tell that….

He looks away, murmuring something about shifting again to patrol our camp, but I stick my foot out to prevent him from moving toward the cave mouth.

"Are we friends or not?" I ask hotly.

"No, we are *not* friends."

"Then as your princess, I demand to know what your f–*freaking* problem is."

"I don't have a problem."

"You haven't said a word to me all day."

"We've been busy."

"Was it not good for you?" I ask, immediately wishing I hadn't said anything.

"Kenna–"

"You're the only person I've ever kissed," I say, unable to stop the words from tumbling out. I've been thinking about it all day. Every minute, every hour, wondering what the hell I did wrong. Wondering why he ran off. I went to an all-girls school. I know what my friends were up to… the things I was too tight-laced to participate in. I think I understand men, and most men wouldn't just turn down an opportunity like the one presented to me and Evander last night, which means…

"Stop," he growls.

"Stop what?"

"Whatever you're thinking…. That's not why I left after kissing you."

I pick at the brown paper wrapping around my sandwich.

"Have you ever kissed anyone before?" I ask.

He grits his teeth.

I shrug. "I just want to know."

"Yes, I have."

"Have you ever... you know?"

"Kenna, please–"

"I just want to know, okay? I haven't... I'm a princess. I never really dated, so I don't know what this means or how to feel...." I almost say he's my first in almost everything. First friend. First crush. First kiss...

"No, I haven't."

I choke. "Really?"

"I've never slept with anyone, if that's what you're asking."

"Why not?"

"That's a very personal question, and I'm–" He cuts himself off, probably noticing how intently I'm staring at him right now. He sighs heavily. "Ghosts take a vow of chastity. At least, some do. The higher ranked agents do. It's to keep our heads focused on our work and not out chasing women."

"But some do?"

He tilts his head in consideration. A very brief smirk touches his lips, like he's remembering something. "Yeah, some do. I'm not giving you details about what my friends got up to."

"I'm not asking about your friends."

He meets my eyes. "Have you ever...?"

I scowl, scoffing, "Of course not. I'm waiting for my mate."

The look on his face when I say it breaks something inside of me that I hadn't realized could be broken.

"I know. I know," I huff out, waving a hand at him. "I can't feel the mate bond, and it's a stupid thing to hold out for–"

"I don't think it's stupid. It's noble of you."

"It's not," I admit. "I'm not enough of a wolf to find my mate, so I'll be alone forever."

"You'll find someone who likes you enough, I'm sure," he says as he puts another bundle of dry sticks on the fire.

I grind my teeth, stopping myself from saying anything stupid that I'll regret, like, "What about us?"

It would make sense if we got together. Sure, he's no Alpha's son, but he's the son of my father's Beta. Granger is the second highest ranking man in our kingdom, and when it comes to princesses getting married, that's exactly the kind of guy the public would assume I'd marry.

Plus, he's supposed to rule with me in Veiled Valley. We're already going to the same place, at the same time, to do the same job...

I open my mouth with every intention of asking if he'll just marry me, for Goddess' sake. It would have nothing to do with love and everything to do with convenience, but Evander has a mate out there still—somewhere.

But Evander raises his head and furrows his brow, and I go silent.

When he turns to look out over the forest beneath us, I feel a prickle of fear lick up my spine, and my powers roil.

"Stay here," he says, and I obey.

Because I'm a coward.

I watch him slink away, his body masked by near total darkness as another storm rolls in and shields the stars from view.

I search through the satchel and pull out a few of the small cakes I was given and unwrap a chocolate one, picking bites from it with my fingers.

It starts to rain. Minutes pass, and the rain picks up to a thundering downpour that sprays mist into the cave and causes the fire to sputter.

I throw a few more sticks on the fire, but it doesn't do much to keep the flames lit.

I pop the last bite of chocolate cake into my mouth and scoot closer to the fire, letting my powers prickle to life and surge to my fingertips, which begin to glow with a shockingly bright silver haze.

A massive fire erupts in the fire ring Evander built, and I grin as my powers stoke the fire back to life.

But ten minutes go by, then twenty, and now I'm getting a little worried.

I rise and dust off my pants. I edge toward the cave mouth, squinting into the darkness.

Suddenly, a man blocks the entrance of the cave, and I jump back, raising my hands in shock and maybe even surrender as the figure steps into the firelight.

I drop my hands and fight for breath.

Evander steps into the cave behind Flynn, followed by another man I don't recognize.

Evander looks me over for any signs of harm before his eyes sweep over the fire I built with my powers. The fleeting look of pride in his eyes is enough to warm me through and through, but I turn away from his gaze before he can see me blush.

I keep telling myself there isn't anything between us, but I feel...

I feel strange. I feel off balance and hazy in his presence. It's the kiss, I'm sure.

But now I'm in a cave full of handsome men, and all three of them are staring at me.

Flynn looks smug as he sits beside me in his leathers–the same onyx black scales Evander wears. "Good to see you safe and sound, Princess Kenna."

"You too. I haven't seen you since you jumped out of a moving car."

"I landed on my feet." He grins and winks at me.

Goddess be damned, I am blushing like an idiot.

Evander clears his throat and glares at Flynn, who doesn't seem to care about what Evander thinks, let alone has to say, about his proximity to me.

"Kenna, this is Agent Connor," Evander says as he motions to Connor, who is also an extremely good looking man with short dark hair and striking blue eyes. Connor gives me a quick nod in greeting and sits down beside Evander.

So, what now?

That question is answered quickly, and I find out that Connor and Flynn have been traveling in the forest for two days looking for us. My jump to Eastonia happened right after my dad put up wards along the border, and his powers notified him that someone successfully breached the wards and gave him a vague location of where it happened.

"There's a village roughly four hours from here on foot. Flynn and I stayed there last night and asked around," Connor says to Evander as they pour over a map.

"One of the Alphas of this territory sent scouts out to spread the word that the two of you were traveling and to leave you be. We caught up to a few scouts and headed your way a few hours ago," Flynn adds.

Evander nods absently as he keeps his eyes on the map.

I hand Flynn one of the cakes in my satchel, and he gives me a grateful smile before eating the entire thing in a single bite.

Connor, however, seems sterner than Flynn, and all business. He points to a spot on the map and tells Evander, "Commander Artyom is stationed here, and Alpha King Ryatt is supposed to meet him there in two days' time. That gives us enough time to get out of these mountains and into the Roguelands if we keep moving."

"She won't shift," Evander says, and I frown. "She'll ride on my back. We can cut the journey in half that way, bump up our mileage." He rolls up the map and hands it back to Connor. "Any word on the Rebel situation?"

"They're out here, for sure. We didn't run into any, but every group we came across was dripping in weapons and had tales about the coven. It sounds like they're spreading out, breaking into factions of five or six people. The Alpha Kings of Tarsian and Crescent Falls say the rebel activity in their kingdoms has been silent since the princesses were dispatched."

I listen intently, watching Evander's face. He's so good at being stony and expressionless, but I know him better than most. Over the past couple of days, I've seen how expressive his eyes can be. It's the only thing that gives his true feelings away, but the average person couldn't tell just by looking at him.

But I can. I can see the hint of fear and concern in his eyes as he stands and stokes the fire, which they've let burn down to embers.

When he looks at me, he holds my gaze, and for a moment, I think he can see right into my mind. Is he picking through the questions there? Is he seeing that I'm thinking about that kiss, unable to banish it from my head?

Can he see how ridiculous I feel right now?

I'm twenty-one. I'm desperate for even a taste of domestic happiness. I'm terrified of being the ruler I was born to be because I know, deep in my bones, I don't have it in me.

I am just a witch. Just a lovesick witch, and I'm surrounded by wolves.

I know what he's going to say before the words leave his lips, so I use my satchel as a pillow and lie down beside the fire, pulling my legs against my chest.

I close my eyes but don't sleep. I listen to the three men—three friends, from the sound of it—talk well into the night.

Against the rhythmic patter of rain, I hear Connor ask, "So, this is her?"

Flynn replies, "He won't admit it. Don't waste your breath, Connor."

I wonder what they're talking about as I drift into a fitful sleep and wake to Evander gently gripping my shoulder.

"We have a long day ahead of us, Kenna. It's time to get up."

2 3

LET HIM HAVE HER

Evander

FLYNN AND CONNOR found us right in time. I feel like I'm hanging on to the only shred of self-control I have left, and the guilt of keeping the truth of what's building between me and Kenna is eating me alive.

Flynn, thankfully, has taken over entertaining Kenna. For the past day, we've been traveling as wolves with Kenna riding on my back, but we're closing in on the border between the Highlands and the Roguelands now, and we paused to take a break, and Kenna demanded to walk.

So, we're walking, and I'm watching Kenna and Flynn tease each other, and I've been purposefully slowing my pace to give them more space.

They get along, and while his obvious flirting grates at every single one of my nerves, she's smiling. She's also giggling and blushing as Connor, and I walk a few yards behind them down a rough trail leading out of the heavily wooded mountains.

"This doesn't bother you at all?" Connor asks quietly as we walk side by side down the trail.

I watch as Flynn tells her some wildly exaggerated tale that has her in stitches. "I haven't seen her laugh like this in a long time. She needs this"

"But… this is *the* Kenna from when we were young trainees?"

"I don't know why either of you think it's your business."

Connor snorts a laugh and claps me on the shoulder. "Do you ever do anything for yourself, man? Look at him right now. He's got her eating out of his palm, and you're just going to let it happen?"

"He wouldn't touch her. He's just entertaining her while we get her to safety."

"If it were any other girl, he'd make a move, you know that for a fact."

I don't say what I'm actually thinking–what words are screaming through my head as I internally battle the mate bond and the reality of our situation.

Instead of saying what I feel–that the idea of anyone else being with Kenna makes me want to tear the world apart–I say, "Flynn's not a bad choice for her, actually. He's the son of an Alpha. He'll inherit a large pack and an even larger territory with close ties to her father."

"You'd let her sneak into his bedroll tonight then, when they think we're asleep?"

I glare at Connor, but he shrugs, giving me a sharp look. Flynn would, in fact, take Kenna to bed with him if it were what she wanted. He's the only high-ranking Ghost who gets away with chasing women because his gifts of breaking into other wolves' mind-links make him a valuable asset to our group and the commanders need him.

"She's your mate, isn't she?"

I halt mid-step, and Connor sighs as he tucks his hands behind his back and turns to face me. Ahead of us, Flynn and Kenna walk out of sight, too engrossed in their conversation to notice we've stopped.

"It doesn't matter if I am or not.. She's a witch. She can't feel the mate bond."

"So because she doesn't feel the bond the same as you, you've decided to deny yourself of a Goddess given blessing–"

"I didn't take you as a religious man–"

"I didn't take you as a coward." Connors voice is sharp and cold, and it catches me off guard.

I step toward him, shoulders squared. "I'm not a coward. I'm a realist. That woman will one day be the Queen of Eastonia, and I am not worthy of sharing her throne. She needs someone like Flynn. If not him, then someone from a similar royal bloodline. I am no Alpha's son."

"You're fucking joking, right? What year do you think it is, Evander? Do we still live in caves? Do we dance naked around bonfires and selectively breed for specific traits and to carry on bloodlines?"

Fury blazes as I stare him down, but he stands firm, continuing, "There's another reason, isn't there? Is it her father? Is he what's stopping you–"

"No one is stopping me from doing anything. I am doing her a favor!"

He blinks at me, then smirks, rolling his eyes toward the empty trail. "Then kiss her goodbye, Ev. I'm sure you'll get your wish and Flynn will take her off your hands the second we meet up with Commander Artyom and her father when we reach the Roguelands."

Connor walks a few paces away.

"Or you can tell me what the real issue is," he offers with a shrug. "I'm not the ladies' man Flynn is, but I've been around the block a few times."

I flex my jaw, feeling uneasy. I'm so good at burying things deep. I'm trained in the art of not letting my feelings and emotions show, but the last several days has rendered that training useless.

I normally keep to myself. I've been fine only letting people see me at surface level.

But I'm teetering on the edge right now, and maybe my mom was right when she encouraged me to start opening up to people.

"I tried to reject her when I first felt the bond when we were younger. I made a vow to her father years prior that I would protect her, and in that moment, I felt nothing but a haze that threatened to suck me under and render me useless. When she's near, she's all I can think about. Her face is all I see when I close my eyes, and her scent is just–" I cut myself off, shaking my head as I meet his eyes. "I now understand why we have to take a vow of chastity."

"Because women are overwhelming."

I smirk, and nod, but this is deeper than that.

"She is the only heir to the throne of all of Eastonia. She has been at risk since she was born. She is the most precious thing in our lands, and I won't break my vow to protect her, especially now that the kingdom is on the brink of war."

"Why would telling her this and acting on the bond break that vow?"

I wish I could just let him into my mind so he could see the tangled web of thoughts I've woven for myself to make sense of my decision to keep this a secret from Kenna.

"Lying to her is better than putting her at risk. I've made my fair share of enemies. Any women by my side would be in danger by association, but the rebel threat is a different animal entirely. I need to have my head on straight in the coming weeks, and acting on the mate bond will prevent me from focusing. I can't risk it. I won't."

"So you'll let her believe you're not mates? What if she finds someone else and falls in love while you're off fighting in whatever war comes our way?"

"I'd prefer she found someone else."

"What are you guys doing?" Kenna's voice flutters through the air, and we turn to find her standing at the crest of the hill she and Flynn walked down several minutes ago. Flynn comes into view beside her, their bodies cast in the shadow from the sun shining in the cloudless sky behind them.

But I can practically feel her smile. She's beaming, exuding so much happiness I can taste it.

"I'd prefer she be with someone who can make her smile and laugh like that," I whisper to Conner, tilting my head toward Flynn. "Someone who can give himself over to her fully and love her like she deserves. I can't be that and keep her safe at the same time. I can't be like that at all. I'd drag her down. She'd lose her spark, and that hurts me more than living with an unrequited mate bond."

The truth settles like ashes around us. If Connor understands, he doesn't say anything, but the look on his face tells me he might.

"We're going to have to camp out again if you don't hurry the fuck up," Flynn calls out.

Conner squeezes my arm and walks away, whistling to himself.

But Kenna waits at the hill when the two men walk out of sight.

She's waiting for me.

WE MAKE camp near a stream in a thicket of spruce trees. The forest all around us is quiet and sparse, but the spruce trees give us a more secluded place to lay down bedrolls than sleeping out near the open trail.

The mountains are behind us at this point, and for the past several miles, we've been met by rolling, hilly plains and the occasional forest, like this one.

We've avoided villages and most roads, and come morning, we'll cross into the Roguelands.

"Alpha King Ryatt is meeting us in the village of Opal Hill," Flynn says as he sits down beside Connor, the three of us sharing space around a small fire.

I look around. "Where's Kenna?"

"She's foraging or something," he says with a wave of the hand, but I rise.

"You left her alone?"

"Is she a child, Ev?" Flynn jokes, but Connor's eyes slide to mine.

I crack my knuckles, looking over my shoulder into the ever darkening landscape all around us. "I can go check on her," Connor offers, attempting to rise, but I shake my head.

"No, I'll go. I'm taking first watch anyway."

I leave the fire before they can say anything and follow her scent through the woods. I find her not far from camp but far enough away to make me feel more than annoyed that Flynn left her out here alone and unprotected.

I step on a twig to get her attention, and she looks over her shoulder, her mouth twitching into a smile.

"I feel like I haven't talked to you all day," she says, rising out of a crouching position. She wipes her fingertips on her cloak, leaving little streaks behind. I look at the bush she was inspecting and notice it's covered in berries.

"Are those edible?"

"Only if you want to die within a minute of ingesting them, yes," she smiles, her eyes locked on mine. But then her smile fades and she looks... she looks... "WATCH OUT!"

Something slams into the back of my head, and I have two seconds to respond before I'm taken to the ground by something huge and heavy.

Kenna screams, but I roll before the enemy stabs a blade into the ground where my head had just been.

I'm on my feet in an instant and barreling toward Kenna, who is slipping away into her shadow, but not fast enough.

Four men dressed in night-black appear out of thin air. One grabs her, and picks her up.

"Kenna!" I shout, but another man grabs me around the waist and slams me back to the ground, pinning me with an arm around my neck.

Two wolves in black armor sprint into view, and chaos erupts as Flynn and Connor battle the assailants, but my eyes are on Kenna.

She's being carried away. She's wriggling and screaming my name, but I—something burns in my side. The pain twists, and I feel myself screaming her name, but my ears are ringing so loud I can't even hear myself.

Kenna screams again, reaching for me as another piercing pain erupts in my back.

Maybe I'm blacking out because I can't possibly be seeing her starting to fight back. She tries to wretch herself out of the man's arms, and he's lost his grip on her hands.

She twists and shoves her palm on his face, over his mouth, and holds her hand there despite his attempts to shake her off.

I blink to try to clear the black spots in my vision, but the darkness in the forest swells despite the moonlight now peeking through the clouds.

The man goes still and drops Kenna before falling backward, lifeless, his face stained with the juice from the berries she was just harvesting.

Kenna just killed someone.

My heart shatters for her just as my vision goes black.

24

POWERS UNSHEATHED

Kenna

I JUST KILLED SOMEONE.

I watch the unfamiliar man twitch on the ground as foam bubbles from his mouth. His eyes glaze over–eyes I wonder if he inherited from his mom… or dad. I wonder if someone who loves him is waiting on him to come home. If he has a mate and children. Brothers, sisters….

I tear my gaze from the dead man and look out over the dark forest at the shadows creeping toward me.

There's more of them. More men. More Rebels.

We're being attacked.

My body acts on instinct as my mind tries to catch up to what just happened, and I whirl to where I saw Evander get stabbed repeatedly while he just–he just stood there and took it.

He stood there, screaming my name as I got carried away and didn't even blink when he was being brutalized because I…

"You're distracting in every way…."

His words from the night we kissed in Tiscoln rush through my head as I take a single step in his direction but pause.

He's not moving. His chest isn't moving.

Oh, my Goddess.

No.

No. No, no, no!

"EVANDER!" I scream, but Flynn and Connor are in their wolf forms coated in armor and sprinting in my direction as I hurtle toward Evander.

Behind me, I can sense the rebels approaching. They're gaining speed. I can taste magic thick in the air.

Something inside of me shifts. Something that wasn't there before. Something heavy and ingrained in every nerve and cell that makes me who I am.

Something, I realize with a start, binds me to the man the rebels just...just *killed*.

I know my eyes are burning with silver fire while I slowly, ever so slowly, turn on my heel to face the rebels. I feel both sides of me–my Firestone heart, and my Shadowsynger blood–converge, creating something unholy and unexplainable.

These are the powers I keep on a tight leash, powers that are so great they're hard for even me to comprehend.

But these people hurt someone I love.

And I'm done being good, and being kind, and pretending to be weak so others don't fear me.

I explode in a shimmer of silver flames that engulf every inch of my body. My Shadowsynger powers stream out of my hands like ribbons of pure, unfiltered darkness.

A startled yelp sounds nearby, and Flynn briefly runs into my line of sight but gets the hell out of my way the second I take my first step forward.

There's no going back. I'm empty, nothing but a writhing shell of strangling powers waiting to be unleashed. My heart is in shambles on the ground next to Evander, and I don't want it back until this is done.

I scream, and it's a siren's song. Shrill and pitched as it echoes through the forest and thunders against the distant mountains.

The trees tremble and bow away from me as I stalk forward, raising my hands and sending my ribbons of shadows barreling toward the forty or so men and wolves now darting through the trees toward me....

And *away* from me.

Screams cut through the burning, crackling noise coming from my powers as I cut through the first line of rebels. Their comrades start to retreat, but I have nothing left inside of me that even remotely wants to show them mercy.

My shadows cut the enemy wolves to ribbons, and my silver fire turns them to ash. A new fire erupts with every step I take, turning the forest around us molten with a cold, biting kind of heat.

Darkness swallows the forest whole as the moon shies away from the carnage, hiding behind a cloud.

None of them are going to survive. I don't know why they bother running.

I walk at a steady, unhurried pace behind them, my powers stretching a quarter mile or more as the last of the rebels fall.

I take a single breath, and my powers disappear, recoiling back into my body like what I've just done is nothing more than a party trick I can turn on and off. The moment my powers dim, I feel the crushing pain of witnessing Evander being hurt over and over again.

But my feet won't move. I'm staring out into the forest, past the piles of ash, past the charred trees and upturned earth.

I can't turn around because, once I do, I'll have to accept that Evander isn't here anymore.

Whatever is broken between us doesn't matter. What the confusing feelings I have for him mean doesn't matter at all.

I just can't lose him. I can't.

Someone calls my name. I close my eyes and turn.

When I open them, Flynn and Connor are leaning over Evander, both dressed in their Ghost armor.

But Evander wasn't wearing his armor tonight. He'd been in plain clothes when he approached me in the forest while I was foraging.

Blood seeps through his shirt. The smell of death lingering around him finally brings me back to my senses, to reality.

I run to him, falling to my knees beside him.

"He's alive, Princess Kenna," Flynn says as he tears away Evander's shirt.

Evander sucks in a sharp, pained breath and just barely opens his eyes. His clouded gaze locks on mine as the first tears start to fall from my lashes. "Don't," he says firmly.

"Evander?" I lean over him. I can heal him. He's very hurt, yes, but I can prevent what surely will be his death if we wait any longer to do something.

"Don't touch me with those tears," he rasps, his voice catching as he tries to lift a hand to push me away but can't do more than make his fingers twitch. "Don't–don't do it. I didn't know–I didn't sense them before it was too late–I'm sorry–"

"Stop," I tell him briskly. "Of course, I'm going to help you–"

"Don't fucking touch me!" he cries out, teeth bared.

It's like a knife to my heart. My lips part, but no words tickle the tip of my tongue. I just stare at him, at the haze in his eyes, and feel….

"You're going to die if you don't let me help you," I whisper, and it takes all of my energy to get the words out.

But Evander starts thrashing, crying out in pain as Flynn and Connor try to hold him down. He's bleeding so much, and every drop of blood I see burns into my soul.

"Don't let her–don't let her do it," he commands his friends, but they're shaking their heads, their faces washed with concern and grief. He starts to tremble, and his words run together, and then his eyes are rolling back in his head. He bucks off the ground, and even mortally wounded and seizing, he's strong. So, so much stronger than Flynn and Connor, who are struggling to keep him on the ground.

Flynn bares his teeth, frustrated, and Connor looks stricken as he fights to keep Evander under control.

"Don't let her–just let me die–" Evander chokes out, his voice lined with desperation. "It's better–for–her–"

"What is he even saying?" I cry out through my tears. He won't hold still long enough for me to get a single tear into his mouth, and my powers are strangled and tired from… from killing so many people.

My heart wrenches as the reality of the last ten minutes hits me directly in the chest.

"Kenna, listen to me," Flynn shouts, straining as he leans his weight on Evander to keep him down. "You have to save his life. You have to ignore everything he's saying right now, and everything he's going to say after–"

"Flynn, don't," Connor growls.

Flynn glares at Connor, shaking his head. "This has gone on long enough. Evander doesn't deserve this! *She* doesn't deserve this!"

"It's not our place!"

I look from man to man. "What are you saying?"

Flynn holds my gaze, his eyes sharp with mingled frustration and subdued rage. "You are his *mate*."

I open my mouth, but I can't find the words I need to convey…. Not even my surprise. It feels like something just clicked into place. Like maybe I've known all along, like my heart has always known that he's mine, and I am his but…

I look down at him and feel like I'm being shredded.

I crawl to him. Evander is on the verge of going under. His breath rattles with each exhale, and his eyes are open but unseeing.

He lied to me. He told me wouldn't lie, and he did. He's been lying for years. He… he kissed me, twice, knowing what I was to him but never told me that I am his *mate*.

He would have rather died than me learning the truth.

My shock and grief simmers until I feel nothing but the cool, smoke scented breeze against my skin.

I let three tears fall into the palm of my hand and tilt them toward his lips. It's enough to keep him alive, but not to fully heal the wounds

I'm sure were caused by poisoned blades. This close to him, I can smell the wolfsbane.

Good. He deserves to suffer a little. Maybe it will be a taste of the suffering I've gone through for months looking for my mate and only getting glimpses of that bond every time I was... every time I was around *him*.

The tears fall onto his tongue and dissolve in a flash of pale gold, and he stills.

I rear back and stand, then walk backward, my heart hammering in my chest. My blood racing is the only sound I can hear as my mind reels over the memories of us, of the balls in Crescent Falls where I felt the bond in my own weird, faint way, and he still….

He knew, and he didn't tell me. He knew I was there to find my mate and it was him the whole time.

He told me he hated me and stayed away for years, making me believe our friendship ending was my fault.

A sob works its way up my throat and strangles me.

Evander groans, shoving Flynn and Connor away as he tries to sit up.

He blinks, reaching up to run his hand over his face, and then his eyes meet mine.

There's real pain there. The kind of pain that cuts so deep there's no magic in the world that can touch it. A pain that festers.

And he deserves it.

"Kenna–"

"How could you?"

He licks his lips, his eyes searching mine. "Please–"

An echo of trembling power coasts through the forest as three shadows appear before us.

My dad looks murderous as he steps into view, his black outfit and cloak shedding the remnants of the power he used to jump all this way. It falls like diamond dust from his cloak as he stalks toward me.

Granger and Commander Artyom look around the clearing, shocked, before Granger rushes toward Evander.

Evander and I are still looking at each other though. I can't look away. I just can't believe–I can't believe he's my mate.

I can barely feel it, but it's there. That little spark, that faint little nudge against my heart.

Maybe that's why he didn't want this with me because I'd never be able to feel it like he can.

Evander mouths my name before his view is obstructed by his father and the commander, and then my dad is in front of me, his hands on my arms, leaning down so we're face to face.

"Are you all right?"

He glances over the top of my head at the chaos I rained down on the rebels and the forest.

"No," I whisper, and launch myself into his arms, hiding my face in his cloak as I let myself come completely undone.

I can hear Granger and Commander Artyom asking what happened, how my dad felt the surge of my powers all the way in Opal Hill, where they'd arrived less than five minutes before I used my powers on the rebels. .

My dad is listening to Flynn and Connor explain the course of events but keeps his arms protectively around me, holding me tight.

"Kenna," he breathes, "how did you–are you sure you're okay?"

"Please just take me home. Please!"

"Evander's hurt. We need to heal him before we jump–"

"He's not coming," I grind out loud enough that all of the men nearby can hear. *"Take me home."*

2 5

GIVING UP THE GHOST

Kenna

"YOU'RE NOT JUMPING LIKE THIS," Dad says sharply as he slams the door shut in the room he just booked for me in an inn in Opal Hill.

I tuck my trembling hands behind my back and squeeze my fingers to stop them from shaking. He spirited us here, thank the Goddess. If I had to spend another second in Evander's company, I would have lost control of my already exhausted powers, but I'm still on the verge of dropping into my shadow, and Dad knows something is wrong.

His silver eyes–the same shape and shade as mine–hold my gaze with an intensity that makes me want to look away and submit, but I stand my ground.

"I want to go home."

"Too bad, Kenna. I'm not leaving Granger and Evander here alone to be tended by whatever healer they have in this village. You need to heal him."

"I already gave him my tears. I don't know what else you want me to do."

"What is the matter with you?" he asks, sounding more than shocked that I'm essentially thumbing my nose at not only him, but his Beta and Evander. "He was stabbed, Kenna. With a knife coated in wolfsbane."

I shrug, but inside I'm falling to pieces. "He'll be fine in a few days and can walk all the way to Moonrise if that's where he decides to go."

Dad narrows his eyes at me. "What the hell is going on right now?"

"Nothing. Flynn and Connor already told you everything. We got attacked by rebels."

He takes a step toward me. "And you used your powers to kill upward of fifty people, maybe more. Are you okay?"

I glare at him. I might be able to force myself to cry, but I've never mastered keeping my real tears at bay. Still, my entire focus is spent on willing myself to look firm, and hard, and not give away the fact that my violent act is ripping me apart. "I'm fine."

He's silent for a moment, searching my face. "I can bring your mom here–"

"Don't. I'll see her soon enough." I tilt my chin toward the ceiling in a show of bravery, but I'm actually trying desperately to stop the tears springing along my lashes from falling down my cheeks. "But I'm not healing Evander. Find another healer. I'm tired."

"Fine."

"Fine."

Dad glowers at me. Any other person would cower away from him if they were able to see the look on his face right now. I just want him to leave so I can crawl onto the itchy, straw stuffed mattress and cry until I pass out.

He turns for the door but pauses, his shoulders slumping. "You saved not only your own life today, but the lives of three of our kingdom's best warriors and countless villagers in the pack nearby. I'm proud of you, Kenna."

My heart is in my throat when he leaves, shutting the door firmly behind him.

I sink onto the bed and lie back, letting my shadow consume me. I'm sure hours tick by, because when we arrived in Opal Hill the moon was still high in the sky, and when my powers finally simmer and ease, it's nearly noon.

I haven't slept. Not a wink. Everything feels wrong right now, and I have no idea how to move forward.

I have a mate. It's what I always wanted. But... this isn't the magical feeling I thought it would be. It's confirmation that I can't feel the bond like most wolves can.

I also have a mate who doesn't want me.

I think about the moment Evander froze and got attacked. It makes my stomach turn, and I, eventually, can't take it anymore and rise from bed, dressing in the clothes Dad packed and brought with him.

A soft, violet dress brushes my ankles. The sleeves are sheer and bunched at the shoulders. I tie my hair–tangled and in desperate need of a good brushing and maybe some really strong conditioner–away from my face and slip into a pair of sandals before walking into the inn proper, which is nothing more than a cozy sitting room with a few bookshelves.

Opal Hill is tiny–no more than forty or so pack members–and it doesn't even have a town square.

I'm sure everyone else in our party is asleep as I walk around the village. I cross a stone bridge covered in wisteria that matches the shade of my dress and find myself in a wooded trail system.

Gardens appear all around me–flowers, vegetables, herbs and spices. It reminds me of the parks and gardens in Moonrise, but on a smaller scale, and I suddenly ache to be home.

Going to Crescent Falls was pointless, wasn't it? I could have stayed in Moonrise this summer. The rebels wouldn't have tried to hunt me down in that case. I wouldn't have killed anyone last night. I wouldn't have spirited Evander and I hundreds of miles from home.

But that night in the alcove, and at the inn, wouldn't have happened. Our conversation in the cave before Flynn and Connor arrived would never have taken place.

I'm so, so angry with Evander, but the fact that I used to like him more than friends... that I loved him, and still do, remains.

I sink onto a bench and tilt my face to the sun.

Well, this has certainly complicated things, hasn't it?

I chuckle despite myself, but when I open my eyes, I find I'm not alone.

Flynn sits down beside me dressed in plain clothes instead of his leathers. He looks rough, like he hasn't slept at all either.

He ruffles his wet hair and looks down at me, searching my eyes. "Long night?" he asks.

"How'd you guess?"

He snorts a laugh and leans against the bench, sighing heavily. "I couldn't sleep. I jumped off that bridge over there to wash up and got chased and cursed at by a woman with a broom. Her daughter seemed to enjoy the show, though," he teases, winking at me.

"You're truly a menace. I have no idea why anyone would let you be a Ghost, of all things."

"I just don't take myself too seriously, unlike your mate and Connor."

"Don't–don't call him my mate, please."

"Why not? That's what he is."

"How long have you known about it?"

"Longer than you, obviously." He gives me a teasing look.

I know he's trying to cheer me up, but I'm still livid.

"Look, I have no experience with mates. But, I'm a wolf, through and through. The mate bond drives people insane, Princess Kenna. And Evander has felt it since he was sixteen. Consider yourself lucky you can't feel it."

"What?"

He nods, but my mind is reeling back to the shocked look on his face and the way he said, "No," the day he showed up after my party. The day all of this went wrong.

He's really felt it for that long?

"I–I can feel it, a little. It's just–I don't really know how to explain it, and I'm certainly not talking to you about it," I huff, shifting away from him.

But Flynn doesn't let up. "I can find you a village woman to talk to."

"I have friends, Flynn."

"...Where?"

I glare at him. "Back home in Moonrise. I'm honestly very popular."

"Well, soon you'll be back in Moonrise complaining to your girl-friends instead of doing something about this situation, like talking some sense into Evander."

"I have no desire to talk to him. He had no desire to act on our bond. I don't understand why he didn't just reject me."

"Well, are you going to reject him?"

"No, I..." I hadn't even thought of it. The thought never once crossed my mind. *I guess* I should talk to him first.

Yes. That's the appropriate thing to do.

I rise, but Flynn stretches out, his face turned to the sun as he says, "If you do reject him, you know where to find me. I wouldn't mind lounging on a throne all day."

"You wish," I grumble and walk back toward the bridge.

I'm sure Evander is at the inn somewhere, so I go back and walk down the hallways looking for any sign of my dad, or Granger, or even Commander Artyom.

But I come across a room toward the back of the inn and hear my dad's voice, and then Evander's voice… lifted in an argument.

I slowly open the door, but neither of them look at me.

Evander looks like hell, but he's standing, his bare chest covered in bandages. His eyes slide to mine, and he sucks in a breath before turning back to my dad.

"When?" he asks in a voice that trembles slightly. "When do I have to give my answer?"

"When we arrive in Moonrise, I assume."

I stand in the doorway, turning to scan the room. Granger is standing near the window with his arms crossed, his eyes on the floor and lost in thought.

"Give your answer to what?" I ask, stepping into the room.

Evander is looking at me again. His eyes are honed on mine and such a deep shade of emerald. It's breathtaking, honestly. I've always thought he was just beautiful, and now that I know we were destined for each other?

I don't want to reject him.

I don't want him to reject me.

We just need to talk about this, but the look on his face as he brushes past my dad and stalks toward me makes me wonder if he has room to even consider that this bond is a good thing.

He pauses beside me, casting me in his shadow. He looks down, his lips parting like he's going to say something, but his jaw flexes.

His hand brushes mine as he walks past me.

The touch sends prickles of electricity rippling over my skin. I try to swallow and find it impossible.

I turn to chase after him, but I hear the doors leading out of the inn slam shut.

"We need to prepare to leave within the hour whether or not he's coming with us," Dad says to Granger.

"He'll come."

"Are you sure about that? Especially now?" Dad eyes his Beta, the two of them sharing some internal conversation I'm not privy to.

"What happened?" I ask as unease settles over the room.

Dad turns and seems surprised to see me still standing there. He runs his fingers through his dark hair. The old tattoos lining his fingers and forearms catch the sunlight filtering through the moth-eaten curtains.

"The mystics have made a decision about the Rite. They've seen who has been chosen to perform the ritual." It's Granger who speaks, and he looks more than forlorn about it.

"Who–" I begin to ask, but then a twisting sensation turns my stomach into a knot. "Evander?"

I look at my dad for confirmation, and he nods.

"Who else?" I ask.

Why am I so hurt when the woman named is not me?

I slowly back out of the room and turn, debating what step to take next.

I'm still trying to understand why Evander hid our bond from me. I'm trying to wrap my head around why he would kiss me and is so devoted to protecting me, but when it comes to us actually being mates he just… can't.

Now, I'm not sure it matters. Not if he's been chosen for the ritual. We might have this all wrong.

But one thing is clear.

The idea of him being with anyone else is absolutely gutting to me.

And that has nothing to do with the bond we share, and everything to do with how I feel about him, and how I've been searching for someone to fill the void he left for years.

He can't… he can't do the ritual. He can't. I can't bear it.

"Are you ready to go?" Dad asks, coming up beside me before I can make a break for the door to chase Evander down.

Granger brushes past us.

"He's going to go make sure Evander is ready to travel. He didn't take the news of the Rite well."

"Dad, I–we're–" I almost say it. I almost tell my dad, the Alpha King of Eastonia, that Evander and I are mates.

But I hesitate.

"What is it?" he asks, looking down at me with concern.

What am I supposed to say?

"Nothing. I just need–I need to talk to Mom."

An hour later, I'm standing outside with Dad while Evander talks with Commander Artyom. My heart lurches as I watch Evander hand the commander his black gloves, and I realize he's… he's done being a Ghost.

He can't go back to that life. Everything is changing now.

His eyes meet mine, and they're lifeless. Empty.

He says a few words to Flynn and Connor, who looks concerned as he gruffly nods and walks toward us.

I watch every step he takes in my direction and drop my eyes as he comes to stand beside me and takes my hand.

His grip is tight. I feel his touch everywhere. I feel *awful*.

This is why he never told me. This–ruling with me, being shackled to a throne–wasn't ever what he wanted.

My dad's powers wrap around us as I look up at him. My lips part to ask if he's okay, but he says, "We need to talk when we get back to Moonrise."

And then the world goes black.

SAYING THOSE WORDS

Evander

I HAVE the urge to yank Kenna into a sitting room, or a closet, or a fucking darkened hallway the second my feet hit the ground in Moonrise.

I can't, though. Not when our mothers are barreling toward us, and their faces are drawn with so much worry that it could easily break my heart, if I still had a heart to break.

I let go of Kenna's hand and feel the absence of her touch like another blade in my side.

But my mom throws herself against me and sobs.

I slowly wrap my arms around her, resting my chin on the top of her head. The throne room takes shape all around me—the soft cream curtains, the murals on the walls and the ceiling, the windows overlooking the lake.

Queen Ella is clutching Kenna's face between her hands, and Kenna is in tears.

Seeing them together—seeing Kenna home—it's enough for me to finally feel like I can breathe again.

"You asshole!" Mom shouts, smacking me hard on the chest.

I grunt in surprise and pain, glaring down at her and grabbing her wrist before she can do it again.

"Mom—"

"I told you—I told you so many times not to—I never wanted you in the Ghosts. I never wanted you to be a warrior, and you nearly got yourself killed, again!"

"Amanda," Dad says gently, tugging her away. "Give the kid a break for a moment."

"You encouraged this," she hisses, yanking her arm out of his grasp.

"Amanda—"

She glares at both of us and turns on her heel, stalking away and cutting around a corner.

Dad meets my eyes as he exhales, "This is between me and her. She's fine, and she still loves you."

"I wasn't worried—"

Dad walks off after her, leaving me alone in the throne room with Kenna and her parents.

My gaze slides to Ryatt, and I find him looking right at me. He tilts his head in a motion to follow.

I have to follow him. He's the Alpha King.

But for a moment too long, my feet stay planted in place, and I make the mistake of glancing at Kenna.

"You've done your duty, Evander. My daughter is safe. Come."

Kenna looks at me, her eyes red and lined with tears.

I shouldn't say anything to her at all. She deserves so much more than this. Explaining myself isn't going to cut it, not now.

But, I tell her, "Our usual spot, tonight. I'll find you."

"Evander," King Ryatt growls, his eyes hard and the color of pure steel. "*Now.*" He turns on his heel and walks away, and I follow, keeping a good distance between us.

I can hear Ella and Kenna murmuring to each other, but their words are lost in the echo of my footsteps as I follow Ryatt to his office. How many times have I walked these same halls to go to this very location? I was raised here. My parents have their own wing of the enormous castle. I used to get yelled at by the maids for riding my bike down this very corridor and using the upcoming stairs as a jump.

Kenna and I used to sneak into Ryatt's office to steal candy from a jar on his desk.

Now, I'm sitting across from him while he stares me down.

"What, exactly, did Kenna do in that forest?"

"Agent Flynn and Agent Connor accurately recounted–"

"I need to hear it from *you*."

My nostrils flare as I exhale, meeting his gaze. "Everything. She used every power she has, somehow converging them into one."

"Did she shift?"

"I don't know. I saw the beginning of it; she killed the first rebel using wolfsbane berries. I–" I have to catch my breath as the memory steals the air from my lungs. I lick my lips and see Ryatt as a father instead of an Alpha King for a moment.

A father who is asking me, Kenna's oldest, and maybe even dearest friend, how she handled taking a life for the first time.

"I blacked out," I admit. "Momentarily. When I came to, she was… she was a shadow walking inside a wall of pure fire, and those shadows… they were everywhere. She cut every single rebel down. Connor and Flynn retreated back to me and tried to keep me calm because I… if I could have, I would have stopped her. I would have stopped her from going on a rampage…."

She did it because someone hurt *me*. I don't know if I can live with that.

"I failed, Your Highness."

"You didn't."

"I failed to protect her. My guard was down. I let her out of my sight, and when I found her again, it was too late. I didn't sense them in the area. I would have laid down my own life rather than allow her to stain her hands with blood, and I am sorry."

Ryatt rests his hands on the table and levels a look at me. "Evander, you've been relieved of your duties in my army. You are now a Beta. Once the Rite is over, you will follow Kenna to Veiled Valley and rule beside her. You have no obligation to me as my subject any longer."

"I made a vow to protect her and failed to do so."

"You were seven years old when you made that vow. I didn't realize how seriously you'd take it."

I stiffen. He holds my gaze.

"Your mother will kill me in my sleep one day, I'm sure of it, and Ella will probably let her. I never meant for you to take it this far–"

"Joining the Ghosts was my decision–"

"It also separated you from Kenna."

I stand, my fingertips prickling with adrenaline. "What is this conversation really about? Are you here to interrogate me about what happened in that forest, or is there something else you want to know?"

He leans back in his chair. "Is there something you'd like to tell me?"

I've already done enough damage. I cannot, and will not, tell Kenna's father that I am her mate.

That will be up to her in the event she doesn't reject me, because at this point, I'm not sure I have it in me to try to reject her again.

"Kenna is a pacifist. She always has been and likely always will be. I have spent the last two decades making sure her future reign is one of peace, and not bloodshed. As long as my wife and I are the King and Queen of Eastonia, we will work to ensure her life is easier than ours was. Kenna has never been in a position to do what she just did. She has barely trained those powers past the point of being able to control them. What she did in that forest is something even I can't do, Evander. Do you understand what I'm trying to say?"

My chest heaves as I take a breath.

Ryatt clenches his jaw, rapping his knuckles on his desk. "She has never lifted a finger toward anyone with ill intent. Why now?" He eyes me coolly, inspecting my face. "Why, I wonder, would she rain hellfire on an army with dozens of men poised to strike if she were safe in the hands of the Ghosts? Your fellow agents could have gotten her out of there."

His eyes are locked on mine.

"It's because someone hurt you, right?"

I shake my head, but he's nodding.

"I'm going to ask you again. Do you have anything to tell me?"

"No."

He taps his fingers on his desk. "Then, I see no reason for you not to perform the ritual."

He could have punched me in the gut and it would have had the same effect.

I bow and back out of the room. He watches every step I take, and his gaze bores into my back when I finally turn around.

A male servant shuts his office door, and the silence in the corridor is deafening.

But Kenna's scent is thick in the air. I turn, my gaze sweeping over the walls for any hint of her shadow.

I don't see her. It could just be the fact that I'm here, in the castle, for the first time in years that has me on edge and unable to focus. Her scent is everywhere. This is her home. But she could very well be eavesdropping.

'I didn't tell him anything,' I say to her over the mind-link... over our bond, and walk off to find my parents.

***

Kenna

I'VE AVOIDED this place for years.

Vines hang from the trees we used to climb as children. The old fountain is still cracked and in shambles, and the forest surrounding Moonrise has taken over our old stomping ground. Moss hugs the fountain and the mosaic tiles that surround it, and little blue flowers bloom across the shaded clearing, blocking out the first glimpses of moonlight stretching through the canopy of weeping willows as I step inside the sanctuary of their branches.

Evander isn't here yet. I'm not sure when he'll arrive.

I sit on one of the boulders surrounding the tree trunk and cross my ankles before running my fingers through my wet, freshly washed hair.

I spent the entire evening with my mom. I told her everything—almost everything. I couldn't bring myself to tell her the truth about Evander, though. She told me to meet up with my friends tomorrow, to talk to Avery and Sophie about my time in Crescent Falls. My two best friends and fellow witches have been curious about my time across the border.

I never told them about my feelings for Evander, though. Not once in the decade or so I've been friends with them. He was always just... the kid I grew up with. The Beta's son. The warrior I wrote letters to.

Now, so much has changed.

I look up as Evander walks through the willow branches, pushing them to the side. The lazy, wispy branches fall back into place behind him, closing us in together.

This is the first time in days we've been truly alone.

There's so much to say, and I don't know where to start.

I stand, breaking out in a cold sweat as I wring my hands together.

He's looking at me with an intensity that could bring me to my knees, but I hold steady.

I swallow, then say, "Reject me, if you have to. I doubt I'll feel it. But I can't—if you don't want this, I think I understand now." I take a step toward him, dropping my hands to my sides. "I have everything in the world. I've never wanted or needed for anything. I've never had to fight to protect what I love and cherish, so I didn't know... I didn't understand how much that meant until I... until I killed all of those people yesterday."

His jaw flexes as I move closer.

"I've never been on an adventure like that before," I whisper. "Out in the woods, sitting around campfires and exploring.... I understand why you don't want to give that up to live in a castle and do paperwork and boss people around—"

"It was never about that, Kenna."

"But it was, wasn't it? Do you remember playing here, Evander? Under this very tree? We used to pretend we were mates, and you'd leave to go off to war, and to go hunting, and I'd stay. I'd stay with my dolls, and I'd write you letters. You were never here, and I never went with you. I was happy under this tree, in Moonrise, pretending to be the queen while you… left. I understand now. We might be mates, but this isn't the life you wanted."

He shakes his head. "No, Kenna."

"Then why did you *leave?*"

I'm standing right in front of him in another step. There's hardly any distance between us. I can feel his warmth. I can almost taste the remnants of the wolfsbane in his body, the poison that's now blurring his scent.

I close my eyes as he reaches up and cups my cheek.

I feel the truth in my heart before he can voice it. I know this isn't what he wants. He wants me, in some shape or form, for sure. Our heated kisses tell me as much.

But there's something greater holding him back.

And it's holding me back from finding actual happiness and giving him the freedom he deserves.

I step away from him.

"I hereby relieve you of your duties as my Beta."

Evander blinks, then cocks his head. "Kenna?"

"I–I reject you–"

"*Stop.*"

27

IF YOU GO, WE'RE DONE

Kenna

"Don't say anything else," Evander growls.

The sanctuary of the willow tree darkens to the point I can barely see his eyes gleaming in the faint moonlight filtering through the leaves. He takes a step toward me, trying to close the distance between us again.

"We have to. You don't want this."

"You have no idea what I want."

"Then tell me," I cut in, my breath catching. "Because I can't–I can't pretend like everything is okay anymore. What do you want? If it's not me, then we need to reject each other!"

"I want you. I want you more than anything, Kenna. You are all I think about. You are on my mind every second of every day–the first thing I see in the morning and the last thing I think about before I fall asleep and *dream* about you. I can't get you out of my head."

"That's what the mate bond is, isn't it? An all-consuming, wholly encompassing–"

"The way I feel about you has nothing to do with the mate bond."

My mind goes blank. All I can see is him, and all I can hear are his words echoing in my ears.

He takes one more step forward, and he's within reach, but he balls his hands into fists. "I have loved you since we were kids. I vowed to your father that I'd protect you when I was seven years old, and my entire life has been shaped to that one vow."

"You were just a kid–"

"I meant it. I went through warrior training. I chose to go into the Ghosts because I knew it would be my best course of action, the best training I could attain, to be able to protect you. I didn't know we were mates until the day I came back to see you, for your birthday, I felt it. That… pull. That heightened sense that you were mine and that feeling like I would lose control if I couldn't have you, Kenna, so I ran. I know what happens to mated men. Every sense is thrown off. I had tunnel vision. I couldn't think—I still can't think straight in your presence. I almost got you killed in the forest. I had no idea there were rebels there, stalking you, waiting for the moment to strike because all I could see, all I could feel, was *you*."

" But you don't want *this*."

"I can't have you and continue to protect you."

"I don't need your protection!" I shout for what feels like the thousandth time. "I–I protected myself. I defended all of us when the rebels attacked!"

He grabs my arms, squeezing tight. "And now the leaders of the rebel army know what you're capable of and will hunt you down because I wasn't able to stop them. They will try again, and again, until they have you."

I shake him off and step away. "This is ridiculous, Evander. Do you hear yourself?"

"Do you think I haven't thought about the repercussions of our bond every single day–"

"Do you love me or not?" I ask, my voice breaking over the words.

He only stares at me, breathing rapidly, his fingers curling into the palms of his hands so hard his knuckles turn white. "There are more important things happening right now. Our kingdom is going to war–"

"I asked you a question," I breathe, my heart hammering. "Do you love me?"

"I do."

His words fall between us and settle there, sucking the air from the space.

"I love you, Kenna, but I can't be your mate and keep you safe. I can't lose focus."

"Then reject me," I growl, tears springing to life along my lashes.

He shakes his head. "I can live with this."

"I can't," I grind out. I have all of this power and still can't stop myself from dissolving into tears, but this is ripping my heart to shreds.

"You only feel like this for me because of the bond between us, Kenna. You can move on, find someone who is worthy of you."

"And you're not?"

"I can't make you laugh. I don't get the same kind of smiles you'd give to someone like–like Flynn."

"Flynn?" Sudden rage boils through my blood. "Why does he have anything to do with this?"

"I saw you and him during our journey out of the highlands. He– you were blushing. You were so happy, laughing at everything he said."

"Are you jealous?" I snap, losing my grip on my anger.

"No!"

"Then why bring him up at all?"

"Because he is someone who deserves you! He deserves that smile; he deserves your life and your love. He would be able to offer you warmth and conversation. He would be able to give you his full attention."

"While you hide in the shadows and make sure no one is going to jump out and attack me?" I seethe. "Do you really think that little of me? That all I want is someone to warm my bed and make me laugh while I remain oblivious to all of the dangers around me? Have you forgotten *who I am?*"

My powers surge, making my eyes glow in the shelter of the willow. A soft breeze rustles the leaves, giving me a single glimpse of the sparkling city beyond before they fall back into place, closing us off from the rest of the world.

Now it's me approaching him, looking up into his eyes. "I am a Firestone witch. I have shadows in my blood. I killed dozens of rebels in a matter of seconds. No one can touch me, Evander, without meeting death. All I have to do is wish for it." My tone is as cold as ice as I close the distance between us. "I was born to be Queen of Eastonia. I will be queen, and I don't need you to pave the path there for me!"

His jaw flexes, but he remains silent as I slowly take his hand. I run my thumb over the curve of his palm, tracing the lines I know how to decipher but refuse to acknowledge.

"Reject me, you *fucking* coward," I hiss, digging my nails into his skin.

He doesn't even flinch.

"You don't feel the bond. It doesn't matter for you if I reject you or not."

"I feel it," I cut in through gritted teeth. Tears blur my vision–hot and desperate. "I feel it. I've felt it for a while. I missed you, Evander. Every day. I thought of you constantly and wanted so badly to just be able to talk to you because *I love you.* You're the only person I've ever loved. You're the only person who has ever just… gotten me, liked me for who I am. Who understood that I'm different. I don't like being scary and cruel. I never wanted my powers to define me or my future reign. I never–"

I have a single moment to suck in a breath before his hands caress my face and his forehead is pressed to mine. I grab his wrists, holding him there, letting my tears fall freely down my cheeks and along my jaw.

I feel time slow as we stand there in the shelter of the willow tree. The world feels like it's spinning out of control beyond the sweeping branches. War is coming, that's clear enough. The Draven coven wants me, and they want to dispose of my parents. My uncle's territory could be at risk as well, and the rebels could be going after Misty in order to get to my uncle.

I hate that Evander's right…about a few things, at least.

"You've been called to perform the ritual during the eclipse," I whisper, my heart tying itself in a knot.

"I know."

"What do you think that means?"

He doesn't pull away, but his thumbs sweep over my cheeks, wiping away my tears. "I think it means this mate bond between us isn't–" He stops himself, swallowing hard. "I have to go."

My lips part as he pulls away, turning his back to me.

"Where are you going?"

"I'm sorry for what happened between us. I lost control. I should never have touched you. It was wrong of me." He takes a deep breath, running his fingers through his hair.

"That's it then? We're not doing this?"

He turns around, keeping a safe distance between us. "I can't do this with you, Kenna. I thought I made that clear."

"What you've made clear is that you're doing everything to ignore the fact that we're mates but refusing to reject me."

"You can't feel the bond like I can!"

"But I feel something!"

"I can't make you happy."

"Do you think that little of yourself?" I shout.

"I think higher of you than I do of myself, and I won't bind you to me for eternity and watch you suffer!" His tone is cutting, decided.

I bristle, my heart threatening to snap. "You're no longer in my father's army. And I've relieved you of your duties as my–my future Beta. What more do you want? What more do I have to say to make you understand that I feel as strongly as you do? I don't want you for the convenience of loving you as my mate. This is different. You just said so yourself. My feelings for you go further than the bond and I–"

He cuts me off with a wave of his hand. "We can't, Kenna. That's final."

"Then you'll do the Rite?"

His gaze bores into mine.

"Does the fact that I was called to the Rite, and you were not, despite the fact we feel the mate bond, not register with you?" he asks calmly, but his voice is still tinged with bitterness, like he'd rather be angry at me than act on the tension simmering between us.

One step, and we're going to throw ourselves at each other. I'd let him lay me down on the grass and claim me as his if it meant not losing him again.

I just don't know how to make him see that.

"We're mates. I shouldn't have been called to perform the Rite. Something is wrong, and I mean to find out what."

"And then what?" I say through tears. I don't have the space to think about what he just said. The mystics are never wrong. My mom trusts them fully. They don't make mistakes.

"Then I'll go to Crescent Falls and fight for your uncle's army when the allied kingdoms go to war with the Draven Coven."

I tilt my chin. My entire heart is crumbling.

Is this feeling of absolute agony the mate bond talking, or something else?

"Then go," I whisper. "And never return. Never speak to me again. The moment you leave this place–" I sweep my arm, motioning to the willow branches, "we're done. Everything we ever were… is over."

He doesn't move.

"Go, Evander. We've said all we needed to say, haven't we?" I run my hands down my sides, sniffling as I look down at the soft grass.

"I never intended for you to know that we were mates. I did what I could to stay away."

"So you could keep lying to me?" When he doesn't answer, I look up at him. "Go away. Please. Just go."

He looks like he wants to say more, but I'm turning away from him, facing the massive tree trunk that has our names carved into the centuries old bark.

"If things–" He cuts himself off the moment I turn back around, my heart filling with hope. His emerald eyes meet mine, and his expression is softer, like he's finally speaking from the heart and not doing everything in his power to be logical for once. "When the war is over," he continues, "if I'm still alive, I will return to you. I will try."

I shake my head. "You're not going to die."

"I will not return until I know you're safe. That's a promise. And I swear that if I do return, I will make this right between us."

I close my eyes, finding it hard to breathe.

When I open them again, Evander is gone.

28

DRUNK CONFESSIONS

Evander

I'D WALK off a cliff if there was one nearby.

I'm sure if I ran deep enough into what was once called the Deadlands—the old home of creatures like rogues—I'd find the swift death I'm looking for.

Instead, I'm drunk in an inn somewhere in the Roguelands... but not nearly drunk enough to wash the taste of every word I said to Kenna out of my mouth.

The inn is full of warriors from all three major kingdoms. The Tarsian warriors are notable by their sandy colored leathers and desert sun-tanned skin. It's interesting to watch them confer with the Rogueland warriors, of course. The alliance between the Tarsian and the Roguelands is precarious, based wholly on how Alpha King Ryatt and Alpha King Jaxon feel about each other at the moment.

Queen Ella split Eastonia in two during the first years of her reign, giving Jaxon full authority of the lands past the river that once walled the Roguelands off from the lost city of Rifthold.

I've heard Alpha Jaxon likes to hold the fact Alpha King Ryatt's wife gave him a piece of the pie over his head.

I snort into my third pint of beer and drink half of it down.

My gaze sweeps over the crowded inn and lands on a gaggle of Crescent Falls warriors. They're practically blushing with excitement. I'm sure the idea of being allowed in Eastonia–a place that for them must seem like a fantasy–overrides the reason they're here at all.

War.

I drain the rest of my beer and motion to a passing waitress who rolls her eyes at me until I toss her what remains in a coin bag I keep in my jacket pocket. She wordlessly walks away and will, hopefully, return with something stronger than beer this time.

But a man sits down at the table across from me, and my drink-blurred vision hones in on shockingly familiar eyes now boring into mine.

"What the fuck are you doing here?" I groan as I lean back in my chair.

Alpha Sydney crosses his arms over his chest and smirks at me, his blue eyes creasing as he takes me in. "I always thought it'd be fun to get drunk with you one day. I might get my wish tonight, but it seems like you're leagues ahead of me."

"I can't believe your daddy let you out of the dollhouse."

"My daddy," he smirks, his tone dropping as he looks over the top of my head at the crowded bar, "needs an emissary in Eastonia while he has troops on the ground in this kingdom, and as his heir, I was the first in line to ensure our warriors are not only taken care of but stay in line."

"Sounds like a vacation seeing as the Draven Coven hasn't made any new moves." The waitress returns with another beer, which I scowl at.

"Whiskeys," Sydney murmurs, giving her a nod.

"You're wasting your time on me tonight, Syd. I'm moving on to the next pack by morning."

"To do what?"

That's a very good question and one I can't answer. I've never not had a purpose. I'm no longer a Ghost. I should be in Moonrise right now preparing to be the Beta of Veiled Valley.

I roll my eyes to the ceiling at the thought. Kenna thinks she has the authority to decide that. She offered me an out, and I couldn't take it even if I wanted to. It's not up to us.

Not unless we tell our families the truth and then reject each other.

"I heard what happened," Sydney says, sipping from the beer I bought, which I already forgot about.

Momentarily, I think he's talking about the falling out between me and Kenna. I stretch out my legs under the table and close my eyes. "It's not worth talking about. It had to be done... for her sake."

"I'm sure she's thrilled to know you're no longer slinking around the allied kingdoms fueling the nightmares of every criminal known to the Alpha Kings."

I open one eye and find him staring at me over the rim of the pint. He cocks a brow.

"Did you think I was talking about something else?"

I clear my throat and wonder, again, if Sydney is able to read minds.

"I'm to be Beta of Veiled Valley. Commander Artyom dissolved my contract with the Ghosts a few months early. Leaving the Ghosts wasn't a surprise."

"Seeing my cousin in action must have been."

I blink then lean forward and rest my hands on the table.

"Word travels fast," Sydney says at the same moment the waitress returns with two tall glasses of whiskey. Sydney waits for her to leave before continuing, "Kenna's powers were felt all over the Roguelands. She's a force–"

"She doesn't want to be known for her powers... or what she can do with them."

Sydney levels me with a look as he picks up his whiskey, swishing it around. "It's a little late for that."

I hold his gaze, seething, "Kenna is good, kind, and a talented midwife. She's not a cruel witch with–with deadly powers."

"I never said she was," he cuts in. "But I can see why the Draven Coven wants her in their clutches so badly. Why they want to be rid of her. They don't stand a chance against my aunt and uncle with Kenna in the way."

"Kenna won't be in the way. She'll be as far from the conflict as she can be."

"Because you will see to the safety and well-being of your mate?" he asks, and my heart stills.

His smirk reaches his eyes, which crease with something I can't say is pleasure.

"What makes you think Princess Kenna is my mate?"

"I've known since we were kids, Ev." He laughs, but the look in his eyes remains cold and calculated. "It's obvious, at least to those willing to look. I can smell it on you, for fuck's sake."

"You can't smell it on me. I've—"

"Barely touched her?" Sydney leans forward with a vengeful look passing behind his pale blue eyes. "You kissed her at that ball. Ryan saw you bring her out to the veranda. That was you, wasn't it?"

"If I hadn't been there, she could have been killed." Or worse. The memory of Gabriel kneeling in shackles in the temple burns through my mind.

"Why aren't you in Moonrise with her right now?"

I take my whiskey and drain it. "I'm on a mission."

"Right," he scoffs, chuckling. "I asked Kenna about that when I saw her. She acted like the two of you hadn't just been through hell and back together. Tell me, does she know that she's your mate?"

"When were you in Moonrise?"

"Two days ago. I spent a few days there with the family."

And I've been roaming the Roguelands for a little over a week looking for any witches who might have looser ties to the Moonrise coven and any dirt on the mystics, but to no avail.

"Does she know?" he asks again, his voice dropping an octave.

"She does."

"And?"

"And? Why is it your business?"

"Because she is my cousin–practically a sister in all the ways that truly count."

"I'm not acting on the bond, so you can save your tough, Alpha dickhead act–"

"She's loved you since she was a child, Evander. What the fuck are you thinking?"

I have the sudden urge to shift and rip the room to shreds.

"You *know* me," I rasp, "and you know her. I am not what she needs."

"And she's not what *you* need."

I exhale through my nose. He quirks a brow.

"You can't spend your entire life protecting her. I get it."

"What exactly do you get?"

"I get that Kenna has never, until recently, used her powers as they were intended. It's incredible, really, how she's able to hold all of that inside. I have moments where my own powers feel like they're going to consume me, and I barely have a handle on them. But for her... that's world destroying power."

He's never mentioned his powers before. I honestly don't even want to ask.

He meets my eyes. "She will be a target for the rest of her life."

"I know."

"She's why you went into the Ghosts, isn't she?"

Silence settles between us. He taps his fingers on his empty whiskey glass.

"I can't protect her if I'm standing by her side as her husband."

"Because?"

"Because my priorities would shift."

"How so?" He motions to the waitress again, who passes our table with a huff and waves her wrist in a promise of more drinks.

I grind my teeth. I'm drunk enough at this point that the words tumble out of me before I can stop them. "I would have a home with her. Children... as many as she wants. We'd have a life together, and one day, that could be taken from me. *She* could be taken from me, and I'm not like them. Like the witches or the rebel covens. I'm not like her. I'm a fox. A wolf on good days. She's… everything. I can't live with the idea of giving her the life she wants, the life I want, knowing I wouldn't be able to protect her in the end. My whole focus the past decade of my life has been to be the strongest, the fastest, and the most lethal. But a decade from now? Two?" I shake my head. "I'm better suited to the shadows. I can watch over her there. She can have the life she deserves, and I can continue to make sure she can live in peace and never have to use those powers."

"But what if she did?"

"What do you mean?"

"What if she actually used her powers and became the witch she's destined to be? You wouldn't have to protect her anymore. You wouldn't need to. You could fucking retire."

"I don't want that for her. I've never wanted that for her. She wants a quiet, peaceful life, and that is the only thing that's ever been important to me."

"Well," he sighs, rolling his neck, "she might get that after this weekend. But not with you. So, you get your wish, even if I think you're a fucking idiot for doing things this way."

"What are you talking about?"

"She's doing the Rite, or whatever it's called. She's the sacred chosen one–"

I'm out of my chair in an instant, and Sydney follows me. His expression changes from the cold, teasing Alpha to something dripping with concern.

"Evander, what–"

"She wasn't called to perform during the Rite. I was."

"Then why aren't you there?"

"Because someone named Vivienne was also called, not Kenna. It was never Kenna."

"I was just in Moonrise. I heard the news the moment Kenna found out."

I grab his shoulders, and at least a half dozen Crescent Falls warriors surround us, talons out and blades drawn.

"What do you know about the mystics, Sydney?" I ask, my fingers digging into the fabric of his shirt.

"What the fuck is going on, Evander?"

"I think this is a trap." I let him go and stagger backward, running my fingers through my hair. "I need to go–to go back to Moonrise. Now."

"I'll come too."

"No, you have to stay with your men." I motion to the confused warriors waiting nearby for Sydney's command to take me to the ground.

"This is Kenna we're talking about," he growls, stepping toward me. "If she's in danger, you're going to need me."

"What the fuck can you do, princeling?" I murmur as whiskey roils through my blood.

Alpha Sydney smirks, his blue eyes glowing with sudden pride, and maybe a hint of excitement.

29

A NEW DESTINY

Kenna

I'M NOT sure how two weeks have already passed since Evander and I fought in the shelter of the willow tree. Two entire weeks. I haven't heard from him or seen him since that night, and maybe that's for the best.

I let my heartache turn to a dull chill that's carried me on a wave of numbness. I walk the golden halls of the castle. I walk the gardens and city streets. I meet with friends for brunch along the shore of the lake and work at the midwifery clinic any chance I can get.

I keep my hands busy with babies and preparations for the Rite.

I keep my mind hollow and honed on maps and the paperwork covering my mom's desk.

I keep a smile on my face anytime I stand in front of my parents' magic mirror, listening to my dad fill my mom in on the movements of the allied armies now gathering in the Roguelands with him at the helm.

In the past week, thousands of warriors from Crescent Falls have entered Eastonia. Battalions have been dispatched, and scouts and

Ghosts are scouring the mountains and valleys for any sign of the Draven Coven.

But no one can find them.

To me, that means this effort by the kings is unnecessary. Why prepare for a war that seems like it's not even going to happen?

But my parents are on edge, especially Mom. And I don't blame her.

I run a brush through my hair as she paces the carpeted floor of my bedroom in her bare feet, grumbling under her breath.

"You should go paint," I offer. "You seem stressed."

"Kenna, please," she mumbles, waving her hand in dismissal before pinching the bridge of her nose. "I'm trying to think."

"About what, exactly?" I continue detangling my hair, brushing the nearly waist length tresses until they shine in the moonlight.

Tomorrow is a full moon.

Tomorrow is the Red Moon Eclipse.

Tomorrow is the Rite, and….

"I don't want you to do it," Mom says, planting her hands on her hips. "I have a say, you know, as queen."

"It's not a big deal. It's not like I have a mate." The lie tastes rancid on my tongue. "Plus, I'll get at least one thing I want out of this if I'm successful."

"And what's that?" Mom meets my gaze through the reflection in my vanity mirror.

"A baby." I know it sounds insane. I know, from the beginning, that I've been searching for love this entire time, but I… I have to be realistic now. Evander is my mate, and he doesn't want a relationship with me, regardless of our feelings for each other. I need to move on.

I need to take matters into my own hands, and if I'm going to be alone, well….

"Goddess, Kenna, do you realize what's about to happen to you?"

"I know what sex is, Mom."

She groans and shakes her head, murmuring some very colorful prayer to the Goddess. "You're not doing it. That's final."

"The mystics said they foresaw me–"

"The mystics saw someone else doing this ritual until a few days ago."

"Now they see *me*, and I'm doing it. I've already made up my mind. Plus, Evander left. It makes sense why the mystics saw a new couple doing the Rite instead of him and Vivienne or whatever her name is."

"Why is this so important to you?"

"It's a sacred ritual, Mom. It hasn't happened in over two decades, and if I was chosen by the Goddess to help bring back the moon, then I will do it. I will."

Mom holds my gaze. Her sea-green eyes are alight with emotions I can't read.

I turn and look up at her. "Look, I know you're stressed out. But I have everything handled. It's going to be fine. I'm going to be fine. I'm looking forward to the Rite, actually. All you have to do is enjoy the festival."

Her nostrils flare as she shakes her head. "You're not doing it."

"Yes, I am."

"Absolutely not."

I feel a flicker of emotion for the first time in two weeks as I slowly rise and square my shoulders. I still have to look up into her face, however, seeing as she's several inches taller than me. "I'm doing it. It's my destiny. The mystics said so."

Mom and I stare at each other.

I know she doesn't want me to do this. A week ago, I'd been sitting in the dining room with Sydney and my mom. He'd come to visit before joining his troops in the Roguelands. Dad was already there, overseeing his commanders in preparation for a journey to meet with Alpha King Jaxon.

We'd been laughing and joking all night, and for the first time in days, I hadn't felt the sting of Evander's rejection.

But then a mystic appeared in the dining room and told us that I, the Princess of Eastonia, had been chosen by the Goddess herself for the Rite.

It's the highest honor in the coven to be chosen for the Rite. The past chosen have been witch queens and the mothers of Alphas–and more.

But I have no idea who will meet me in that sacred cave–in the remains of an ancient temple deep underground.

Part of me wonders if this is why I can't feel the mate bond like Evander can. Maybe he's right, and the Goddess made an error when she threw us together, and now she's making up for the mistake.

But Mom hadn't been happy and spent two entire days looking for answers about the sudden change.

All while I reveled in it, feeling excited and hopeful.

But seeing her now, and the emotions roiling behind her eyes, sends that hope crashing down.

"What happened to you?" she whispers, and it's like a blow to my heart.

"What do you mean?"

"You know what I mean," she says. "You were so excited to find your mate this summer and become the Luna of Veiled Valley."

I sit back down on my vanity stool and turn to the mirror to finish getting ready for bed. "I'm just being realistic. With everything going on in the Roguelands and Evander not being my Beta anymore–"

"What?"

I cringe. I hadn't told her that part. I haven't told her anything at all about Evander, actually. "I told Evander he doesn't need to be my Beta. I can find a new one. It won't be that difficult–"

"Why would you tell Evander he doesn't need to be your Beta?!"

"Because he doesn't want to be my Beta. He never wanted to. He doesn't want to be around me at all, and I gave him a way out!" I snap, my voice echoing through my room and bouncing off the domed ceiling. I swear the crystal chandelier begins to tremble as my temper flares.

But I refuse to cry.

Even though I really want to.

"Kenna–"

"Don't," I say, holding up a hand. "It's done. Evander left. He went back to the Roguelands already, to do Goddess knows what, and I'm here, Mom. I have returned. I will ascend the throne in Veiled Valley–alone. I will continue my training to take your place one day. This is what everyone wanted and expected of me, and I'm doing it."

Mom sucks in a breath, and her expression cracks. Grief flares behind her eyes in a way I've never seen before. "If this isn't what you want, Kenna, you don't have to be the Luna of Veiled Valley."

"We both know that's not true. I'm the only other Shadowsynger besides Grandpa and Dad. The throne is mine, I've never had a choice."

She swallows hard. "What happened to you?"

"Why are you asking me that again?" Hot tears sprout along my lash line.

"Because–"

"Because I killed people. I used my powers and took out… forty rebels at least. Forty people who might have had families who are wondering where they are and why they're not coming home. I did that."

A tear slides down Mom's cheek. I've rarely seen her cry. Honestly I can't remember the last time I saw her cry.

I run my tongue along my teeth, trying to stem my anger but it's too late. For the past two weeks, all anyone has been asking me is, "Where is Evander?" Evander this, Evander that. Where did he go? What happened? Have you spoken to him? Blah, blah, blah….

My shadow starts to curl over my skin. It knows I want to just disappear right now.

"Kenna Mystica Westfall," Mom says, using my full name, which usually means I'm in huge trouble. "What the fuck is going on with you?"

I have a single second to suck in a breath before my entire facade comes crumbling down and I break, my eyes flooding with tears.

"He doesn't want me. He–I asked him if he loves, and he said he did, but he still left. I told him, if he left, he could never come back. He left anyway–"

"Are you talking about Evander?"

"Yes, I'm talking about Evander! Who else?!"

Mom looks shocked as she edges a step closer to me despite the sparkling darkness of my powers now roiling around me like a shield.

"He–he–he told me he can't protect me if we're together because it would distract him or something. Do you know why he feels like that? Because I'm a fucking coward, Mom! I don't want to fight anymore. My powers are too much for me and I–I killed so many people. So many. In a matter of seconds, forty people were dead, and I did it without thinking. I'm a monster–"

"You are not a monster," she growls, but her eyes are wide as she tries to close the distance between us.

"He kissed me," I choke, the words broken by sobs. "I felt it. I kept telling him I felt the bond between us but it's not in the same way he can feel it, and because of that, and because I'm too much of a coward to own up to what I am and accept it, he won't accept our bond, Mom."

She stills, her eyes locked on mine. She searches my face for the words I can't say because if I do, I'll fall apart.

"Evander is your mate." It's not a question. It's a statement. A cold, hard truth that settles between us.

I can't do more than nod.

"Where is he, Kenna?"

"How am I supposed to know?" I shout, wrapping my arms around my body in a tight embrace just as my shadow erupts and swallows me whole.

Mom can't see me, but she knows I'm here because I can't stop sniffling. Another sob threatens to strangle me while she reaches out a hand, searching for me, and eventually cups my cheeks.

"Did he reject you?"

"I don't know. I just know this hurts so much, and I don't want to feel like this anymore. I have to do something else, something for me. I'm doing the Rite."

Mom nods, and my tears gather between her fingers as my shadow starts to recede.

"What do you need?" she asks in a small, soft voice. "Do you want me to send a hellhound out to find him? I'm sure Amanda is gunning to track him now and give him a piece of her mind, anyway."

My lips curve into a watery smile despite the anguish in my heart. "No."

"What about… food?"

I shake my head.

She nods, but her eyes are still clouded with tears as she sighs. "You've the stories about your father and I. I know Amanda and Commander Artyom have been rather colorful in their renditions of our first few weeks together. It was… hell, Kenna. I have no other way to describe it. I didn't love your dad back then. I hated him, actually. Our love for each other now has nothing to do with the mate bond between us. The bond simply brought us together, and we had to fight to get to where we are now."

She slides two fingers under my chin so I'm forced to look up at her, even though she still can't see me.

"You and Evander have practically shared a soul since you were babies. You love each other in a deep, ingrained way. He will come back."

"He won't, Mom." I take a step back just as a trio of maids arrive. Long strips of white fabric hang from their arms, while the third and last to enter holds a basket full of toiletries.

Tonight, I prepare for the Rite.

I shed my last tear for Evander and turn to the maids, my shadows fading. They look slightly nervous as they shift from foot to foot.

Mom leaves without another word, but her thoughts on the matter are clear.

I know without a shadow of a doubt she's going to go talk to Amanda about this and come up with some scheme to get us back together.

But I let any shred of hope and longing fade away and follow the maids into the bathroom, letting them undress me as they run a fragrant bath.

The hot water washes away my tears, and when I emerge from the depths, I let go of any feelings I once had about finding my mate and settling down.

I have a new destiny, and tomorrow night, I will emerge with the moon as the future queen.

And Evander will be... gone. Forever.

3 0

THE RITE

Evander

I THINK I might want to kill Sydney.

For someone so stoic and all business, he's also extremely sarcastic and has found every opportunity to push my buttons the last twenty-four hours or so.

Thank the gods we can't mind-link because I'm sure he'd be rattling off insults and jests in my ear every waking hour we spend traveling back to Moonrise.

We're close to the sacred valley now. Close enough I can sense the wards Ryatt put up around the city to keep it hidden.

I pull on a shirt as I look out over the mountainous horizon. Summer is in full swing, and the rolling mountains are nothing but emerald green trees.

There's a lake in the distance that sparkles like diamonds over a sheet of the purest turquoise, but no sprawling, golden city in sight.

"We're here," I grumble, stooping to tie my boots.

Sydney shifts out of his wolf form several feet away and makes a show of stretching, completely naked, before pulling clothes out of the pack he'd carried on his back since we left the Roguelands.

Neither of us can jump, so the entire trip was done on foot and paw. I stayed in my fox form for the majority of it, enjoying how much faster I could navigate the forest than Sydney.

Once we walk down this last hill, we'll pass through the wards, and the city will come into view. That's how it works. Only those with connections to the coven or direct invitation from the king can breach the wards.

I squint up at the canopy of trees over our heads. The sun is setting. Tonight is the Rite, and I only have a few hours, if that, to find Kenna and stop her before it's too late.

Too late for what, I'm not sure. But something feels wrong.

"Hurry," I growl, glancing at Sydney as he buttons his shirt.

"What's the rush?" he teases, hiking his backpack over his shoulder. "Oh… yeah, right. Your mate is about to get sealed in a cave with a man that's not you."

"I'm not here because of that," I retort, but the idea of anyone else touching Kenna rips through my body like claws. "Kenna could be in serious danger, and I'm not wasting any more time."

Sydney steps to my side, and we walk down the hill, following a well beaten trail that seems like it leads deep into the forest.

The only problem is that it *does* only lead into a dark, endless forest. The trees are so tight here that I can't see past them, and after an hour, I've realized we've been walking in a circle.

We can't get through the wards.

"What's going on?" Sydney rasps, his blue eyes alert as they scan the shockingly quiet forest.

My nostrils flare as I look up at the canopy. The sun has nearly set. Once the Eclipse starts, we're too late. I have to get to Kenna before that happens, before she goes into the cave.

There's a real possibility that I've been locked out of Moonrise. If she told anyone about us and asked her parent's to keep me away, this could be Ryatt's doing.

I find that hard to believe, though. Kenna isn't that kind of woman. She's not cold and petty. She wouldn't separate me from my family.

Sydney fumbles with something in his pocket. He curses as he drops a bronze, circular object that falls to the ground with a thud.

"What is that?" I ask, intrigued.

"A compass," he grumbles, smoothing dirt away from its surface. "My dad made it for me. Watch." He holds it up in the air, and the lid pops open. I hear gears spinning, and suddenly a whoosh of air rolls through the forest.

I look at Sydney as the trees sway around us. His eyes are glowing in the darkness sweeping across the woods.

What kind of power is this?

My ears pop, and I feel an electric pulse shoot up my spine as he lowers his hand and drops the compass back into his pocket. He blinks, and his glowing eyes return to normal.

"What the fuck did you just do?"

He shrugs. "I just broke through the wards. Come on, we don't want to be late."

He sets off in a jog down the trail we've been traversing in a circle for an hour, and I follow, but all of the hair on my body is standing on end when the trail turns from raw earth to the smooth cobblestone lining the streets of Moonrise.

We break out of the trees, and the city rises before us. It's busy—every shop is open. The streets are teeming with people and festivals take place in every square.

Paper lanterns hover over the lake, casting crimson streaks of light across the surface of the water. It's as still and as smooth as glass.

But I'm on edge, and beside me, Sydney has lost all traces of humor as well.

"I should have been allowed past the wards," he says in a whisper over the thrum of music coming from the city. We walk toward the lake instead, toward the ancient street leading to Old Moonrise.

"I told you something was wrong," I reply, running a hand across my belt. My fingertips brush over the hilt of all six blades I'm carrying. "Go to the castle. Find Queen Ella and alert her about the wards. I could be wrong, and I could easily be the reason you weren't allowed access because they want me out, but if there's a threat–"

"I got you, you're fine. Find Kenna."

Sydney takes off with another word, and I'm alone.

My gaze sweeps over the lake, to the bonfires dotting the far edge. The moon breaches the peaks of the mountains as I walk steadily along the lake.

In the distance, along the side of the mountain hugging the lake, I can see the outline of several torches. They're being carried by mystics–easily seen in their white and silver robes.

They have Kenna.

I'm not too late.

I hope.

Kenna

MY HEART POUNDS ERRATICALLY as I walk up a set of stairs carved into the side of the mountain. Behind me, at least a dozen mystics in their robes and masks follow holding torches to light our path.

I've only heard stories about the Rite and the rituals that take place during this sacred night. For a few moments, the Goddess sleeps, her powers waning to nothing under the pull of the Eclipse. The lines that blur the realms of the living and the dead are so fine you can reach your hands between them, or so they say.

I can feel my powers recoiling as the Eclipse begins.

But it's nothing compared to the sudden nerves settling deep in my bones. I have an urge to turn around, to run home, but it's too late.

I spent the entire day in the company of the mystics. They chanted over me, sliding their thumbs over my forehead as they blessed me and the union that will take place tonight.

In some ways, I am a child of the last Rite that took place. Evander *is* the child of that Rite.

I wonder if that's why we're mates, but the thought is fleeting. I've reached the entrance of the ancient temple.

My pale white robe is removed from my shoulders to reveal nothing more than a thin, white slip that covers my body and drags on the ground behind me. Moonstone dust covers my skin, and it shines in the torch light.

I look at the entrance of the temple. It's dark and empty, and an echo of air streams out from its depths. I've never been inside. Even the mystics don't go inside.

This place is only for the chosen.

I find it hard to swallow.

"Princess Kenna," one of the mystics says as she hands me a torch, "you will know where to go."

I nod because I can't find words right now. My blood rushes, and my heartbeat echoes in my ears as I turn to look down at the lake, which is alight with lanterns and bonfires. Everyone is celebrating and honoring their dead loved ones and ancestors tonight. Everyone is counting on me to help bring back the Goddess's powers, I guess. *However the legend goes.*

It's not that I don't believe in the gods and goddesses. I worship the Moon Goddess as a shifter, of course.

I'm just nervous. I'm terrified, actually. Maybe Mom was right.

"Is he already down there?" I ask breathlessly.

"The other chosen will be here shortly. He had a long journey."

I narrow my eyes at the mystics, but because of their masks, it's impossible to read their expressions. A soft breeze comes from the temple entrance, and then the mystics are gone, turning to little puffs of mist.

A chill snakes up my spine as I turn back to the temple. Now or never.

I edge into the temple and feel a change. The air is different here—colder, stiller. There's an emptiness about this place that takes hold of me, and I can't shake it off as I run my hands along the ancient marble walls and walk down a long flight of stairs into a vast darkness.

My torch barely gives me enough light to see, and I'm not sure where I'm going, but eventually my feet meet solid earth.

I'm in some kind of tunnel, I think. The walls glimmer with crystal as I walk toward a new source of light.

I've been told the temple gives way to ruin deep underground, and that a cave is where the ritual takes place.

Whoever told me that was right.

The second I set foot in the cave, small warming fires erupt, their flames a strange shade of blue. For whatever reason, I imagined some sacrificial altar in the center of this space where I'm meant to lie prone and have sex with what could be a complete stranger, but the ground is covered in furs that are warm to the touch as I pad across them in my bare feet.

Today has been a day full of prayer already, but I find myself asking the Goddess why She chose me and why She changed Her mind and brought me here, instead of the other woman.

The Goddess works in mysterious ways, and that truth rings loud and clear over the sound of hurried footsteps sounding behind me, echoing through the tunnel.

I whirl around so fast the torch I'm holding burns out, and in the blue-hued light of the fires I find myself looking at the man meant to be father of my child if we're successful.

Amanda told me what it felt like to be down here during the Eclipse. She said it felt like she'd been... drugged. Like all of the power she ever had simply went away, leaving her numb, leaving her empty and desperate for feeling.

That's how I feel now as I drop the unlit torch. It hits the ground and rolls away.

Evander stares at me, panting, his eyes glowing in the firelight.

I feel...

It's like a blow to my heart. It's electric, something life giving and undeniable. Little gold threads weave through my heart and pull tight, binding me to him.

Why now? Why would I feel the mate bond like this now?

"Are you here to reject me?" I whisper, and it takes a tremendous effort to do so.

But his eyes are on my mouth as I say the words. He looks slightly lost and off kilter as he takes a single step in my direction.

I'm suddenly acutely aware of how little I'm wearing. My nipples peak under the thin fabric of my dress, and the straps have fallen down my shoulders. His gaze sweeps over my body in a way that makes me tingle with desire.

"No," he rasps. "I'm not here to reject you."

"Then why?"

His lips part, but he shakes his head. "You—what have you done to me, Kenna?"

I'm trembling, my knees suddenly weak. "Please, Evander. I am yours. I would be yours regardless of the Rite. I…" I meet his eyes. "I want this. I want *you*. If this is the only way I can have you, if this is the only night we will ever be together, please."

He closes the distance between us in three steps.

And then his lips brush over mine. "Lie down."

3 1

YOU BELONG TO ME

Kenna

What I don't know, as I kneel on the furs, is that Evander came here looking for me only to find out he's still part of the Rite. Mystics surrounded him at the lake shore and followed him to the temple entrance, hurrying him along, telling him he was late.

He came here for me. Maybe to stop me from doing this, or for another reason I don't know.

It's clear, however, that he feels some sense of relief finding me well and whole, regardless of the situation.

But I can tell he's trying to free himself from the yoke of the eclipse that's blurring the lines between us right now. He's trying to be logical about this. He's trying to hold onto some kind of rationality but is failing just as miserably as I am as I lie back against the furs.

He's watching every move I make. I can feel his heart thundering through our bond.

I feel like I'm in a haze as he covers me with his body. I reach up and run my fingers through his soft, golden hair. He smells so good—like the forest after a heavy rain. Like the warm comfort of my bedroom during a storm when the only lights are that of those silly candles I love so much.

He smells like home to me in every way. It's the bond, of course, but there's more to it. How could I not see this before? When we were young, when I was just a teenager writing him letters and waiting with bated breath for his return?

This hazy, overwhelming feeling has to be the eclipse. There's no other explanation for it.

But I'm also… so incredibly happy to see him.

His knee draws up between my thighs as he holds himself up on his elbows. He nudges my head to the side, his mouth brushing up my neck to that spot just behind my ear that makes shivers lick up and down my spine when his tongue darts out and smooths over that space.

I close my eyes and drink in every sensation, my fingers tangled in his hair.

But then, for a moment, I hurtle back to reality.

Just before his mouth meets mine, I press a hand to his chest. "We don't have to do this."

He pauses, opening his eyes. I curl my fingers into his shirt.

"Evander, I–we don't have to do this. The Rite, I mean. I know you don't want–"

"I was wrong," he says, lowering his face to my neck. He sucks gently, his teeth raking over my skin.

I suck in a breath and let it out in a moan as heat pools between my thighs, and I start to grind against his knee.

"I have dreamt of you like this," he rasps, running a hand down the curve of my hip while holding himself upright with the other. "I loved falling asleep because it meant *this*. It was the one way I'd let myself have what I wanted."

He bunches up the dress until my hips are exposed. I'm totally naked beneath, and he groans with satisfaction, but I'm still unsure.

"Wait–"

He pauses again, looking down at me with sudden clarity.

"Why did you come back?"

He holds my gaze for several seconds, taking a resigned breath. "I found out you'd been called to perform the Rite and I didn't like it. I felt like something was wrong about it, just like when I was called and you weren't chosen. My own mate–" He grits his teeth and his eyes fill with a kind of heat I've never seen in him before. "My mate," he rasps again, lowering his lips to mine. "My behavior toward you has been inexcusable, Kenna. I don't deserve you. I likely never will. That is why I left, but I can't…. Now that I've tasted you, I can't be without you. I can't put that kind of distance between us."

"But this is everything you don't want."

He shakes his head. "You are everything I've ever wanted." His mouth meets mine in a kiss so hot and demanding I feel like I'm floating. The room around us fades to nothing, and then it's just us, and his hands are on my body, tearing at the dress.

But then he stills and looks into my eyes again. "You have every right to push me away, to reject me. I will accept it if you do. Until that night under the willow, I had no idea how strongly you felt, and I couldn't handle knowing how deeply I'd hurt you. Our kingdom is on the brink of war. Your life is at risk. If we do this, I can't promise you I can give you the life you want, the life you deserve, but I can keep you safe. I swear that I can keep you safe."

"Evander, I don't care about that," I whimper, caressing his face, but he shakes his head.

"I do. That's why I've pushed you away. I want you to have children and a warm home. I want you to have a soft life, where you're safe and content with someone who makes you laugh. I don't know if I can be that man, but I can try."

His words echo through my heart and ignite something deep inside of me that I can't explain. It's more than the bond, just like Mom said. The bond is so complex and confusing, but this feeling is totally, utterly clear.

"I love you," I tell him, and he exhales deeply, closing his eyes as he kisses me softly, tenderly.

"I love you," he whispers against my lips.

In the distance I swear I hear the beating of drums. Maybe I'm imagining it. Maybe it's my own heartbeat rattling the walls of the cave, but my body starts to move in tune with the strange, ancient music.

Evander's kiss turns to something heated and animalistic. He tears my dress again, pulling it away. I unbutton his shirt, my fingers slipping over the soft fabric in my haste to touch him, to lay my hands on his bare skin and feel his heat.

His hand glides over my chest to my breasts, and he lowers his head to suck my skin, his tongue darting over my right nipple until it hardens, and I moan his name. I grind against his knee, chasing whatever friction I can find to ease the throbbing ache between my legs, but I need more.

He shifts his weight, pressing kisses down my body until he's... he's...

"What are you doing?" I gasp, trying to sit up, but he pins me to the furs by stretching an arm over my weight.

When his tongue parts my folds I lose any sense of self completely. My mind goes blank, and all of my attention is on the feeling of his tongue grazing my sex until I am trembling with ecstasy I've never experienced before.

His teeth glide over my clit, and I cry out, pinning his head between my thighs. "Evander!"

"Oh, my gods," he groans, kissing up my thigh and back down again before going back to work.

"For—for a man who took a vow of chastity," I pant, "you seem to know what you're doing."

"I'm a virgin, Kenna, not a monk," he laughs hoarsely.

I look down to find him staring up at me, his eyes glazed with feral intensity. He holds my gaze while sliding two fingers inside of me, stretching me to the point of pain. I arch my hips into his touch even though it hurts, unable to stop myself. Pressure builds and builds until I feel like I might explode as he slowly, achingly slowly, thrust his fingers in and out.

"Take off your pants," I command to the best of my abilities.

He arches a brow.

"Take them off," I repeat, trying to keep my head on straight as he continues working me into a frenzy with his fingers. He's watching me fall apart and loving every second of it. "Evander–"

He removes his fingers and is suddenly on top of me, nudging my legs further apart. He dips his head, hovering over me while he pulls his belt free of the loops. "Let me make one thing clear, Kenna. You might be a future queen, but there is one place I plan on ruling in our future home. You are mine, and this body–" he bites down on my neck and I moan loudly at the pressure. "This body is mine. You will do as I say."

For whatever reason, Evander bossing me around is like fire in my blood. I nod, whimpering and closing my eyes as he continues to bite down on my neck while kicking out of his pants.

He's so warm, practically fevered. His naked body settles against mine, and I feel utterly whole and protected beneath him.

But then I feel *it*, and some of that heated confidence wanes.

I went to an all-girls college, for Goddess' sake. I've heard all the stories about what happens in a bedroom–or a bathroom stall in a crowded inn.

I'm still not prepared for Evander's brutally hard cock resting against my thigh.

He's going to tear me to pieces with that thing, and I think I'm going to love it.

My breathing picks up as adrenaline takes over.

"Do you know what to do?" I whisper.

He lets go of my neck to look down at me.

"Yes, I know what to do. I'm going to try not to hurt you, but this *will* hurt, Kenna."

"Just for a minute, right?"

He nods. "Yeah, just for a minute." But now he looks uncertain. "We don't–I'm not sure if we should. I don't want to hurt you." He starts to pull away, but I gather him back.

I want to say we have to do this. This is the Rite. The eclipse is happening as we speak, and it's probably why we're acting so insane right now, but I don't.

"I want you. I want to do this."

I sit up a bit and kiss him soundly, my tongue sliding into his mouth, over his teeth. He groans and wraps his arms around me as he lays us back down.

The head of his cock nudges my entrance. He lets out another groan as he holds me as close as possible, breathing in my scent. "You're so wet," he rasps, pressing a kiss just below my ear. "You were so wet in that inn when we were traveling. It took all of my strength not to claim you as mine right there on that straw mattress."

"I wanted you to," I breathe, closing my eyes as he slowly nudges his cock inside of me. The fullness is something I wasn't prepared for, and I wince as he pulls out.

"Kenna," he groans, pressing in again, deeper this time. "Look at me."

My eyelids flutter open, and I look into his eyes as he thrust his hips against mine, hard.

He holds still, giving me a moment to get used to the fullness of him inside of me. It doesn't hurt as much as I thought it would.

But when he does it a second time, I cry out, and he's past that barrier.

And I'm his.

"Oh, Kenna," he says against my shoulder as his hips grind into mine. "Fuck, you feel… you feel so good, Gods." He nips at my ear as he thrusts into me with fervor.

My eyes flutter closed as I wrap my arms around his neck, pressing kisses to his jaw. The slight ache gives way to something deeper, a new kind of heat that blazes through me like wildfire. Again, that delicious pressure builds in my core and spreads through my thighs until I'm wound as tight as a bow string, and the sounds coming out of my mouth are unintelligible pleas for more.

Then it hits me. Pleasure washes over me like a tidal wave and then explodes. I come so hard I'm sure I'm blacking out. My vision fills with stars as I meet Evander's eyes, unsure if this is how it's supposed to feel, but if it is, I want to do this again, and again, and *again*. My muscles spasm around his cock, and he buries himself deep inside of me, holding himself there as I come undone around him.

When I open my eyes again, trying to catch my breath, he's looking down at me with so much emotion behind his eyes it's nearly enough to bring me to tears.

But then he flips me over onto my stomach and enters me again.

"Evander," I groan, arching my hips to meet him thrust for thrust. He pulls me up so my back is flush with his chest and grips my throat, whispering the dirtiest things I've ever heard in my life in my ear while his free hand toys with my clit until my head starts to spin.

"You're mine," he says, over and over again. "You belong to me."

"I'm yours," I rasp, and I feel a sudden surge of my powers returning at the very moment I come for the second time, and he flattens me to the ground, covering me with his body.

But his mouth trails hot kisses over my bare shoulders as he pumps into me once, twice, then a third time.

"Evander, please!" I beg, already on the edge of oblivion again. The pressure feels impossible. I want him so badly, I need him....

A searing pain erupts on my left shoulder, and my mind explodes with light and color.

Those fine threads woven between our hearts blaze with new life.

Evander just marked me. His teeth are still piercing my skin as my powers suddenly roar to life, and they feel new and whole and...

He comes, spilling himself deep inside of me, filling me with a new kind of warmth, and gathers me up as he rolls us over.

I stare up at the ceiling in shock.

"I need to mark you," I manage to say. "I need to–"

A thunderous boom echoes down the tunnel into the cave.

32

THE WORLD FALLS APART

Kenna

EVANDER LOOKS down at me and goes perfectly still.

"What was that?" I whisper. It could easily have been the fireworks the elder council in the coven ordered for the festivities.

Another Earth rattling boom shakes the underground temple to the point dust and bits of rocks tumble from the ceiling.

I don't even have a second to take a breath before Evander rolls off me, pulls me to my feet, and grabs his shirt. He yanks it over my head and deftly buttons it, but his body is so still, and his head is cocked to the side as he listens to whatever is happening beyond the sanctuary of the cave.

His mark on my shoulder burns, and blood seeps into the white fabric of his shirt, which is large enough that it brushes over the top of my knees as he steps away and quickly puts on his pants. "Where is your cloak?"

"Evander, what is going on? It's just the fireworks–"

"Listen, Kenna," he whispers, slowly raising a hand to the ceiling. "Listen."

I find it hard to swallow as I strain to hear anything over the pounding of my heart.

Another roaring boom shudders through the air. I meet Evander's eyes as my heart races. I know he has better hearing and sharper senses than I do. He can shift into not only a wolf, but a fox, and has the gifts of both powers simultaneously. He must sense more than the thundering echoes of whatever's going on beyond the cave.

He reaches down and snatches my cloak, draping it over my shoulders. "I came here," he explains in a low, gravely tone, "after spending two weeks canvassing the Roguelands for mystics who might have broken with the coven."

"Mystics don't break ties with the coven, Evander. That's ridiculous!"

"Listen, please," he rasps, clasping my shoulders. "I already told you I felt like something was wrong. Something felt off about how the couple performing the ritual was chosen. We are mates. We should never have been separated like the mystics foresaw. This is a trap."

My blood runs cold as I slowly turn to look at the entrance of the tunnel.

"What–what do you think is happening out there?"

"We're going to find out."

I expected him to tell me to stay here, to wait for him to return. Maybe even to hide, but... he grabs my elbow and leads me toward the tunnel just as the strange fires burning around the cave go out, and we're swallowed by darkness.

Evander doesn't stop moving. Those threads that bind our hearts pull tight in a silent command to stay with him.

'Mom,' I say down the mind-link. 'Where are you? What's happening?'

We reach the steps leading out of the ancient temple, Evander leading me through pitch dark, he says, "I can't mind-link with either of my parents right now."

"I just tried reaching my mom–"

"I need you to be prepared for what we're—"

Something–someone–grabs my hair and yanks me backward so

violently I cry out in pain. Evander whirls, his eyes glowing in the dark–the only source of light–and shifts.

But I'm being dragged by my hair, and I can't get my feet back underneath me. There's a heavy feeling in the air, like all of the oxygen has been sucked from the corridor, and it's pressing down on my powers.

I reach up and grip the wrists of my assailants, trying to force my powers to the surface.

Evander lunges in his wolf form; the thick, golden undercoat on his belly brushes over the top of my head, and then a shriek echoes through the darkened corridor. The shriek gutters with what can only be blood, and then the grip on my hair slackens to the point I can untangle myself and get back on my feet.

I barely turn around to look down before Evander is nudging me away, leaning into me so I have to grab his fur to prevent being knocked over.

The last thing I see before climbing onto his back, before he takes off at the speed of light, is a faint shimmer of opal and moonstone in the shape of a sightless, mouthless face.

A mystics mask.

Evander just killed a mystic.

A mystic that was trying to take me.

Oh, my Goddess–

Evander breaches the entrance to the temple, and suddenly we are out in the open, in the returning moonlight, and its chaos.

I look up and see bright, shimmering light rebounding off the invisible wards my father put around Moonrise like a large dome. Fractals of light fall down onto the lake like embers, sizzling on the water's surface.

Moonrise is being attacked. 'Get me to the castle, now!' I shout, or better, scream down our bond.

Evander sprints at his full strength down the side of the mountain while I hold on for dear life. My dad is in the Roguelands with the armies preparing to go to war with the Draven Coven once their stronghold is found. My mom would have been overseeing the festivities for the Rite as planned, but I can't reach here. The mind-link between us is empty and silent.

Something is terribly wrong, and I can't focus. A new power within me is coming to the surface, something I've never felt before—or I have, but not like this. This feeling makes me want to claw my way out of my skin.

Evander skirts the edge of the lake, weaving between the panicked crowd of festival goers as they run for any kind of cover they can find.

But then I feel a shift in the air. The cold taste of metal fills my mouth, and a shudder ghosts over us, followed by a cracking boom that pierces the air.

And the wards.

Fire fills my vision as the wards come down, and Moonrise is left totally, utterly out in the open.

We reach the city center just as warriors begin to spill from every building after desperate attempts to get everyone inside the shops and markets that line the numerous squares.

'Go to the castle. Shift into your shadow. Wait for me there,' Evander says into my mind as he skids to a stop.

I'm off his back in an instant and sprinting toward the steps that lead up to the castle—my home—situated in the very center of the city.

"EVERYONE INSIDE!" I shout as I run past people hurrying through the square. Warriors brush past me, but I don't stop to ask where the queen is.

I reach the castle and storm inside, coming to a stop in the front foyer where the massive, golden staircase funnels up nearly five stories.

Maids rush back and forth. A group of them, teary eyed, slides to a stop when they see me. "Go, go hide. Now!" I shout, unclasping my cloak. "Go down to the tunnels and get to the lake, to the docks."

"Princess Kenna, you must come with us!"

"I can't leave. Where is my mother?"

"She isn't here," one of the maids says, her voice breaking over the words. "She was at the lake with Lady Amanda—"

"Go. Go now," I tell them hoarsely. "Get out of the castle. We are under attack."

They rush back into the shadowed corridors leading off the foyer as I run up the stairs. The only solace I have is that my dad is well aware someone has broken through his wards. Any second now, he will be here. Any second....

A blast knocks me flat on the ground. The stained glass windows that stretch all the way to the highest point of the ceiling at my back explode in a shower of glass. I cover my neck, breathing rapidly, willing my powers to take hold, but I'm drained, somehow.

It's the eclipse. My powers haven't returned to their full force. Whoever is attacking right now is taking full advantage of.... Wait.

Wait a minute. This is what Evander was talking about. He's right.

Neither of us should have been called to do the Rite separately. That's insane. We're mates.

But separated...

My breath hitches in my throat as I hurry to my feet and sprint down the hallway toward my mom's office, to the magic mirror.

Separated. They--whoever is attacking us–wanted me and Evander separated tonight during the eclipse. My powers were tamped down, practically useless, and Evander wouldn't have been there to protect me if we were apart.

Evander realized that. This is why he left. He went to find someone who could explain why he'd been chosen but I hadn't, and when I'd then been chosen....

"Oh, my Goddess! What the fuck is going on!" I murmur as I shove through the door to Mom's office. The curse word feels surprisingly good on my tongue.

But I hear lifted, furious voices echoing from the shattered foyer as I slip into the room and shut the door behind me, locking it tight. I shout down the mind-link to my dad.

Nothing.

My parents are radio silent as I turn toward the mirror and try to use my powers to ignite the strange forces within.

But all I can see is my own reflection.

I'm starting to panic now. My powers just won't work. This shouldn't be happening, even with the eclipse. The eclipse is over now, for Goddess' sake!

"Find the fucking princess. We need her alive!" someone shouts from down the hall, followed by hurried footsteps.

I wring my hands and squeeze my eyes shut, trying to pull my shadow around me, but nothing happens.

No, no, no, no–

Someone slams themself against the door so hard the hinges whine in protest.

"Come on," I whisper, shaking out my hands. "Come on...."

The door shatters in a burst of splintered wood and glass.

Four burly, violent looking men enter the office. They don't have to look hard to find me. I'm standing in the open in nothing but a cloak and Evander's shirt, my bare toe curling into the carpet.

"Well, look what we have here," their leader, a middle-aged man with wiry brown hair and a long, unkempt beard says as he edges into the room. "The pretty little princess all by herself."

"How convenient," one of his companions drawls, giving me a wicked smile.

I don't move. I don't say a word as they step closer to me.

"Ha, she's not as powerful as we were told, huh? Look at her. Cowering like a little doe."

A soft, communal chuckle lights through the air between the men.

Movement in the doorway behind them catches my attention, but I don't let it show. Two wolves are hiding in the shadows, inching toward the men. They have no idea what's currently behind them...

"Well, you found me. Shucks." I give the men a sparkling grin and clap my hands together. "What now? Where to next? I'm growing bored."

The leader gives me a quizzical look.

One of his men steps forward, licking his lips. "We were told to bring her in alive, right? Gabriel didn't say anything about what kind of shape she'd be in, though. Why don't we have a little fun with her first?"

"I'll go first," another of them growls.

But behind them in the shadowed corridor, Evander, in wolf form, bares his teeth. The wolf beside is familiar somehow, but I can't quite place him.

It's only when he steps into the light spilling from the open door that I see his startling blue eyes.

'Sydney, where is my mom?'

'She's not in Moonrise. She and Amanda are gone. We don't know where.'

My blood runs cold.

'My dad?'

As if on cue, the castle shudders as power rips through the sky above us. All the little trinkets in my mom's bookcase tremble. The men look around nervously.

"Get her in silver cuffs. We need to go before the king gets here."

"He's already here!" one of the men shouts. "Did you not feel that–"

A snarl snakes from the corridor, and the men turn as Sydney and Evander stalk into the office, teeth bared and gleaming.

I exhale, glad they've finally revealed themselves.

'Close your eyes,' Evander says down the bond, so I do, but I can still hear them tearing those men to ribbons in front of me.

When I open my eyes again, Evander and Sydney are coated in blood that doesn't belong to them, and there's not much left of the men.

'We need to get to your father. He's here, fighting alongside the warriors.' Sydney eyes me for damage before turning and trotting out of the room.

Evander, however, stays.

"My powers haven't come back," I tell him out loud as I carefully walk across the bloody carpet in his direction. I run my hand through the fur over his neck, and his mark on my shoulder burns with sudden longing.

I desperately wish we'd had more time together tonight.

Now, I have no idea what the rest of the night will hold.

'Your mom's been taken, Kenna. She went willingly with Gabriel in exchange for the attack to end. We need to go.'

'They're still attacking–'

'They're hunting for you. Your dad is injured, but he was able to get here–'

'How was he injured?'

Evander looks into my eyes. He's such a large wolf–taller than me standing, which is incredible. 'The Draven Coven is attacking the major kingdoms. The Roguelands are at war. Crescent Falls…'

I blink, my hands trembling as my powers finally start to edge to the surface. Anger, grief, and worry converge into something enormously powerful.

And new.

A shredded sound echoes through my ears. My vision temporarily goes dark, and I blink rapidly to clear it.

But when I look down at my hands I find… paws.

Paws of the darkest, most depthless type of black.

I look at Evander in shock, and I swear, beyond the worry in his own eyes, pride shines there.

I just shifted, and it didn't hurt.

It felt *good.*

33

THE FACE OF EVIL

Evander

I'm NOT sure what I expected Kenna's wolf to look like. I hadn't expected this, however.

Her night-black fur shines in the faint light cast from the windows where magic is whizzing through the air as a battle ensues outside. Her fur is so dark that it sucks the light from the room and turns it to diamond dust that falls from her as she moves toward me, her silver eyes blazing with mingled worry and surprise.

She's small—smaller than the average wolf, for sure. The top of her head barely reaches my shoulder as she brushes against me.

I feel her power the second she touches me.

Unmatched strength. Ungodly powers I'm sure even she doesn't comprehend. She is a hybrid of several forces combined into one tiny wolf, and I have no idea what to do with her now.

I have it in mind to find the nearest closet and lock her in it, preventing her from putting herself in danger, but we need to find her father.

Sydney returns from surveying the castle for more threats, his golden wolf an incredible contrast to Kenna's night-black. He meets my eyes in the darkness and says into my mind, 'Well, it's about fucking time.'

Kenna whips her head around, her ears flattening and teeth bared.

'We can mind-link now,' Sydney continues, speaking to both of us. He meets my eyes again and I swear, beyond the lupine glaze in his eyes, I can see him smirking as if in his human form. 'You marked her, huh? Welcome to the family.'

'We don't have time for this. Where is my dad?' Kenna's voice is a growl through my mind.

Without further conversation, Sydney turns and leads us out of the castle, which is a tangle of shattered glass and the occasional body.

'Wait,' Kenna says in a strained voice as she passes the body of a young maid, but Sydney and I flank Kenna and prevent her from turning around. 'Please!'

'She's gone, Kenna,' Sydney says, his voice breaking between the words.

My heart wrenches as I feel Kenna's despair flow through our bond.

But people start funneling into the castle foyer in a ripple of noise and sudden chaos, and the three of us stop short of the entrance.

Warriors carry their wounded. Families rush in with injured loved ones and unharmed children. I step in front of Kenna as the crowd hurries inside, the air filling with the sounds of agony and desperation.

When I look at my mate, her eyes are wide and set with determination.

She's not coming with us to find Alpha King Ryatt. She has to stay here and use her gifts to heal her people.

'Go. Go shift and change. I'll bring your father here,' I tell her. She turns and hurries back up the stairs behind us, disappearing in a flash of onyx.

Sydney and I dart out into the war-torn city under the shimmer of the broken wards. The fighting has lessened, but there's still magic in the air as we race through the city center to the more sprawling, rolling neighborhoods that hug the forest beyond.

Warriors are thick in this area. Wolves canvass the streets, and their human companions carry wounded and help families out of their destroyed homes.

'Where is he?' I ask Sydney as we leave the city proper and cut into the trees. Silence chokes the air. Even the birds stay as quiet as possible.

My answer comes only moments later when we reach an active battle.

The rebels are trying to retreat, but the Moonrise warriors are on a warpath spearheaded by Alpha Ryatt and my father in their human forms.

It's madness. I can't tell who's friend or foe in the chaos. The dense forest makes navigating the rocky, hilly terrain impossible as I weave between trees and follow Sydney to the front line where our allied warriors push the rebels back, trying to herd them away from Moonrise.

It's working.

I'm barreled into from the side and knocked down, my head smacking against a rock. Teeth lock around my neck and thrash, but I stand, shaking off the attacking wolf before lunging on him and taking him to the ground.

It goes on like this for some time. My body is in shambles—my fur clotted with blood—by the time I finally fight my way through the fray and reach my father's side.

He's bloody and beaten but whole.

'Dad!' I shout, but right as he turns to me, another wolf bounds out of the darkness.

This wolf is different. Large, lumbering, and missing most of his fur. His eyes burn red as he opens his massive jaw and tears into my dad.

I act on instinct, digging deep for all the strength I have left, and leap toward him, catching the back of his neck in my jaws. I pull him off my dad and throw him to the ground. Sydney rushes to my side, and together, we take him apart while he thrashes.

But out of the corner of my eye, I see Ryatt rushing toward us in his human form, his shadowsword drawn and raised.

A whisper of darkness surrounds me for a split second before whatever figure was coming up on me dissolves into nothing and reappears behind Ryatt.

'WATCH OUT!' I scream down the mind-link to Ryatt, but it's too late. A flash of magic so dark it consumes what little moonlight there is to be had tears through Ryatt, curling around him and strangling him right before my eyes.

Dad pulls himself up, swaying on his feet, and runs to Ryatt.

Gabriel meets my eyes from his position behind Ryatt before he disappears in a cloud of smoke and ash, and the forest falls silent.

The enemy warriors disappear as if they'd never been there. Even their bodies turn to mist, leaving nothing but trails of blood behind.

But my focus is on Ryatt as he falls to his knees. Dad catches him before he falls over face down in the bloody dirt.

"My wife!" Ryatt roars, his voice guttering with blood and absolute despair. "He has my wife!"

"Look at me, Ryatt. We need to get you to the castle!" Dad says, clasping his friend's face between his hands. "Where—where are you hurt? How?"

The king closes his eyes and doesn't open them again.

I DON'T UNDERSTAND any of it. Gabriel's powers are immense. Even if he was born of a witch, he shouldn't be this powerful.

Questions blur my mind until the early hours of morning. Rain pounds every quiet street. If there is a sun today, it's hidden behind thick, unending clouds the color of steel.

The rain washes the blood from the streets as I walk in my human form, stopping to peer into shops, to check on the families starting to come out of their ruined homes.

After the battle, Sydney and my dad took Ryatt back to the castle to be healed, if that's possible. In a sick, twisted way, I feel fortunate that Dad is distracted by Ryatt right now so he isn't dwelling on the fact that my mother–his mate–is also missing alongside the queen.

Queen Ella wouldn't let anything happen to my mom, and that's the only shred of hope I have as I walk into the castle after hours of canvassing the city for survivors and wounded in need of help.

It's quieter inside than I expected. Maids sweep the shattered glass from the foyer. Voices drift from every room, and I follow the sound to the formal ballroom toward the back of the castle. It's the largest area inside the massive dwelling, and right now, it's full of people spread out with blankets and what meager belongings they could gather before leaving their homes.

A group of women walks around pushing carts laden with food and drinks. Others are passing out more blankets and bedrolls.

I have no idea where my mate is, or where my father is, but none of these people are especially hurt, so the injured aren't being kept here.

I keep moving, passing through the ballroom into the west wing of the castle. The long hallway is alight with activity as I cut around a corner, noticing every door to every sitting room and office in this section of the castle is open.

Healers move from room to room in an unhurried fashion carrying baskets of herbs and potions. The smell of healing tonics hangs thick in the air as I pick my way down the hallway, pausing to look in each room.

A tall, red-headed woman steps out of one room and notices me, her shoulders slumping in relief. I recognize her as Avery, one of Kenna's local friends and fellow witch.

"Where is she?" I ask.

"She's down the hall. She needs to rest. I've been telling her to go upstairs and get some sleep."

"I'll handle it," I tell her as I brush past and continue at a steady pace, stepping past countless healers and common folk walking between the rooms to check on friends and family.

I find her slumped on a stool in a sitting room at the very end of the hall. Three older children are fast asleep in a nest of blankets and pillows on the ground surrounding what I assume is their mother, who is healing from what looks like burns. My gaze sweeps over the sleeping children and my heart shudders when I notice the bandages covering their arms and legs.

A rage I've never known before boils to life.

Gabriel will pay for this. I will find him.

Kenna holds a bundle in her arms as I approach her and lean down to gently wake her up. The newborn baby in her grasp stirs, a soft whine cutting through the air. Kenna wakes to the sound and jerks when she sees me, but her face flushes with relief.

"You need to sleep," I whisper.

She adjusts the baby–who is still so pink that I wonder if it's just been born–in her arms and shakes her head. I notice the tears then. Streams of silver that have dried on her skin.

"Where is this child's mother?"

"Dead," Kenna whispers. Her hollow gaze settles on the baby. "I didn't get to her in time. She was in labor when the attack began, and we can't find her husband so–so I've been taking care of the baby while healing–"

"Kenna, this is too much. You need to let the other healers help."

She starts to shake her head, but another healer walks in. "Princess Kenna, he's right. You've been at it all night. Please, go rest. Things are settled."

"How is my father?" she asks with effort.

I turn to the healer, catching her eyes. She catches the silent plea behind my gaze and purses her lips before saying, "He's going to be fine. Your tears healed the worst of the injuries. Everyone is sleeping now. He is sleeping, I assure you."

It might not be the whole truth, but it's enough for Kenna to rise with the baby in her arms.

The healer steps forward, but Kenna is reluctant to hand the child to her. I place my hand on her lower back. "Kenna, I passed several families with infants. There are mothers out there that are able to nurse this baby. That's what the baby needs right now. There's nothing more you can do."

Kenna swallows against a sob as she nods and gently lays the infant in the healer's arms.

I realize how Kenna is feeling when we walk out into the hallway. She leans against me for support, and I scoop her into my arms and carry her through the castle, past the ruins of the foyer and the once towering stained glass windows.

Her room is untouched and warm as I close the door behind me with my foot. I lay her down in bed, taking off her shoes and socks. She's wearing a simple pair of cotton pants and a loose shirt, probably something she grabbed in her haste to redress and tend to the wounded.

But as I pull the covers over her exhausted body, she reaches up and grabs my shirt. "Will you stay with me?"

She looks so tired and broken. I wouldn't think about leaving her, but…

"I'll stay. I'll sit in the chair by the window. I won't leave the room."

"Just lie with me, please."

"Kenna," I say hoarsely, clearing my throat. "I can't be in the same bed with you right now."

"Why not?" She looks up at me so innocently.

"Because I've just claimed you as my mate and I'm… not sure I can control myself, regardless of the circumstances." In fact, I've spent the last several hours trying not to go scorched-earth on everyone around me because I'd been separated from my mate only moments after marking her.

Everyone who told me men go absolutely feral after marking their mates were correct. Feeling her soft, warm weight in my arms as I carried her upstairs was enough for my cock to go rigid against the stiff fabric of my pants, and I am absolutely aching to be inside of her.

And there're hundreds of people downstairs—displaced, homeless, and injured.

"Please?" she whispers, and it's my undoing.

I take off my shirt and pants, sliding in beside her in nothing but a pair of boxers and hold her against my chest.

Her fingers drift over my bare chest, tracing the lines of my muscles. Each touch sends a flurry of sensation dancing up and down my spine and ignites that need to claim her all over again.

"I want to mark you," she whispers, and I close my eyes against the urge to roll over and pin her to the bed.

"We have plenty of time for that later. You need to sleep now."

"I can't sleep," she says softly, her fingertips drifting lower, brushing over the waistband of my boxers.

Fuck it all.

I rise up on my elbow and look down at her, taking in how the stormy, gray morning light drifts over the soft planes of her face. She's the most beautiful thing I've ever seen in my life.

And she's mine.

I lower my lips to hers. "Where do you want to put your mark on my skin?"

3 4

THE TASTE OF HIM

Kenna

I ARCH my back and brush my mouth over Evander's jaw. His proximity is overwhelming to every single sense, and I drown in him. He lowers himself to cover me wholly with his body, pushing the sheets down to the end of the bed with his feet.

This feels different than it did in the cave. Despite our obvious desire for each other that has spanned weeks at this point, we were performing the ritual together. It was something we had to do.

But this… this is just for us. Because we want to. Because, despite everything that happened last night and what's happening now, we need this from each other.

His touch is the perfect distraction. His hand roaming down my side is enough for my mind to go blissfully blank.

Every other feeling is set aside for now, and that's okay. For a few moments, we can just be mates. Soon, I'm sure every waking minute of my life will be consumed by worry for my parents and my kingdom.

Falling back into the spiral of anxiety and grief, I clutch his face and draw him close, kissing him soundly. Our teeth clash, and I bite down on his lip, drawing out a moan from him.

"I'm trying to be gentle with you, Kenna. Don't tempt me."

"Tempt you to do what?" I ask innocently, going as far as to bat my eyelashes at him as he pulls away to look down at me.

"Tempt me to take you in every way I've been imagining. In every place I've been envisioning in my dreams of you." He grinds his hips against mine, his hard cock pressing against my thigh. "But you're going to be sore and I... I just want to take care of you right now. We have time for the rest of that."

"I want to know about your dreams," I whisper, trailing my lips over his neck.

His throat strains as he swallows, letting out a little gasp as I continue my exploration of his skin– his shoulders and his chest– with my mouth. My tongue darts out to swipe over his flesh. He's salty from sweat but tastes divine, and a fresh heat builds deep in my belly.

"You're making this very hard for me, Kenna," he groans, closing his eyes. I look up at him, and I've never seen him so relaxed, so at peace. His eternally pinched brow has softened to the point he looks... far younger than before, so much closer to his actual age, like he's never experienced death, war, and violence.

Pride swells in my heart at the thought that I am the reason for his peace, at least right now. I'm sure I'm also the reason for that pinched brow and icy expression more often than not.

"I want to know," I whine, arching my knee as he settles deeper between my legs. We're still separated by our clothing, but he's bare save for his boxes as I run my hands down his back.

But I pause as my hands drift over a network of scars.

"What happened to you?"

He shushes me, leaning in to kiss me again. "Nothing you need to worry about. I'm a warrior."

Still, the thought of him hurt makes my heart twist.

"Don't think about it, Kenna."

"I feel like I barely know you now," I admit.

He nuzzles my neck, inhaling deeply. "I'm not all that different."

"But–"

"Look at me," he commands in a tone that immediately makes me submit. It's hot, admittedly, and that heated rush ripples through my body again. "You are my mate, but you're also so much more than that to me. You will learn sides of me no one else has ever seen, and my past–what happened to me in the field and occasionally in training–is part of that." He kisses the mark he left on my shoulder. It burns to life, still unhealed and raw.

"I love you," he continues. "But you don't have to take care of me."

I'm not sure how to say what I feel about that sentiment. If I did have something to say, it's stolen from my lips as his kisses cover my collarbone, his tongue dragging over my skin. His teeth graze down to my breasts and any rational thought leaves my mind.

"Let me be the one taking care of you," he says softly, and reaches down to tug my pants down over my hips.

I gasp as he brushes a kiss over my belly while yanking my pants and underwear down and off. He works his way back up, removing my shirt and lingering on my breasts to knead and suck them until I'm panting his name, and my eyelashes are fluttering.

The way he touches me is something I'm not prepared for. Maybe it's because we've only ever been with each other, and only once. Every sensation for me is new. And to him? It's like he's desperate to explore and uncover every inch of my body in the most enthusiastic way.

He kisses my neck as he squeezes my hips, the head of his cock sliding through my wetness and nudging my clit.

"You're so beautiful," he whispers against my skin. "You're so soft, so full, and I–" His breath catches in his throat, and he exhales deeply, groaning with relief as he sinks his cock inside of me until he's buried to the hilt.

The feel of him is exquisite, but he was right. I am sore. Sore, but thrumming with want as he pulls out, my muscles clenching to try to keep him inside.

He chuckles low in his throat as I whimper, rocking my hips against him. "Please," I rasp, digging my nails into his sides.

He thrusts again, slowly, grinding into me, and curses under his breath. "You've done something to me, Kenna. I can't get you out of my head. I want to stay deep inside of you forever."

I almost choke on a moan as he picks up his pace, lowering to rest on his elbows as his body slides over mine. We're both slick with sweat, and I'm so close to coming undone at this point that I wonder if he's going slow, drawing this out, just to watch me unravel and beg.

"I dream about you on your knees," he rasps in my ear, thrusting into me hard enough the headboard smacks against the wall. "With my cock between your beautiful lips."

My eyes flutter closed as his voice–heavy with want and full of smoke–laces over my neck and shoulder.

"I dream I'm pinning you against a wall and fucking you until you're screaming my name," he pants, teeth gritted as he lowers his forehead against mine. He clutches my ass and rocks against my hips. "I've dreamt of you sprawled naked in my bed with nothing but moonlight covering your skin, and claiming you while you slept, waking you up with my cock buried in your pussy."

Goddess, he's going to make me come with just his words. My heart pounds to the rhythm of his thrusts.

"I want you to come for me," he commands.

"Evander," I whimper, opening my eyes as he lowers himself further until we're chest to chest. I wrap my arms around his shoulder, spasming around him as I come. I cry out his name like it's a prayer to the gods.

"Quiet," he pants, murmuring unintelligible words of praise in my ear as he body strains.

I'm still coming undone. Pleasure I've never felt roars through me like a firestorm, igniting every nerve until I'm buzzing with electricity.

I want to scream. I want the echoes of my pleasure to bounce through the mountain valley around us, but I bite down on his shoulder hard enough he grunts and hisses as my teeth sink into his skin.

His blood is beautiful. The taste of him blooms through my mouth, setting fire to my senses and awakening something primal.

He comes, grunting and growling my name as he pumps into me, then stills.

I open my eyes to find him looking down at me, his eyes hooded and heavy with mingled desire and exhaustion. I glance at his shoulder. A half-moon wound drips with blood in the stormy darkness.

I marked him.

There's no going back now.

"I'm sorry," I begin to say, but he shakes his head and slowly pulls out, blowing out his breath.

"Never say that to me," he whispers, brushing his lips over mine. His muscles strain as he untangles us and lies beside me, gathering me into his arms. We lie like that for a long time, neither of us speaking, while we listen to the rain thunder against the windows.

I'm so tired. So exhausted. I feel a crushing kind of sleep creeping in as he pulls the blankets over our bodies. Reality hits me almost as hard as the fatigue numbing every muscle.

"What are we going to do, Evander?" I ask after a long moment.

"Whatever we can," he replies, his voice distant and sleepy.

I fall asleep before my mind can begin to whirl over our current reality and the world outside of my bedroom. Below us, hundreds of people are displaced and wounded. My mom is missing, but I know, deep in my heart, that she's okay.

Dad, however….

I wake sometime later, unaware of what time it is, or how much time has passed since I fell asleep in Evander's arms. He's dead asleep beside me, but the door to my room creaks open to reveal a figure dressed in the gray uniform the maids in the castle usually wear.

I sit up, pulling the sheets with me to cover my naked breasts, and squint at the maid in the dark. I recognize her as Mary, one of the kitchen maids.

"Is everything all right?" I ask as she edges around the door.

She blushes deeply and refuses to look at Evander even though she knows he's there. "Yes, Your Highness. But we were unable to locate the husband of the woman who died in childbirth last night. She has no local family, and no one knows what to do with the child. I wanted to tell you that some of the healers are talking about sending her to the orphanage in the Roguelands–"

"Wait," I tell her, blowing out a breath. "Just wait. I'll be down soon." I feel a certain responsibility to the baby. I was the first person to hold her. I held her as her mother died. Her mother had been in the throes of a difficult labor when the attack began and was wounded, and there had been nothing I could do at that point. She'd died only minutes after I got to the stuffy sitting room where she'd been laboring.

Losing a mother like this... I can't fathom it. I'm an only child because my own mother nearly died having me, and my dad wouldn't let her go through that again.

"I will decide what is done with the baby," I tell the maid. "Give me a few minutes, and I'll be downstairs. Were you able to find a nursing mother? If so, fetch her for me–"

Another set of footsteps echo from the corridor beyond the door, and I stiffen, recognizing them completely. I don't have a single second to cover myself further before my dad barges through the door, stepping past the maid, who squeaks in surprise and quickly ducks out of the room.

"Dad!" I hiss, but it's too late. He looks at me, then at Evander, and curses, his eyes full of sudden fury.

I give him an exasperated look and shout, "Get out!"

Evander stirs, reaching over to lay his arm over my lap. My cheeks blaze with embarrassment.

"In my office," Dad rumbles. "Now."

35

WILD GOOSE

Kenna

I ADJUST my apron strings to stop my hands from trembling. The corridor outside my dad's office is unusually quiet and empty. Normally, warriors and higher ranking wolves would be walking back and forth or waiting on the benches along the wall for a meeting with him. Commanders would be speaking in low tones outside the door, not sparing a passing glance to the others waiting in the wings.

And beyond the windows behind me, the city of Moonrise would be loud, shiny, and glowing with activity, but now it's gray and silent.

The wound on our precious, sacred city festers with every passing second my mother, the queen, is gone.

I chew my lip and rock on my heels.

"You had an opportunity to tell me the truth and you chose to lie–"

"She is my mate, and I will decide what is best for her!"

I close my eyes and let out my breath. I've been listening to Dad argue with Evander for the last ten minutes. Dad promptly shut the door in my face when I tried to follow Evander inside, so... whatever issue he has with finding Evander in my bed isn't my business, apparently. At least, not yet.

I should go downstairs and help. I told Mary I'd be down to assist them with the care of the baby, and that was twenty minutes ago.

I pick at the hem of my apron and narrow my eyes at the door, wondering if they'll even notice if I walk away, but the door opens wide, and Evander storms out. He comes to a stop in front of me, reaching for me as he leans down to speak into my ear, but my dad darkens the doorway behind him and snarls, "Go, now."

Evander turns to look at him with a vengeful expression, his emerald eyes narrowed in a scowl of epic proportions.

But he turns back to me and his eyes soften. "I will see you soon. Tonight–"

"General Evander," Dad seethes. "*Now.*"

"General?" I look from Evander to my father. "What?"

Evander leans down and kisses my cheek, and then he's walking away, his footsteps echoing off the walls.

I huff a breath and turn back to my dad as he reaches out and grabs my arm, yanking me into his office.

The door slams shut behind him in a phantom wind. The air is sucked from the room as I round on him, shouting, "What the hell is going on? Why did you just call my mate a *general?*"

"Because Evander and I are going to Crescent Falls," Sydney says.

I whirl toward his voice to find him leaning on the corner of Dad's desk looking worse for wear. Dark circles line his eyes, and his dark copper hair is ruffled and unkempt. He hasn't slept.

"Why are you here?" I growl.

Dad walks around his desk and sits down with a soft groan, and I remember that he was injured badly last night. "Are you all right?" I ask him, but he gives me a withering look that would make most men cower.

"How long have you known he's your mate?"

"Why are you sending him away? Is that why? Because we're mates and you don't approve?"

"He lied about it. He sat here in my office and lied to his king–"

"Evander has done more for this family, for me, than you'll ever know," I snarl, edging toward the desk. "You have no right to send him away. You have no right to force him back into your army and use him–"

"Crescent Falls was attacked last night, Kenna," Sydney says in a low whisper, his eyes on his lap.

"Several rebels were captured by your uncle's warriors and interrogated," Dad continues.

I look from man to man. "What does this have to do with Evander?"

"He's leading a group of Ghosts into the city to try to locate the twin sister of Gabriel."

My brow furrows. "A sister?"

My mind reels over what I know about the Draven Coven. Atticus, their leader, was the twin sister of Petra, who terrorized my mother and went behind Queen Ravenna's back to lead King Kane's armies into Moonrise twenty or so years ago. Atticus survived and vanished.

Now his son Gabriel leads the rebels, and Gabriel has a vendetta against the royal families of the Allied Kingdoms.

But I never knew he had a sister.

"Why–"

Sydney clears his throat and meets my eyes. "Apparently, this woman defected from the Draven Coven as a young teenager and has been hiding in Crescent Falls for close to a decade."

"Then she's not behind these attacks," I counter, looking at my father. "Why bother finding her?"

"We have information from the rebels that Isaac and Ryan interrogated that leads us to believe this woman has powers that Gabriel needs, and he won't stop his assault on Crescent Falls until he finds her."

"So we have to find her first," Sydney says, looking grim.

"That's stupid," I tell him. "And a huge waste of time–"

"The Draven Coven is a disease born from the time when Kane ruled," Dad seethes. "We are going to do anything we can to stop them."

"And where the hell is Mom?" I shout, losing my temper. My eyes flare with silver flames.

"She's fine," Dad grumbles, tapping his fingers on his desk. "I'm in contact with her."

"She's gone, Dad! She was taken by the Draven Coven—"

"She went willingly in exchange for them stopping their attack on Moonrise."

"Well, they didn't stop attacking," I growl. "Now what?"

"Your mother has a plan," he says calmly. Too calmly. His eyes betray the steadiness of his tone, however. He flexes his jaw and grinds his teeth like he's doing everything in his power not to jump to wherever he thinks Mom is. "Your mother has been through this before, and I doubt this is the last time she'll lead herself into danger."

"So you're just going to sit back and let her deal with this herself?"

"They have Lady Amanda as well and are likely using her against Aunt Ella," Sydney says steadily. "Our hands are tied."

"So, that's it, then? Mom is on her own, and you're sending Evander away—"

"I have the full force of my armies surrounding the only known location of the Draven Coven," Dad growls. "Evander has a job to do. We need to find this woman if she's really as powerful as they say so we can have full control over this situation and eradicate Gabriel's coven."

"And if she's just a wolf?"

"She wouldn't be," Sydney cuts in.

I slowly turn to meet his gaze. "What are you not telling me? What exactly does Gabriel want?"

"Gabriel has powers he shouldn't have," Dad says as he leans back in his chair. "Shadowsynger powers, for one. Our bloodline is solid. You, me, and your grandfather are the only living people who possess shadows and the ability to jump, save for your mother, but that's only because of the bond I share with her."

Something clicks into place. All of those stories I was told about my parents and their fight to end King Kane's reign converge, illuminating a disgusting truth.

"Is Gabriel... related to King Kane somehow?"

Kane and his stolen powers, his sick, twisted experiments on his enslaved subjects...

"We believe Petra and Atticus may have been his children," Dad says. "And if Gabriel is really Atticus's son, which is up for debate even within the rebel circles, Gabriel believes his father is the rightful Alpha King of this kingdom, and thus he would be the heir."

My blood chills as my gaze sweeps the room. "What, exactly, is up for debate about that?"

"Petra's mother was in the fringes of the Moonrise Coven. Her family believed in strict...breeding," Dad cuts himself off, taking a breath. "Breeding for the sake of stronger powers. Your mother has had a hunch for many years now that Petra's family secretly defected from the Moonrise Coven and aligned with Kane, and Petra's mother offered herself as a breeder before she returned to the Coven and bore his twins."

Male witches rarely come into powers, which is why Gabriel is such an enigma.

"But what of Gabriel and his supposed sister?" I ask, closing in on the desk. "Sure, he wants to be Alpha King someday, but you said some of the rebel's don't believe he's truly Atticus's son–"

"Your mother believes Gabriel is actually Petra's son... and Atticus is still his father."

My mouth pops open. "Gross!"

Sydney snorts, but Dad's gaze bores into mine. "It's not something to laugh at. This family breeds for power, like I just said."

"But Kane wasn't powerful. His power was stolen. And Petra's powers of ice were minimal in comparison to anything we're capable of–"

"We've had reason to believe, for several years now, that Atticus and Gabriel are in possession of some kind of relic that gives them their powers. Like the mask your mother...." Dad tapers off and looks suddenly uncomfortable.

I image my mother, her face hurdling into view, and see those strange silver scars that line her hairline.

King Kane's mask... the one that harvested the powers of his slaves.

She became the mask, absorbed it somehow, when she uncovered the ancient Firestone cities and brought them back to life.

My stomach hollows out as I look at my father. "What if it's not just a relic?" I step toward the desk, my mind going a million miles an hour.

But Dad already knows this. He looks down at his desk as the realization strikes me straight in the chest. "His sister... he was draining power from his sister, and that's why he's looking for her. That's why he tried to kidnap me and Misty."

"If Misty has powers outside of her wolf gifts, they haven't shown themselves," Sydney cuts in.

"Still, it makes sense, doesn't it? Kane drained Mom of her powers once. If he does have a relic, he'd still need power. And if his sister is as powerful as the rebels say then...." I look at Sydney. "You and Evander *can't* find her. You understand that, right? She's hiding from him. She doesn't want to be found, and she shouldn't be found!"

"If she is like you, or your mother, she must be found and contained."

"That's awful, and you know it," I spit, turning my gaze back to Dad. "And I won't allow you to send Evander looking for her, forcing him to be a part of this madness!"

"It is not up to you," he says sternly, his eyes going icy. "She is a threat to the Allied Kingdoms."

"I won't allow it. He is my mate. I get a say in this!"

"He is my Ghost, and I am the king. Pack your things, Kenna."

"Where are you sending me?" I sneer. He has to be joking. All of this has to be a bad dream I'll wake up from at any second.

"To Veiled Valley as planned. Your ascension ceremony is in two weeks, which gives your mother plenty of time to do whatever it is she's doing and return to us. Your grandfather is on his way here as we speak to assist me in the recovery of Moonrise and our people."

"I am the best healer you have. You cannot, and will not, send me away!"

He rises and towers over me with only the desk between us to separate me from his rage. But I'm also raging. My blood rushes as I square up to him. He looks down at me and says, "You may be my daughter, but as Luna of Veiled Valley, you are still my subject, and I am your king. You will do as I say."

"Evander is my mate and will rule beside me. I will not ascend the throne without him–"

"Evander will never be Alpha of Veiled Valley," he snarls. "Not after what he's done."

"What has he done?" I shout, my shadows burning to life.

But Dad's eyes soften as he searches my gaze. "Do you not care that he toyed with your heart for years? You are my daughter, and he has proven he does not deserve you–"

"You will never understand the depths in which he had to travel to make his way back to me, Dad. How dare you separate us! I will never forgive you for this!"

"Kenna, wait," Sydney tries to say, but I'm already moving toward the door. I throw it open, tears blurring my vision as I rush into the hallway and slam the doors shut behind me for dramatic effect, of course.

I thought Evander might have come back. I thought he'd be waiting in the hall for me, but... I'm alone.

I'm alone. Mom is gone and in danger of her own making. Dad hates Evander and is sending him on a wild goose chase for a woman who does not want to be found. And, worst of all, Sydney seems to be backing my father up.

I swallow hard and wipe my clammy hands on my apron. I'm dressed for a day full of healing and hard decisions, but my mind is wrecked by nerves, guilt, and worry.

I put on my best mask–one of cheer and optimism–and walk the empty hallway to the recesses of the castle.

I find Mary and turn my attention to the one thing that truly matters this very minute.

"Where is the baby?"

36

SHE'S OURS

Evander

I LOOK DOWN at a pair of familiar black gloves. They feel heavy in my hands, but that might just be the crushing ache of what's to come and why these have been given back to me.

The barracks in Moonrise suffered damage in the attack, but they're still intact enough to house the unmarried and unmated warriors who reside in the city. I came here because I had to meet with Commander Artyom to get these fancy gloves back, and since every warrior is out in the city canvassing for hiding enemies, I'm alone.

I sit down on a random cot and stretch out my legs, going over the conversation I just had with King Ryatt.

I know this mission wasn't given to me because I am the best in the field and the only chance of the Allied Kings finding this woman, whose name isn't known. I am being forced away from Kenna while her father, the king, decides whether or not I'm worthy of her affection.

I don't blame him. I don't deserve her love. I've decided to live with that truth as long as it means I can still have her, but he's right.

I slip my fingers into the gloves and flex my hands.

Footsteps sound nearby, and I turn to find Sydney walking steadily in my direction.

"You should sleep. You look like shit," I grumble as he sits down on the cot opposite mine.

"I went to bat for you, you know. Ryatt isn't seeing clearly right now given that my aunt is in captivity."

"So is my mother," I remind him, meeting his sapphire eyes.

He nods knowingly and sighs, "Do you think finding this woman is a good idea?"

"I've been tasked—"

"I'm asking you personally. Your mate made some very good points."

"What does Kenna think?"

"That she doesn't want to be found. As far as my father knows, from the rebels his forces apprehended, she crossed the border at the age of eleven and has been missing for nine years. She was just a child and likely had help escaping. I don't think she's a threat."

"But if she is, we have to act."

"I understand that," Sydney grinds out but shakes his head. "It just doesn't sit well with me."

"Well, your role in this will be purely diplomatic." I rise but notice him picking at his nails. I continue, "From what I was told, you have sway with the other packs in Crescent Falls. All you'll be doing is researching their numbers, going through their population lists, and looking for possible female adoptees that are her age—"

"I met someone," he says suddenly, refusing to meet my eyes.

I ease back onto the cot and stare at him. "Who?"

He lets out his breath in a rough exhale. "I believe... I don't know. I didn't catch her name. I was drunk," he says with a short laugh. "I've never been that drunk before, and it was Ryan's doing, honestly. But I met her at the same ball the rebels attacked. She was the reason I wasn't there. I took her back to Ryan's house, and I... we slept together, and I felt that tug, you know? I've been wondering if she's my mate, but I have no idea who she is or where to find her."

"And this situation has you thinking about her?"

"I'd rather be looking for her," he says, meeting my gaze. "I agree with Kenna when it comes to Gabriel's sister. She doesn't want to be found. It's likely she has no idea her brother is behind this, if she remembers him at all. Selfishly, I see this as an opportunity to find that woman from the ball. I'd have the necessary resources at my disposal."

"Why didn't you catch her name?" I ask.

"I'm sure she told me, I just don't remember," he groans, running a hand over his face. "I had Ryan look into it but he has no idea who she is, either. And he knows most of the women in Crescent Falls."

I smirk, but Sydney looks withdrawn as he stands. "Enough about me. I just wanted to say I'm doing what I can to get you out of this but Ryatt is on a warpath and my Dad isn't easy to sway, either. Once Ella is back and safe, I'm sure he'll change his tune."

"Don't count on it." I stand, taking off my gloves and slipping them into my pocket. "Do you know where my mate is?"

"She's at the castle helping the other healers." He follows me out of the barracks. The city is quiet and empty, which is an odd sight. "Look, you and I have to leave tomorrow morning. Don't–don't put yourself between Kenna and my uncle in the meantime."

I eye him for a moment. "I already told him how I feel about that sentiment. She is mine."

"He's her father."

"She is my mate."

Sydney takes a breath and lets it out slowly. "I don't envy you, Ev. Ryatt gives my father a run for his money when it comes to being protective of their children."

"This is my battle to fight," I tell him right before he edges around a corner and disappears into the city center.

I walk to the castle where I'm sure I'm not welcome. I don't care. If Kenna and I have one night together, I mean to make the most of it.

I slip through the ballroom–past the families waiting to find new shelter since their homes were destroyed in the battle—and into the corridor lined with rooms now dedicated to healing the sick and wounded.

But I don't find Kenna among the ranks of the healers who are far too busy to pay me any mind. But I stop one of them, taking her by the elbow. The young witch can't be more than sixteen and stares up at me with a fearful expression. "Where is the princess?"

"She's—she's upstairs, in her quarters."

This is odd, but I let the witch go and make my way up to Kenna's rooms, which are tucked in a quiet, private wing dedicated to her personal use. She has a bedroom, of course. A large, airy bathroom. But she also has a small library and sitting room attached to her room, and that's where I find her.

With the baby.

The sun sets in the distance, casting a hazy glare through the windows as the storm clouds from this morning finally part. Her eyes are closed, and her expression is soft, relaxed, as she gently rocks the sleeping infant in her arms.

I edge toward her, careful not to make any noise, but one of her eyes opens. "Evander," she whispers, a ghost of a smile touching her lips.

She looks beautiful. Her face, cast in the shadow of the sunset, is the most glorious thing I've ever seen. Her dark hair is loose and falling over her shoulder in thick, bouncy waves that touch her waist, and her eyes are alight on mine, as smooth and gray as polished silver.

I sit on a stool across from her and rest my elbows on my knees as I hold her gaze. "What are you doing, Kenna?"

She sighs, her gaze sweeping over the sleeping baby in her arms. "I don't know," she admits, adjusting the newborn's weight. "I couldn't leave her alone down there. I didn't want to be—to be parted from her. Not yet."

I keep my gaze on Kenna's face, watching a myriad of emotions play out behind her eyes.

"We believe the baby's father might have been one of the warriors who perished last night," she says in a whisper. "We're still trying to find any family that might claim her, but so far, nothing."

"Was her mother part of the coven?"

She shakes her head. "Her mother was a shifter. I think she might have come here with her mate for some reason, possibly with some of the Rogueland warriors for the festival…. I just don't know." She closes her eyes and heaves a breath. "There's an orphanage here in the coven, but I can't… I don't want her to go there."

A half empty bottle of milk sits on the table between our chairs, and the surface is cluttered with clothes and a few clean diapers that look impossibly small.

Still, seeing Kenna like this feels natural, like she was always meant to sit by a window holding a baby, rocking the child back to sleep.

My heart squeezes.

"You want to keep her, don't you?"

Kenna shifts her weight, her eyes locked on the window beside us. "This happened to my Aunt Maddy. Did you know that?"

I shake my head.

"She was born at the castle in Crescent Falls when Grandma Isla was pregnant with Uncle Isaac. Her mother died in childbirth, and Grandma couldn't save her, and her father… well, he was killed by Grandpa Maddox. I don't know all the details but… they didn't keep her. They found her a loving family but her adoptive parents died and she was… she grew up in the care of a stepmother who used her like a slave and sold her to breeder traders."

I absently pop my knuckles as Kenna's worry and grief rips through our bond.

"I don't want that for her," she whispers, holding the baby a little tighter. "I was there when she was born. She–she wrapped her tiny hand around my finger, and I just–I can't–"

"Keep her."

Her eyes meet mine. "What? But–"

I reach out and smooth my hand over the soft, peachy blonde hair on top of the baby's head. Kenna goes perfectly still, watching every move I make as I lean forward to carefully take the baby from her arms. "Evander?"

But my focus hones in on the child. She's smaller than average, especially for a wolf. I test her weight in my arms and sit back down with her, tucking her in the crook of my arm before meeting my mate's gaze.

"She's yours."

"She's not mine," Kenna says with a little laugh.

"The Goddess works in mysterious ways. I know you believe that more than most."

"Her parents died," she argues, her eyes shining with tears.

"And you were there when she came into this world. Tell me, how many babies have you delivered?"

"Hundreds," she chokes, confused.

"And how many mothers have been lost?"

She looks down at her lap. "Not–not many. Not in my care–"

"But those babies–those orphans, they didn't have this kind of effect on you, Kenna. I can feel it through the bond–"

"But she's not *ours*, Evander." She looks suddenly broken, a silent plea shining through her tears. "She's not your daughter."

"Do you think that matters to me?" I lean forward, eye to eye with my mate.

"Does it not? She wouldn't share our blood–"

"You are my mate, and if the Goddess has chosen you to raise this child as your own, then I am her father and will treat her as such. I will love her as my own. If this is what you want... if this is where your heart is, which I know it is, then she is *ours*, Kenna."

Kenna swallows hard, her throat bobbing as silent tears slide down her cheeks. "It's ridiculous, isn't it? Thinking I can just–just take this baby girl and say she's mine–"

"Brie," I say, my tongue rolling over the word as I look down at the baby, grazing her cheek with my knuckle. "*Our* daughter's name is Brie."

"Like... the cheese?"

I glare at Kenna. "Like the flower that grows in a river glen, in the old tongue."

"Oh," Kenna whispers, cracking a smile.

I look down at the baby and nod. It's decided. Maybe, now that I've held her, I finally understand the strange sensation that's been sending a hum through our bond since last night that had nothing to do with marking each other and everything to do with this.

This gift, I realize, as Brie startles awake and briefly opens her eyes.

But she settles back into my touch, her cheek resting against my chest.

Kenna slides off her chair and kneels in front of me. When she looks up at me, her eyes full and overflowing with tears, I feel her confusion, worry, and absolute despair flow down our bond.

The past day has been some of the best times of my life, and also the absolute worst. I know she feels the same.

She lays her head on my lap and hugs my leg, dissolving in silent sobs.

So, I sit there, holding my daughter and my mate, and look out the window at our city where I was raised and wonder what the fuck I can do to make this place safe for them again and banish the threats against Kenna, her family, and our kingdom.

Because I will, even if it kills me.

37

IT'S ALREADY BEGUN

Ella

Dim lighting casts the space in a strange, unnerving glow.

I pace along the wall, running my fingers over the strange carvings that seem lost to time and make little sense to me, despite over two decades of learning every custom and legend about Eastonia and its dark history.

Even Amanda's not sure what these murals and carvings mean or depict, but we're in agreement that we're deep underground in the ruins of some old temple to some lost god.

Amanda rushes out a breath and slumps into a dusty armchair, which looks out of place in the sitting room where we've spent the last two days. Maybe it's been two days. I haven't seen the sun since before the eclipse began and everything absolutely unraveled.

"I can't shift," she breathes, closing her eyes. "My powers are shot."

"Me neither," I grumble, tucking my filthy, dust covered fingers in the pockets of the simple dark cotton pants I'd been wearing the night of the festivities. I thank the Goddess I hadn't yet changed into the massively extravagant ball gown I planned to wear to the party at the castle after the Rite.

Amanda, too, is dressed plainly. I recently braided her long, copper blonde hair into a neat-ish braid, but we're both coated in dirt, blood, and the dust that seems to cling to everything in this room.

I lean against an antique desk and wonder, for the thousandth time, where the hell the Draven Coven got all of this antique furniture, and close my eyes.

I reach down my bond with Ryatt and tug hard.

"Anything?" Amanda whispers.

I shake my head and open one eye, fixing her with a look that conveys the fact that we are well and truly alone now.

I'd been able to mind-link with Ryatt, through our bond, up until a few hours ago, but now it's eerily silent.

My powers, too, feel tired and useless.

I almost run my fingertips over the fine network of scarred symbols on my forehead but think better of it when I notice the dirt caked beneath my fingernails.

"You'd think they'd be dying to talk to me," I shrug, kicking the corner of a faded crimson rug. "Being the queen, and all. I'm shocked my head isn't on a spike yet."

"Don't talk like that," Amanda scolds, frowning. "You promised me we'd make it home."

"Consider this a needed break from the kids," I grin, but Amanda shoots me a dirty look and crosses her legs, turning her head away from me.

"My idea of a break from the kids was a trip to Maatua with Granger and staying in your mother's fancy guest house for a week."

"Well, there's still time for that. We just need to figure out what the hell these people want, first–"

The massive double doors at the entrance–the only way in, or out, of the room–burst open to reveal nothing but darkness beyond.

I don't bother straightening. Food and drink have been brought in on a regular basis–good food. I was even offered a cup of coffee a few hours ago, which was my only hint that it'd been morning at the time.

Fresh cream and sugar, too.

So far, we haven't been poisoned, neglected, or tortured.

But we also haven't seen anyone but servants.

I watched a middle-aged man of considerable strength walk in, his glassy, nearly white hair tied back away from his face.

A cloak of all black shields his body, but his identity is unmistakable.

I'd remember him anywhere because his face is ingrained in my memory like a scar. He gave me a single shred of hope during one of the darkest times of my life while I was locked away, underground, just like I am now.

"Queen Ella," Atticus says with a bow.

The doors shut behind him with a snap.

"What kind of game are you playing?" I edge toward him, my eyes shining with the last traces of my powers. "Where are we?"

"Underground near the Tarsian border," he replies with hesitation. He sweeps a pale hand around the once-luxurious sitting room with a slight smirk on his lips. "This place once belonged to King Kane and was outfitted to his desires in the event he was ever overthrown from his seat as the King of Rifthold."

Amanda snorts somewhere behind me.

"And now this is where your coven of mole-people are based?"

Atticus eyes me for a moment. His eyes are a pale shade of gray that seems slightly off and unnatural, so different from my mate and daughter, whose eyes are like a raging storm.

He looks like Petra, and it ties my stomach in knots to even look at him directly.

"I am not the leader of the Draven Coven. I never was and never will be."

I cock my head. "That's bullshit. You ordered an attack on Moonrise. You tried to kidnap my daughter and niece–"

He shakes his head and looks suddenly resigned. "I would never." He takes a single step in my direction but stops short of where I'm now standing with my arms crossed. "I made you a promise two decades ago that nothing would happen to your child. I've kept that promise."

"Like hell you have," I snarl.

I glance over my shoulder. Amanda nods her agreement but stays silent.

"This is a precarious situation, and I have little control," he grinds out. "I am trying to help you–"

"How?"

He holds my gaze, searching my eyes. "Gabriel is going to be an even bigger problem if he's not stopped, and I don't have the manpower or resources to stop him."

"So you dragged us here for our help?" Amanda cackles. "Goddess above, I've officially heard it all."

"Is this a game to you, fox?"

"Do not address her," I seethe, and he slowly turns his eyes back to meet mine. "You have attacked my kingdom, threatened my family on both sides of our borders, and have now separated us from our children. What the fuck do you want?"

Atticus's icy expression shatters as he crosses between us and sits down in an armchair. I glance at Amanda, wondering if she caught the shift in his demeanor as well.

I have to add that Amanda is an excellent mother with an uncanny ability to read the emotions of others. Her brow pinches in concern as she briefly throws me a look and edges toward Atticus, who drops his head in his hands and exhales deeply.

I'm used to Alphas playing tricks like this on me to pull at my heartstrings.

But if Amanda believes Atticus is in distress, he must be.

I raise my hand at Amanda in a motion to stop when she begins to reach for him.

Atticus slowly looks up at us. "You'd better sit down."

Amanda settles herself back in her dusty chair, and I choose to perch on the desk, my arms still crossed tightly beneath my breasts. "Whatever you're about to tell me, save your breath. I already know that you're the son of Kane–"

"You don't know the half of it."

I look into his pleading eyes and feel what Amanda must have felt. This man is in trouble.

Maybe I hadn't read him wrong twenty years ago, and I'd been right about that sliver of understanding between us when he'd led me to face his sister for what would be the last time.

"I am the son of Kane. He fathered me, and Petra and I were raised in Moonrise, but I was separated from Petra and my mother as a young child and… I trained under Kane. I'm not the only son he fathered. There were so many of us—witches, shifters of all kinds…. He put us through tests, weeding out the weakest, needing a new heir to replace Ryatt." I square my shoulders at the mention of my mate, but Atticus continues, "I was a slave until you killed Kane and destroyed Rifthold, but I escaped and went home to my family because that's what I thought I should do."

Amanda chews her lip and meets my gaze. A chill runs up my spine.

"By then, Petra was on the run. There were enough unsettled loyalties for her to start to band a small coven together. At that point, I knew I wouldn't be welcome in Moonrise, and the rest of the heirs of Kane either died in Rifthold or went into hiding, so I followed my sister into hell." He grimaces and runs his fingers through his hair.

"You stood by and watched as she tortured those witches," I snarl.

"I got many of them out," he admits.

I glance at Amanda. She looks just as confused as I feel.

"Petra gave birth to a son, in secret, a year before you showed up," he says. "I won't go into detail about Gabriel's father because I'm sure you already assume—"

"That you're his father?"

Atticus slowly looks up at me, his face going a pale shade of green. "Are you out of your mind?"

I shrug. "I've heard the rumors that the two of you were… close."

He makes to stand, but Amanda bares her teeth at him, her canines blazing sharp in the dull light surrounding us.

"Gabriel is not my son. I believe he might be Kane's son, given the timeline. She would have been working with Kane at that point. But she wanted a daughter–needed a daughter–since the males born of witches possess no gifts, and sent Gabriel away. To where, I don't know, but whoever raised him did so while placing a silver spoon in his mouth and telling him he was the future King of Eastonia when they tucked him into bed each night."

"What rule do you play then? Are you saying Gabriel is in control of the coven?"

"I am his advisor," he murmurs.

"So you–"

His eyes light on mine as he stands. "I must make one thing perfectly clear to you, Ella. Gabriel will succeed in his quest for control of Eastonia if he is not stopped. This isn't a game."

"Your inbred nephew is nothing compared to my mate and my daughter–"

"Your daughter has no idea how much danger she's in," he says softly, shaking his head. "Please–"

"You are complacent in this–"

"Gabriel wants my daughter," he breathes, his shoulders going slack. He stumbles a step backward and falls back into the chair.

I arch a brow, looking at Amanda. She nods at me, taking an easy step toward Atticus. "Why?"

"For the same reason he wants the royal princesses," he murmurs, meeting my eyes. "He has a relic, Ella. Like your crown. A scepter–and he uses it to draw the powers from others to increase his own."

"I didn't know you had a daughter," I say. I figured something like this was happening. Ryatt and I have been following the Draven Coven for years, putting shreds of information together to try to see the full picture of their movements and desires.

But I also thought it was Atticus at the helm, and this was some personal vendetta against me, not that his son was vying for what he believed is his rightful throne.

"Sasha," he whispers like it pains him. His eyes cloud over with tears, but none of them fall from his lashes, like he's spent years reckoning with her loss. "She was ten when I sent her over the border to get her away from him. He'd harvested her powers from her for the first time a week before I got her to safety." He runs his fingers through his ashen hair and looks at me. "Her mother was a shifter. Lora, my mate. I kept them hidden from Gabriel and his cronies for as long as I could, but even as a twelve-year-old, he had so much sway. Lora died at the hands of his henchmen, and I was dragged back to hell with Sasha when she was only a few days old."

"She's in Crescent Falls?" I say, shocked. He nods, and suddenly everything starts clicking into place. "He's looking for her, isn't he? The breeder auctions, the balls, trying to kidnap the princesses? This is all connected."

"Her powers are… immense. Like yours. But she's just a wolf. Gods, I prayed for a son to spare her from this. There are so few women in the coven now. They're considered precious, highly valuable. They all die so young because of his sick experiments. But Sasha, and woman like your daughter, and possibly your niece, can survive his torture and–" He stops himself like he's telling me too much.

His gaze locks on mine as he continues. "He wants Sasha. He needs her to take the throne of Eastonia, but he has enough support now across the border to start a war with the Alpha King of Crescent Falls. We're all in danger. This isn't a game, Ella. The war has already begun."

"How do we stop him?"

WHAT IF THEY TAKE HER?

Kenna

I WAKE up in the morning to hazy sunlight blaring through my windows. I blink, reaching up to rub my eyes but then pause and look over at the other side of the bed.

Evander slept here last night, but he's no longer here, and his side of the bed is cold and empty.

He's leaving today. Soon, I assume, given the fact I overslept, and it's probably close to 9:00 AM. I roll over onto my side, lifting up on an elbow to peer over the edge of the bassinet beside my bed.

Brie is snoozing with a peaceful expression on her perfect face.

A soft creak alerts me to someone entering the room, and thinking it's Evander, I sit up a little straighter, but it's only Avery.

"Hey," I whisper, pushing the sheets down to free my legs as I swing them out of bed. "I didn't expect to see you until later."

"It's a quiet morning down in your makeshift infirmary," she says with a soft smirk. She edges toward the bassinet and peeks inside, her smile growing. "Are they supposed to sleep this much?"

"Yes. It's really all newborns do," I yawn, stretching my arms over my head. "But she was up several times last night. Evander took a few trips down to the mother acting as a wet nurse with her to help settle her."

Avery sits on the edge of the bed in her healer uniform, her starched apron a pearly shade of white.

Avery is my oldest friend, other than Evander. I met her in kindergarten, and we grew up together, but our training went in totally different directions. She's a surgical healer, a highly specialized trade that uses an even more specialized kind of magic, and she knows very little about babies.

She smooths a rogue lock of red hair away from her face and watches me as I flutter around the room, pulling out fresh clothes and an apron from my closet to get ready for another day of healing downstairs.

"How come you never told me about Evander?"

I pause, my fingers brushing over the fabric of my apron. "I should have. I'm sorry."

Avery exhales, shrugging as I turn to face her with my uniform in hand. "I wish you had, only so I could have been there for you."

"I'm fine, really. I was fine before." I'm not sure why I never told her, or any of my friends, about my real feelings for him. I guess it kept me safe–locked away in my own delusion.

But everything is different now.

"Well, everyone's heard about what happened between your father and Evander at this point." She huffs, eyeing Brie as the baby starts to stir. "I was just down in the kitchen. Everyone's talking about how your dad tried to send Evander away."

"He didn't just try," I counter, shrugging out of my pajamas and pulling a pair of panties and deep blue slacks up to my waist. Avery's seen me naked a time or two, so I don't bother with modesty. "He *is* sending him away, today. Right now, I'm sure. I need to find them both."

Avery gives me an odd look as I put on a bra and pull a matching shirt over my head and begin to tie my apron strings. She gingerly picks a squirming Brie out of the bassinet and settles her against her shoulder. "No, he's not! Like I said, I was just in the kitchen. They're preparing the biggest breakfast I've ever seen in my life! Enough to feed everyone housed in the castle right now and the Ghosts who just arrived in town this morning with your mom."

My heart falls into my stomach. "My mom is here?"

She nods, her mouth popping open to say something I'm sure is along the lines of, "You didn't know?" But I'm already taking Brie from her arms and racing toward the door.

"Where are they right now?" I ask, my heart thundering against my ribs as my breath catches.

"I have no idea!" she exclaims, but I'm already cutting through my living area and yanking open the massive double doors leading out into the corridor and the depths of the castle. Why did no one tell me? Why wasn't I woken up the second she arrived?

I jerk to a stop as Evander appears holding a tray of breakfast. He looks remarkably relaxed for someone about to get banished to another kingdom and separated from his mate under the guise of a mission.

"What are you...? Where is...? What's going on?" I trip over my words, my mind going a hundred miles per hour. Evander looks over the top of my head as Avery comes out of the room behind me, mumbling something about taking Brie downstairs for her own breakfast as she takes her out of my arms and hastily walks out of sight.

"Good morning," Evander says slowly, skeptically, as he steps up to me.

I blink a few times, wondering if I'm dreaming. "I thought you and Sydney were leaving this morning? Why didn't you wake me up?"

"Kenna, your mom is here, and she's safe. I found out early this morning when I was bringing Brie back upstairs and didn't want to wake you after the night we had with her," he says, giving me a knowing smile. "The Ghosts found her after she alerted your dad to her whereabouts."

"Then the Draven Coven has been found?"

He shakes his head. "They were let go. That's all I know. She's resting, and I haven't been briefed on whether plans are changing, but for now, I'm staying here."

I throw my arms around his waist. He carefully holds the tray above my head. "When can I see her?"

"I'm sure they'll find you soon enough."

A guard hurries down the hallway in our direction. We turn as the young man skids to a stop, his shoes screeching on the tiles. "Princess Kenna," he says with a short bow, "General Evander–"

"What is it?" Evander asks, dropping his voice into his usual icy, all-business tone.

"I didn't know who else to go to. Alpha King Ryatt and Beta Granger have been in his office with the Queen and Lady Amanda since the arrived–"

"What is it?" Evander repeats through gritted teeth.

I peer at the guard, who looks between us, his shoulders rigid. "We have a few Draven prisoners on the other side of town, as you know. One of them is willing to talk, but only to her." He points at me and all the fine, downy hair on my body stands on end as I slowly look up at my mate.

"Why?" Evander asks.

⁂

IT'S GOING to be a hot one today. I can already feel the heat oozing off the pale stone pavers lining the winding streets of Moonrise as Evander holds a door open for me, which leads into the dark recesses of what's been used as an office building pertaining to royal affairs. Generals, commanders, and lawyers use this space. Tight offices crowd a narrow, unlit hallway as we follow the guard down the hall and up a flight of stairs.

More guards appear, leaning against door frames and chatting in small groups over cups of coffee. Some of them give me a passing glance, but most of their attention is on Evander.

I haven't seen him at work. Not really. I've never given stock to his professional reputation. All I know are the rumors and tall tales of my mate during his time in the field.

Seeing the shock, awe, and respect on the faces of the guards does something to my heart that's hard to put into words.

On one hand, I'm proud to be walking beside this man. This man who instills fear in his enemies and has the respect of his men. But on the other hand, I remember the scars on his back, and how empty and dark his eyes were before he finally let himself love me, and wonder if years of training, killing, and commanding has done irreversible damage to the man I love–the boy I once knew.

Evander gives a silent commander to a trio of guards standing in front of one door. They move out of the way, and he goes inside.

I follow him into the dark and shield my eyes as a bright, fluorescent kind of light flutters on.

A man sits in silver shackles on a metal chair. His shaved head is bowed to his lap, and his fingers are bruised and bloodied.

The room smells sharply of blood, in fact. I wonder if it's his. I wonder, briefly, if they've been torturing information out of him.

He raises his head, and my assumptions are confirmed.

He's beaten to a pulp–one of his eyes swollen shut and his lips violently split–but I sense no magic on this man. He's a shifter. A wolf. I can smell the difference.

He tries to whistle at me as I edge to a stop, but his blooded mouth only sputters. Evander scowls, reaching out an arm to stop my progress. "What do you want, wolf?"

"I heard a rumor," he whispers dryly, his beady black eyes darting between me and Evander, "that one of our own is in your castle, Princess."

"Any surviving Draven rebels have been imprisoned here," I say with so much firmness in my tone that I sound almost identical to my mom. It takes me off guard, but I quickly right my expression.

"You're mistaken," he rasps, revealing broken teeth as he smiles.

"Who?" Evander snarls.

"One of our own women," the man spits, disgust flaring to life in his eyes. "She's pregnant."

My stomach hollows out. I place a hand to Evander's lower back to steady myself.

"I didn't realize the coven enlisted female warriors," Evander drawls.

"Of course not. The women are for our own enjoyment, to keep up morale. Gabriel is a generous king." His broken smile makes me sick to my stomach.

"There's no such woman here," Evander says. I wonder if he's thinking the same thing I am as I start to knit my fingers together.

There *was* a pregnant woman who wasn't part of the coven. No one knew her, or her home pack, or her family.

Brie's mother.

"She belongs to the Draven Coven. Gabriel will soon find out one of his women is unaccounted for. The baby she will bear is a girl child, which is sacred. He'll come for her."

"Gabriel is the least of your worries right now," Evander sneers. "I was told you were willing to talk; so talk. What is Gabriel planning?"

The man smiles at Evander then shifts his eyes to me. "You think you're so safe in your gilded cities, don't you, Princess? Gabriel broke through your father's wards like butter. But what he wants—what he was looking for—isn't here, and your powers, Princess, are not the kind he wants to possess as his own. Although… a daughter from your womb is something he'd like in the future."

I feel Evander's rage ghost through our bond, but I step out from behind him. "He's looking for his sister, isn't he? She's not here."

"He knows that, but the battle in Moonrise provided the perfect distraction for the moves he's making in Crescent Falls, didn't it? Pity your own mother decided to surrender instead of fight."

"Tell us where he is," I command.

"I will tell you where his hideout is if you tell me where the woman is," he snarls.

"Like he said, there is no pregnant woman who isn't part of our coven here," I snap. "If you can't give me Gabriel's location, you're of no use to me or my family."

"Your mother's location, then, as a token of goodwill—"

I crouch, eye to eye with the man. "You're too late for bargaining chips. My mother is here. Someone in your ranks let her go, and she's currently debriefing my father, the king, on what happened to her. You will die shortly, I assume, unless you're of some use to us. So, I'll ask you again, where is Gabriel?"

His nostrils flare like he's trying to pick up a scent on me.

Evander catches this and puts a hand on shoulder in a command to rise and back away, and I do.

The man narrows his eyes, a crooked smile tugging at the corners of his bloodied mouth. "You smell like milk and a baby."

"I'm a midwife," I rasp, but the nerves in my tone are clear enough.

His smile grows. "Lucky for the Draven woman, I guess."

I turn from him before my concern can blossom across my face and hurry from the room. I close my eyes as I cross the threshold, and an echoing snap cuts through the air–the sound of flesh on flesh. I can almost feel the burn of the slap Evander laid across the prisoners face on my own skin as I walk blindly down the hall and down the stairs, holding my breath until I finally reach the blaring sunlight.

Evander is behind me in a few seconds but doesn't stop me. He silently follows me through the streets–past the freshly reopened store fronts and families throwing open their shutters as they clean the battle debris from their townhomes.

He doesn't say a word until we're at the steps leading up to the castle.

"Kenna, he could be talking about anyone."

"You know he's not. You know he's talking about Brie's mother–"

"You are Brie's mother now," he cuts in, grasping my shoulders and whirling me to face him. "She is ours. You heard him–her mother was nothing but a slave. Her coming here, seeking the help of our healers, was her final gift to that child."

"What if they take her?" I whisper, fear clouding every sense.

He drags me against his chest. "I won't allow it."

Groups of people walk up and down the stairs, the city having returned to its usual bustle.

We have no privacy here, and this conversation can't continue in the open.

"Have you been summoned by your parents yet?" he asks.

I shake my head.

"Come on," he says, knitting his fingers in mine.

3 9

TELLING ELLA

Kenna

THE WILLOW TREE wasn't touched during the battle. I'm not sure how I would have felt if we'd walked up and found it destroyed. Some of the tension in my chest eases as Evander parts the curtain of branches and ushers me inside the shaded haven of our youth.

My gaze sweeps over the cool, shady clearing before I turn to my mate and finally let out a deep breath. It seems like I've been holding it since I woke up this morning.

"What do we do?"

Evander paces with his hands tucked in his pockets, his brow pinched in thought. "You and Brie will go to Veiled Valley, immediately."

"But–"

"It's the best option other than sending you both to Maatua," he cuts in.

I rest my back against the tree trunk, crossing my arms under my breasts. "I won't just run away and let others fight my battles. I've spent my entire life doing that!"

"We have to think about Brie now," he says, meeting my eyes. "And our future children."

"Future children?" I murmur, furrowing my brows. "It's a little early to be thinking like that, isn't it?"

"It's a little early to have a newborn under our care after being mated for only a few days, but that's our reality, and we have to be realistic. We can send Brie away, if you'd prefer."

"No!"

"Even to be with your family in Maatua? Gabriel might be able to jump, but not that far. I'd bet my life on it."

"She was born alone in this world, and I won't put her in that position again." My heart squeezes tight as Evander edges toward me. "This isn't fair to her."

"If the Draven Coven is keeping women like cattle and willing to risk battle to keep them, and the children, under lock and key, then we need to do something, Kenna."

Everything hurts. My head pounds as Evander sinks into the grass, stretching out his legs. His shoulders slump. It's a rare moment, I realize. He is so practiced in the art of wearing masks, just like me. But for a second, he lets that mask slip, showing me his real emotions.

He's stressed. Tried, anxious, and on the verge of breaking.

Just like me.

"If I go away, what will you do?"

"That's not up to me. Your mother's return means my mission in Crescent Falls might not be going forward. It depends on whatever information she relays to your dad."

"So you'll let my parents dictate our next move?"

"They're your parents, but they're my king and queen. If the Allied Kingdoms are facing a long, drawn out war with the Dravens, then we need to be prepared to be separated for a while."

This wasn't supposed to happen. Just a few weeks ago, I was in Crescent Falls looking for my mate while the timer ran out on my freedom. Evander was also on a timer, counting his days in the Ghosts, and preparing to rule beside me in Veiled Valley.

We were going to be together again regardless of our feelings.

Now....

"I can't lose you." My heart shatters as his emerald eyes lock on mine. Grief courses through my body, making me feel weak and sick to my stomach. "Not now. Not ever. I can't–we haven't had enough time."

"You're not going to lose me." He moves to his knees as I walk toward him.

"Promise me," I demand, kneeling in front of him. He takes my hand, tracing the lines on my palm.

I have a long love line. It stretches across the surface of my hand, strong and steady.

Some say it's the silliest kind of magic. Even wise, old witches in the coven don't also put stock in the ancient art of tea leaves and palm reading.

But I've kept that hope in my back pocket for years now.... Hope that I'd find my mate and get a lifetime with him.

My mate is a warrior, though.

His touch moves from my hand to my forearm. His fingers glide over my skin, bunching up my sleeves. "I love you. Whatever happens next, know that I'll return to you."

Tears sting my eyes. "I want you whole," I whisper, sniffling. "Not in a casket."

A soft smile brushes over his mouth. "They'd have to catch me to kill me, Kenna."

He takes me into his arms, nestling me against his chest.

We sit there for a long time–long enough that I start to feel prickling in my legs from lack of use and the obvious, gnawing hunger from missing breakfast.

I feel a slight tickle deep in my brain that's wholly familiar.

"I'm being summoned," I tell him, my eyes closed, and my entire body relaxed in his touch.

"Damn. I was just thinking about how much I'd like to lay you down in the grass and see what you look like with just the sun on your skin."

Heat blossoms throughout my body as he absently strokes down my side. "I'm sure they want to see you, too."

He groans softly as I untangle myself from him. "I'm going to go get Brie and introduce her to my mom," he says.

"Maybe... do you think our moms know what happened... between us?" I find it hard to believe that my dad, given his freak-out over Evander and I being mates and acting on our bond, told my mom anything about it.

"Well," Evander says, standing and dusting off his pants., "they're about to find out, aren't they?"

I sigh, my stomach in knots. "Maybe we shouldn't say anything."

"Us being mates is the least of their problems. Come on." He takes my hand, pulling me after him.

We walk back to the castle together, neither of us saying much. My brain is wrapped in anxiety that slithers over my body like a snake. Evander notices, tugging me to a stop in one of the narrow corridors on the first floor of the castle, near my mom's office. "We're going out tonight," he says.

"What?" I laugh. "Like, out to dinner?"

He leans down, brushing his words over the top of my ear, "You need to shift, Kenna. You need to stretch those powers. You're burning out. You're wound so tight, and I can sense the tension in your body right now, in your powers. I'm going to take you out, into the woods, along the ridges and in the valleys we used to run in as children, and you're going to shift with me."

He presses a kiss to my temple and starts to pull away, but I grab his shirt, yanking him back to me.

His soft chuckle ignites a fresh wave of desire as he pins me against the wall and kisses me tenderly.

I melt in his arms. For a single second, nothing else matters but this, but then someone softly clears their throat.

My cheeks flame as Evander sighs, turning to face his dad.

Great.

"Evander," Granger says like he's holding back either a laugh or a groan. "King Ryatt would like to speak to you."

"Of course, he would," Evander grumbles, running his fingers through his hair. "His office, I assume?"

Granger nods, but his eyes, so like his son's, slide to mine.

Evander lets me go and walks away without another word. I linger in the hallway, rocking on my heels.

How embarrassing. We have absolutely no privacy, even in this enormous castle. Suddenly, going to Veiled Valley as soon as possible is exactly what I want.

Granger steps toward me with his hands tucked behind his back. He bows his head slightly, looking more than a little uncomfortable, but says, "Congratulations. I am honored to have you in our family, Kenna."

"Oh, thanks," I whisper, surprised. "You're–you're not mad?"

"No, of course not. Amanda and I are delighted. It was the best news to come home to after everything that happened."

A weight lifts off my shoulders. "Good. Good… so my mom knows?"

"Of course." If Granger were capable of laughing, I'm sure he would be. He looks incredibly serious as he says, "Your dad is the only person opposed."

"Great, well… where is my mom?" I shift uncomfortably from foot to foot.

Granger watches me for a moment, unsure if he should say what's obviously on his mind, but eventually motions me to follow him.

"She's resting. She and Amanda refused to see a healer, rest, or eat before telling us what happened. She's in here. "

"I don't want to bother her," I say, halting my progress down the hallway leading to my parents' private rooms. "I–I should be helping the other healers, anyway–"

"Our warriors are starting to move people out of the castle and back into homes in the city. The wounded are being moved in a few days, once the hospital roof is mended. I assure you, there isn't much for you to do right now other than see your mom."

"Okay…."

I continue to follow him but wring my hands. I'm not sure I even want to know what happened. Would I have ever put myself in her position? Sacrificed myself for my kingdom, allowing myself to get kidnapped and taken into the lair of the enemy?

I like to think I would, but my mom is... everything I'm not. Strong, brave, and capable.

And all the while, I've been here, healing the wounded and rolling in the sheets with my mate.

I try to swallow past the lump in my throat but find it impossible as I reach her door and softly knock. Granger walks away as a maid opens the door and ushers me in.

"Is she asleep?" I ask.

"No, although King Ryatt would like her to be. She's writing letters."

"Letters?" I make a face, confused, and follow the maid through the sitting room to the bedroom door, which she promptly opens for me.

Mom sits at her desk, her head bent as she scribbles. She turns to look at me, a wave of relief washing over her tight expression. "Oh, thank the Goddess you're in one piece." She rises and runs to me, hugging me tight enough that I wince. "How are you? What happened during the Rite? How did you escape?"

"I–well, Evander was there–"

"I know." She sighs heavily as she steps away motioning for me to sit on the edge of the bed as she sinks back into her desk chair. Her room is decorated tastefully if not minimally. A mural of the night sky stretches across the ceiling, outlined by roping trim of muted silver. The walls are a deep red that makes the cream colored carpet seem slightly out of place, but it's a cozy room.

I cross my legs, picking my nails while she scribbles something else on an insanely high stack of paper. "Your dad said Evander found you in the old temple and got you out shortly after the attack began.

"Evander believed the Mystics were... working against us." I leave out the rest. She would know Evander and I performed the Rite. I'm sure Dad assumes we did, given that he found us in bed together after the battle.

"He was correct," she murmurs. "A few, at least. I dealt with it this morning. The outliers are dead or fled. We're missing at least one mystic right now."

"I'm sorry this happened, Mom."

"It'll be fine. My captivity was... enlightening."

I wait for her to tell me about it, but she continues scribbling on those papers. "What are you doing?"

"Writing to your uncle," she says under her breath.

"Why not use the mirror?"

She sighs, tapping her pen on the edge of her desk. "We don't know what Gabriel is fully capable of yet, if he's able to intercept our magic and spy, you know? So, your dad and I decided that we'll be sending correspondence to Isaac through your grandparents in Maatua."

"Then the borders are officially shut down?"

"Yes, they are." Her voice is edged like a fine blade. She's holding something back, some deeply rooted anger I'm actively trying to make sense of.

She's stressed. We all are.

I don't want to add to that, so I do what I do best.

Deflect.

Even if it means I'm about to rock her world.

"Evander and I are mates."

She looks at me over her shoulder with a smile. "Oh, I know. Trust me. Your dad about lost his mind." She chuckles, her eyes shining with joy. "I'm happy, sweetheart. So happy–"

"And we have a baby."

Mom's mouth pops open, her brow pinching tight. "You *what?*"

THIS IS YOUR GRANDDAUGHTER

Evander

RYATT ONLY WANTED to see me to tell me what I already know.

I'm not leaving yet, but if it were up to him, I'd be on the next ship sailing out from Tarsian into the uncharted sea south of Eastonia with no return date.

I'm needed. It's the only reason I'm still in Moonrise. While Ryatt is the king, he has commanders to appease, and all of those commanders are currently fighting over who gets to use the Ghosts.

"I'm not a fucking roofer," Flynn groans, squinting against the sun as he drops another box of singles on the roof we're currently patching.

"You look the part," Connor remarks from a few feet away, his brow damp with sweat and eyes shining in the setting sun.

Flynn scowls and wipes his face with the back of his hand, smearing tar across his cheek. "This is absolute bullshit. Where the fuck is Commander Artyom? I know this wasn't his idea."

Connor's eyes flicker to mine. He gives me a knowing smirk. "I take it your soon-to-be father-in-law didn't take so kindly to the news?"

Flynn belts a colorful string of curses as his hammer comes down on his thumb for what might be the fourth time in the last twenty minutes.

"He loves me," I say sarcastically, waving an arm around the tight roof overlooking the lake. A three story drop greets us below, and the warriors who dropped off our supplies *accidentally* took the ladder we used to get up here with them when they left.

We can get down. It'll take a while, but we're not going to be stuck up here forever. He must think a twisted ankle and bruised knees will keep me out of his daughter's bed.

I roll my eyes to the skyline where golden light reflects off the vibrant roofs and towers of the city center.

I told Kenna we'd shift tonight.

I'm not going to miss out on that.

"Why are we being punished for Evander's inability to keep his hands off the princess?" Flynn complains, flexing his bloodied hand. "One second, I was cozy in the Roguelands awaiting another opportunity to be stationed in Crescent Falls, and now I'm here, fixing the roof of a seafood restaurant."

"The Ghosts are still going to Crescent Falls," I murmur, but my attention is fixed on the building just a few feet away from the one we're perched on. A single open window leads into someone's kitchen. I gauge the distance, weighing my options.

"To find some girl?" Flynn shakes his head.

"She must be important," Connor adds.

I stare at them both. "I know as much as you know." It's true. I've told them everything. After leaving Kenna with my dad, I went to Ryatt's office as summoned, found out Connor, Flynn, and several Ghosts in my usual unit had just arrived in town, and was given my next mission.

That had turned out to be helping clean up the giant mess the Draven warriors left behind during their raid.

As far as I know, we're still going to Crescent Falls, but the mission is delayed now that Queen Ella is home and relaying what she learned to her mate.

Until then, we wait, which means I have more time with Kenna and Brie.

The sun lowers over the mountains at the edge of the lake and casts the sky in ribbons of the deepest pinks and purples, and I make my move.

"What the fuck are you doing, man?" Flynn says somewhere behind me as I rise from my knees and eye the distance between this roof and the window.

I look at Flynn and Connor over my shoulder. "I'll see you guys sometime tomorrow. I'm sure I'll have more news for you then. Right now, I have an appointment, and I'm late."

I take off at a sprint across the roof against the shouts of alarm from Connor and Flynn. I leap, resisting the urge to shift, and duck through the window while giving the three-story drop below me a single glance.

My feet hit the tiled floor hard enough the knick-knacks in the butter-colored kitchen rattle on impact.

Bowing slightly in apology at the older couple sitting at a nearby table eating dinner, I race through the snug apartment and out into the city center.

Night falls in earnest before I reach the castle. I enter through my family's private wing, which is quiet and empty. Mom and Dad must be with Ryatt and Ella, I'm guessing. Which might mean Kenna is with them, which means my plans to sneak her out to shift tonight might not come to fruition.

I check her rooms and find them just as empty, but as I'm starting to lose hope, I do a quick sweep of the infirmary.

My mate is dressed in a light cream dress with a white apron, her dark hair pulled back into a tight bun at the nape of her neck. She leans over an injured warrior as she speaks in soft tones to another healer–something about the dosage of herbs they're giving him. She straightens and turns around. I wonder if she can sense me nearby like I can when she's near.

I've been curious about what the mate bond feels like for her. For me, it's overwhelming. Like my entire body is tethered to hers. Every emotion, every feeling, every sense courses through our shared bond, and I feel it in full.

But I have no idea how she feels, whether my emotions mingle with her own. I try not to think about it, honestly. There is a small, insignificant part of me that harbors doubt because of the fact she can't, and never will, feel as strongly for me as I do for her.

But her smile as she meets my gaze melts any doubts.

She wipes her hands on her apron, rising on her toes to look over my shoulder as I approach.

"How'd you escape the recovery effort?" she asks in a teasing tone. "I heard whispers you were seen on a few roofs today."

"I was," I admit, resisting the urge to sweep her into my arms and run out the castle with her. "We had a date, though."

"Right." She unties her apron and bunches it in her hands as she leads me out of the infirmary, stopping to toss it in a laundry hamper at the very edge of the room. "There's something we need to do first, something my mom has been bugging me about."

"What's that?"

We walk side by side down a tight corridor leading back to the grand foyer–a servants corridor–and she pauses in a shadowed alcove. "I told my Mom about Brie." Her tone is slightly strained, which alarms me. Before I can say anything, she continues, "She wants to meet her, obviously. She's surprised, and I'm sure she's told your parents about our plans to adopt her. I told her Brie would be staying with the wet nurse until Dad releases you from your duties today in hopes she'd talk to him about how he's acting right now... but you obviously escaped purgatory on the rooftops."

"Your father has every right to not like me," I tell her, tucking my hands in my pants pockets. "I would do the same for Brie, I'm sure, if she were ever in love with someone who treated her the same way I treated you."

"You were protecting me. I understand that now–"

"I could have done things differently."

"Well," she smiles, toying with her dress. "You have the rest of your life to make it up to me, don't you?"

I smirk, and the playful expression behind her eyes makes me feel a little more relaxed about our current situation.

A few minutes later, Brie is in my arms, fed and asleep, and we're on the hunt for Ella. The massive castle's network of winding hallways and narrow stairwells were built in a time when an entire pack would live in one dwelling together. Dozens of rooms branch out before us as I follow Kenna upstairs to the private quarters belonging to her family.

My parents are there already. I knew they would be. The personal library of the royal family has always been a meeting point for them and Kenna's parents. I used to come here as a child and read or play quietly while our mothers conversed, but the colossal room that stretches four stories high and houses millions of books seems smaller than usual.

And much, much more crowded, especially as Ryatt rises from an armchair near the dormant fireplace with a glass of whiskey clutched so tightly in his hand his knuckles are white.

Dad leans against a bookshelf but straightens as Kenna closes the door behind us and takes my arm. I find myself clutching Brie a little tighter than I normally would.

Her soft pink cheeks crinkle as she yawns, her brow pinching together before she lets out a soft whine.

Mom stands overlooking a long table where Ella is sitting with at least a dozen books splayed open between them.

Everyone looks at us. Nobody says a word for what feels like a very long time.

I scan the room before landing on Ryatt. I look directly into his eyes for several seconds before slowly bowing my head in his direction.

Kenna stiffens beside me but clears her throat. "Hi, uhm... I thought now would be a good time to introduce everyone to your new grandchild–"

Mom and Ella rush away from the table in a flurry of vibrant fabric and noise. I can't think straight over the hushed murmurs of surprise and awe.

My eyes are still locked with Ryatt's, however. When Kenna tries to take Brie out of my arms, I tighten my grip on the baby on instinct.

Ryatt notices. He slightly narrows his eyes but relaxes his grip on his drink and turns to say something to my father.

"Let me have her, Evander. It's all right," Kenna whispers, giving me an exasperated smile as she takes Brie into her arms and rests her against her shoulder.

My mom has tears in her eyes as she and Ella pepper Kenna with questions. Kenna, in turn, tells them the story of how Brie came to be.

But she left one very important thing out.

"We believe Brie's mother and father were part of the Draven Coven."

Everyone in the room looks at me. Kenna's nostrils flare as she pats Brie's back, her eyes flicking to her mother's face.

Ella slowly turns her gaze from Kenna to me. "How do you know?"

Ryatt speaks from his armchair, "We need to speak to our daughter–alone."

Silence hugs the curved, wide room. I glance at my dad, still standing near Ryatt's side. He flexes his jaw as he nods and strides toward Mom, taking her by the arm.

Kenna steps into me, trying to lock her fingers with mine, but I shake my head. "The usual spot, tonight. I'll wait for you."

I reach for Brie, but Ryatt growls, "The baby stays here."

My mate's eyes narrow on her father as Ella whips to Ryatt. "What is your problem, Ryatt?"

"Come on, sweetheart," Mom says to me, giving me a little nudge to follow her and Dad out of the library.

I hold Kenna's gaze until the library door closes behind us with a snap.

"Are you going to continue allowing him to speak to us like that?" I ask Dad.

"He is our king, and Ryatt is my closest and dearest friend. You and Kenna have no idea what you're getting yourself into if that child belongs to the coven. We already have enough to deal with-"

"Not now, Granger," Mom sighs, roping her arm through mine. "Tell me about her, Ev. Tell me everything."

41

A RUN IN THE MOONLIGHT

Kenna

MY HEART IS in shambles as I walk up the slight rise to the willow tree. The forest groans all around me in a stiff breeze that promises cooler weather and storms tonight. It would be a welcome relief from the heat and a distraction from the raw conversation I just had with my parents about everything that happened and will soon happen.

I've been blessed to have never experienced the torment of war. Sure, small tangles and skirmishes have occurred during my parents' reign, but nothing like this. Nothing that promises what could be years of battle and bloodshed while Gabriel fights his way to my parents' throne.

He'll never take it. He'd have to overthrow the entire royal family in both kingdoms to succeed.

But he'll lay waste and leave bodies in his wake.

I move the branches out of the way and step inside the cool sanctuary of the willow.

"Evander?" I call out.

He steps out from behind the tree trunk, his hands tucked in his pockets. His gentle smile in my direction is the only glue holding me together as I hug myself and step toward him, heaving a breath. "We need to talk."

"I figured," he says, his voice soft and lighthearted despite the resigned look in his eyes. My lips part to start explaining what I just heard and now think, but he says, "If you've changed your mind about what kind of relationship you want with me, you just need to say so. I won't force you–"

"No!" I nearly shout, stopping short of him. I blush, then clear my throat, "No, it's not that at all."

I sink to the ground with my back against the tree trunk and close my eyes for a moment, breathing deeply. The rich, damp forest scent all around me mingles with Evander's warm vanilla and leather as he sits beside me, hugging his knees.

"It's about Brie," I tell him, my throat feeling tight. "My parents made some good points about our decision to adopt her as our own."

"Like, she doesn't have Firestone or Shadowsynger blood, and therefore can't inherit titles from Veiled Valley or the Firestone Throne of Eastonia?"

I open my eyes, meeting his gaze. "How come I never gave that any thought and you did?"

"Because the first thing on your mind when it comes to her is keeping her safe and loved now, not twenty years from now." He stretches out his legs and leans his head against the tree. "I had a similar conversation with my parents."

"They think this is all so abrupt, don't they?"

"My parents?" He looks down at me and smiles slightly, chuckling, "My parents got together during the Rite, remember? They were living together in Veiled Valley within a few days of that and expecting me to arrive in a matter of months."

"Oh, yeah." I let out my breath in a whoosh. "But they didn't take in a baby within days of being mated."

"They weren't at war."

He takes my hand, squeezing. "Brie is ours."

"I know, I just think… my dad made valid points about her future. She won't be my heir, Evander. Is this fair to her?"

"Is it fair for her to be with two people who can love her and raise her surrounded by family and protection?"

"You know what I mean."

"Are you reconsidering?"

"No, I'm not." I draw in a breath. "I'm not. I feel it in my soul that she's meant to be with us."

"Then what's bothering you?"

I close my eyes, screaming internally. "My dad is being a hard-headed jerk right now."

"He has every right to. His kingdom is under attack and his family threatened–"

"He has a serious problem with you!"

"I'm mated to his daughter. Of course he'd rather see me banished to another kingdom than accept it's time to let you go, Kenna." He shifts her weight, turning to face me. "Your dad doesn't scare me. He never has. His feelings toward me are surface level, all right? Deep down, he's probably elated that we're together, but I understand his current feelings because I feel the same way."

He tries to tuck my hair behind my ear and caress my cheek, but I pull away, asking, "What do you mean by that?"

"He was separated from his mate, and she was in danger. His home was attacked, and he was injured. His family is at risk, and he's scared, Kenna."

My dad is never scared. At least, I've never thought so. But I look into my mate's eyes and see the stark compassion there.

"Are you scared?"

"Yeah, I am. I'm not scared to go into battle. I'm not scared of the idea of putting my life on the line to protect my family and my king-dom. But I'm scared of what this means for you, and our daughter, and our future together. If your dad needs to take his frustrations out on anyone, I'd rather it be me than anyone else. I can handle it." He shakes my shoulders a little, lowering his forehead to mine. "And we can handle raising Brie. One day, when she's old enough to understand, we'll tell her everything. She'll have freedoms neither of us had, Kenna. Freedom to choose her own path. That's a blessing in itself."

I fight the urge to cry. Evander's right. Sometimes it's incredibly annoying how often he's right, but still....

He takes me by the chin and forces me to look at him. "Now, we have something we need to do."

I sigh. "Shift?"

He nods. "It's time."

"I don't know if I can just... shift like you can. When I shifted a few days ago it was because I was—I was scared, I think. It just happened."

"You can shift because you marked me. You're mated now; that's an exclusively shifter trait. Our powers are bound."

"I didn't realize you paid attention in your Wolf Arts classes."

He smirks, his eyes glistening like raw gems in the moonlight drifting through the willow branches.

"We'll take it slow, okay?"

Under the protection of the willow, we slowly undress. Evander doesn't shy away from staring as I remove my clothes. In fact, he gathers them up and folds them neatly next to his, murmuring encouragement as I try, and try, to ignite those lupine powers again.

I wonder how it feels for him, being able to shift whenever and wherever he wants. He can shift into two creatures, which is insanely rare. Unfathomable, really. Tonight, he chooses his wolf, and a part of me is disappointed.

When we were kids, he came into his fox powers. It made games of chase practically impossible. I used to watch from the hedges, picking berries and wild herbs with Grandma Cressendra while Amanda coached Evander in his new found ability, and felt more than jealous of their stealth and speed.

But they might be the only fox shifters in the world, and Evander grew up hiding that side of himself, just like his mom did.

But his wolf... it's glorious. Golden with copper undertones that shimmer in the moonlight.

He looks down at me, his eyes still the same deep shade of green, and patiently waits.

I look down at my hands—at the shadows curling around my fingers—and feel…

'Dig deep,' he says. 'It'll happen.'

'My other powers won't let it overwhelm them.'

'Remind those powers who's in control, Kenna.'

I look up at him again as I take a deep, restorative breath, and strain my senses, burying my powers of fire and shadow as deep as I can and willing my wolf to take over.

I'm not sure how to describe the feeling of whole-body transformation. It's like when my shadow takes over. It's not totally painless, but it doesn't hurt, either. It's like every bone in my body goes to mush, and my muscles contract then relax, and a wave of pleasure wraps its way around every inch of my skin in ribbons that tighten and flex, building something new.

I hear Evander's thankful exclamations through the bond over the blood thrumming in my ears—ears that can suddenly hear everything. I pick up scents I never thought possible—flowers and trees miles away, the smell of other wolves and people nearby, Evander….

'Open your eyes,' he commands, so I do.

I'm no longer standing straight up on two legs. My hands and feet have been replaced with taloned paws of the darkest black. A slight breeze whispers through my fur, tickling the skin beneath, but I'm warm. Warmer than I've ever been.

Before I can question it, Evander turns and runs at a speed that doesn't seem possible.

'Follow me,' he says, the words a gentle, yet commanding, hum through my mind and body, and then a slight tug in my chest has my paws moving.

I feel like a baby deer or toddler just learning to run. I trip over my own feet as I follow Evander through the woods, bumping into trees and getting tangled in heather and alder crops.

My vision eventually catches up with the transformation and the dark night shifts to what could be a clear, cloudless day. Night-vision, basically. How strange. Why do people even bother shifting back to their human forms when we could just be... this?

By the time we've put a few miles between us and Moonrise, I've gotten the hang of being on all fours. I leap over a creek, marveling at how the water shines like diamonds, and land gracefully instead of skidding to a stop on my side.

Soon, I'm zigzagging through the forest, jumping over boulders and testing my stealth.

All while Evander simply jogs ahead, occasionally looking over his shoulder to make sure I'm still within sight and not desperately tangled in vines or bramble bushes.

I've never been this far in the forest before. Moonrise is surrounded by dense woods that can easily disorient any rogue travelers. I know we must be approaching the edge of the wards surrounding Moonrise, but Evander keeps going.

He says nothing to me, likely to keep me focused on learning how to navigate the world in this new body. We dip down into a shallow mountain valley where the moonlight illuminates a lake high above the distant city. The water shines a bright silver, and a waterfall feeds the lake, sending a soft hum of movement through the still night air.

I look up at the stars as I follow Evander to the lake, crossing a field of boulders left behind by an ancient glacier.

I trip, twisting my front right paw. Evander lets out a snort, and I turn to look up at him.

'We're almost there.'

I trot after him, more carefully this time, until we reach the lake's edge.

I think we're about to stop, but he skirts the lake, walking along the smooth, ancient rocks I wonder if anyone other than us has touched.

'Where are we going?' I ask through the mind-link.

'You'll see. This is probably my favorite place to be... other than between your legs.' If he could wink at me right now, I'm sure he would.

If I could blush, my entire face would be bright red, but his flirty comment has heat and desire spreading through my body like wildfire.

Evander notices and looks over his shoulder at me once more, his eyes alight, but then he cuts behind the waterfall and disappears.

For a moment, I hesitate. I really don't want to be in another cave right now, not after the battle that ensued while Evander and I were underground during the Rite.

But I follow him anyway, and once I pass behind the cold spray of the falls and see what he brought me here to experience, I gasp.

My entire body ripples with energy as my human form takes over. I don't know how to control that aspect yet, obviously, and apparently a little bit of emotion is all it takes to cause the transformation.

Naked, my skin prickling with the cold air coming off the falls at my back, I look around. My mouth parts as my eyes dance with shimmering light.

It's a small, shallow cave, but the walls aren't pure, raw earth.

Crystals coat every surface. Moonlight cuts through the falls and makes the crystals look like they're dancing.

And Evander stands in his wolf form in the center of it all.

I meet his eyes and can't stop the delirious smile from stretching across my face. "How long have you known about this place?"

He shifts back to his human form in a soft flash of light and stalks toward me. "Since the day after your sixteenth birthday," he replies, running his fingertips over my upper arms. "I left Moonrise and just ran, ran until I found this lake. I found this place and wondered if I'd ever have a chance to bring you here."

"It's so beautiful," I gasp, but the words turn to a gentle moan as he leans down to brush his lips across my temple and the top of my ear.

"You did so well," he rasps, his touch on my skin shifting to something harder and more demanding.

And my body responds.

We're alone. Finally.

"Kiss me," I command, and his eyes darken with heat.

4 2

———

AN OPEN WINDOW

Kenna

EVANDER'S MOUTH crashes against mine. The roar of the waterfall behind us fades to nothing but a gentle hum as the sound of his pleasure–a low, guttural growl–fills my ears and blur my senses.

We're both stark naked and slightly sweaty from shifting. There's nothing between us now–nothing stopping us from just being with each other.

He picks me up and kneels with me in his lap, his hands on my hips to hold me in place.

"You're so beautiful when you shift," he whispers, nipping the shell of my ear. "Like a pure, moonless night."

His kisses dust over my jaw and neck, igniting a fire in my body I never want to stanch. I wiggle my hips, grinding against him, making mewling, desperate sounds of desire as his skin brushes over mine.

I'm aching for him. Every touch and smooth, heat-filled word out of his mouth sends me into a frenzy.

I'm having a hard time calming down and being in the moment

right now. All I want is him inside of me. I want him rough and demanding. I want him to bite me—to mark me—again and again.

He lets out a low chuckle when I bite down on his shoulder in emphasis. "We'll play later," he says softly, his voice low and full of desire. "You're worked up from shifting. It's a natural response–"

I bite down harder, and he winces. "Kenna," he groans, clutching my hips a little harder. The head of his cock presses against my entrance, but he holds me in place, refusing to allow me to slide onto him like I want to.

"Please, Evander?" I whimper, giving him my best doe-eyes.

It doesn't work on him.

He smirks, kissing me slowly, taking his sweet time.

All while I beg and pant and desperately try to chase any friction while he teases me with his cock.

"You're so wet," he says, sliding me over his shaft. He lets out a very satisfied groan.

"Please?" I beg again, on the verge of biting him once more. I don't know what's gotten into me, but if he doesn't give me what I want now, I might cry.

I've never felt like this before. It's hard to describe, really. It's like all of my senses are honed on him and what he can do to me, the pleasure he can give, and how it feels to have him dominating me in every way.

This, I realize, is a mate thing.

Right now, my wolf powers are still in total control.

I can feel the mate bond at its full strength.

How do people live like this? Doesn't it get in the way of their daily lives?

I sink my nails into his back as he rocks his hips against mine.

"I can't take it anymore," I whisper. "I need you."

He kisses me again, harder this time, and I match his energy. His tongue swirls over mine, drawing out a moan from my lips as he clutches me to his chest. But then he pulls away and flips me over so quickly I let out a sharp yelp.

"On your knees, mate."

My heart rate skyrockets. I obey, my gaze fixed on the crystalline floor that bites into my knees as I kneel with my back to him.

I feel him rise up behind me, his hand on the small of my back as he pushes me forward to rest my weight on my elbows.

I am totally exposed to him at this angle. His hands clutch my hips, squeezing. "Good girl."

My breath comes in a rush as I lean down further until my breasts graze the ground. One of his hands gathers my hair, twisting it tight. The other smooths over the globes of my ass in a gentle caress.

I slowly look at him over my shoulder and my heart skips a beat.

He doesn't meet my eyes. He's transfixed–looking at me, my body, like he's in a trance.

His gaze lowers to mine. His eyes are cloudy with desire and darker than I've ever seen them, but the corner of his mouth twitches into a dark, ruthless smile.

"Please?" I mouth, shaking with anticipation.

His lips part as he grazes the head of his cock over my pussy once, twice, then sinks into me in a single, hard thrust.

This is what he's always wanted but could never voice. My complete submission.

I'm more than willing to give it to him.

"Gods," he growls, closing his eyes as he thrusts into me, his dick stretching me to the point I'm dizzy with pleasure. He hits that spot that makes me start babbling incoherently, and the echoes of my pleasure bounce off the walls, mingling with the sound of his thighs hitting the back of mine.

His grip on my hair is tight enough to sting but the pain only makes this sweeter. I close my eyes, moaning his name.

It's a white-hot kind of pleasure I'm unprepared for. My body shakes, and I start to lower myself until my belly hits the cold, slightly damp crystal floor.

He follows, lost in his own pleasure, until he's covering me with his body and pumping into me fast and hard.

"You feel so good," he rasps against my ear, groaning and cursing. "Fuck, Kenna, I'm not going to last much longer–"

With gritted teeth, he pulls out, flips me over onto my back, and enters me again before I have a chance to catch up to his movements. He grips the back of my thigh, drawing my knee up to give him deeper access, and buries his face between my breasts.

"Evander!" I scream, choking on his name as a climax builds at a rate I hadn't been expecting. My entire body is on fire–my muscles so tight I can barely breathe.

His tongue darts over my left nipple before he sucks it into his mouth, grazing the tender skin with his teeth.

I let out my breath in a hiss and wrap my arms around his neck, canting my hips to meet him thrust for thrust.

"I'm–I'm going to come–" I manage to say, breathless, closing my eyes as that delicious tension snaps, and my climax ripples through my body like a rogue wave breaking against the shore.

He gasps, wrapping an arm around me to push me into his chest, and in one final thrust, he completely unravels at the same moment I do.

His slow, rhythmic thrusts fill me with warmth. My muscles spasm, squeezing him tight.

He looks down at me as if in a haze. We lay like that for several seconds–panting–trying to catch our breath.

But then he kisses me so tenderly tears prickle along my lower lashes. I run my hand up his neck, into his hair.

"I love you," he whispers against my lips.

"I love you," I tell him, meaning every word.

I feel it in my soul. I can feel the fine threads of our bond humming with delight.

My mate.

I found him, after all this time.

I'll never get over it, I'm sure.

We spend the next hours lying in each other's arms talking about everything and nothing at all.

When the sun begins to rise, we shift, and make our way home.

We change back into our clothes beneath the willow and return to the castle as the first rays of morning sun dust over the rooftops.

Together, we fetch Brie from the nursing mother who's been pumping milk and breastfeeding her at night and take her to the informal dining room on the second floor.

Evander mind-links with his parents to meet him there, as do I, and as we sit down to eat, they all join us for a quiet, slightly tense forced-breakfast.

But I'm sitting next to Evander, my knee resting against his thigh under the table. He's holding Brie in his arms while she sleeps with her chubby cheek squished against his arm.

When he speaks, or laughs, she smiles.

My heart has never been so full.

But our perfect night and near-perfect morning couldn't be all rainbows and sunshine.

"The Ghosts are required at the barracks," Dad says from the head of the table where he's been sulking all breakfast. "Alpha Sydney is preparing to return to Crescent Falls with his warriors to begin the search for the Draven woman, Gabriel's sister."

I glance at Evander, then my mom, taking Brie in my arms. She blinks up at me, frowning a bit when she realizes Evander isn't holding her anymore.

"Not Gabriel's sister." Mom clears her throat and looks directly at me. "We have a meeting with Alpha Jaxon and his son using the mirror in half an hour."

"I thought we weren't using the mirror anymore?" I sit up a little straighter.

"I made a deal with Atticus," she begins, her eyes sweeping the table. I notice Amanda looking down at her plate, her expression unreadable. "He let me go in exchange for our help finding his daughter... Gabriel is his nephew."

I look at Evander. In the days since Mom's return, I've only heard parts of the truth, I realize. Now, I'm getting the full story. She tells me what she learned when she was held hostage.

"Atticus is imprisoned in Tarsian, in Alpha Jaxon's pack," Mom concludes. "Kenna, I want you to come to this meeting with me."

"I will," I say, my head spinning.

Mary, the maid, meekly slides through the door at the edge of the room. She blushes when all eyes turn on her. "Uhm, I'm very sorry, Your Majesties. I'm here to put the baby down for her nap."

"Oh," I murmur, wondering how much time I've lost track of after sitting here listening to my mom tell me about Gabriel, his parentage, his use of ancient relics to suck powers from people, and our plan moving forward.

Even Evander is quiet and lost in thought as Mary approaches the table. I stand, laying a fussy Brie in her arms. "Put her down in my room, please. I'll be there in about an hour."

Mary nods and walks away with Brie. Evander tracks her movements before rising, followed by Granger, and then my dad.

Evander squeezes my shoulder and leans down, whispering, "I'll see you later this evening."

"Okay," I reply, but an uneasy feeling tightens my chest as he walks away with the rest of the men.

Amanda mentions something about needing to meet with the wives of the warriors who lost their lives during the battle and excuses herself, leaving me and my mother alone.

I hate using the mirror. Sure, it's an easy way to communicate with our family across the border, but talking to Alpha Jaxon and his son and heir, Cole, is never fun.

Cole is handsome but cold and just as stern and emotionless as his father.

I stand in Mom's office, just behind her, listening to them argue about what's to be done, how many warriors to add to their armies, and how to stop the Draven Coven from breaching the border into Crescent Falls.

All the while, I find myself staring Cole down. He's my age, maybe a few years older. One day, he'll be King of Tarsian while I'll be Queen of Eastonia. One day, we'll have to be allies.

He sneers at me. I sneer back.

"Atticus is not available," Alpha Jaxon says shortly. "He's losing his mind, I'm afraid."

"What do you mean?" Mom asks skeptically.

"Our healers believe he might have been slowly poisoned, likely with nothing more than wolfsbane, but he's detoxing, essentially, and having hallucinations."

"Alert me when he's well again," Mom grumbles, waving a hand in dismissal. "I expected something like this. Atticus might be male, but he has witch powers. It's likely Gabriel was poisoning him to keep him subdued."

Jaxon nods, and without further conversation, his image in the mirror disappears.

I shiver involuntarily. "I really don't like him."

"I don't mind Jaxon," Mom smirks. "Cole, on the other hand, is a dickhead."

I snort a laugh and follow her out of her office, but I expect her to turn to her own quarters, or, better yet, go back into the depths of the castle to continue her duties as queen for the day, but she follows me instead.

"What are you doing?" I ask. I'm anxious to get back to Brie. That meeting took longer than I expected, and there's still so much to do today.

"I have some time before I meet with the mystics we have under lock and key in Old Moonrise," she says with a shrug. "I thought I'd spend some time with you and Brie for a little while, if that's okay. Your grandma Isla wants to meet her soon."

"You told her?"

"She sensed something new was happening within the family," Mom smiles. "I didn't really have to tell her much about it. She's very excited to meet your daughter."

A weight lifts off my chest. At least Mom is on board with this.

But that nagging, uncomfortable feeling hits me again when we walk through my quarters. No maid met us at the door. It's silent in here, actually, save for a soft breeze coming through an... *open* window in my bedroom.

I halt as unease crushes me from the inside out.

Brie's bassinet is empty.

A crimson stain… blood. There's a trail of blood leading from the bassinet to the window where–where the balcony is–

Mom's powers burst to life as she shoves me behind her.

Mary is lying lifeless on the balcony, Brie's blanket clutched in her arms.

43

UNDER THE WARDS

Evander

My mind is a roaring, tangled mass of chaos as I tear through the castle with Kenna at my side. It's full night—nearly 3:00 AM—but the castle is alight with activity as warriors canvass every inch of every room and winding hallway.

Kenna's tears have dried, but her eyes are wide and hollow as I guide her to my family's wing, neither of us saying a word.

Brie was taken last night, and so far, she hasn't been found. A maid is dead—killed in my mate's bedroom. Neither of us have eaten or slept.

Worse yet, the prisoner I interviewed in the barracks is gone as well.

All signs point to the Draven Coven for the kidnapping and murder.

I yank Kenna into the foyer of my family's quarters. It's quiet—my parents are out, probably sitting in Ella's office or Ryatt's war room deciding what needs to be done, but I'm sick of waiting.

Kenna's despair is like a blade in my chest.

I take her upstairs into my bedroom which hasn't changed at all since I was a young teenager and I left home for training. I haven't been home much at all since then.

I shut the door behind us and immediately start gathering supplies. Extra clothes, extra weapons, coins and a variety of medicines and herbs.

Kenna watches me in total silence. She doesn't question why I've kept a stash of these things hidden around my childhood room. Deep down, we both understand the reasoning behind this. Being royal comes at a cost, and thankfully there were only a few times when some threat had our families packing up in the middle of the night to put the children into hiding.

This is different, though.

"They're going to know we've left," Kenna says absently. Her normally sunny, bright voice is completely robbed of feeling as she crosses her arms under her chest and hugs herself tight. "We can't leave the castle without someone seeing us."

"It doesn't matter," I tell her, stuffing my supplies in a backpack designed to be worn while in wolf form. "Brie is probably dozens of miles away by now. We've waited too long." In her parents' defense, with Ryatt's wards in place, it should have been impossible for anyone to pass through the wards around Moonrise undetected. Something is wrong, though. The hundred or so miles that surround Moonrise and fall under Ryatt's protection have been canvassed thoroughly.

I know, because I've been out there in the woods looking for my daughter since the moment I heard the news.

"Don't ask me to stay behind."

I zip the backpack and turn to her, holding her gaze. She's shaking, picking at her shirt, and anxiety oozes off her, turning the air in the room to ice.

"You're not staying behind. I need you," I tell her, meaning every word. "But I don't know what we're walking into. This is obviously a trap, Kenna. They know we're going after her. They know Brie was in our care, or at least the care of the royal family, and knew someone would come looking for her." I hike the backpack over my shoulder.

"We need to be prepared for the worst. You need to be prepared to fight."

She sucks in a breath. "I'm prepared."

"Good." I search her eyes, hating every second of this. I don't want her to go, to be in danger, but I can't stomach leaving her behind.

Kenna's a ball of nervous energy when we leave the castle, passing guards and frantic maids. We don't reply when people shout at us to ask where we're going. They should know, and when the sun rises, and we're no longer in Moonrise, our families will know as well.

By then, we'll be long gone because Kenna has a secret.

"SHE'S NOT FAR," Kenna says as she pulls the hood of her cloak over her head. Her eyes shine a molten silver in the darkness as her powers surge.

She's bonded with Brie. She holds her in her heart, and somehow, her powers are honed in on Brie like a tracking device.

But we're deep in the woods now. We haven't shifted yet. We've passed a few patrols, but now that the sun is starting to rise, the past mile or so has been quiet and empty of others.

I step into a clearing on the very edge of Ryatt's ward. I can feel the change in the air as we near the magic, invisible wall. Stepping through it is impossible. Without permission to leave the Wards, we'd end up walking in a circle, growing more and more disoriented.

I'm not confident Kenna and I will be able to leave Moonrise. If Brie has been taken across the wards somehow, there's nothing we can do without getting Ryatt involved.

I really don't want to have to do that.

"I don't understand," Kenna whispers, looking around. A creek burbles nearby. A log-jam forms a small, clear pond that's surface ripples with small fish in the ever growing morning light reaching through the dense canopy of trees.

I set my pack down and scan the area. No scents of other wolves or warriors. The birds chirp and sing as the first rays of light touch their wings, oblivious to any nearby threats.

"What's wrong?" I ask her.

Her face is cast in shadow beneath her hood as she turns to me, defeated. "I can't feel her as strongly, but I feel like she's—she's been here. Right here." She points to the ground. "Then she just vanished. Her scent isn't strong here. I can't pick it up."

"Me neither," I admit, perplexed. "There's no way they could have carried her through the wards. Ryatt would have been notified someone was trying to leave."

A crunching sound echoes through the woods, and I immediately sense a new presence.

"What are you doing here?" Kenna breathes, startled, as Sydney edges out of the woods in a cloak, dressed for a journey.

His blue eyes sweep over Kenna as if looking for injuries, and when his gaze cuts to mine, I glare.

"I thought you were in the Roguelands."

"I was. I asked your father to spirit me back to Moonrise when I heard what happened. I was about to leave for the border to return to Crescent Falls with my men, but this was more important."

I guess this is perfect timing then.

"Do you have your compass?"

Kenna looks between us. Sydney sighs. "I've already tried. It doesn't work. I thought the two of you had already crossed, so I tested the wards. They're even stronger than before after what happened in the castle. I heard your voices and—"

"You came here to help us?" Kenna says, looking a little shocked.

I know things have been tense between them since Ryatt lit into her about our relationship. She made it sound like Sydney took Ryatt's side, but I know that's not the case. Sydney is simply stuck in the middle, a prince of Crescent Falls essentially trapped in Eastonia.

"Your parents don't know you're out here, do they?" he asks her.

She shakes her head.

I say, "We waited all day for someone to act. Queen Ella already sent word to the Alphas of the Roguelands and Jaxon of

Tarsian about Brie's disappearance and the murder. King Ryatt spent the day preparing for a counter attack on the Draven Coven."

"And Evander and the Ghosts in Moonrise spent the day looking for our baby," Kenna whimpers.

My heart wrenches, but I keep my gaze steady on Sydney's face.

He looks at me and a memory floods my mind. We're boys, running through the woods together. Ryan didn't want to come with us and chose to stay behind to be doted on by our mothers during one of Kenna's family vacations here.

We'd gotten lost for a while, having gone so far from the city-center that we ended up in these very woods.

"The tunnels," we say in unison.

"What?" Kenna asks, but Sydney and I are already moving. I grab my pack, motioning for Kenna to follow.

I can't believe I'd forgotten about the tunnels. In my defense, it's been fifteen years, at least, since the day Sydney and I found them but were too scared to explore.

It takes another thirty minutes to reach the strange, leaning trees about two miles up the creek. The forest is denser here. The morning light barely touches the forest floor as I follow Sydney through the trees to a place where the trees have been bent at odd angles to create a strange, wooden tunnel.

Kenna halts when she sees it. It's just as eerie as the time Sydney and I stumbled across it as children.

He is pleased as he pants and rests his hands on his knees. "I can't believe I didn't think of this."

"I know," I say, heaving a breath.

Poor Kenna is out of breath behind us after thirty minutes of matching our pace. "What is this place? I don't like it."

"Eastonia is covered in old ruins and temples. A lot of them are connected by intricate tunnel systems," Sydney begins.

"From the time of the fall of the Firestone queens. The various covens built the tunnels as means of escape in times of war," I add.

Moonrise has over a dozen ancient, buried temples dotting its territory. Most have been explored, but this place... It's wholly untouched.

"It's like a vortex into another world," Kenna breathes, her feet firmly planted in place as she looks through the tunnel formed from bent trees. "I don't like it."

"This is the only plausible way they escaped through the wards. If there's an old ruin down there, there will be tunnels." Sydney takes a few steps forward.

"They went under the wards?" Kenna doesn't sound like she believes this for a second.

"We need to try," I tell her. "It's the only option we have."

Kenna nods, her eyes downcast to her hands. I watch her, noticing the lines of grief and pain around her puffy eyes–eyes red from crying.

It's been the worst day.

I don't know how to comfort her.

I only know that I won't stop until Brie is safe in her arms, and they're both on a ship to Maatua to wait out this ever nearing war.

Movement over the top of her head catches my eye a moment too late.

"Kenna, run!" I shout, swinging my pack from my shoulders as my wolf form takes hold and I shift, my clothes shredding to ribbons. Six wolves tear toward us through the trees, jaws slack and teeth gleaming in the morning sunlight.

But they're not just wolves.

Hellhounds. All six of them. Their bodies are mangled and furless, their eyes shining with the powers of the witches who command them.

Sydney shifts and races forward, putting himself between the hellhounds and Kenna.

She doesn't move. Her eyes dart to mine.

'Go. Go through the tunnels. Follow that sense you have about Brie, and find her. I'll hold them off,' I beg her.

Kenna's expression is pained as I leap forward and come to

Sydney's side. The hellhounds reach the clearing and bound toward us.

I don't see any witches, but they have to be nearby.

Or these creatures have been separated from their masters by the wards somehow, and they're out for blood.

'Sydney,' I say through the mind-link as the hellhounds circle us, 'we're going to let them take us.'

'I know,' he says. 'Is she gone?'

I look over my shoulder at the tunnel.

Kenna is nowhere to be seen.

44

ASHES TO ASHES

Kenna

I HOLD my breath as I run through the dark, my cloak billowing out behind me like a crimson curtain. The tunnel of gnarled, bent trees is longer and tighter than I anticipated, and I have to crawl on all fours toward the end.

But the tunnel doesn't drop into the inky dark underground as expected. I trip, falling down a shallow ledge and land hard on my knees.

The tunnel entrance is a few feet above me, hidden in a tangle of heather and bramble bushes, but I'm still wholly in the forest.

But it's changed. The dense woods I'd just been in with Evander and Sydney give way to sparse trees and a rolling, hilly landscape of soft green grass.

I'm past the wards.

I can't feel the strain of my dad's magic on my shoulders any longer.

I look up at the tunnel and can barely see the entrance through the glare of the morning sun.

'Evander?'

Nothing.

'S-Sydney?'

I wait on my knees, my voice carrying through the mind-link into a vast nothingness.

An hour passes. The sun creeps higher through the tall, spindly trees above my head as I wait, and wait, and wait.

My heart cracks with the knowledge that Evander isn't coming. I feel it in my bones as I wrap my cloak tight around my body despite the climbing heat. Sydney, too, won't be coming through that tunnel. I'm alone.

There has to be more entrances like this through my dad's wards. Tunnels and passages steeped in ancient magic even his powers can't touch. It's the only way the Draven Coven could have gotten in and out unnoticed. It answers one question I had, at least, which was how the mystics who went behind my mom's back were able to help the Draven Coven get into Moonrise before they used magic to tear down the wards and attack.

A hollow feeling settles low in my belly as morning turns to midday, and I still haven't moved. Hungry, hopeless, and unsure how to move forward, I rise, and my shadow consumes me.

I have no idea where I am. I walk for another hour, picking through the forest, walking up the hills to look out over what I realize is an increasingly barren landscape. If I go forward in this direction, I'll have no cover from the sun. I'll be out in the open, vulnerable, save for my shadow.

But as I crest another rise, a tickle deep in my brain halts me in my tracks.

'Mom? Mom—oh, my Goddess, I need your help!'

'Where are you?' Mom says frantically. 'There was an attack just within the wards—'

'We were going to find Brie, and then we got attacked by hellhounds. I think I'm in the Deadlands somehow. Nothing is familiar.' I look around, taking in the cragged, barren mountains and golden plains stretching into the horizon. How did I get so far from the

Roguelands, and why? Did the tunnel through those trees take me here? Is it some kind of portal?

I shake my head and squint up at the sun. My body aches from draining my powers. My shadow starts to recede, but I pull it back up, forcing it to stay in place and keep me hidden.

'I can feel Brie. Like I'm bound to her somehow, and we were able to follow her scent for a while, but now everything is hazy–'

'Listen to me, Kenna,' Mom says hastily. 'Your father is in the Roguelands. There was another attack by the Dravens. He's declaring war.'

My heart shatters but I nod, even though she can't see me.

'You need to find a way to the river. If you follow the river north, you'll eventually reach Moonrise again.' She sounds strained, like she's holding back tears. 'I'm using my powers to put more shields around Moonrise. I'll find the hellhounds, but I can't help you jump home–'

'Gabriel has Evander and Sydney.' I take a deep breath, turning my fear and stress into something new, something dark. 'He has Brie. I'm not coming home without them.'

'I know.'

Shock ripples through me. I swear I can hear the smile in her voice. 'I wouldn't have come home with your father.'

'What do I do?' I ask, yanking on my resolve. *Don't fall apart. Don't cry. Will your powers to roil and fester into something dark and deadly.*

'Do what you have to do, Kenna. You were born for this. Do not trust anyone–'

The mind-link suddenly cuts out. I whirl back toward the woods and find a mystic standing several yards away in the shadows, her silver cloak shimmering in the sunlight.

Her mask of moonstone reflects the sun in a blinding fashion. I squint and shield my eyes.

I have an overwhelming feeling that this isn't good.

"Princess Kenna," she says in a voice both young and old, male and female. It sends shivers up my spine as she bows low and slowly straightens. She must sense me because of her powers, despite my shadow. "We've been looking all over for you. Your family is worried sick."

"I'm lost," I say, unease spreading over my skin in soft ripples of energy that ignites my strained powers.

She nods, probably smiling demonically behind her pretty mask. "Your mother tasked me with bringing you home. Come, now. Everything will be all right." She stretches out a hand–long, pale fingers smudged with… dirt.

I sweep my gaze over the cloak and the dress she's wearing beneath it. Dirt, grime, and splotches of dried blood. Upon further inspection, it looks like she's been outside for a long time. Her hem is torn and muddy, and even her mask doesn't glisten with its normal luster.

'Where is your hellhound?" I ask.

She drops her arm, her hand curling into a fist before she tucks it behind her back.

"Mystics don't have hellhounds. Hellhounds are gone, Princess. Surely you're educated enough to know your mother eradicated that practice. Come, we have to go."

"Where is my daughter?"

The mystic looks down at me, her face hidden by her mask. I notice the blood on her neck then. A handprint, like someone tried to kill her by strangling her, or tried to stop her from killing them.

"She's back at the castle. It was a huge misunderstanding."

"And my mate?"

Nothing. She says absolutely nothing for what feels like ages.

I feel a shift in the air between us. I can almost taste her rage as she takes a single step toward me.

I hold my ground.

"You're lost and delirious, Princess." She grabs my arm and squeezes so hard I feel my bones rubbing together. Her power collides with mine, and I suddenly find it hard to breathe.

Mystics are an enigma. They don't cast spells or make potions. They can't shift, and they don't possess the kinds of senses shifters do.

They read the stars. And they can appear anywhere, using their powers to jump.

"You gave Gabriel the ability to jump. He harnesses that power from a mystic."

She digs her nails into my arm, but I don't even flinch.

"Come, Princess. Let me make this more comfortable for you."

I feel her power trying to overpower my own. She's trying to spirit us away, to where, I don't know, but I'm too much for her.

She growls, her nails cutting into my skin.

But then she lets go and draws a huge, thin sword from her cloak.

Well, this is new. I never knew mystics were armed.

"Bad idea," I warn, raising my hands. "Do you know what will happen to you if you kill the only heir to Eastonia?"

"Gabriel is the rightful king." She swings the sword.

I jump back, the tip grazing over my belly and cutting through my dress. "Missed me."

Her snarl echoes off the hills around us.

My powers burn to life, and I find myself smiling. "Tell me where my mate and child are, and I'll let you live."

She chuckles, swinging her sword–made of pure silver– again. "You don't have it in you, Princess. You've always been so small, so scared, and so, so kind. You don't have it in you to kill."

"I never said anything about killing." I grin, my canines lengthening as my wolf powers prickle to life. "I'm a wolf, too, remember. I like to play with my food."

She lets out a growl and screams, lunging for me with her sword raised.

In that very moment, my shadow erupts, mingling with my wolf powers until I'm nothing but pure night, pure power, and a tiny bit of canine.

Her sword cuts through the air as I shift and leap out of her way. My wolf is black as night but covered in a silver shadow that oozes with stardust. Silver fire flames to life as I land behind her and turn around to face her again.

She edges away, shocked. I'm a little shocked, too. I didn't know I could combine my powers.

What else can I do?

My fur stands on end as I let the full brunt of my powers come to surface. I don't need them all, obviously. But this is for research... at least, that's what I'm telling myself.

Leashes of shadows funnel from my body like rays of pure death.

The mystic drops her sword and tries to run, but my shadows have her surrounded.

I edge forward, allowing my shadows to creep closer to her, to box her in. My silver fire slithers toward her, burning everything in its wake in its path. Her silver sword melts and withers to ash at her feet.

"Wait!" she cries out, raising a hand.

I'm beyond mercy as I say, "Where is my mate?" My human voice booms from all around us. I can talk in wolf form. I add that to the list of strange powers and continue. "And where is my daughter?"

"I can't–I don't know–I was supposed to get you alone and kill you."

"Like the mystic in the cave during the Rite? No one was supposed to show up to perform the ritual with me, were they? The mystics purposefully made Evander believe he was doing the Rite without his mate and vice versa! You needed me alone. You knew I'd accept the nomination. You knew I wouldn't ever put my own feelings first. I always did what was right for the coven and you used that against us!"

"P-Please!"

"No," I say, my voice thundering over the hills and the forest behind me. "It's too late for that. What you've done is unforgivable. How many more mystics are working for Gabriel?!"

"We didn't have a choice!"

"Bullshit. You're the most powerful witches in our world! You gave him his powers!"

I swipe a paw at her face, knocking off her mask. It shatters beside her, the crystals turning ashen and dissolving beside her.

She's a little older than me. Her skin is so pale I can nearly see through it. Round, wide, deep-set brown eyes meet mine in fear.

"Was the world that much better under Kane?" I ask. "A world where your kind were captured, enslaved, and drained of your powers?"

"Gabriel has a following," she warns, baring her teeth. "He has an army."

"He is one against many," I correct, snarling. "My father's army and my uncle's army would decimate him—"

"He has a relic like your mother's mask," she pants. "It's an orrery."

Confusion clouds my senses for a split second.

"Only his sister can power it. It's her gift. He used her powers eleven years ago to charge it, overthrowing Atticus as head of the coven. But the orrery is running out of power. He's getting weaker. Our powers as mystics can only help him so much. He needs her and will tear your uncle's kingdom apart to find her. He thought he could use you, or Princess Misty, but he needs a specific… skill set."

"What can she do—"

The mystic pulls a dagger from her cloak and screams, sending it through her own heart.

I rush away from her, my chest squeezing tight.

Her eyes go dim as she collapses.

My powers retreat. The sun shines again, covering the ashen clearing in streams of gold.

The mystic's chest rises and falls once, then twice, before she stills and then…

Her body disappears, her clothes going slack as her flesh turns to pale moondust, dust that drifts away on the wind.

I shift back to my human form involuntarily and fall to my knees, unable to catch my breath. My whole body is on fire. My bones ache as I try to rise, but I'm exhausted.

But I catch a glimmer in the outer pocket of her clock. I crawl toward it, my fingers brushing over a smooth, worn surface of some kind of circular object.

It's Sydney's compass.

I was right when I thought they'd been captured and taken.

My heart skips a beat as I dress in the Mystics tarnished, bloody dress and cloak, my own clothes torn to shreds.

I clutch the compass as I look out over the landscape before me.

"Where are they?" I ask the Goddess, and the compass grows suddenly warm in the palm of my hand.

45

―――――

YOUR MATE OR YOUR BABY

Evander

WATER POURS down the walls in steady, frigid streams. My head aches, and the smell of blood hangs thick in the air as I try to open my eyes for the fourth time in the last five minutes.

I think my skull might be cracked. I reach up to rub my throbbing temples but wince when I flex my hands.

My fingers are shattered.

"Syd?" I croak into the darkness.

"I'm still alive," he replies groggily.

I open my eyes to slits. Faint light fills my vision. It's enough to cause a searing pain to ripple through my brain. "Where do you think we are?"

"One-hundred-percent underground," he answers shortly somewhere beside me.

I reach for him, unsure how far away he is, but the manacles binding each wrist to heavy chains only allow me to stretch my arms so far.

We've been here for a day at least. No food or drink has been

349

offered. No one has come to see us or talk to us. The gaping wounds on my legs and chest from when we were brought into submission by the hellhounds itch, and my joints ache with fever.

We surrendered to give Kenna time to escape so she could find Brie.

We surrendered because we knew, without having to even talk about it, that we would be brought directly to Gabriel.

But right now, we're weakening.

"You should have gone home," I tell Sydney. "You didn't need to get tied up in this."

"I couldn't just leave knowing how bad things were going to get."

I slowly turn my head, every vertebrae singing in agony. "What do you mean *you knew?*"

In the fading light, I see him lying on his side a few feet away. His eyes are closed, and his mouth is open as he takes a ragged breath. "I saw something like this–an attack–a few months ago in my dad's orrery."

Sydney looks like shit–I'm sure I look the same, or worse–but I wonder if he might have been hit on the head harder than I have. "You see things in the stars?"

He coughs, then groans, murmuring something about ribs being broken. "Uh-huh."

"You're a mystic."

"No, I'm not. I might see shit, but I can't make heads or tails about what it means. It's a useless, annoying gift, if I'm being honest."

I have vague memories of my parents talking about King Isaac and his odd ability to read the stars. They chalked it up to him being a beast, one of the two guardians of the Moon Goddess.

But these traits are inherited, apparently.

"Are you willing to elaborate?" I ask, losing what little patience I have.

"I just knew I needed to be in Eastonia. Something pulled me here, and everywhere I go, Gabriel seems to go, too. Or, he wants to be there."

I blink, unable to process what he just said. My head spins as I try to focus on Sydney, but his body goes fuzzy.

"I think we're dying," he says in a mere whisper.

"Likely," I reply.

Silence swells between us, broken only by the water falling at our backs. Filthy, sulfur-scented water that stings when it touches my wounds, but in chains, I can't move away.

"I don't want to find her," he says absently.

"Who?" Not Brie, surely. We're not wounded and ill enough for Sydney to be giving up on his cousin's infant daughter just yet.

"The woman from the ball," he breathes. "My mate."

I close my eyes and sigh. If I learned anything in my training as a Ghost, it's that a dying man will admit anything. It's a reckoning, a final attempt to lessen one's burdens as death closes in.

I need to get us out of here, now.

"Why not?" I ask, just to keep him awake and talking.

More dripping water clouds the air between us. "Look at what you've been through for Kenna. What my parents and my aunt and uncle went through." He takes another ragged breath, letting it out slowly. "Danger follows my family everywhere we go. I can't put her through that. I won't."

"I'm sure your dad thought the same thing when he was young."

He snorts a laugh, which is a good sign, but a door nearby wetly creaks open before he can reply.

Wordlessly, someone unlocks the manacles and lifts me up. My legs are worthless. I still can't keep my eyes open as I'm dragged by at least three people out of the room. I hear Sydney groaning and hissing in pain behind me, which is a relief. He's also been taken from the room, but to where?

The changing light behind my eyelids tells me we're being dragged down a long, narrow hallway. It eventually opens up into an echoing chamber where multiple conversations suddenly cease.

A low, cackling laugh I hear in my nightmares whispers through the air.

"It's about fucking time," I grumble, opening my eyes as far as they'll go, which isn't much.

Gabriel tsks, drumming his fingers on the remains of what looks like an ancient sacrificial altar. "Such foul language for a high born wolf. I guess you wouldn't really act like a noble, would you? Having been essentially raised in filthy barracks."

"Where the fuck is my daughter?"

"Your daughter?" he laughs, the sound like talons being raked down a chalkboard. "You mean the child stolen from my coven?"

"She was never yours!" I shout, but Gabriel just shakes his head.

"This is my coven. The women and the children they supply us are for me to use as I please. I would have let the child go, if you and your filthy blood mutt of a mate hadn't shown interest in her. She must be very powerful if the royal family wants her, which means I need her."

"She's just a baby," I say, my voice trembling.

"Our babies are just as powerful as adults," he laughs, shaking his head. "But, you're just a shifter. How would you know that? Silly me. Perhaps a demonstration is in order."

My blood runs cold as he snaps his fingers and a thin, gaunt man appears, Brie shrieking in his arms.

"No!" Sydney shouts, wriggling in his restraints.

I watch in horror as the man lays my daughter on the altar in front of Gabriel. 'Sydney, if you have other powers you haven't mention, now would be the time to fucking use them!' I scream down the mind-link.

Kenna

MY POWERS SURGE. I have sudden tunnel vision as I look up at the ruins of the temple. It's built into a rock face and sheltered by gnarled, dead trees. I can feel them–the Draven Coven. I can feel Gabriel's power.

I close the compass and slide it into my pocket, then pull the hood of the dead Mystics cloak over my head.

I don't have the mask. I wish I did, given I'm about to creep into enemy territory disguised as a mystic.

Thankfully, the entrance to the temple casts me in darkness until I reach a torch attached to the wall. I yank it free, wincing as a few fragments of embers sear my fingers, but edge down a wet, steep set of stairs.

It's a terrible place to house what could be hundreds of people, based on the smell. Voices carry behind doors made of curtains on pieces of wood. Small fires crop up as I walk down what I believe might be the only hallway–leading to what, I have no clue–while people huddle against the sudden chill in the air.

I wish my mom would have hunted and destroyed every old ruin in Eastonia. It's silly, of course. Most of the temples have been pulled from the ground and are now protected, turned into libraries and museums, or resumed being places of worship.

But for some reason, these temples resisted my mom's Firestone powers.

I step over a pile of bloody, discarded laundry and wince, my nose crinkling. It smells awful down here. Horrible.

But I catch hints of… vanilla.

I almost gasp in relief, turning into a doorway. I lift the torch, careful to keep my face hidden, and feel my heart crack.

Blood coats the floor around two sets of chains and silver manacles. Evander and Sydney were here. I can still smell their scents.

Evander's blood is on the floor.

Rage simmers to life as I slowly turn and walk out the door, finding myself face to face with two guards. I lower my head so they can't see my face.

"What are you doing here, mystic?" one of them sneers. "Gabriel has been waiting for you."

"Did you bring the princess?" the other asks.

"I didn't need to. She is dead," I say.

"Prove it," one of them sneers. "You were supposed to bring back her head."

Oh, fuck. I didn't think of that.

Slowly, I raise my head, my face catching the light of the torch.

My shadows curl around the two men, strangling them before they can utter another word. They silently drop to the ground, motionless.

"Damnit," I curse, reaching up to yank my hood lower over my face. I should have asked where Gabriel is right now, but he has to be nearby, right?

I follow Evander's scent and walk down a rough, crumbling set of stairs leading into smoky darkness and through another stinky, filthy corridor.

I'm met by more guards, but they don't question me. They simply open heavy, wooden double doors and usher me inside a huge, cavernous room.

"No," I say, my throat closing around the word.

Evander, held by three guards with chains bound to his wrists, whips his head toward me.

"Kenna," he mouths at the moment I lift my face to the light in the room.

Sydney looks over his shoulder at me with great effort. He looks horrible. He's near death. Both of them are. Their wounds have festered.

What am I going to do?

But then I see Gabriel... and Brie. His hand rests over her stomach while she lies crying on an altar in front of him.

'Kenna,' Sydney says into my mind. 'I can't break us out. Not yet. I think we've been dosed with wolfsbane. I just need a minute to-to get my powers back. I'm close.'

"Well, how nice of you to join us. I was hoping to have just your head in attendance today, but this will do for now," Gabriel says smugly. He motions to his guards. "Grab her–"

My shadow erupts around me, closeting me in shimmering, heatless silver fire.

"Let them go," I shout.

Gabriel laughs, his eyes narrowing. "No."

I could kill him. I could kill everyone in this room. But I don't know how to protect Evander, Sydney, and Brie from my flames and shadows.

I need Evander and Sydney's help to get her out, but they can't get out of their restraints.

Dread settles heavy in my stomach. My powers flicker out. Gabriel motions to his guards, and Evander is shoved forward at the same moment Gabriel rounds the altar and pulls a blade from his belt.

"I'll give you one single mercy before I kill you, Princess Kenna." He toys with the blade as the guards force a thrashing Evander to his knees. "You choose. Your mate or this worthless baby who has no blood ties to you?"

Evander meets my eyes, pleading, begging me to choose her.

"I–" I try to get my powers to come back, but I'm in such despair that my powers only fizzle, little sparks springing from my fingertips.

Gabriel shakes his head, chuckling.

I hear the sound of gears groaning, and locks clicking, at the same moment Gabriel grabs Evander by the hair and slashes his blade across my mate's neck.

46

SECRET POWERS

Sydney

KENNA'S anguished screams slows time to a halt the moment my powers finally break through the manacles on my ankles and wrists.

It's too late.

I'm too late.

Evander falls face first, unable to save himself from hitting the floor.

I feel like everyone is moving in slow motion. Kenna sprints forward, her shadows billowing out around her as her face twists with despair. Guards move in, blades drawn in her direction.

And Gabriel is grinning like a madman as he turns back to Brie.

Fuck, no.

My body screams in pain as I lurch forward, shouting in rage, agony, and desperation as I collide with the nearest guard. The man falls to the ground with a crunch. I leap off his body, his ribs cracking beneath my feet as I jump, begging the Goddess to help me gather enough power to shift.

We're all so weak right now. Gabriel knew exactly how to enact this sick, twisted plan. He knew Kenna and Evander would come for Brie. Maybe, somehow, he knew I'd show up, too.

He knew Evander and I would either fight until we were on death's door or surrender, using our defeat as a means to get us here.

I can't let it end this way. Not after what our families went through to restore some kind of peace and order so we could grow up safe, grow up ignorant of the dangers of this world.

I blame myself as I run toward Gabriel, my wolf powers a single hum of energy, not nearly enough to shift. Out of the corner of my eye, I see Kenna falling to her knees beside Evander. Tears stream down her cheeks, glowing faintly, as she gathers his limp, lifeless body in her arms.

"No!" I shout, sending my fist flying, colliding with a second guard. He falls, hitting his head on the edge of the altar with a cracking, wet sound that echoes off the walls around us.

Shadows weave through the fray, taking out enemy after enemy as I fight my way to Gabriel, who snatches Brie in his hands so roughly she shrieks in fear and discomfort. The sound causes Kenna to scream, and I feel the full force of her powers cascade through the room.

I take down another guard with my bare hands; the last guard in my way. I briefly meet Kenna's eyes from where she kneels with Evander in her lap, her hands coated in his blood as she cradles his head.

She looks like something out of a nightmare. I can't describe the pain behind her eyes. She just lost her mate. She used her already weak powers to take out Gabriel's guards to allow me time to get to Brie, to stop Gabriel from taking her daughter.

She doesn't have enough power left to heal Evander.

That's what I see in her gaze. Anguished resolution. Evander died so Brie can live and I can't–I can't let her down.

Powerless, weaponless, and hazy from the wolfsbane surging through my veins, I throw my body at Gabriel as he starts to disappear, his body turning to stardust.

But I grab his arm, surprising him, and yank him back before he can jump to Goddess knows where with Brie.

I send my free hand flying, punching him square in the center of his face, crushing his nose. He cries out, and I only have a split second to catch Brie as he lets go.

Brie is frantic, bright purple from crying, but whole.

"KENNA!" I scream, then launch my newborn second-cousin into the air like a football.

Kenna leaps, eyes wide, and catches Brie.

But a hand closes around my neck, squeezing so hard my vision fills with black spots.

Gabriel shoves me to my knees with strength I don't think is possible for any man to possess.

"Fucking inbred scum," I snarl, clawing his forearm.

"You had so much potential," he clucks, his fingers bruising my neck. "You and your father, both. It was such a shame he never used his powers at their full strength. All of that Goddess given power. A prophecy born, and he only ever shifted into his beast to show off his powers to your mother."

I'm starting to black out. I can hear Kenna screaming my name somewhere nearby. I can feel her shadow powers at work, cutting through guards. Somewhere, in the distance, I sense a faint, trembling whirl of power coming our way, slicing through the earth like a derailed freight train.

I choke on a laugh.

"What's so funny?" he sneers, squeezing tighter.

My head spins as I try to catch a breath. "You–you're just a man with stolen powers. I was born with mine."

He leans in, "I know what you are and who belongs to you, wolf. You'll never be able to protect them. I will hunt them for the rest of my life, until my dying breath, and when I catch them, I'll make you watch me take them apart, piece by piece, as I drain their powers to ashes."

I might be dying, because his words don't make any sense, and Gabriel's face twists as a blinding light sears through my skull.

When my vision clears, I don't feel any pain. I'm… I'm not under this Goddess forsaken mountain in a temple deep underground. I'm in Crescent Falls.

I'm in Ryan's house.

I bump into the kitchen counter, and *she* catches me around the waist, giggling. Neither of us have been able to get a word out since we left the ball. Drunk and deliriously happy, we've done nothing but laugh. Laugh at each other, and the people we passed on the way here, at Ryan's poor excuse for a gate to his territory that I was able to open with a flick of my wrist.

"Can I–can I kiss you?"

She swats my chest, "I've been waiting for you to make a move–"

My lips crash into hers. Sloppy, unsteady. Our teeth clash, and she laughs against my lips and I…

I feel it.

Like a light just erupted in my chest. Like fine threads are weaving through my heart and I…

I clutch something cold and hard in my hand as the memory fades. I'm still with Gabriel. I'm not with the beautiful woman I met at the ball. I can barely remember her. Her face is a blank slate in my mind but I feel her, as if she's calling out to me.

"Give up, princeling," Gabriel grunts, trying to crane my neck to the side. My spine strains.

But I move my shoulder–a hard, deliberate motion–and send the blade I just pulled from his belt into his side.

Gabriel lets go of my neck. I gasp for breath, my throat swollen and sore.

He screams in pain, yanking the blade free at the same moment a rush of air blasts the doors to the altar room open wide and fills it with black mist.

I meet Gabriel's eyes. He holds my gaze.

"You better find her before I do." He pants, then smiles, and disappears.

"SYDNEY!" Kenna screeches.

I try to rise, but I can't breathe. I clutch my neck where his fingers left welts and bruises and double over, choking.

Kenna screams my name again, but then hands are on my shoulders, and suddenly the room swirls into darkness. I feel like I'm being pulled apart, then roughly put back together again, and then I'm flat on my back looking up into a dense canopy of trees.

Uncle Ryatt's voice sounds out nearby. Commander Artyom briefly comes into my line of sight, but he's quickly replaced by Connor, one of the Ghosts close with Evander.

"You're all right, man," he tells me, pressing something cold against my neck. "You're healing up just fine on your own."

"My p-powers–"

"They'll come back. Stay here, okay?"

Connor's gone, and my vision remains hazy.

People are walking by, crouching to check on me. Their faces are a blur, and all around, the air is full of noise. I can't separate the voices and conversation. I feel like I'm spinning.

"Kenna?" I say to the void, wondering if her name even left my tongue.

Slowly, I start to regain feeling in my arms and legs. I grip grass between my fingers. I flex my toes. The gashes and welts on my body start to burn, reaching a peak, then feel like nothing at all.

I sit straight up, blinking into hazy evening sunlight.

Warriors wearing Eastonia's royal emblem dart through a wide open clearing. Several rough looking men kneel in cuffs, their heads bent against the sun. I turn around, squinting into the trees, and see the cragged mountain where the temple rests in the distance.

A moan cuts through the air to my left.

My heart sinks as reality settles heavy on my shoulders.

I slowly rise and turn.

A group is gathered several yards away. A sheet of coppery blonde hair glints in the sunshine as Lady Amanda bends, resting her cheek against Evander's chest. Granger kneels beside her, his hand pressed against her back. He's so still, so incredibly still as he looks down at his son's–his son's body.

Another trembling moan cuts through my soul as Ryatt kneels on the other side of Evander. I can't see who he's talking to, who he's trying to pull away from Evander.

But I know it's Kenna.

"I can't!" she sobs. "Please, I can't leave him like this. I can—I'm trying to save him. I have to try!"

"You've been trying," Ryatt says, his voice incredibly strained. "Kenna, I am so sorry. He's gone."

"Noooooo!"

I fight to stay upright as Kenna's desperation clouds the air. My heart hammers in my chest as I edge forward toward the group—toward the family and friends gathered around Evander.

My friend.

My oldest friend.

Kenna has his head in her lap. Her tears fall into his hair as she cries, her chest shaking with sobs.

Before I kneel beside her, I look up to find Aunt Ella standing pale and resigned, dressed in a cloak of the deepest crimson. Her hair is loose and billowing in the sharp, mid-summer breeze, and her eyes are dark.

She's holding Brie.

"Get my grandma," Kenna says, her voice edged with frantic desperation. "Grandma—Grandma Isla. Please, Dad! She can—she can help me—"

Ryatt has tears in his eyes as he shakes his head.

There isn't time to spirit our grandmother from Maatua.

There isn't time to begin with.

I fall to my knees beside Kenna.

Connor and Flynn stand in the distance beside a grave looking Commander Artyom. No one speaks. No one can possibly utter a word at a time like this.

I glance at Granger and Amanda. Granger's eyes are lifeless as he stares down at his son, his hand curling into his mate's dress as she silently sobs against Evander's chest.

I look at Kenna, reaching for her, clutching the back of her neck. She sniffles as she looks up at me, her eyes red and bloodshot.

"This can't be happening," she whispers, devastated. "What do I do?"

What would I do in this situation? When all hope is lost? What if it were my mate lying on the grass on what could easily be the most perfect summer day I've ever seen, lifeless?

I still question my gifts. I'm a tangled mess of them. Half-cocked powers that make little sense.

But I lay my hand on Evander's chest while holding Kenna's gaze.

She swallows, hiccupping, but her eyes go wide with sudden understanding. "Can you...?"

"Lay your hand over mine," I tell her.

Everyone around us starts to move, confused, as Kenna gently places her hand on mine.

We're weak. Our powers have been strained, pushed to their limits, hampered by potions and poison.

My hand warms, soft blue light pouring from my palm. Kenna, too, reignites what's left of her powers, merging them with mine.

Thank you, I say silently, *Grandma.*

This is the most useful gift of all.

Kenna's tears that have dripped down onto Evander's pale, lifeless face begin to shine as our combined healing gifts flow through him.

I watch my cousin. I watch hope flare behind her eyes.

And I promise myself... *I swear,* on the Goddess, that I will never find my mate. I will never put her through this, even if it means I'll never know what it's like to be loved like Kenna loves Evander.

4 7

A LOVE LIKE OURS

Kenna

A HEAT like no other spreads through our joined hands. I almost pull away from Sydney, surprised by the searing pain. My heart hammers against my ribs, but I stay focused, looking down at my mate and praying so hard the words jumble together.

I barely notice how everyone but Amanda has backed away. Even Granger, who looks like he's ready to flatten Eastonia to kill the rest of the Draven Rebels with his bare hands, is resting on his knees with his hand wrapped around Evander's ankle.

But Dad stays by my side. My dad, who wanted to send Evander away, now rests his hand on Evander's shoulder and squeezes.

"Come on, son."

"Evander," Granger whispers, squeezing Evander's ankle. "Don't do this to your mother. Don't do this to Kenna."

My heart wrenches. I let my tears flow freely, several of them dripping down onto Evander's lips.

Sydney is shaking with the effort of this beside me. His eyes are pinched closed, and similar unintelligible prayers are mumbled from his lips. He strains, his brow pinched, and the heat between our hands grows so strong I think I might be getting burned.

I think of the night at the ball when I'd been crying in that corner. I remember that man in a mask coming to me, asking me to dance, and how safe and comfortable I'd felt in what I believed to be a perfect stranger's arms.

I wish I could go back to the night, just for a moment. I wish I could take off the mask he'd been wearing and kiss him again, for the first time, and know it was him.

I wish I could have a chance to dance with him again, one last time.

Because this isn't working.

"Sydney," I whimper, clutching his hand, knitting our fingers together over Evander's chest as our powers flicker out. "Nothing is happening."

Sydney chokes on a breath and hangs his head.

I keep clutching his hand, my body aching from sobs that wrack my ribs and spine.

Maybe not feeling the full brunt of the mate bond right now is a good thing because the pain of losing Evander is already too much to bear. I can't breathe. My lungs won't work. My heart is being crushed, twisting in on itself.

I look up at my mom with tears in my eyes as she clutches Brie to her chest, silent tears streaming down her face.

"I'm sorry," I manage to say to everyone around me, to Evander. "I am so sorry—"

But Evander's chest moves-rising as he breathes in deep.

Time stills. I feel like I'm imagining it.

I look at my mom again, and her eyes are full of silver fire.

"A little more," she says in a mere whisper. "Give him a little more, Kenna. He's there. He's trying to fight his way back to you. Keep trying."

I look around at the totally still people kneeling around me. Dad slowly blinks before closing his eyes, moving in slow motion as he hangs his head and outstretches a hand to Evander.

Again, I look at Mom. She nods.

Determination courses through me as I untangle my hand from Sydney's and take Evander's face in my hands. I look down at him, at his closed eyes, and let out a scream that shakes the trees and echoes off the mountain tops. I want every kingdom, every sleeping god and goddess, to hear me.

"Wake up!" I command, and the very last of my powers surge. "WAKE UP!"

His chest trembles, then relaxes, and then his lips part as he suddenly sucks in a ragged, shallow breath and coughs.

Time snaps, speeding up to normal, and Evander cries out, clutching my arm so tight I feel my bones scrape together.

Shouts fill the air, mingling with several surprised yelps and cries of shock.

"It's me," I blubber, leaning down to rest my forehead against his. "It's me. You're okay. You're okay–"

"Kenna?" Evander rasps. He coughs painfully, wincing.

"Thank the Goddess," Sydney says hoarsely, scooting back and falling over on his side.

The next several seconds are chaotic. Amanda throws herself on Evander again and sobs. He bursts into tears beside her, and Dad...

"Thanks the gods," he breathes, slouching, holding his head in his hands beside me.

"Kenna," Evander says hoarsely, opening his eyes to slits.

"Yeah?" I sniffle, my cheeks aching from smiling so hard.

"I'm fucking done. We're going to Veiled–Veiled Valley. I'm going to sit on that throne beside you and that's it. I'm never fighting again."

Flynn and Connor laugh nearby.

But I'm beaming, barely able to breathe. "That sounds nice," I tell them, and lean down to brush a kiss to his lips.

BRIE LOOKS UP AT ME, and I look down at her. Her eyes will be a soft hazel, I think, now that they're beginning to change. In the sunlight streaming through the windows, I can just make out a hint of green near her pupils. She'll be blonde, at least for a while. Peach fuzz hair has started to sprout, and golden eyelashes catch the light as her mouth pulls into a sleepy smile.

Rocking her to sleep is methodic and relaxing for both of us.

The door to my sitting room silently opens.

Sydney walks in, closing the door behind him. "Hey."

"Hey," I whisper.

He looks much better than he did yesterday. His coppery brown hair is brushed back away from his face, and he's clean shaven, dressed for a journey.

I swallow hard as he sits down in the armchair across from me and crosses an ankle over a knee.

I can't look at him without thinking about what happened yesterday evening. I hadn't known he had healing gifts. He never told anyone.

When my own powers were abysmal, he stepped up. I placed my hand over his, and together, we fought like hell when all odds were stacked against us.

"How is he?" he asks, his eyes downcast on Brie.

I heave a breath, blinking rapidly to stop tears from flowing down my cheeks. "He's resting."

Sydney nods absently but still won't meet my eyes.

We almost lost Evander. We came so close.

It doesn't feel real that he's still with us. Our powers didn't do much to heal his numerous injuries, and he'll likely have a scar across his throat forever, but we rekindle what small flicker of life was left in him. We gave him a fighting chance.

Now, he's in the bedroom, the next room over, asleep. I doubt he'll wake up for some time. He's on so many tonics to keep him at rest while the potions and herbs I've been using on him do their job and heal his body.

"I'm leaving in twenty-minutes," Sydney says. "Your dad is jumping me to Veiled Valley. I'm taking a boat to Maatua from there."

"So soon?"

He says nothing but cracks his knuckles.

"Say hi to Grandma and Grandpa for me, won't you?"

"Of course. I'll be back in a month for your ascension ceremony."

Oh yeah, that. Nothing in the world, even almost getting killed by Gabriel, would stop me and Evander from taking over Veiled Valley, apparently.

Finally, Sydney meets my eyes. "Gabriel is still out there."

"I know."

He grits his teeth. Something is obviously wrong, something he's not willing to share.

"We're safe here, you know. Dad and Granger took out the rest of the coven. Commander Artyom and his forces have been canvassing the Roguelands, but so far, it's pretty much confirmed that the Draven Coven is gone, for good."

"Gabriel is still alive."

"I know," I repeat, sensing the rising anger in his tone.

"I tried to kill him."

"Did he... did he say something to you?"

"Many things." He rolls his neck and looks out the window. "I love you."

"I love you," I say, but he stands and leaves without another word.

But Dad catches the door on Sydney's way out. Sydney steps past him as if in a hurry and disappears.

Dad sighs and closes the door behind him.

"Does he really have to leave so soon?" I ask. "He seems out of sorts."

"His parents want him home, and he's an Alpha. Now that the rebel threat is taken care of, he's no longer needed here."

"But Gabriel's out there–"

"And Sydney has been tasked with tracking down Gabriel's cousin." Dad sits down, sighing. His eyes are a deep steel color in the sunlight as he looks down at where Brie is sleeping peacefully in my arms. "Sydney will be fine. I wanted to talk to you before I left to escort him to Veiled Valley, though."

I rock Brie with more fervor. Dad and I have been at each other's throats for some time now, which is highly unusual. If I'm fighting with anyone, it's normally Mom.

"I treated you and Evander unfairly."

I smirk. "You think?"

"Kenna, please, just listen." He's trying to look serious right now but failing. His mouth quirks as he leans back, sighing. "I would have never stopped you from being with him. Evander has always loved you. He's loved you on a level even your mom and I didn't fully understand. I knew, from the moment he swore he'd protect you, when was a child, that Evander was... going to get in the way of himself when it came to acting on the mate bond we all knew was there."

"You knew?"

"I assumed," he admits. "No one has ever been as committed to someone like he was committed to you without a mate bond in place. I honestly didn't feel that way for your mother, my own mate, until after we officially accepted our bond."

"Do you approve of him, then?"

"Of course, I do."

"And you'll be nice to him?"

"If he proves to be a good son-in-law and Alpha of Veiled Valley, yes."

I playfully scowl, but that heavy feeling in my chest lifts as Dad rises.

"Let me take her. Your mom and Amanda want her, and you should rest."

I allow him to lift Brie from his arms with practiced grace. When I was her age, my parents were trying to find a way home after fighting for their lives through Tarsian with me in tow. Brie is lucky, I think. She's surrounded by so much comfort and love.

Dad leaves, and I quietly edge into my room. I pull the curtains closed, blocking out the sunset, and crawl into bed beside Evander.

I curl my body around his, spooning him, which is very difficult because he's so much taller than me.

But in the quiet dark, I close my eyes, knowing we're safe.

He squeezes my hand to let me know he knows I'm there.

"Don't ever do that to me again," I murmur against his back, and his answering chuckle vibrates through the room, warming me through and through.

We'll have a quiet life. We'll wake up slow and eat breakfast together. We'll fill Brie's new nursery in Veiled Valley with toys and take her on walks to the city every day.

Once a year, we'll gather in Maatua for Winter Solstice and watch our family grow, year by year, adding new members and gifts as time flutters by.

One day, we'll have another baby. Maybe he'll be the new Alpha of the Veiled Valley, or she'll be the future Queen of Eastonia.

The future might be unclear, but what I do know is that this is exactly where I'm meant to be.

I drift off to sleep, clutching Evander tight, and thanking the Goddess for letting me find him, to know him, as my mate.

4 8

———————

ASCENSION

A MONTH LATER

Kenna

A RUSH of cool air greets me as I step out on the balcony overlooking the city of Veiled Valley. The valley is a sea of green against the mist rising from the river far below–mist that swallows whole a dozen or so bridges connecting the city on either side of the pristine, near tropical mountains.

I take a deep breath, my ribs aching as the corset I'm wearing cuts into my skin. Why do we bother wearing these anymore?

I pinch the fabric of my silver-blue gown between my fingers. The fabric billows out around my waist, creating a ball-gown effect that's honestly very beautiful, if not totally inefficient. I can barely walk in this gown–this gown of silver stars and fresh-water pearls that glimmer in the moonlight–but I guess that doesn't matter. I won't be doing much walking until the after-party tonight, after my ascension ceremony.

The mist keeps rising, covering the sparkling city in a milky white hazy, but the moon is full and beckoning me to shift–to tear out of my dress–and sprint into the woods.

It's not that I don't want to go through with this. Not at all. After everything Evander and I have been through the past few months, sitting down together on Veiled Valley's Shadowsynger thrones and falling into a mundane routine feels like we're stepping into heaven hand-in-hand.

I don't want to think about war, or politics, or the ever changing political landscape behind the mystical veil that surrounds my new pack.

I just want to wake up with my mate, eat breakfast, do paperwork, and pepper Brie with kisses.

Another whoosh of air spirits from the house, ruffling my skirts.

"I know, I know," I mumble, turning to the ancient doors of stained glass behind me. The magic that resides in this strange castle of onyx stone rustles the curtains in our bedroom in annoyance. I'm running late. It took ages to turn my unruly brown waves into the intricate updo–a nest of braids and pearl clips and a crown–and don't even get me started on my makeup.

Once upon a time, I lived for this. For primping, fancy clothes, and shoes.

But now I've seen the worst of the world and this feels... unimportant.

"Kenna?"

Evander slips into the bedroom, dressed in a suit of the deepest blue, which makes his green eyes pop. Even from the edge of the balcony, I can see his eyes shining in the soft light of the massive chandelier in the center of the domed ceiling in our bedroom.

His blonde hair is swept away from his face, and he's clean shaven for the first time in weeks.

He looks, at least for a moment, like the Evander who covered my eyes that night when he ran over a Draven wolf when he was desperately trying to get us to the port. The night we fell through the roof of the chicken coop. The night I crawled to him, laying my hands on him knowingly for the first time and feeling that pull that would bind us together for eternity.

My mate, in all his glory, smirks as he strides in my direction.

"Don't laugh," I beg, my cheeks going bright pink. "I look like a wedding cake."

"You don't," he tries to assure me, but his eyes glimmer with mischief as he stops in front of me, giving me a brief inspection. "You look beautiful."

"I begged to just wear my after party dress." I turn back to the city, gripping the railing. "But Mom and my grandmas teamed up against me. Only Aunt Maddy was on my side."

"What's bothering you about the dress?" He comes up behind me, his body a welcoming, comforting presence as my nerves threaten to start pulling me apart.

"The corset is too tight. It's cutting into my skin. I can barely breathe."

"That's an easy fix." He pushes the silken, transparent cloak of stars that attaches to my shoulders and flows down my back in a train that would give most brides a run for their money and starts loosening the laces.

"You're rather good at that for someone who was a virgin when we first slept together–oh!"

He gives my laces a little tug. "Don't tempt me, Kenna," he rasps, leaning in to brush the words over my neck. "We'll play later."

"Don't tempt me," I counter, testing the tightness of my corset by taking an easy breath. Much better. "I'd give anything to just stay in our room for the night. We've barely had time to move in and unpack our things."

"Should I go downstairs and cause a distraction to give you time to escape?"

I turn to face him, shaking my head. He would, too. If I asked–if I told him I didn't want to do this–he'd sneak me out of the castle.

"I'm just nervous."

"I know. So am I. Being the First Mate of Veiled Valley is a huge weight on my shoulders."

I swat him. "You'll be Alpha, Evander."

"Maybe in name. You're the true Alpha here, Kenna."

The balcony around us trembles with impatience. I roll my eyes, murmuring a prayer to the Goddess, and nod to myself. "The house is right; it's time. Where's Brie?"

"Isla has her. She won't let anyone else hold her."

I smirk as I follow Evander out of our bedroom and through the winding, onyx corridors leading to the throne room where practically everyone in Veiled Valley will be waiting for us.

"That sounds like my grandma."

"Cressendra looked like she was about to fight Isla for a chance with the baby," Evander chuckles. "I'd pay to see that, honestly."

"I'm not sure who'd win," I admit with a laugh, the tension in my chest lessening.

We reach the side door to the throne room. I can hear the thrum of conversation, music, and excitement from within. It's been centuries since Veiled Valley held a ceremony like this. I'm the first Shadowsynger Luna to ascend the throne since the time of the Fire-stone Queens.

So, I invited the whole freakin" pack. Every man, woman, and child is squished into the colossal throne room and adjacent ballroom.

And everyone is waiting for me.

A flash of blonde hair tinged with white catches my attention. I turn, smiling as Grandma Isla rushes in my direction. Poor Brie, now two months old, is dressed in a fluffy pale blue dress with a huge bow on the top of her hairless head.

"I thought I'd have to drag you out of that room, Kenna." Grandma Isla huffs then smiles, carefully handing Brie to Evander, who cradles her.

"I'm ready. I just needed a minute," I tell her.

Her smile sends a warmth spreading through my heart as she reaches up to caress my cheek. "I'm so proud of you. We're all so proud of you."

Tears sting by eyes as I nod, unable to form the words I need to thank her, but she's on a mission.

"Ready?"

"We're ready," Evander answers for me, giving my shoulder a little nudge with his elbow.

Grandma moves in front of us and opens the door wide.

Now or never.

I step into the throne room beside my mate holding my daughter. We walk up the stairs leading to the twin thrones as a hush falls over the crowd.

In the sea of onlookers, I spot my parents standing together whispering to Uncle Isaac and Aunt Maddy.

Ryan and Sydney edge through the crowd, towering over pretty much everyone else in the area. Even Misty came, and I briefly see her and Piper, Evander's little sister, sneaking glasses of champagne while everyone else is distracted.

I'm not sure what's meant to happen next, but a priestess meets us in the center of the platform dressed in robes of deep blue, black, and violet–the official colors of the Shadowsynger line.

I expect her to say a few words, but she simply motions for me to follow her into the crowd.

Confused, I turn to Evander, who nods for me to follow her. My nerves erupt again. I wonder if they're going to cut me open and do some blood ritual.

But when we pass through the center of the crowd, my dad steps to my left side, and on the right

"Don't be nervous," Grandpa Westfall murmurs, leaning into me to whisper the words into my hair.

He looks so much like my dad. Handsome, even in his old age. Dad takes my arm and squeezes, but his expression is serious, icy.

Only his eyes show his true feelings. Pride shines there as he looks from me, to his father.

The crowd parts, allowing us to walk out onto the sweeping, moon-drenched veranda. Intricate tiles swirl into a mosaic of a full moon surrounded by the cycle at the edge of the veranda. The tiles shine like diamonds in the light of the moon.

I turn to look over my shoulder and notice the excited crowd is following us, crowding the open doors overlooking the veranda.

My dad and grandpa come to a stop and guide me to stand in the center of the full moon.

"The last person to go through this ceremony was my father," Grandpa Westfall says in a voice that carries to the crowd. "Tonight, we crown a new Luna to the Shadowsynger throne."

Metal sings through the air as Dad unsheathes his sword of pure midnight. Gems of the deepest blues and purples glimmer as he slowly tilts the sword tip down, holding Grandpa's gaze.

This is pretty serious, I realize, my cheeks glowing with a nervous blush.

"Kneel, Kenna Westfall, my daughter," Dad says steadily.

I drop to my knees. In the crowd, I see Evander and Brie standing between Sydney and Ryan, all three of them wide-eyed and excited.

"Are you going to cut off my head?" I whisper.

Grandpa Westfall shushes me.

Dad says something in a language long lost to time–something that sounds like music. Something that makes my shadows swirl to life. Some people in the crowd echo his strange words, and I spot several people in tears–happy tears. Tears of awe. Tears that tell me this pack never thought they'd ever see this again.

"For the pack," Dad says, laying his sword on my right shoulder. "For the family," he says, laying it on my left. He gently rests the tip against my heart, his eyes meeting mine. "For the Goddess."

I hold his gaze as my powers tremble, reaching for the sword. I fight the urge to gasp as my shadows start to seep into the onyx sword, igniting the gems to the point they glow.

"Rise, Kenna," Grandpa says with a smile I've only seen a few times in my life.

I do.

I rise, and Dad kneels, extending his sword to *me*.

"But–"

"It's yours," he says, smiling. "Take it."

My hand curls around the hilt. It's lighter than I expected. The crowd waits on pins on needles–for what, I'm not sure–but I raise the sword to the moon, and the tiles beneath my feet begin to glow.

A single tear rolls down my cheek. I meet Evander's gaze and find he's also teary eyed as he smiles at me, letting out a surprised laugh.

The crowd erupts in a riotous applause, and then I'm laughing too.

"Luna Kenna of Veiled Valley!" he shouts, and soon everyone is shouting and hollering, dousing me in praise.

"Holy shit," I breathe, choking on a laugh.

"I've never heard those words come out of your mouth," Dad smirks.

"Now what?" I ask, lowering the sword. I was wrong about it being light. My arm aches, and I nearly drop it before he takes it and sheaths it down his back.

"I'll hang onto this for tonight. Now, you go sit on your throne beside your mate."

I search his eyes–so like mine–and see the pride there. "Thank you, Dad."

He says nothing, but his answering smile has fresh tears pricking my lashes.

"Go dance with your mate, Kenna," he laughs, giving me a nudge.

Beaming, I turn from him to Evander, who is waiting for me in the doorway. Sydney takes Brie from his arms and gives me a knowing bob of his head as he walks away with the baby.

I step up to Evander's side. He takes my hand, knitting his fingers with mine.

"We've only danced together that one time," I tell him.

"Let's make up for lost time, then."

49

HOPE FOR THE FUTURE

Kenna

"I'M GOING BACK to Crescent Falls at the end of the week," Sydney says over the rim of his whiskey glass, his blue eyes a stark contrast to his all black suit. "To look for Sasha."

"Ah," I say, giving him a hard look. "You sure?"

"Am I sure I'm looking for her? Yes. It's my mission."

Ryan crosses his arms, rolling his eyes to the ceiling.

Evander leans against one of the enormous black marble columns in the ballroom, his eyes sliding to mine.

There's barely anyone in here at this point. The musicians are being fed copious amounts of champagne in thanks for their near ceaseless playing over the past four or five hours, and the once riotous crowd has dispersed.

It's 2:00 A.M. Everyone is going home. Even our family members have retreated to the numerous guest rooms.

So, it's just me, Evander, Ryan, and Sydney.

And... Flynn. Our Beta, since Evander's siblings are still too young to hold that position.

Flynn's all right, I guess.

"I think she may have been adopted, but Ryan hasn't found anything about that yet." Sydney toys with his glass, looking at his twin.

Ryan nods. "All of that is public record in Crescent Falls. But so far, I've found nothing, and I have to say I'm looking forward to replacing you in Eastonia for a while."

"What about group homes?" Evander cuts in. "Orphanages?"

"Not in Crescent Falls," Sydney sighs. "We don't have those. Celestoria has them, from what I know. But Atticus would have had to arrange for her to cross those borders, and I doubt he had the manpower and alliances in Crescent Falls to move her that far out of Eastonia."

I hate talking about this. I don't want Sasha to be found. I don't think she should be. She's not a threat, and sniffing around while Gabriel is still out there, covenless and hunting her, means we're putting her in even more danger.

But this isn't up to us anymore. She's in Uncle Isaac's kingdom, and it's his decision.

He's not okay with a rogue witch in his territory, especially one with enormous powers and a cousin hell bent on destruction in order to find her and take over the Allied Kingdoms by using her powers.

"I'm going to bed," I say abruptly, giving my cousins a false smile. "This conversation is exceedingly boring."

"Breakfast tomorrow?" Ryan asks me as Evander and I turn to make our leave.

"Lunch," Evander says. "We're sleeping in as late as we can."

Ah, that sounds delicious.

I open my mouth to tell them goodnight, but Evander swoops me into his arms. I yelp in surprise as he practically runs out of the ballroom with me against his chest.

I clutch his dress shirt as he tears up the stairs in the foyer and down a darkened hallway. Sconces flare to life as we hurtle toward our bedroom.

"You're insane!" I giggle.

"I've been going insane seeing you in that dress," he growls, squeezing me. "I had to fight the urge to take you upstairs all night."

Nice. I knew my after-party dress would have an effect on him. It's silken and flows over my generous curves like a finely fitted glove, the silver fabric a perfect match to my eyes. I even let my hair down, and we spent the entire night dancing.

It's truly been the best night of my life.

"Please tell me you didn't wear gowns like this to all of the mating balls you went to last spring," he says, turning on his heel and skirting through the door to our room, which the magic of the house graciously opened for us so Evander wouldn't be tempted to kick it down.

Our bedroom is huge—a sweeping, wide room with a four poster bed and dark paint and fabric that bleeds into a domed ceiling with a mural of the stars overhead. The stars glow on their own accord, mimicking the night sky. In fact, the ceiling will eventually fade from a starry night to a stunning morning, if it's sunny.

If it's rainy tomorrow, well, there's a chance we'll wake up to dark storm clouds rolling across the ceiling.

I love it.

I almost say something about how bright the stars are tonight, but Evander tosses me onto the bed, and the thought is gone.

He's on me in an instant, kissing me so deeply I can barely catch my breath.

"How much do you like this dress?" he asks, running his hands down my sides. "How upset would you be if I tore this dress to pieces getting it off you?"

"You'd be buying me a new one!"

He gives me a teasing pout. "Oh, no. How will we possibly afford that?"

I gasp out a laugh as he tears the dress down the middle, freeing my breasts.

His mouth is instantly on my skin—tasting, exploring, his tongue flicking over my nipple and teeth grazing the tender skin on my belly as he makes his way lower, and lower, hooking his thumbs around my panties and pulling them down my thighs.

"I have a surprise for you," I whimper, closing my eyes against the rippling pleasure flooding my body as he kisses my inner thigh.

"What is it?" he growls, his voice low and full of need. He drags his tongue up my leg, stopping precariously close to my center.

I arch my hips involuntarily, desperate for his touch.

"I've been keeping a secret," I pant, twinning my fingers in his hair as he dips his head to press his tongue through my folds. I jerk against the motion of his tongue, letting out my breath.

"Bad girl," he rasps, his teeth grazing my clit.

I whimper as he squeezes my thighs while he works me into a frenzy. It's like he's been starving for me, waiting for this moment all night.

But just when the incredible, body-numbing pleasure starts to build, he pulls away and leans over me, covering my body with his own.

Still dressed, he kisses me deeply, his tongue swirling over mine as I quickly unbutton his shirt and start yanking on his belt.

"Are you going to tell me this secret of yours, mate?"

He reaches down and pulls his belt from the loops, tossing it across the bed. He shoves his pants down just far enough to free his cock from his boxers and sinks into my pussy without ceremony.

We both let out a breath. He groans, slowly pumping into me a few times while I adjust to his size.

"Gods, Kenna–" he rasps, burying his face in the side of my neck.

I wrap my legs around his waist and close my eyes, sinking my teeth into his shoulder.

It's slow and tender despite the buildup of dancing all night, our bodies writhing against each other when the party took on a new, darker vibe.

But my body is thrumming. Pleasure builds and bursts, coursing through my thighs and belly. I cry out, my voice echoing off the walls, and I'm exceedingly thankful for this old castle with its thick, impenetrable walls.

Evander comes undone shortly thereafter, his hands squeezing my hips as he thrusts me into the mattress. I ride out my orgasm with his.

Only when we're sweating and untangling ourselves from each other does he ask again, while I settle myself in his arms, "What was your secret surprise?"

"Oh, that," I smile, blushing as I prop myself up on my elbow to look down at him.

I memorize the planes of his face. His regal nose. His bright, emerald eyes fanned by lashes a few shades darker than his golden hair.

He's handsome. Beautiful. He's everything I've ever wanted.

"Evander," I whisper. "I'm pregnant."

Evander's eyes go wide briefly, but he's still. His face undergoes a great change as my words settle in.

I'm not sure what I expected. I didn't think he'd jump up and down with glee. I also didn't think he'd be upset or say it's too soon. We have a two-month-old, for Goddess' sake, who we adopted two days after the Rite.

His hand brushes down the slope of my hip and back up, resting over my belly.

"Really?"

I nod, tears stinging my eyes. "Really."

"How long have you known?" There's so much emotion in his voice.

A sob works its way up my throat, tightening around my words as I say, "Two weeks. Almost three. I wanted it to be a surprise, I just didn't know how to tell you."

"That's why you've been sick. I thought it was nerves. I thought your new scent had something to do with you ascending to the throne…." He tapers off, his eyes going wide again. "You're pregnant?"

"Yes, Evander," I laugh. "We're having another baby next spring."

He looks at me, searching my eyes. As if it finally clicks, he crushes me to his chest, wrapping his strong arms around me and holding me there.

He whispers a nearly silent prayer to the Goddess, choking on the words as I start to cry the happiest tears that have ever rolled down my cheeks.

We lay like that for a long time, talking in whispers about our future, about Brie's future, and the future of our newest addition.

And when the sun starts to rise, and we haven't slept, we get out of bed anyway, too excited to sleep.

I dress in comfy pajamas and a robe to fight the fall chill in the air. Evander and I walk hand and hand downstairs to the informal dining room where our family is slowly gathering for breakfast.

So much for sleeping in as long as we can.

Evander fixes me a plate while I feed Brie a bottle and listen to my mom and Aunt Maddy talk about the success of the ball last night. Grandma Isla and Grandma Cressendra discuss the upcoming move to Maatua where she and Grandpa Westfall have decided to retire. They'll be living next door to Grandma Isla and Grandpa Maddox. My grandfathers discuss how good the fishing is as they sip their coffee.

Ryan and Sydney trickle in, hungover, but happy to see everyone gathered around a table together.

I have a flash of memory of a trip to Maatua as a child. We always ate outside in the morning when the weather was fine, filling up a picnic table while Grandpa Maddox divvied out his famous pancakes.

The table is fuller now.

I pass Brie to my mom, who holds her against her shoulder, gently patting her back as she continues her conversation with Aunt Maddy.

Evander leans over to whisper in my ear. "Should we tell them?"

Part of me wants to, just to see their reactions to our news, but it's early, and outside of this room, beyond the misty veil of this precious gem at the very end of Eastonia, war is still on the horizon.

I look around, taking in the faces of my family, noticing the dark circles and new fine lines created by strife, grief, and uncertainty.

I have no idea what the next year will look like. I don't know when Gabriel will make his next move. I don't know who at this table might not be here in the end.

But the sun shines today. There isn't a single cloud in the sky.

And right now, it's peaceful.

"Let's wait for a rainy day," I tell him.

He rests his hand on my lower belly, leaning over to press a kiss to my temple.

"A rainy day," he agrees.

We'll share the news on a day when everything seems hopeless. Because, in Brie and our future child, I see and feel nothing but hope.

That's enough to carry me through whatever comes next.

5 0

SYDNEY'S QUEST

Sydney

Four Months Later

DAD'S ORRERY clicks and spins, the internal gears grinding against the soft patter of winter rain on the windows. I watch the strange tangle of metal for another few minutes, tucking my hands in the pockets of my old leather jacket before taking a breath and walking toward the stairs.

It's only 8:00 A.M. The sun barely crests the snow-capped mountains in the distance when I reach the main foyer. Maids and workers rush past me with courteous bobs of their heads.

The world keeps spinning and spinning.

A flash of memory clouds my vision. I watch Gabriel drag his knife across Evander's throat. Kenna's scream sears into my mind like a brand.

I blink, and the memory vanishes, replaced by the pale cream rug and ceiling height windows overlooking the private drive.

I remind myself I'm back in Crescent Falls, and nothing is amiss.

"Oh, I thought that might have been you in the orrery." Mom's voice drifts toward me on a coffee scented breeze. "Did you hear the news?"

"What news?" I slowly turn my head to her, noticing her eyes are softly creased as her lips pull into a smile.

Her grin falters a bit when she notices my hard expression.

"Kenna and Evander just found out they're having a boy. Isn't that wonderful?"

I nod, clearing my throat. "I thought they might." I knew they would, actually. I saw it in the stars, not that anyone needs to know that. I still don't exactly know how to read the heavens. My dad never mastered it, and he passed those strange powers down to me.

I see so many things and can never make sense of most of it.

"You should stay for breakfast," Mom offers as I start striding toward the door. "Sydney, please. You've been out running around Crescent Falls and the surrounding packs looking for that girl from Eastonia for months–"

"It's still an active mission," I remind her, doing my best to flash her a charming grin. I fail, of course. Ryan is so much better at buttering up our parents. "I have pack matters to attend to this morning. I was just stopping by to–to–" Why am I here? I keep forgetting. I often walk into a room and get blinded by memories of being under the mountain with Gabriel and completely forget why I'm there and what I meant to do.

I run my fingers through my hair as Mom narrows her eyes at me. "You need sleep, honey."

"I sleep," I lie. "I'm just busy. If you want to help me, you can ask Dad and Uncle Ryatt to take me off this case. I'm an engineer, not a detective."

"I'll see what I can do," she murmurs, but her stormy blue eyes bore into the back of my head as I hurry through the door and down the rain-soaked front steps.

I walked all the way here, I remember that much. It snowed for a while when I approached the castle earlier this morning to use the orrery.

I kick at a pebble as I walk briskly down the private road leading off the royal property, letting my memories flood back. I woke up at 4:00 A.M. and had two cups of coffee. I worked out, then went on a run, and by then it was…6:00 A.M. Yeah, 6:00 A.M. Then I came here to…

"Sasha," I say, letting the woman's name roll off my tongue. "That's why I came here."

Because I can't fucking find her, and I've been looking for four months. I've canvassed every pack, spoken to every Alpha, Beta, lowest ranking rogues and everyone in between. No one remembers an eleven-year-old orphan from Eastonia. No one knows who she is or where to find her.

So I looked toward the stars, again, for the millionth time, to see if they finally had an answer for me.

Instead, two hours of my day vanished in what felt like a single blink.

I wave to the guards at the security gate and wait for the gate in question to roll back, then stride into the sprawling network of town-homes and mansions that hug the royal grounds.

A mile later, the rain turns back to wet, clumpy snow, and I step into the city-center.

I don't have pack matters to deal with today. That was a lie. For the past four months, most of the day-to-day activities have been the burden of my Beta, Asher. As for work at my engineering firm, it tends to run smoothly without me trapped behind a desk all day.

So, I walk the streets of Crescent City looking for someone who doesn't want to be found.

I'm not sure why it matters so much to me to find her. Before Gabriel captured me and Evander, I was in agreement that Sasha shouldn't be located and that she wasn't a threat. Sure, she's a powerful witch. But she's the sister… no, the cousin of Gabriel, and he's still out there. Finding her and protecting her from him means protecting the Allied Kingdoms from his wrath, or so I tell myself.

I can't witness something like what happened to Kenna and Evander again.

So, I keep walking.

I haven't bothered to shave in several days. I scratch the stubble along my jaw, trying to make sense of what exactly I need to be doing right now, and decide I need coffee, first and foremost. I can't remember the last time I slept more than a couple of hours at a time.

I eventually walk into the Neutral Zone and go to that coffee shop I found when I'd come here looking for Evander all those months ago. It feels like a lifetime has passed since then. I order a hot coffee and wait at the counter, thumbing through the notifications on my phone as conversations carry on around me.

"Sydney?"

I look up from my phone and raise a finger as the barista sets my coffee down and moves on, but my eyes catch a burst of color against the onslaught of gray beyond the coffee shop windows.

There's a shop across the street I hadn't noticed before. Wet snow drips down windows that show off an array of foliage and flowers. The door leading inside the shop is bright pink and hand-painted with forget-me-nots and daisies.

Intrigued, I sip my coffee as I walk across the street. It's a flower shop, obviously. I have no reason to go inside other than... well, I have nothing else to do.

A bell chimes as I walk in and close the door behind me with a crunch.

"I'm back here if you need me!" A lifted, feminine voice drifts through the air as I walk around the store. Bundles of flowers and herbs sit in narrow buckets and shelves are covered in a wide variety of potted houseplants.

My skin prickles with heat and a sudden surge of energy as I pass under several grow lights that cast the peachy pink walls in stripes of vibrant blue.

But then I hear a crash and a muffled curse.

A curtain separates the main room from what I assume is a storage or work area of some sort.

I take a slow sip of my coffee as I watch the curtain. It doesn't move. "Are you all right back there?"

"Just fine," the voice grumbles.

The curtain parts and….

"I just cut my finger," a woman says as she crosses the room. "I'm so clumsy."

I watch her walk behind the counter and crouch with effort.

My mind is blank in a way I've never experienced before. I know her. I swear I know her from somewhere. Her ashen blonde hair catches the snowy light coming from the windows as she rises with a first aid kit.

"I'll be with you in just a second, sir. I'm bleeding all over the place–" She meets my eyes with a "customer-service" smile that immediately cracks. Her eyes–a strange shade of violet–go wide. "A-Alpha Sydney, I didn't know–"

"Here," I tell her, closing in on the counter in a single step. I set my coffee down and reach for her hand. "May I?"

"I can put a bandage on by myself," she says with a nervous laugh, but I shake my head. Reluctantly, she allows me to take her hand, and when her skin touches mine I feel… I feel…

Hazy. Like I'm missing something. Like I'm locked out of my own head.

"This is pretty deep. How'd you manage it?" I graze my thumb over a gash in her forefinger.

"Sheers–oh!" She yanks her hand away, shocked, and holds it protectively against her chest.

I can still see the wound, however. Pale white power shimmers on her skin as the wound quickly knits itself together.

"You're welcome," I tell her, grabbing my coffee. "Sorry if I startled you."

She gives me an odd look then examines her finger. "You didn't," she says slowly, reaching behind her to untie her apron strings. "I just don't come across people with extra gifts very often."

"It's more common now that the Veil is gone," I say absently, but my eyes are still searching her face, mentally tracing every line. She's beautiful. Absolutely stunning in a way I can barely put into words. She's an artist's rendition of what the Moon Goddess might have looked like as a human–ethereal and unique, with a thin, sculpted nose, high cheekbones, and wide eyes.

Eyes the color of lavender. I've never seen that before.

I think.

I should ask her out. Or at least talk to her, for fuck's sake. If Ryan were here, he would be all over her by now or urging me to make a move.

But I find her oddly familiar. I just can't place it.

"Can I help you find anything in particular?" she asks a bit unsteadily, her back to me as she hangs up her apron on a hook behind the counter.

"I'm, uh, actually, do you ship to Eastonia?"

She looks at me over her shoulder. "Eastonia? No, never. Plus, the borders are closed again."

"Right." I click my tongue. "Never mind."

"What, exactly, do you need to send to Eastonia? They have very strict environmental laws when it comes to shipping flora–"

"I know," I say, chuckling.

"Of course, you do, being the prince and all."

Her tone is… not teasing, no. She's nervous, and it's painfully obvious as she keeps her back to me and keeps her hands busy by picking up random items and setting them down again.

"My cousin and her mate just found out that they're having a son. I was going to send them flowers. Something blue, I guess."

"Congratulations," she says in a near whisper, and turns back around.

She's pregnant–visibly so. Her sage green dress barely hides the swell of her belly as she eases onto a stool and looks up at me expectantly. I hadn't noticed it before because of the apron. "I'm sure they have florist in Eastonia."

"Yeah, I'm sure." I run my fingers through my hair. "Never mind. I–you have a nice shop. Have a good day–"

"Wait. Wait–" She tries to stand but winces as she grips the counter. "You should take some flowers back to the queen, at least. On the house, of course. Or for yourself. As a thank you for mending my finger–"

"No, it's fine, really, I–are you hurting?" I fight the urge to leap over the counter and help her back onto the stool, but she shakes her head.

"I'm just sore. My bed in the apartment upstairs is… well, it came with the building, and it's terrible."

"You should replace it," I say stupidly, and her eyes narrow slightly.

"I'd love to, but people generally don't come in to buy flowers in the winter. I make most of my income during the festivals in the summer and–" she waves a hand over her belly, "I've had expenses come up."

"Ah." I nod. "Does your mate help you out around here, or is it just you?"

"Just me."

"Where is he? Does he–"

"I don't have a mate," she says, and her lips twitch into a ghost of a smile. "It's just me."

I feel like an asshole. "Did you do the flowers for the festival this past summer?"

"A bit, yeah. Enough to keep this place afloat during the winter, I hope. I just opened this past spring."

"And you're alone?"

"I already answered that," she laughs, her eyes suddenly a shade lighter than before. I'm sure I'm imagining it.

But she's even more beautiful now that she's smiling, and I feel a nagging ache in my chest at the sight.

Like I know her. Like I remember that smile.

I walk toward the door before I can say anything else, but stop mid-step and turn back around.

I meet her gaze, holding it. "Have we met before?"

The silence between us is deafening. She chews her lower lip–a motion that sends my body into a sudden frenzy.

"No, Your Highness. I don't think we have."

"What's your name?"

Thank you for reading! Son of the Alpha: The Alpha King's Breeder Book Nine *is now on preorder. Find it here. Keep reading—Chapter 1 drops now!*

SON OF THE ALPHA CHAPTER 1:
THE COLD, HARD TRUTH

Sarah

It's warmer down here under the grow lights. Electricity hums through the air as I move from plant to plant, pruning, plucking, and watering. Outside the frosty windows, the Neutral Zone is every shade of silver in the unforgiving cold.

Someone passes bundled against the frigid, windy air. Their red hat disappears into a rush of snow being swept by the wind down the street.

I shiver despite the slight warmth in the air.

I've been cold for weeks. Cold, hungry, and stressed beyond belief.

The baby swaddled in a sling across my chest wriggles before falling back asleep, his cheek pressed against my breast.

I move to the utility sink in the storage room and wrench on the pump, but the water doesn't start. The pipes are frozen solid.

"Shit," I whisper, closing my eyes and trying to swallow past the lump in my throat.

Mr. Foxglove, my landlord, was supposed to be here this morning to fix the heat to the building. My one room apartment upstairs has been freezing cold since Tuesday last week, the day after my son was born. I've resorted to turning the oven on and letting it run empty to heat the space. Empty, because I have no money for food. Every single cent I have to my name is going toward my rent, which has doubled every month since the snow started to fall.

"I'm sorry," I croak, tearfully, to my thirty, wilting plants. No water for them today again. My precious blooms of begonia and lily tremble in answer. My orchids are fried. I can't bring those back from the dead, even if the water returns.

It wasn't supposed to be like this. A year ago, I rented this space and the apartment upstairs. I painted the walls and the exterior door my favorite color–pink. The most magnetic fuchsia the world has ever seen.

I got a contract to provide the florals for some of the balls at the summer mating festival. People came in droves to buy bouquets for their newly found mates in the weeks that followed.

But then the rebel threat brought Crescent Falls into war.

People stopped buying flowers.

The royal family stopped throwing balls and parties, as did the Alphas of the dozen or so packs that surrounded the city.

And Mr. Foxglove started raising my rent.

I sink onto the rickety stool behind the counter and stare out at the wind whipping the snow against the window.

The baby stirs again, letting out a frustrated grunt. I reach for my shirt, pulling it away enough to free my breast so he can nurse and wince, my eyes watering, at the sharp pain of it.

I'm so hungry. I'm so, so cold. The patchwork coat I've been stuffing with fluff from my mattress upstairs barely shields me from the cold, but it's all I have.

I've sold everything. Every piece of furniture, every item of clothing, just to have a roof over my head.

All because I had a dream… and then got pregnant.

And the kingdom went to war.

And no one cares about flowers in the winter.

I bite back a sob and gently bounce the baby, trying to get him to settle. I know he's hungry too. My milk is barely there, probably because I don't eat very often.

The exterior door wrenches open sending a burst of freezing cold air into the shop.

"You said you'd be here this morning," I say, trying my best not to send the words off my tongue in the snarl my landlord deserves.

Mr. Foxglove–a man of maybe fifty with black hair and devilishly green eyes–smirks at me, taking his time shutting the door. The cold air funnels around the room, ruffling the leaves of my already frail plants and blossoms. "You're not my only tenant."

"The heat has been out for over a week. Ms. Elosie upstairs has been burning newspaper in her woodstove to try to keep warm." I clutch my baby tighter against my chest to fight the chill now creeping into my bones. "We're freezing here. The pipes are frozen, and we have no water–"

"Well, if that's the case, I doubt I'll be able to get anything fixed today." He checks his filthy nails, smiling at me. "At least it's somewhat warm in here, right? With all the lights you have burning up your utility bill."

The baby makes a grunting noise before he starts to whine.

Foxglove rolls his eyes, leaning his hip on the counter. "I'm not here to fix shit, Ms. Greenly. You owe me rent for this month."

"I'm not paying you a single cent until the building has working heat and water!"

"Then get out," he smiles, teeth flashing.

I look at the window again, at the raging wind storm outside. He's still giving me a cool smile when I meet his gaze once more.

"Where," he says slowly, tapping a finger on the counter, "is my money, Sarah?"

I reach into the pocket of my coat with trembling fingers and clutch the wad of cash resting there. I slam it onto the counter.

He picks it up, weighing it in his hands before counting. "Great start, but you're short by at least half."

"Wh-what?" I stammer? "No, it's all there–"

"Nope. You're short. If you want heat and water, you'd better come up with the rest by tomorrow–"

"You've tripled my rent over the last three months!" My voice edges on despair. That's all the money I have. It should have been more than enough. I should have a few dollars left over for food, but now...

He pockets the money and leans down so one of his elbows rests on the counter. He reaches for me, twisting a lock of my ashy blonde hair around his hairy, ring-laden pinky finger. "My offer still stands, you know. You want water, heat, and a roof over your head? It would only take a few minutes flat on your back to make that happen–"

I pull myself away and step back until I hit the wall, nostrils flaring with hatred and disgust as I fight to catch my breath.

He clicks his tongue and shrugs. "Well, in that case, pay the fuck up, or you and your bastard will be out on the street come sunset tomorrow. Mark my words."

He turns on his heel and leaves the shop, not bothering to close the door behind him.

Tears burn down my cheeks as I rush after him, shoving the door closed against the howling, bitter wind. My son wails in his sling as cold bits through my coat.

I lock the door and draw the blinds, whispering reassurances to the screaming baby before going through the side door leading to the stairwell. It's dark, empty, and lifeless.

The dark steps blend with the peeling gray paint as I hurry up to my apartment holding back a torrent of tears.

I knock on my elderly neighbor's door and yank it open, glancing inside. Ms. Eloise is curled up in a blanket on her bed like usual, her woodstove barely puffing enough heat into the room to keep frost from coating the windows.

I watch her chest rise and fall then slowly edge out of the room and turn toward my own door.

My apartment is a stark contrast to the bright florals of my shop below. The walls are gray with patches of wood and stone showing beneath the peeling paint and fraying drywall. The floor is old, faded wood that leaves splinters that bite into my feet if I ever walk barefoot.

A twin mattress rests on the floor. I sold the bedframe a few weeks ago. No art hangs on my walls any longer, only a few faded photos from a time in my life that feels like a lifetime ago.

I close the door behind me and rub my cold hands together before moving to the oven and turning it on. It'll take a few minutes for the room to heat up, so I shrug off my coat and take my baby from his sling, and curl into a ball around him in bed while he nurses.

Silent tears fall down my cheeks and seep into the mattress as I stare at the pictures on the walls.

Me, only ten or so months ago, dressed to the nines in the center of a gaggle of young women my age. Me, a year ago, posing outside the pink door to my shop downstairs, beaming with pride.

Pictures of me with friends whose faces have blurred with time. Friends I shared apartments with, drank with, and gossiped about everything from boys to music to the royal family the tabloids always love to gossip about.

I cup my son's head and close my eyes.

None of those friends have been around for months. Once I began to show... once I stopped going to the bars and clubs with them or out to brunch...

Everyone simply vanished.

But one face remains in the sea of lost memories.

Hadley comes through the door without needing a key. The lock has been broken for weeks.

Her dark brown curly hair pokes out beneath a pale blue hat, and the tip of her nose is bright red.

I rise up on an elbow, taking my coat and the raggedy quilt I found in the trash with me. "What are you doing here?"

"Goddess, Sarah, it's freezing in here!" Her smile fades as she looks around. Her hazel eyes meet mine again, giving me that same pained look she always gives me. "I brought food."

"You shouldn't have. You'll get in so much trouble for being out–"

"My brother can kiss my ass." She tries to smile, but it falls flat. I sense the nerves in each word as she edges toward the row of countertops that act as my kitchen. She sets a paper bag of groceries on the counter, pulling out a carton of milk and a bag of oats. Butter, salt, six eggs…

"I got you some vitamins. My–my friend said these are the good ones." She sets them down on the counter before turning around, but my heart is aching.

"Does he know you're here?" I ask, sitting up and fixing my shirt. The baby is fast asleep beside me, his tiny fists under his chin.

Hadley shakes her head. "I can't stay long. I have a shift at the bar, and you know how my brother gets about me being outside of our territory." She looks around, her eyes glistening in the darkness. "I'm trying to get you out of here, okay?"

"I never asked–"

"You can't stay here, Sarah!"

"My shop," I tell her, fear and heartache twisting its way through my heart like a heated blade. "I can't just leave everything I've worked for behind." I flash her my best "I got this, seriously," smile even though inside, I'm falling to pieces.

"Did you get the contract with the royal family? The upcoming ball?" Her eyes are full of so much hope.

I shake my head.

Providing the flowers for Queen Madeline's upcoming party would have made it possible to get out of this hellhole. Now, I'm in too deep. I'm out of money. Foxglove has me backed into a corner, and I have a baby to think about.

But I'm packless. Hadley is my only support, and her brother has her under lock and key.

I can't pull her into my drama, anyway. I can't even think about it.

It's better for everyone that I remain alone.

She shakes a smaller paper bag. "I got you a burger and fries," she says softly.

But a distant, rhythmic thudding echoes up the stairwell.

"I think that might have been the shop," I say, peeling myself out of bed carefully so as not to disturb the baby.

"I'll stay with him," Hadley says as I open the door and look down the stairs into the growing dark.

Another knock, but not from the private residents entrance that faces the alley.

A few seconds later, I'm standing in my shop squinting through the frosty windows at the wind-blown street.

A man walks away, his hands tucked in his pockets and his head bent against the wind.

Thank you for reading! *Son of the Alpha: The Alpha King's Breeder Book Nine* is now on preorder. Find it here.

ALSO BY BELLA MOONDRAGON

The Alpha King's Breeder series:

Bought by the Alpha: The Alpha King's Breeder Book 1

Loved by the Alpha: The Alpha King's Breeder Book 2

Lost by the Alpha: The Alpha King's Breeder Book 3

Luna of the Alpha: The Alpha King's Breeder Book 4

Legacy of the Alpha: The Alpha Kings's Breeder Book 5

Daughter of the Alpha: The Alpha King's Breeder Book 6

Descendants of the Alpha: The Alpha King's Breeder Book 7

Shadow of the Alpha: The Alpha King's Breeder Book 8

Son of the Alpha: The Alpha King's Breeder Book 9

The Luna's Vampire Prince series:

The Culling

The Kingdom

The Conquered

Pregnant With Four Alphas' Babies

Chosen As the Breeder

Mated to Four Alphas

Threats Against the Breeder

At War for the Breeder

The Stolen Breeder

Four Alphas, Four Babies

Becoming the Luna Queen

Descendants of the Breeder

Desired by the Devil series

Whispers of the Devil

Banter of the Devil (releases 10/15/2024)

The Mafia Kings series

Indebted to the Mafia King

Loved by the Mafia King (releases 9/15/2024)

Claimed by the Mafia King (releases 11/15/2024)

Sign up for Bella's newsletter here.

Follow Bella on Facebook here.

www.ingramcontent.com/pod-product-compliance
Lightning Source LLC
Chambersburg PA
CBHW070403310726

48977CB00003B/535